Joseph Wright

A Grammar of the Dialect of Windhill in the West Riding of

Yorkshire

Joseph Wright

A Grammar of the Dialect of Windhill in the West Riding of Yorkshire

ISBN/EAN: 9783337327071

Printed in Europe, USA, Canada, Australia, Japan

Cover: Foto ©Andreas Hilbeck / pixelio.de

More available books at **www.hansebooks.com**

A Grammar

OF THE

DIALECT OF WINDHILL,

IN THE

WEST RIDING OF YORKSHIRE

*Illustrated by a Series of Dialect Specimens, phonetically rendered;
with a Glossarial Index of the Words used in the
Grammar and Specimens.*

BY

JOSEPH WRIGHT, M.A., Ph.D.,
DEPUTY PROFESSOR OF COMPARATIVE PHILOLOGY
IN THE UNIVERSITY OF OXFORD.

'Nur das Beispiel führt zum Licht;
Vieles Reden thut es nicht.'

London:
PUBLISHED FOR THE ENGLISH DIALECT SOCIETY
BY KEGAN PAUL, TRENCH, TRÜBNER & CO., CHARING CROSS ROAD.

—

1892.

To My Mother

PREFACE

—·—

My chief object in writing the following Grammar has been to furnish specialists in English philology with an accurate account of the Phonology and Accidence of one of the most interesting of the Yorkshire dialects. And in order to make the work as useful as possible to this class of scholars, I have taken special care to include in the Phonology fairly complete lists of the words which are in common use in the dialect and also exist in the literary language. This method of treatment has sometimes involved me in great difficulties; because in the case of words which seem to have had an abnormal development I could not always decide with certainty whether the seeming irregularities had arisen within the dialect itself, or whether the words in question had been introduced from the literary language at various periods, or were merely borrowings from some neighbouring dialect. These are difficulties which every writer of a scientific dialect grammar has to contend with. But it would manifestly have been dishonest on my part to have omitted any word or form which did not seem to have had a regular development. The result is that the grammar contains dozens of words the vocalism of which I have not been able to

a 3

explain satisfactorily, but I have nevertheless registered
them in separate paragraphs, as being in common use in
the dialect and of equal importance to the English philo-
logist. Out of a great many such examples I will only
mention a few here : nuəz (OE. nosu) *nose*, biəd (OE.
beard) *beard*, ut (OE. hāt) *hot*, friət (OE. fretan) *to fret*. for
which we should expect in the dialect noiz (§§ 105, 109).
bād (§§ 61, 68), uət (§§ 122, 126), freit (§§ 82, 87). On the
other hand, the present grammar will, I trust, help to throw
some light upon Old English vowel quantities, besides
showing how dialects still keep apart many vowel sounds
which have fallen together in the literary language. Of
the latter I will only mention a few examples, although
a great many may be found in the grammar :—jād (OE.
geard) *yard*, jiəd (OE. gerd) *yard, three feet.* wāk (OE.
weorc) *work*, wēk (OE. wyrcan) *to work.* meil (OE. melu)
meal, flour, miəl (OE. mǣl) *meal, repast.* reit (OE. reoht,
reht) *right*, rait (OE. wrītan) *to write*, rīt (OE. wyrhta)
wright.

In the treatment of the native element contained in the
grammar I have generally started out from Old English,
which in some respects presents fewer difficulties to the
writer of a modern dialect grammar than Middle English
with its numerous dialects. Had I, however, been a
specialist in this period of our mother tongue, I should
probably have been able to settle many minor points which
remain unsolved in the present grammar. But still, in
spite of my shortcomings in this respect, I hope that the
book will be a welcome contribution to English philology.

In the treatment of the French element in the dialect
I found, after trying many experiments, that the only

satisfactory plan was to start out from the present pronunciation of literary English. The words have come into
the dialect at various periods and through various chan-
nels, and it is accordingly almost impossible to treat them
historically. I have therefore contented myself with
registering the present dialectical pronunciation of the
French element, and for this purpose I have adopted, as
the standard of literary English pronunciation, the sound-
system in Sweet's Primer of Spoken English, which is fairly
typical of the Southern pronunciation of educated people.
A comparison of the development of the French and English
elements in the dialect is interesting from many points of
view. I will only draw attention to §§ 61, 203 and §§ 58,
202 ; but many other paragraphs will be found equally interesting both to English and French philologists. Any one,
who is not thoroughly acquainted with the dialect, may
possibly think that I have introduced into this part of the
grammar many words which are not in common use; but
such is not the case. I have been particularly careful in
this respect. I will only mention one instance out of
many where I may seem to have erred: **raiet akt** *riot
act,* which is one of the commonest expressions in the
dialect, a regular household phrase. What mother has not
said to her naughty child hundreds of times, **if tə duz ðat
ə·giən al rīd ðī traiet akt ən reit ən oel ?**

In the chapter on the consonants the chief interest
naturally lies in the gutturals. In this part of the grammar I have tried to give complete lists of the words which
differ in their development from literary English, I mean
such words as: **flik** *flitch,* **reik** *to reach,* **brig** *bridge,* **flig**
fledge, **duef** *dough,* etc.

It was originally my intention not to give any specimens of the dialect in this volume, but to reserve them for
a second which was to contain a complete glossary of
such dialect words as are not in use in the Modern literary
language, together with extensive specimens of the dialect.
With this end in view I have been collecting materials for
a great number of years, but various circumstances prevent me from entertaining the hope of being able to
publish them for some years to come. I have therefore
decided to give a few specimens in the present volume,
trusting that they may be found useful to those readers
who may wish to make themselves familiar with the
dialect. To anyone who takes the trouble to read them
I venture to say that they will be found both amusing and
instructive.

The Index, which has been a laborious piece of work,
contains all the words occurring in the grammar.

As a guarantee for the general accuracy of the material
contained in the book, I need only state that I spoke the
dialect pure and simple until I was practically grown up.

In conclusion I have the pleasant task of expressing my
most cordial thanks to three friends—Professor Napier,
Professor Holthausen, and the Rev. A. L. Mayhew—who
have given me much valuable help in the work.

JOSEPH WRIGHT.

OXFORD,
January 1893.

CONTENTS

ABBREVIATIONS, ETC.

———◆◆———

Angl. = Anglian.
Dan. = Danish.
dial. = dialect.
Fr. = French.
gen. = genitive.
Germ. = German, Germanic.
Goth. = Gothic.
Lat. = Latin.
lit. = literally.
lit. Engl. = literary English.
Low Germ. = Low German.
ME. = Middle English.
MHG. = Middle High German.
Mid. Du. = Middle Dutch.
M. Low Germ. = Middle Low German.
Norw. = Norwegian.
occ. = occasionally.
OE. = Old English.

O. Fr. = Old French.
O. Fris. = Old Frisian.
OHG. = Old High German.
O. Icel. = Old Icelandic.
O. Ir. = Old Irish.
O. Low Germ. = Old Low German.
O. Norm. Fr. = Old Norman French.
O.N. = Old Norse.
O. North. = Old Northumbrian.
O. Swed. = Old Swedish.
pl. = plural.
pret. = preterite.
pp. = past participle.
sing., sg. = singular.
Scot. = Scotch.
Swed. = Swedish.
W. = Windhill.
WS. = West Saxon.
> = has become.

The asterisk (*) prefixed to a word denotes a theoretical form.

———————

WORKS REFERRED TO IN THE GRAMMAR.

Cotgr. = A French and English Dictionary, composed by Mr. Randle Cotgrave; with another in English and French, edited by J. Howell.

EEPr. = Early English Pronunciation, by A. J. Ellis.

E.E.T.S. = Early English Text Society.

Etym. Dict. = Etymological Dictionary of the English Language, by W. W. Skeat.

Florio = A Worlde of Wordes, or most copious and exact Dictionarie in Italian and English, by John Florio, London, 1598.

Grundriss der germanischen Philologie, herausgegeben von H. Paul.

The Dialect of the Southern Counties of Scotland, by J. A. H. Murray.

N.E.D. = New English Dictionary, edited by J. A. H. Murray and H. Bradley.

P. B. Beitr. = Beiträge zur Geschichte der deutschen Sprache und Literatur, herausgegeben von H. Paul und W. Braune.

Prompt. Parv. = Promptorium parvulorum sive clericorum, dictionarius Anglo-Latinus princeps, auctore fratre Galfrido, grammatico dicto, ex ordine fratrum predicatorum, Northfolciensi, circa a. d. MCCCCXL, ad fidem codicum recensuit Albert Way, London, 1865.

Sievers, OE. Gr. = Angelsächsische Grammatik, von E. Sievers.

Stratmann = Dictionary of the Old English Language, by F. H. Stratmann (new edition, by H. Bradley).

Sweet, H.E.S. = History of English Sounds, by H. Sweet.

Sweet, NE. Gr. = New English Grammar, by H. Sweet.

Synopsis of Old English Phonology, by A. L. Mayhew.

Town. Myst. = The Towneley Mysteries (printed for the Surtees Society).

The following list of letters may be useful to those who consult the book without first reading the chapter on pronunciation :—

ə = the e in German Gabe.
ȫ = the i in lit. Engl. bird.
j = the y   ,,   you.
ŋ = the ng, n ,,   sing, song, drink.
š = the sh   ,,   she.
tš = the ch   ,,   choose.
þ = the th   ,,   thin.
ð = the th   ,,   then.
dž = the j   ,,   just.

GRAMMAR

INTRODUCTION.

§ 1. WINDHILL is a manufacturing village in the township of Idle and parish of Calverley in the West Riding of Yorkshire, three miles North of Bradford.

The dialect belongs to the Eastern North Midland group, which embraces the whole of South Yorkshire. Dr. Ellis (EEPr. v. p. 364) distinguishes nine varieties: The Western group containing var. 1. Huddersfield and var. 2. Halifax. The North Central group containing var. 3. Keighley, var. 4. Bradford, var. 5. Leeds, var. 6. Dewsbury. The South Central group containing var. 7. Rotherham and var. 8. Sheffield. The Eastern group containing var. 9. Doncaster and the Eastern slip.

Of these nine varieties the Windhill dialect is most closely related to numbers 3. 4. 5.

CHAPTER I.

PRONUNCIATION.

A. The Vowels.

§ 2. The Windhill dialect contains the following vowel sounds :—

Short vowels	a,	e,	i,	o,	u, ə
Long ,,	ā,		ī,		ū, ō
Short diphthongs	ai,	ei,		oi,	ui
		eu,	iu,	ou	
		eə,	iə,	oə,	uə
Long ,,	āə				
Triphthongs	aiə,		iuə,	ouə	

NOTE.—To these must be added l, m, n, ɯ in the function of vowels. For examples see the corresponding consonants §§ 17–19.

§ 3. In the following paragraphs will be given a brief description of the Windhill vowel-system. For which purpose I have adopted the notation as given in Sweet's Primer of Phonetics. In the autumn of 1886 Dr. Sweet was kind enough to render me considerable help in the analysis of the W. vowel sounds; thus enabling me to fix

the sounds far more accurately than would otherwise have
been the case, had it not been for his kind assistance.
The late Dr. Ellis, to whom I dictated the Dialect Test
(EEPr. v. pp. 389–90) and the dialect words in his Classified Word List (pp. 391–4), was also of some help to me.
But a comparison of his appreciation of the W. vowels
with that of Dr. Sweet and my own will show that we
differ on several minor points.

All the diphthongs and triphthongs have the stress on
the first element. In my transcription I have written ie,
ue, &c., but the first element is really a medium long
vowel, which stands in the same relation to the corresponding short vowel as the lit. Engl. vowel in feet does
to fit or seek to sick.

§ 4. a (mid-back-wide) like the a in German Mann,
but with the tongue slightly more advanced.

lat *late*, faðe(r) *father*, mak *to make*, as *to ask*, laðe(r)
ladder, dlad *glad*, tšap *chap*, ratn *rat*, paste(r) *pasture*,
apren *apron*, kwaleti *quality*, vari *very*.

ā (mid-back-wide) like the a in German Name and in
lit. Engl. father, but with slightly more advanced position
of the tongue as in short a. After our ā there is also
a trace of a glide (āᵊ), which however is not sufficiently
developed to be conveniently represented in print.

rām *room*, fāl *fowl*, bān *child*, wām *warm*, wāk (noun)
work, fādin *farthing*, sāvnt *servant*, pāðe(r) *powder*.

ai = a + i:

raiv *to tear*, mais *mice*, tais *to entice*.

aie = ai + e:

aien *iron*, faie(r) *fire*, raiet *riot*.

āe = ā + e:

dāe(r) *dare*, sāe(r) *sour*, tāe(r) *tower*.

§ **5.** e (low-front-narrow) like the ä in Swed. lära and the first element of the diphthong in lit. Engl. care but short. Ellis identified it as mid-front-wide, but Sweet and myself agree in the above analysis.

elp *to help,* **bed** *bed,* **brek** *to break,* **emeŋ** *among,* **weš** *to wash,* **bleg** *blackberry,* **geðe(r)** *to gather,* **ðen** *then,* **šepste(r)** *starling,* **len** *to lend,* **gezlin** *gosling,* **depþ** *depth,* **lek** *to leak,* **frend** *friend,* **treml** *to tremble,* **bleŋkit** *blanket,* **fešn** *fashion,* **lenit** *linnet.*

ei = e + i :

feit *to fight,* **beid** *bead,* **eit** *to eat,* **leitš** *leech,* **reik** *to reach,* **lein** *to lean,* **ei** *high.*

eu = e + u :

eu *ewe,* **feu** *few,* **seu** *to sew.*

ee = e + ə :

beed *to bathe,* **dee** *day,* **breed** *to resemble,* **bleet** *to bleat,* **tlee** *clay,* **leek** *to play,* **beekŋ** *bacon,* **kweet** *quart,* **meeste(r)** *master.*

§ **6.** i (high-front-wide) like the i in lit. Engl. bit:

lig *to lie down,* **wik** *quick. alive,* **iŋ** *to hang,* **sitš** *such,* **fligd** *fledged,* **dwinl** *to dwindle,* **litl** *little,* **sili** *silly,* **ive(r)** *ever,* **rik** *smoke,* **divl** *devil,* **tšimli,** *chimney,* **šimi** *chemise.*

ī (high-front-narrow) like the ie in German Biene. It is a pure long vowel, not like the ee in South. Engl. feed, which is a diphthong (ij):

mīld *mild,* **nīt** *night,* **fīld** *field,* **wīl** (adv.) *well,* **frīt** *fright,* **bīld** *to build,* **īmin** *evening,* **kīl** *to cool,* **lītnin** *lightning,* **sī** *sigh,* **nī** *knee,* **bīf** *beef.*

iə = i + ə :

biəd *beard,* **iəþ** *earth,* **swiə(r)** *to swear,* **friət** *to fret,* **fliə(r)** *to laugh or sneer at,* **driəd** *to dread,* **tliən** *clean,* **briəd** *bread,* **biə(r)** *beer,* **viəl** *veal,* **fiəs** *fierce.*

iu = i + u :

tliu *a ball of string* or *worsted*, spiu *to vomit*, tiuk *took,*
lium *loom*, iniu (pl.) *enough*, briu *to brew*, frute(r) *future,*
bliu *blue*, riubub *rhubarb.*

iuə = iu + ə :

siuə(r) *sure*, piuə(r) *pure.*

§ 7. o (low-back-wide-round) like the o in lit. Engl.
not :

frozn *frozen*, lop *flea*, bodi *body*, wotə(r) *water*, solt *salt,*
moni *many*, jolə *yellow*, sori *sorry*, tof *tough*, fotnit *fortnight*, kotn *cotton*, ont *aunt*, rost *to roast.*

oi = o + i :

þoil *to give ungrudgingly*, boil *to boil*, toist *toast.*

ou = o + u. But here the first element is low-back-narrow-
round like the aw in lit. Engl. law :

koud *cold*, doutə(r) *daughter*, floun *flown*, kouk *coke,*
grou *to grow*, þout *thought*, loup *to jump*, out *ought*, tout
taught, poutš *to poach*, skoud *to scald.*

ouə = ou + ə :

fouə(r) *four.*

oə = o + ə, the first element of which is the same as the o
in ou :

koəf *calf*, woəf *insipid*, boək *beam*, boəld *bald*, poəm
palm, soəv *salve*, moək *maggot*, boən *born*, noəðə(r) *neither,*
snoə *snow*, goəm *heed*, care, goəki *left handed*, oəðə(r) *to
order*, džoənəs *jaundice.*

§ 8. u (high-back-wide-round) like the u in lit. Engl.
put :

fun (pp.) *found*, flutə(r) *to flutter*, tul *to*, fuml *to fumble,*
ut *hot*, muðə(r) *mother*, uðə(r) *udder*, butšə(r) *butcher,*
buzəd *butterfly*, nuvl *novel.*

ū (high-back-narrow-round) like the u in Germ. gut. In

the W. dialect it is a pure long vowel and not a diphthong
(uw) like the oo in Southern Engl. food:

šūl *shovel*, əbūn *above*, būkþ *bulk, size.*

ui = u + i.   The first element of which is not the u in
put.   Dr. Ellis identified the first element as mid-back-
narrow-round like the o in Germ. Bote, but this is certainly not the sound.   At first Dr. Sweet gave the same
analysis as Dr. Ellis, but he was afterwards inclined to
think that it might be mid-back-narrow-round with outer
rounding like the o in Swedish sol.   But this too is hardly
our sound.   The nearest analysis seems to me to be the
tongue position of high-back-narrow-round, like the u in
Germ. gut, ou in French sou, with the lip position of mid-
back-narrow-round:

bluid *blood*, uin *to harass, treat badly*, gruin *snout of
a pig.*

ue = u + ə.   The first element is the same as the u in ui:

nuəz *nose*, smue(r) *to smother*, due(r) *door*, juək *yolk*,
kuem *comb*, duef *dough*, dlue(r) *to stare*, kued *cord*, tluək
cloak, pue(r) *poor.*

§ 9. ə (mid-mixed-narrow) like the e in German Gabe,
but with the tongue slightly more retracted.   It is not
identical with the -er in lit. Engl. better, which is mid-
mixed-wide.   It occurs in both stressed and unstressed
syllables:

jestedə *yesterday*, sterək *heifer*, fərə *furrow*, wəri *to
worry*, bəd *but*, spərit *spirit*, valə *value.*

ə̄ (low-mixed-narrow) like the i in lit. Engl. bird, but
with the tongue rather more advanced.   It only occurs in
stressed syllables:

gə̄s *grass*, bə̄k *birch*, wə̄d *word*, mə̄ðə(r) *murder*, wə̄k
to work, kə̄smes *Christmas*, gə̄t *great*, kə̄nz *currants.*

B. The Consonants.

§ 10. The W. dialect contains the following consonants :
b, d, f, g, j, k, l, m, n, ŋ, p, r, s, š, t, þ, ð, v, w, z, ž.

§ 11. b (lip-stop-voice) like lit. English b. It occurs initially, medially, and finally :

bān *child*, beəd *to bathe*, bun (pp.) *bound*, brig *bridge*, bleb *blister*, breəd *to resemble, act like another person*, brīt *bright*. kubəd *cupboard*, riubub *rhubarb*, uzbn *husband*. dub *a small pool of water*, nub *to nudge*.

§ 12. d (gum-stop-voice) like lit. English d. It occurs in all positions :

duəf *dough*, dī *to die*, diu *to do*, dwɪnl *to dwindle*, džais *joist*, dlas *glass*. bodm *bottom*, fādin *farthing*, widə *widow*. nobəd lit. *not but, only*, grund *ground*, od *to hold*, snod *smooth*, bogəd *ghost, apparition*.

§ 13. f (lip-teeth-open-breath) like lit. Engl. f. It occurs in all positions :

feu *few*, foil *foal*, feit *to fight*, flig *fledge*, fan (pret.) *found*. duəfi *cowardly*, woəfi *insipid*, fift *fifth*, druft *drought*. kaf *chaff*, duəf *dough*, koəf *calf*, laif *life*.

§ 14. g (back-stop-voice) like lit. Engl. g. It occurs in all positions :

geən *near, direct*, galək *lefthand*, gāl *the matter which gathers in the corner of the eye*, guid *good*, goəmləs *foolish, silly*. blegs *blackberries*, bogəd *ghost*, pigin *small water can*, flegstn *flagstone*. ig *mood, temper*, ug *to carry*, lig *to lie down*, neəg *to gnaw*.

§ 15. j (front-open-voice) like lit. English y in you. It only occurs initially :

jest *yeast,* jestədə *yesterday,* jolə *yellow,* juɒ *young.* I have sometimes heard the sound medially in teəljə(r), teelə(r) *tailor.*

§ 16. k (back-stop-breath) like lit. Engl. k. It occurs in all positions:

kā *cow,* kest *to cast,* kei *key,* koud *cold,* koul *to rake,* kīl *to cool.* skrat *to scratch,* bakə *tobacco,* beekɒ *bacon,* oks *ox.* flik *flitch of bacon,* reik *to reach,* wik *quick, alive,* bēk *birch.*

§ 17. 1 (gum-side-voice) like ordinary English l. It occurs as a consonant in all positions, but as a vowel in unaccented syllables only:

leek *to play,* loin *lane,* len *to lend,* leeð *barn,* luənsəm *lonely.* leelek *lilac,* loup *to jump.* olin *holly,* bīld *to build,* twilt *quilt.* koil *coal,* steil *to steal,* wīl (adv.) *well.*

Examples of vocalic l are: kitl *to tickle,* adl *to earn,* satl *to settle,* spinl *spindle,* rasl *to wrestle.*

§ 18. m (lip-nasal-voice) like lit. Engl. m. It occurs as a consonant in all positions, but as a vowel only in unaccented syllables:

meitš *to measure,* mun *must,* muin *moon,* māt *to moult.* treml *to tremble,* īmin *evening,* sīmin-dlas *mirror.* steim *to bespeak,* gam *game,* freem *to make a beginning,* goem *heed, care.*

Examples of vocalic m are: bodm *bottom,* fadm *fathom,* fipms *fivepence,* wiəpm *weapon,* kindm (OE. cynedōm) *kingdom.*

§ 19. n (gum-nasal-voice) like lit. Engl. n. It occurs as a consonant in all positions, but as a vowel only in unaccented syllables:

niə(r) *kidney,* nīt *night,* nɒɒ-neel *corn on the foot,* nub *to nudge,* noəðə(r) *neither.* snoə *snow,* inif *enough,* moni *many,* sind *to rinse, wash out,* spinl *spindle.* gēn *to grin,* bin *within,* fādin *farthing,* runin *running.*

Examples of vocalic n are : frozn *frozen,* brusn (pp.) *burst,* ratn *rat,* seldn *seldom,* getn (pp.) *got,* tšozn *chosen,* p̄azn *thousand.*

§ 20. ŋ (back-nasal-voice) like ng, n in lit. Engl. sing. song, drink, drunk. As a consonant it only occurs in accented, and as a vowel only in unaccented syllables :

bleŋk *blank,* briŋ *to bring,* teŋz *tongs* fiŋə(r) *finger,* iŋ *to hang,* bleŋkit *blanket,* þiŋ *thing.*

Examples of vocalic ŋ are : brokŋ *broken,* beəgŋ *bargain,* drukŋ *drunk, drunken,* wokŋ *to waken.*

§ 21. p (lip-stop-breath) like lit. Engl. p. It occurs initially, medially, and finally :

poəm *palm,* poəz *to kick,* penəþ *pennyworth.* speən *to wean,* spitək *spigot,* api *happy,* apl *apple,* stapl *staple.* lop *flea,* elp *to help,* sweəp *the handle of a machine,* saip *to ooze or drain out slowly.*

§ 22. r (gum-open-voice). Before a following vowel r is a gently trilled sound. Final r is also slightly trilled, but not so strongly as before a following vowel. This is always the case when the word containing it is used alone, or stands at the end of a sentence. In these positions it is never weakened into a mere voiced glide as in lit. Engl. fear, nor does it disappear altogether as in lit. Engl. far. In order to distinguish strong and weak r the latter is uniformly written (r) in this grammar :

raiv *to tear,* roət *to bray,* roəm *to roam,* reik *to reach,* rām *room,* brek *to break,* reŋ *wrong.* sarə *to serve,* marə *to match,* fəri *first turn,* barə *barrow.* ger up *to get up.*

swie(r) *to swear*, pie(r) *pear*, smue(r) *to smother*, wee(r) *to spend money*.

§ 23. s (blade-open-breath) like the s in lit. Engl. sit. It occurs in all positions:

sal *shall*, sud *should*, sīt *sight*, seem *lard*, sāk *to suck*, snod *smooth*, steim *to bespeak*, strie *straw*, speik *to speak*, siuge(r) *sugar*, swiel *to gutter (of a candle)*. koese *causeway*, brusn (pp.) *burst*, rāst *rust*, omest *almost*, þrosl *thrush*. as *ash*, *ashes*, guis *goose*, ās *house*, oks *ox*, oes *horse*, ius *use*.

§ 24. š (blade-point-open-breath) like lit. Engl. sh in she. It occurs far more frequently initially and finally than medially:

šuin *shoes*, šimi *chemise*, šap *shape*, šak *to shake*, šuðe(r) *to shudder*. tšons *chance*, tšeeme(r) *chamber*, tšiuz *to choose*, fešn *fashion*. weš *to wash*, rediš *radish*, fotš *to fetch*, bleitš *to bleach*, mitš *much*.

§ 25. t (gum-stop-breath) like lit. English t. It occurs in all positions:

tak *to take*, temz *hop-sieve*, toist *toast*, teu *to work zealously*, tlueþ *cloth*. fotn (pp.) *fought*, fiute(r) *future*, wāte *weekday*. gēt *great*, fouet *fourth*, ut *hot*, lat *lath*.

§ 26. þ (teeth-open-breath) like the th in lit. Engl. thin. It occurs initially and finally:

þak *thatch*, þāzn *thousand*, þout *thought*, þriep *to contradict, dispute*. broþ *broth*. māþ *mouth*, dieþ *death*, swāþ *the skin of bacon*.

§ 27. ð (teeth-open-voice) like the th in lit. English then. It occurs initially only in words which had formerly the weak stress; medially between vowels; and finally after vowels:

ðai, ði *thy*, ðis *this*, ðen *then*. šuðe(r) *to shudder*, pāðe(r) *powder* feðe(r) *feather*, soðe(r) *solder*. buið *booth*, leeð *barn*, smuið *smooth*.

§ 28. v (lip-teeth-open-voice) like the v in lit. Engl. vine. Initially it only occurs in words of French origin:

vari *very*, viel *veal*, vois *voice*. ave-meil *oatmeal*, navi *canal*. neiv *fist*, raiv *to tear*. þraiv *to thrive*.

§ 29. w (lip-back-open-voice) like lit. Engl. w in wet. It only occurs initially and medially:

wāk (noun) *work*, weɔ *thong*, wen *when*, wīl *wheel*, wik *quick, alive*, wām *warm*. ewee *away*, dwinl *to dwindle*, twais *twice*, kweet *quart*, kwaleti *quality*, swiet *to sweat*, swetš *a small sample of cloth*.

§ 30. z (blade-open-voice) like the z in lit. Engl. zeal, freeze. Initially it only occurs in ziel *zeal*. It is common medially and finally:

uzbn *husband*, meze(r) *measure*, rīzd *rancid (of bacon)*, frozn *frozen*, fuzi *soft, spongy*, buzed *butterfly*, gizn *to choke*. temz *hop-sieve*, ez *us*, siðez *scissors*, tšiuz *to choose*.

§ 31. ž (blade-point-open-voice) like the s in lit. Engl. measure. It only occurs after d and n:

džoul *to knock, strike*, džais *joist*, džudž *judge*, sādžn *sergeant*, eedž *age*, tšeedž *charge*, inž *hinge*, sinž *to singe*; but in words of French origin we have indžn *engine*, moendž *mange*.

CHAPTER II.

1. Short Vowels.

a.

§ 32. Windhill a corresponds to:

1. OE. æ(a) in originally closed syllables, § 57 : as *ashes*, fan (pret.) *found*, gam *game*, lat *late*, sal *shall*, sam up, (OE. samnian) *to pick up*, þak *thatch*.

2. Rarely OE. a(æ) in open syllables, § 71 : faðə(r) *father*, mak *to make*, tak *to take*.

3. Shortening of OE. ā, § 125 : as *to ask*, spatl *spittle*.

4. Shortening of OE. ǣ, §§ 135, 144 : blast *blast*. bad *bad*, laðə(r) *ladder*.

5. Rarely shortening of OE. ēa, § 186 : tšap *chap*.

6. Lit. Engl. æ in French words, § 194 ; galək (O. Fr. galc) *left hand*, ratn *rat*, valə *value*.

7. Lit. Engl. a in French words, § 195 : bastəd *bastard*, pastə(r) *pasture*.

8. Rarely lit. Engl. ei in French words, § 196 : aprən *apron*.

9. Lit. Engl. o (through the influence of the preceding w) in French words, § 202 : **kwaleti** *quality*, **warend** *to war-rant*.

10. Lit. Engl. e before r in French words, § 208 : **tarie(r)** *terrier*, **vari** *very*.

e.

§ 33. Windhill e corresponds to :

1. Germanic e, and the i-umlaut of a in originally closed syllables ; and also when e was originally followed by a single consonant + a suffix containing an l, m, n, r, §§ 72–3 : **delf** *delf*, **elp** *to help*, **leðə(r)** *leather*, **melt** *to melt*, **weft** *weft*.

bed *bed*, **ketl** *kettle*, **lenþ** (by assimilation) *length*, **mens** *neatness*, **set** *to set*.

2. Rarely OE. e in open syllables, § 88 : **brek** *to break*, **get** *to get*.

3. Germ. a before a following g, ŋ, š, §§ 59, 197 : **beg** *bag*, **bleg** *blackberry*, **emeŋ** *among*, **reŋ** *wrong*, **seŋk** *sank*. **eš** *ashtree*, **weš** *to wash*.

4. Rarely OE. a(æ) in other cases, § 60 : **eltə(r)** *halter*, **geðə(r)** *to gather*, **wesp** *wasp*.

5. Rarely OE. o, § 108 : **ðen** *then*, **wen** *when*.

6. Shortening of Germanic ǣ (W.S. ǣ, O. North. ē), § 134 : **bleðə(r)** *bladder*, **šepstə(r)** *starling*, **slept** *slept*.

7. Shortening of OE. ǣ (i-umlaut of ā), § 143 : **fleš** *flesh*, **len** *to lend*, **les** *less*.

8. Shortening of OE. ē, œ̄ (i-umlaut of ō), § 148 : **bled** *bled*, **gezlin** *gosling*, **met** *met*.

9. Shortening of Anglian ēo (= WS. īe) § 192 : **depþ** *depth*, **ten** *ten*.

10. Shortening of OE. ēa, § 186 : **lek** *leak*, **red** (adj.) *red*.

11. Shortening of OE. ēo, § 192: **brest** *breast*, **frend** *friend*.

12. Lit. Engl. ə in French words, § 206: **demək** *potato disease*, **mel** *to meddle*, **treml** *to tremble*.

13. Lit. Engl. æ before g, ŋ, š in French words, § 197: **dregŋ** *dragon*, **bleŋkit** *blanket*, **fešn** *fashion*.

14. Rarely lit. Engl. i in French words, § 212: **lenit** *linnet*, **rebit** *rivet*.

i.

§ **34.** Windhill i corresponds to:

1. OE. i, § 89: **bin** (OE. **binnan**) *within*, **bitn** *bitten*, **find** *to find*, **lig** *to lie down*, **wik** *quick, alive*.

2. OE. e (i-umlaut of a) before an original ŋ (now ŋ or nž), § 76: **iŋ** (ME. **hengen**) *to hang*, **sinž** *to singe*, **þiŋk** *to think*.

3. Rarely OE. e in other cases, § 77: **kil** *to kill*, **sitš** *such*, **wilə** *willow*.

4. OE. y (i-umlaut of u), § 117: **brig** *bridge*, **flig** (ME. **fligge**) *fledge*, **ig** (OE. **hyge**) *mood, temper*.

5. Shortening of OE. ī, § 160: **dwinl** *to dwindle*, **fift** *fifth*.

6. Shortening of OE. ȳ (i-umlaut of ū), § 177: **litl** *little*, **wiš** *to wish*.

7. Rarely shortening of Germanic ǣ, § 136: **ridl** *riddle*, **sili** *silly*.

8. Rarely shortening of OE. ǣ (i-umlaut of ā), § 145: **ive(r)** *ever*, **ivri** *every*.

9. Rarely shortening of OE. ē, older īe, § 150, note: **rik** *to smoke (of a chimney)*.

10. Rarely shortening of OE. ēo, § 192: **divl** *devil*, **sik** *sick*.

11. Lit. Engl. i in French words, § 211 : konsiðe(r) *to consider*, livə(r) *to deliver*, tšimli *chimney*.

12. Lit. Engl. e before nasals in French words, § 209 : lints *lentils*, šimi *chemise*.

O.

§ 35. Windhill o corresponds to:

1. West Germanic o in originally closed syllables ; and also when o was originally followed by a single consonant + a suffix containing an l, m, n, r, § 100 : bodm *bottom*, fotn (pp.) *fought*, lop *flea*, frozn *frozen*, olin (ME. holen) *holly-tree*, snod *smooth*, tšozn *chosen*, þrosl *thrush*.

2. Rarely OE. o in open syllables, § 110 : bodi *body*, popi *poppy*.

3. OE. a preceded by w and not followed by g, ŋ, š, or r + consonant, § 58 : swolə *swallow*, swop *to exchange*, wo(r) (accented form) *was*, wotə(r) *water*.

4. OE. ea(a) before ls, lt, § 58 : fols *false*, molt *malt*, solt *salt*.

5. Rarely OE. a in other cases, § 58 : oməst *almost*, oləs *always*, moni *many*.

6. Rarely OE. eo(e), § 80 : jolə (OE. geolu) *yellow*, fotš *to fetch*.

7. Shortening from OE. ā, § 125 : sori *sorry*.

8. Shortening of OE. ō, § 169 : foðə(r) *fodder*, tof *tough*.

9. Rarely shortening from OE. ēo, § 192 : foti *forty*, fotnit *fortnight*.

10. Lit. Engl. o in French words, § 214 : boni *nice, pretty*, džosl *to jostle*, kotn *cotton*, poridž *porridge*.

11. Lit. Engl. ā before n + consonant, in French words, § 200 : dons *dance*, ont *aunt*, tšons *chance*.

12. Rarely lit. Engl. ou in French words, § 217 : gol *goal*, rost *to roast*.

u.

§ 36. Windhill u corresponds to :

1. OE. u, § 111 : **drukɒ** *drunk*, **fun** (pp) *found.* **grund** *ground*, **kudl** *to embrace*, **kum** *to come*, **þunə(r)** *thunder*, **ug** *to carry*, **undəd** *hundred*.

2. Rarely OE. o, § 107 : **flutə(r)** *to flutter*, **uvm** *oven*.

3. Rarely OE. i, § 97: **kud** (OE. cwidu) *cud*, **tul** (ME. til) *to*.

4. Rarely OE. y, § 121 : **bluš** *to blush*, **bunl** *bundle*.

5. Shortening from OE. ā, § 126 : **ut** *hot*, **wun** *one*.

6. Shortening of OE. ō, § 169 b; **munþ** *month*, **muðə(r)** *mother*, **sluf** (OE. slōg) *slough*.

7. Shortening of OE. ū, § 174 : **fus** *fuss*, **plum** *plum*, **uðə(r)** *udder*, **uzbn** *husband*.

8. Lit. Engl. u in French words, § 227 : **butšə(r)** *butcher*, **puš** *to push*, **put** *to put*.

9. Lit. Engl. ɐ in French words, § 226 : **buzəd** *butterfly*, **mutn** *mutton*, **uml** *humble*.

10. Rarely lit. Engl. o in French words, § 215: **nuvl** *novel*.

ə.

§ 37. Windhill ə corresponds to :

1. Rarely OE. e, § 81 : **bəri** *berry*, **jəstedə** *yesterday*.

2. Rarely OE. i, § 91: **stərək** (OE. stirc, styric) *heifer*.

3. OE. u before a following r, § 113 : **bərə** *borough*, **fərə** *furrow*.

4. OE. y before a following r, § 120, (2): **bəri** *to bury*, **wəri** *to worry*.

5. Lit. Engl. i before a following r in French words, § 213 : **əperit** *spirit*.

2. The Long Vowels.

ā.

§ 38. Windhill ā corresponds to:

1. OE. ū, § 171: ās *house*, dāst *dust*, kā *cow*, rām *room*, rāst *rust*, slām *slumber*, þāzn *thousand*.

2. OE. medial -ug-, § 114: fāl *fowl*, kāl *cowl*.

3. Rarely OE. u before n + consonant, § 115: ānd *hound*, drānd *to drown*.

4. OE. a, ea before r + consonant, § 61: ād *hard*, bān *child*, wām *warm*.

5. OE. e, eo before r + consonant, § 74: āt *heart*, dwāf *dwarf*, wāk (noun) *work*.

6. OE. ēo before r + consonant, § 189: dālin *darling*, fādin *farthing*.

7. O. Fr. er before a following consonant, § 207: pāsn *parson*, sāvnt *servant*.

8. Lit. Engl. au in French words, § 235: dāt *doubt*, gān *gown*, pāðǝ(r) *powder*.

ī.

§ 39. Windhill ī corresponds to:

1. OE. i before ld, § 92: mīld *mild*, wīld *wild*.

2. OE. i before ht, § 93: brīt *bright*, nīt *night*, sīt *sight*.

3. OE. medial -ig-, § 94: stīl (OE. stigel) *stile*, tīl *tile*.

4. OE. e before ld, § 78: fīld *field*, wīld *to wield*.

5. Rarely OE. e in other cases, § 79: bīzm *besom*, wīl (adv.) *well*.

6. OE. y before ht, § 118: flīt *flight*, frīt *fright*.

7. OE. y before ld, § 119: bīld *to build*.

8. Germanic ǣ (WS. ǣ, O. North. ē), § 130: īmin *evening*, nīdl *needle*, þrīd *thread*.

9. OE. ē, § 155 : ī *he*, wī *we*.

10. OE. ē, œ̄ (i-umlaut of ō), § 147 : blīd *to bleed*, gīs *geese*, kīl *to cool*.

11. Anglian ē, ēo (=WS. īe), § 150 : bəlīv *to believe*, lītnin *lightning*, sīn *seen*.

12. Rarely OE. ī, § 158 : sī *to sigh*.

13. OE. ēo, § 187 ; dīp *deep*, nī *knee*, trī *tree*, wīl *wheel*.

14. Lit. Engl. ij in French words, § 232 : bīf *beef*, pīs *piece*.

ū.

§ **40.** Windhill ū corresponds to :

1. Rarely OE. o, § 106 : šūl *shovel*, stūp (ME. stolpe) *a post*.

2. Rarely OE. u, § 112 : būkþ (ME. bulke) *bulk, size*, ə-būn (OE. on-bufan) *above*, wūl *wool*.

ə.

§ **41.** Windhill ə̄ corresponds to :

1. OE. ær before a following consonant, § 69 : gə̄s (OE. gærs) *grass*.

2. OE. ir before a following consonant, § 90 : bə̄k *birch*, þə̄d *third*.

3. Rarely OE. or before a following consonant, § 104, (3) : wə̄d *word*, wə̄ld *world*.

4. OE. ur before a following consonant, § 113, (1) : də̄st *durst*, snə̄t (ME. snurtin) *to snort, snore*.

5. OE. yr before a following consonant, § 120, (1) : bə̄dn *burden*, bə̄þ *birth*, mə̄ðə(r) *murder*, wə̄k *to work*.

6. OE. ī (?) with metathesis of r, § 161 : kə̄sməs *Christmas*, kə̄sn *to christen*.

7. OE. ēa with metathesis of r, § 185 : gə̄t *great*.

8. Lit. Engl. ə in French words, § 228 : fəniš *to furnish*, kən *currant*.

3. The Diphthongs.

ai.

§ **42.** Windhill ai corresponds to:

1. OE. ī, § 156: ais *ice*, bait *to bite*, raiv *to tear*, sail (ME. sīlen) *to strain*, swaim *to climb a tree*, waif *wife*.

2. OE. ȳ (i-umlaut of ū), § 175: aid *hide, skin*, mais *mice*.

3. Rarely OE. i, § 95: ai (accented form) *I*.

4. Lit. Engl. ai in French words, § 229: paint *pint* sailm *asylum*, tais *to entice*.

ei.

§ **43.** Windhill ei corresponds to:

1. OE. e (Germanic e, and the i-umlaut of a) in originally open syllables, § 87: beid *bead*, eit *to eat*, meit *meat*, neiv *fist*, steil *to steal*.

2. OE. e before ht, § 86: feit *to fight*, reit *right*.

3. Rarely OE. æ (ea), § 67: eit (O. North. æhto, æhta) *eight*.

4. WS. ǣ, O. North. ē before a following k, § 132: leitš *leech*, speitš *speech*.

5. OE. ǣ (i-umlaut of a) before a following k, § 138: bleitš *to bleach*, reik *to reach*.

6. Rarely OE. ǣ in other cases, § 139: lein *to lean*, spreid *to spread*, kei *key*.

7. Rarely OE. ēa, § 182: ei *high*, nei *nigh, near*.

oi.

§ 44. Windhill oi corresponds to:

1. OE. o in originally open syllables, § 109: **foil** *foal*, **koil** *coal*, **oil** *hole*, **þoil** *to give ungrudgingly*, **þroit** *throat*.

2. Lit. Engl. oi in French words, § 216: **boil** *to boil*, **oil** *oil*.

3. Lit. Engl. ou in French words, § 219: **doit** *to dote*, **toist** *to toast*.

ui.

§ 45. Windhill ui corresponds to:

1. OE. ō, § 163: **bluid** *blood*, **duin** *done*, **uin** (ME. hōnen) *to treat badly, harass*, **tuiþ** *tooth*.

2. Lit. Engl. uw in French words, § 221: **buit** *boot*, **fuil** *fool*, **gruin** *a pig's snout*.

eu.

§ 46. Windhill eu corresponds to:

1. OE. e, eo,+ w, § 85: **eu** *ewe*, **streu** *to strew*.

2. OE. ēaw, § 180: **deu** *dew*, **feu** *few*, **teu** (OE. tēawian) *to work zealously*.

3. Rarely OE. ēow, § 190: **seu** *to sew*, **tšeu** *to chew*.

iu.

§ 47. Windhill iu corresponds to:

1. OE. iw, § 96: **tliu** (OE. cliwe) *a ball of string or worsted*.

2. Rarely OE. u, § 116: **þriu** *through*.

3. OE. īw, § 159: **spiu** *to vomit*, **tiuzdə** *Tuesday*.

4. OE. ō before a following **k, m**, and when final, § 164: **iuk** *hook*, **tiuk** *took*.

gium *gum*, lium *loom*.

diu *to do*, iniu (pl.) *enough*.

5. OE. ēow, § 190: bliu *blew*, briu *to brew*, niu *knew*.

6. Lit. Engl. juw in French words, § 237: flute(r) *future*, ius *use*, iuz *to use*, viu *view*.

7. Lit. Engl. uw in French words, § 239: bliu *blue*, friut *fruit*, riubub *rhubarb*, siu *to sue*.

ou.

§ 48. Windhill ou corresponds to:

1. OE. al before a following d, § 64: koud *cold*, oud *old*.

2. OE. o before ht, § 101: bout *bought*, doute(r) *daughter*.

3. OE. o, older ō, before ht, § 167: brout *brought*, þout *thought*.

4. ME. ow (OE. -og-), § 102: floun *flown*.

5. OE. ol before a following consonant, § 103: bouste(r) *bolster*, kouk *coke*, out *holt*.

6. OE. ōw, § 166: flou *to flow*, grou *to grow*.

7. O. Norse au, § 184: loup *to leap, jump*.

8. Rarely OE. āw, § 123: out *aught*, soul *soul*.

9. Rarely OE. ǣ before a following ht, § 140: tout *taught*.

10. Lit. Engl. ou in French words, § 220: boul *bowl*, poutš *to poach*.

11. al before d in French words, § 199: skoud *to scald*.

eə.

§ 49. Windhill eə corresponds to:

1. OE. a in originally open syllables, § 70: beed *to bathe*, eeg (OE. haga) *the berry of the hawthorn*, neeg (OE. gnagan) *to gnaw*, reeðe(r) *rather*, speen (OE. spanan) *to wean*, teem *tame*.

2. ME. ai. ei from OE. æg, § 65 : deə *day,* eəl *hail,* sneəl *snail.*

3. ME. ei from OE. eg, O. Norse ei, § 84 : breəd (OE. bregdan) *to resemble,* reən *rain,* beən (O. Icel. beinn) *near, direct.*

4. Rarely WS. ǣ, O. North. ē, § 133 : bleət *to bleat,* eə(r) *hair.*

5. Rarely OE. ǣ (i-umlaut of ā), § 141 : leədi *lady,* tleə *clay.*

6. O. Norse ei, § 127 : leək *to play,* weək *weak.*

7. Lit. Engl. ei in French words, § 204 : beəkŋ *bacon,* eənšn *ancient,* pleəs *place.*

8. O. Fr. ar before a following consonant, § 203 : geəd *guard,* kweət *quart,* tšeədž *to charge.*

9. ·Lit. Engl. ā in French words, § 195 : meəstə(r) *master,* pleəstə(r) *plaster.*

iə.

§ 50. Windhill iə corresponds to :

1. Rarely OE. ea, æ, a, § 68 : bieəd *beard,* iərin *herring.*

2. OE. e before r not followed by another consonant, § 75 : biə(r) *to bear,* swiə(r) *to swear.*

3. Rarely OE. er before a following consonant, § 74 ; iəþ *earth,* liən *to learn.*

4. Rarely OE. e in other cases, § 82 : frieət *to fret,* riəp *to reap.*

5. Rarely OE. i, § 98 : fliə(r) (Norw. flira) *to laugh or sneer at.*

6. WS. ǣ, O. North. ē, § 131 : drieəd *to dread,* miəl *meal, repast,* wiə(r) *where.*

7. OE. ǣ (i-umlaut of ā), § 137 : diəl *deal,* iəl *to heal,* sie *sea,* tliən *clean.*

8. OE. ēa, § 179: **briəd** *bread*, **striə** *straw*, **þriəp** (OE. þrēapian) *to contradict*.

9. OE. ēo before a following r, § 188: **biə(r)** *beer*, **diə(r)** *dear*.

10. Lit. Engl. ij in French words, § 231: **biək** *beak*, **fiətə(r)** *feature*, **viəl** *veal*.

11. Lit. Engl. iə in French words, § 233: **fiəs** *fierce*, **tliə(r)** *clear*.

oə.

§ 51. Windhill oə corresponds to:

1. OE. eal, al in the combinations lf, OE. lh, lk, ll, lm, lv, § 62: **koəf** *calf*, **woəf** (OE. wallu) *sickly to the smell, insipid to the taste*, **boək** *balk, beam*, **boəld** (ME. balled) *bald*, **poəm** *palm*, **soəv** *salve*.

2. ME. aw (of various origins), § 63: **moək** (ME. mauk) *maggot*, **soə** *he saw*, **kroəl** *to crawl*.

3. OE. or before a following consonant, § 104: **boən** *born*, **oəs** *horse*, **þoən** *thorn*.

4. OE. āw, § 123: **bloə** *to blow*, **noə** *to know*, **snoə** *snow*.

5. O. Norse au, § 184: **goəm** *heed, care*, **roət** *to bray*.

6. O. Fr. al before k, m, l, § 198: **goəki** *lefthanded*, **boəm** *balm*, **boəl** *ball*.

7. Lit. Engl. long open o in French words, § 225: **doəb** *to daub, smeer*, **džoənəs** *jaundice*, **poəz** *to kick*, **foətn** *fortune*, **oəðə(r)** *to order*.

uə.

§ 52. Windhill uə corresponds to:

1. Rarely OE. o, § 105: **uəp** *hope*, **nuəz** *nose*, **fluət** *to float*.

2. Rarely OE. o before a following r or r + consonant, § 104 (2): **smuə(r)** *to smother*, **buəd** *board*, **uəd** *hoard*.

3. Rarely OE. u before a following r or r + consonant, § 113, (3): **muən** *to mourn*.

4. OE. **eol**, § 83: **juək** *yolk*.

5. OE. **a** before mb, § 66: **kuəm** *comb*, **wuəm** *womb*.

6. OE. **ā**, § 122: **buən** *bone*, **duəf** *dough*, **nuən** *none*, **suəp** *soap*, **tluəþ** *cloth*, **uəm** *home*, **uəs**, **uəst** (OE. hās) *hoarse*.

7. OE. **ō** before a following r, § 165: **dluə(r)** (ME. glōren) *to stare*, **muə(r)** *moor*.

8. Lit. Engl. long open **o** in French words, § 223: **kuəd** *cord*, **fuəs** *force*.

9. Lit. Engl. **ou** in French words, § 218: **nuətis** *notice*, **tluək** *cloak*.

10. Lit. Engl. **uə** before a following r in French words, § 222: **puə(r)** *poor*.

āə.

§ 53. Windhill **āə** corresponds to:

1. OE. **a**, **ea** before a following r, § 61 : **dāə(r)** *dare*, **aə(r)** (accented form) *are*.

2. OE. **e**, **eo** before a following r, § 74: **wāə(r)** *worse*, **stāə(r)** *star*.

3. OE. **ū** before a following r, § 172: **kāə(r) dān** *to bend down*, **sāə(r)** *sour*.

4. Lit. Engl. **auə** before a following r in French words, § 236: **āə(r)** *hour*, **tāə(r)** *tower*.

4. The Triphthongs.

aiə.

§ 54. Windhill **aiə** corresponds to:

1. OE. **ī** before a following r, § 157 : **aiən** *iron*, **spaiə(r)** *spire*.

2. OE. **ȳ** (i-umlaut of **ū**) before a following r, § 176: **faiə(r)** *fire*, **aiə(r)** *to hire*.

3. Lit. Engl. **aiə** in French words, § 230: **raiət** *riot*, **umpaiə(r)** *umpire*.

iuə.

§ 55. Windhill **iuə** corresponds to:

1. Lit. Engl. **uə** before a following r in French words, § 240: **siuə(r)** *sure*.

2. Lit. Engl. **juə** before a following r in French words, § 238: **kiuə(r)** *cure*, **piuə(r)** *pure*.

ouə.

§ 56. Windhill **ouə** corresponds to:

Rarely OE. **ēow** before a following r, § 190: **fouə(r)** *four*.

CHAPTER III.

The Vowels of Accented Syllables.

In treating the vowels in accented syllables it is necessary to distinguish between vowels which were originally in closed syllables, e. g. OE. **dæg** *day*, **helpan** *to help*; and those which were originally in open syllables, e. g. OE. **dagas** *days*, **etan** *to eat*. In the former case OE. **æ** (a), o, e, usually appear in the W. dialect as **a, o, e**, whereas in the latter case they have generally become **ee, oi, ei**. When through inflexional endings the vowels **æ** (a), o, e were in OE. now in a closed syllable, now in an open one, the W. dial. has mostly generalised the vowel of the open syllable.

1. The Short Vowels.

a.

§ 57. West Germanic **a** (= West Saxon **æ** (a), and **ǫ** before nasals) in originally closed syllables usually appears as **a** in the W. dialect.

Examples are: **adl** (ME. adlen, O. Icel. öðla) *to earn*, **afte(r)** *after*, **akoen** *acorn*, **aks** *axe*, **am** (Sievers, OE. Gr.

§ 427) *am*, am *ham*, amə(r) *hammer*, and *hand*, anl *handle*,
ansə(r) *answer*, antm *anthem*, anvil *anvil*, ap (ME. happen)
to *wrap with clothes*, apl *apple*, arə *arrow*, as *ashes*, as-
midin *ash-pit*, at *hat*, avə(r)-meil (cp. ME. havere *oats*) *oat-
meal*, pret. bad (§ 373) *invited*, bak *back*, pret. ban *bound*,
band *string, cord*, barə *barrow*, bas *door mat, hassock*, baþ
bath, be-gan *began*, blak *black*, brak *broke*, brakɒ (OE.
bracce, gen. braccan) *a kind of fern*, bran (OE. brand)
niu *quite new*, bras *brass*, pret. brast *burst*, brat (O. Ir., OE.
bratt) *pinafore*, braznt *brazen, impudent*, daft *foolish, silly,
cowardly*, dam (O.Icel. damr) *large pond*, dlad *glad*, dlas
glass, dlazn to *glaze*, dlaznə(r) *glazier*, draft *draught, draft*,
fadm (ME. fadme) *fathom*, falə *fallow*, pret. fan *found*, fan
fan, fasn to *fasten, conclude a bargain by paying earnest
money*, flaks *flax*, flask *flask*, flat *flat*, gab (cp. O. Icel.
gabba) *impudence*, gad (cp. OE. ge-gada *companion*) *to
gossip*, galəs *gallows*, gam (OE. gamnian) *game, to gamble*,
ganə(r) *gander*, pret. gat *got*, pret. ga(v) *gave*, jarə *yarrow*,
kaf *chaff*, kal to *gossip*, kan *a can*, kan (unaccented form
kn more frequently with assimilation kɒ) *can*, kani *knowing,
intelligent, skilful, nimble*, kanl *candle*, kap *a cap*, kasl
castle, kat *cat*, krab *crab*, krabd (ME. crabed) *angry*, krabi
ill-tempered, kraft *craft*, krak to *crack*, kram to *cram, press
close together*, kramp *cramp*, lad (ME. ladde) *lad*, laf (with
a from the pp.) to *laugh*, laftə(r) *laughter*, lam *lamb*, land
land, lap *lap, lappet*, lap (ME. lappen) to *wrap up*, las
(ME. lasse) *lass*, last *last, latest*, lat *late*, lat (OE. lætt) *lath*,
latə(r) *latter, later*, man *man*, marə *marrow*, nap *nap*,
narə *narrow*, nat *gnat*, pak (ME. pakke) *a pack, bundle*,
pan *pan*, paþ *path*, pratli *gently, softly*, raftə(r) *rafter*, ram
ram, rami (cp. OE. hramsa *wild garlic*) *having a strong
taste or smell*, raml to *ramble*, ran *ran*, sad *sad*, sakləs
(OE. saclēas *innocent*) *simple, silly*, sam up (OE. samnian)

to pick up, gather together, **sal** (emphatic form, see § 391)
shall, **sale** *sallow*, **sand** *sand*, **sap** *sap*, pret. **sat** *sat*, **satl**
(OE. **sahtlian** *to make peace, reconcile*) *to settle*, **skaftin**
shafting, **skab** *scab*, **skraml** *scramble*, **skrat** (ME. **scrattin**)
to scratch, **slafte(r)** *to slaughter*, **slak** *slack*, **slave(r)** *slaver*,
spak (§ 372) *spake, spoke*, **span** *to span*, pret. **span** *span*,
spare *sparrow*, **staf** *staff*, pret. **stak** *stuck,* **stamp** *to stamp*,
stand *to stand*, **šade** *shadow*, **šaft** *shaft*, **šale** *shallow*, **šap**
shape, **tale** *tallow*, **tan** *to tan*, **tap** *tap*, **tate(r)** *tatter*, **tlam**
(see N.E.D. sub **clem**) *to famish*, **tlap** *clap*, **tlate(r)** *to clatter*,
trap *trap*, **tšavl** *to nibble at, gnaw, chew*, **þak** *thatch*, **ðat**
(see § 354) *that*, pret. **þrast** (§ 367, 4) *thrust*.

§ 58. **a** preceded by **w** and not followed by **r** + consonant (§ 61), **g**, **ꞃ**, **š** (§ 59), has become **o**. It has also
become **o** when followed by **ls**. It :

swole *swallow*, **swom** *swam*, **swon** *swan*, **swop** *to exchange,
barter*, **wokꞃ** *to waken*, **woks** *wax*, **wonde(r)** *to wander*,
wont *want*, **wo(r)** (emphatic from § 396) *was*, **wot** *what*,
wote(r) *water*, **wotš** *watch*.

fols *false*, **molt** *malt*, **olt** *halt*, **solt** *salt*.

a has also become **o** in **omest** *almost*, **oles** *always*, **moni**
many.

§ 59. **a**, followed by **g**, **ꞃ**, **š**, has become **e** :

beꞃ (cp. O.Icel. **banga** *to hammer*) *to throw violently*,
beꞃk *bank*, pret. **breꞃ** *brought*. pret. **deꞃ** (§ 367) *reviled,
reproached*, **dreꞃk** *drank,* pret. **eꞃ** (§ 367) *hung*, **eꞃ** *to hang*,
eꞃk *hank*, **eꞃkl** *uncle*, **eꞃke(r)** *anchor*, **emeꞃ** *among*, pret.
fleꞃ (§ 367) *threw*, **geꞃ** *gang*, **geꞃ-wee** *thoroughfare, passage*,
keꞃke(r) (ME. **cancren**) *to become rusty*, **kreꞃk** *crank*, **leꞃ**
to long for, **leꞃ-setl** *a long bench with a high back*, **leꞃ**
(this form is gradually going out of use. The younger

people say loŋ) *long*, neŋ to *gnaw as a pain*, neŋ-neel (see N.E.D. sub **agnail**) *corn on the foot*, preŋk *prank, trick*, pret. reŋ (§ 367) *rang*, reŋ *wrong*, reŋk *rank*, reŋl (ME. **wranglen**) *to pull the hair of the head*, pret. seŋ *sang*, seŋ (this form is now seldom heard among the younger people. Its place is gradually being supplanted by soŋ) *song*, seŋk *sank*, pret. sleŋ *slung*, pret. sleŋk *slunk*, speŋk *to beat, hit*, spreŋ *sprang*, pret. steŋk *stunk*, pret. steŋ *stung*, streŋ (archaic, stroŋ is now generally used) *strong*, pret. sweŋ *swung*, sweŋki *small beer*, šeŋk *shank*, pret. šreŋk *shrunk*, teŋ (cp. ME. **tange**, O.Icel. **tangi** *sting, dagger*) *a sting, to sting*, teŋz *tongs*, pret. tleŋ *clung*, tleŋk *to beat, flog*, þreŋ *busy*, þeŋk *to thank*, weŋ *thong*. muŋe(r) *monger* is a loan-word.

beg *bag*, bleg *blackberry*, breg *to brag*, deg (cp. Swed. **dagga** *to bedew*) *to sprinkle with water*, dreg *to drag*, fleg *flag*, geg (ME. **gaggin**) *to gag*, reg *rag*, seg (ME. **saggin** *to sink down*) *to distend*, stege(r) *to stagger*, šeg *shag*, tleg (Lowland Scot. **clag**) *to stick to, as thick mud to the boots*, tlegi *sticky, dirty (of roads), stopped up with dirt*, weg *to wag*, wegŋ *wagon*.

eš *ash-tree*, leš (ME. **laschin**) *to comb*, meš (cp. § 125) *mash*, peš (ME. **paschen**) *to dash, strike hard*, pleš (Swed. **plaska**) *to splash*, reš *rash*, smeš *smash*, weš *to wash*.

§ 60. In the following words we have e which in many of the examples is no doubt the i-umlaut of a: besk *to bask*, elte(r) (Prompt. Parv. **heltir**, Town. Myst. **heltere**, Stratmann) *halter*, esked (cp. ME. **aske** *lizard*) *newt, eft*, espin *aspin*, etš (ME. **hacchen**) *to hatch*, fest *fast*, geðe(r), *to gather*, te-geðe(r) *together*, kest (ME. **kesten**) *to cast*, kredl *cradle*, swetš (OE. **swæcc** *taste*) *a small sample of cloth, cotton*, etc., weðe(r) *whether*, wesp *wasp*, ev *have*, ez *hast, has*, ed *had*.

§ **61. a + medial r** has become **ā** before consonants:
ād *hard*, **ādn** *to harden*, **ām** *harm*, **ām** *arm*, **āp** *harp*, **āt**
thou art, **āvis(t)** *harvest*, **bāk** *bark*, **bāli** *barley*, **bān** *child*,
dān *to darn*, **fān** *fern*, **jād** (OE. **geard**) *yard*, **jān** *yarn*, **kāt**
cart, **māk** *mark*, **pāk** *park*, **spāk** *spark*, **stāk** (always used
in combination with some other word, as **stāk mad** *very
angry*, **stāk neəkt** *quite naked*, cp. OE. **stearc** *strong, severe*),
stākɳ (OE. **stearcian**) *to grow stiff, stiffen*, **swām** *swarm*,
swāþ (OE. **sweard**) *the skin of bacon*, **swāþi** *swarthy*, **šāp**
sharp, **tādʒ** *towards*, **wād** *ward*, **wāf** *wharf*, **wāk** (OE. **wærc**)
pain, as verb *to ache*, **wām** *warm*, **wān** *to warn*, **wāp** *warp*,
wāt *wart*.

But it has become **āə** before medial and final r in: **āə(r)**
are, **dāə(r)** *dare*.

§ **62. eal, al** has become **oə** in the combinations **lf**,
OE. **lh, lk, ll, (l), lm, lv**:

lf: **koəf** *calf*, **koəf** *calf (of the leg)*. **oəf** *half*, **oəpni** *halfpenny*, **oəpeþ** *halfpennyworth*.

lh: **woəf**, **woəfi** (OE. **walh** *sickly taste*) *sickly to the smell,
insipid to the taste*.

lk: **boək** (OE. **balca**) *balk, beam*, **stoək** *stalk, stem*, **toək**
to talk, **woək** *to walk*, **tšoək** *chalk*.

ll, (l): **boəld** (ME. **balled**) *bald*, **foəl** *to fall*, **foəl** *a veil*,
goəl *gall*, **koəl** (cp. **kal** § 57) *to call*, **oəl** *all*, **oəl** *hall*, **smoəl**
small, **stoəl** *stall*, **woəl** *wall*.

lm: **poəm** *palm*.   **lv**: **soəv** *salve*.

§ **63.** ME. **aw** (of various origins) has become **oə**:
doən *dawn*, **droə** *to draw*, **kroəl** *crawl*, **loə** *law*, **moək**
(ME. **mauk** Stratmann) *maggot*, **oək** *hawk*, **oəl** *awl*, pret.
soə *saw*, **tloə** *claw*.

§ **64. al** has become **ou** before a following **d**:
boud *bold*, **foud** *fold*, **foud** *to fold*, **koud** *cold*, **oud** *old*.

The regularly developed form **oud** *to hold* is now only used in the phrase **oud on** *stop!* The usual form **od** *to hold*, is a new formation from the past participle **odn**, where the stem vowel has been regularly shortened before the following **n**.

§ 65. ME. **ai, ei** from OE. **æg** has become **ee**:
breen *brain*, **dee** *day*, **deezi** *daisy*, **eel** (OE. **hægl**) *hail*, **feen** (OE. **fægen**) *glad*, *fain*, *gladly*, **fee(r)** *fair*, **mee** (shortened in **mebi** *perhaps*, *possibly*) *may*. **meen** *main*, **neel** *nail*, **peel** *pail*, **slee** (a new formation from the past participle) *to slay*; **sleen** *slain*, **sneel** *snail*, **teel** *tail*.

§ 66. **a** became lengthened to **ā** before **mb** already in early ME., as is shown by the forms in the Ormulum. This **ā** fell together with OE. **ā** = Germanic **ai**, and has accordingly become **ue** (see § 122) in the Windhill dialect: **kuem** *comb*, **wuem** *womb*. **lam** *lamb* is a new formation from the plural, where the short vowel was regularly retained, cp. Ormulum acc. sing. **lamb** (i. 274) beside acc. plural **lammbre** (ii. 109). The word-lists in vol. v of Ellis' Early English Pronunciation show that all English dialects have a short vowel in this word.

§ 67. **a** has become **ei** in **eit** *eight*, **eit'** (with suspended t) *eighth*. In **meitš** *to measure* the **ei** seems to point to an OE. **ǣ** (cp. §§ 132, 138).

§ 68. **a** has become **ie** in **bied** *beard*, **gie(r)** *gear*, **ierin** *herring*.

§ 69. **æ** (a) has become **ō** in **gōs** (OE. **gærs**, ME. **gers**) *grass*; and **oi** in **loin** (OE. **lane**, **lone**) *lane*, which has had the same development as old **o** in open syllables. See § 109.

§ 70. Short **a** in originally open syllables has usually become **ee** But see § 71.
Examples are: **beed** *to bathe*, **beek** *to bake*, but **bak-stn** (lit.

bake-stone) *the iron plate on which oat cakes are baked,*
bee(r) *bare,* pret. **bee(r)** *bore,* **bleed** *blade,* **bleez** *to blaze,*
deel *dale,* **dlee(r)** (ME. **glarin**) *to stare hard,* **dreeg** (OE.
dragan) *to drawl,* **dreek** *drake,* **eeg** (OE. **haga**) *the berry
of the hawthorn* (the tree is called **tšīz ən brɪəd trī** lit.
cheese and bread tree), **eeke(r)** *acre,* **eel** *ale,* **ee(r)** *hare,*
eet *to hate,* **bə-eev** *to behave,* **fee(r)** *to fare,* **fleek** *flake,*
freem (OE. **framian**) *to make a start* or *beginning,* **nītin-
geel** *nightingale,* **geep** *to gape,* **ə-geet** *in action, at work,*
geet *gate,* **greev** *grave,* **greez** *to graze,* **keek** *bread of
every kind,* **kee(r)** *care,* **kreev** *to crave,* **leedl** *ladle,* **leem**
lame, **leeð** (O.Icel. **hlaða**) *barn,* **meed** *made,* **meeg** (OE.
maga) *maw,* **meen** *mane,* **nīt-mee(r)** *nightmare,* **meet** (M.
Low Germ. **mate**) *mate,* **neeg** (OE. **gnagan**) *to gnaw,* **neekt**
naked, **neem** *name,* **preet** (cp. Swed. **prata**) *to prate, babble,*
reek *rake,* **reeðe(r)** *rather,* **seeg** (OE. **sage**) *a saw,* **seek** *sake,*
seel *sale,* **seem** *same,* **skeelz** *scales,* **skreep** *to scrape,* **sneek**
snake, **snee(r)** *snare,* **speed** *spade,* **speen** (OE. **spanan**) *to
wean,* **spee(r)** *to spare,* **steek** *stake,* **steel** (pret.) *stole,* **stee(r)**
to stare, **steevz** *staves,* **sweep** *the handle of a machine,* **šeed**
shade, **šeem** *shame,* **šee(r)** *share,* **šeev** *to shave,* **teel** *tale,*
teem *tame,* **teen** *taken,* **weed** *to wade,* **weel** *whale,* **ween** *to
wane,* **wee(r)** (ME. **waren**) *to spend* or *lay out money,*
weev *wave,* **weeve(r)** *to waver.*

§ 71. **æ** (**a**) appears as **a** in: **gavlek** (OE. **gafoluc** *spear*)
crowbar, **mak** *to make,* **ransak** (O.Icel. **rannsaka** *to search a
house*) *to ransack,* **tak** (O.Icel. **taka**) *to take,* **šak** *to shake,*
šakl *shackle,* **sadl** *saddle,* **stapl** *staple,* **faðe(r)** *father,* **laðe(r)**
foam, froth. On the stem-vowel in the last five words cp.
the similar double development in German in such words as
Schemel, Vater, nehmen, beside **Semmel, Vetter, kommen.**
See Paul-Braune's Beiträge, vol. ix. pp. 101–135.

e.

§ 72. West Germanic e and the OE. e which arose from the i-umlaut of a(o) have fallen together in the W. dialect as also in all other Mod. Engl. dialects, at least so far as can be ascertained from the word-lists in Ellis' EEP. vol. v.

§ 73. e (= old e and the i-umlaut of a(o)) in originally closed syllables usually appears as e in the W. dialect; and also when e was originally followed by a single consonant + a suffix containing an l, m, n, r.

1. Old e:

beg (OE. bedecian) *to beg*, bele *to bellow*, bel *bell*, delf *a stone quarry*, delv *to delve*, elde(r)-trī *elder*, elm *elm*, elp *help*, etn *eaten*, enent *anent, opposite*, evm *heaven*, felt *felt*, feðe(r) *feather*, freš *fresh*, getn (pp.) *got*, jel *yell*, jelp *yelp*, kres *cress*, leðe(r) *leather*, melt *to melt*, nest *nest*, nevi (OE. nefa, gen. nefan) *nephew*, rekn *to reckon*, sel(sen) *self*, seldn (OE. seldon) *seldom*, sevm *seven*, skelp (ME. skelpen) *to beat, flog*, skep (O. Icel. skeppa) *a large wicker basket for holding spinning bobbins*, etc., smel *to smell*, smelt *to smelt*, spek *speck*, swel *to swell*, swelt (OE. sweltan) *to faint, be overpowered by heat*, twenti *twenty*, þreš *to thresh*, þrešld *threshold*, weft *weft*, west *west*, weðe(r) (OE. weder) *weather*, weðe(r) (OE. weðer) *the wool of a sheep which has already been shorn at least once before*.

2. i-umlaut of a(o):

bed *bed*, bef (Germ. bäffen *to bark*) *to cough*, bek (O. Icel. bekkr) *beck*, beli *belly*, belesez *bellows*, belt *belt*, bend *to bend*, benk *bench*, best *best*, bete(r) *better*, blend *to blend*, dregz *dregs*, drenš *to drench*, eb *ebb*, edž *edge*, edž *hedge*, eft (O. Icel. hepti) *haft*, eg (O. Icel. eggia) *to urge, incite*,

eg (O. Icel. **egg**) *egg*, **el** *hell*, **els** *else*, **em** *hem*, **en** *hen*, **end**
end, **esp** (O. Icel. **hespa**) *hasp*, **evi** *heavy*, **fel** *to fell*, **kemp**
(ME. **kempe**) *short coarse white hairs in wool*, **ketl** *kettle*,
leg (O. Icel. **leggr**) *leg*, **lenþ** (by assimilation) *length*, **men**
men, **mens** (OE. **mennisc** *dignity, honour*) *neatness*, **neb**
bill, beak, **nek** *neck*, **net** *net*, **netl** *nettle*, **pen** *pen*, **peni**
penny, **rest** *rest*, **retš** *wretch*, **seg** *sedge*, **sek** (O. Icel. **sekkr**)
sack, **sel** *to sell*, **send** *to send*, **sent** *sent*, **set** *to set*, **slek**
small coal, **slek** (OE. **ge-sleccan**) *to extinguish a fire*, etc.
with water, **snek** (ME. **snekke**) *the latch of a door*, **spend** *to
spend*, **stem** *stem*, **step** *step*, **strenþ** (by assimilation) *strength*,
stretš *to stretch*, **šel** *shell*, **šelf** *shelf*, **tel** *to tell*, **temz** (cp. OE.
temsian *to strain, pass through a sieve*) *a coarse hair sieve*,
tletš (cp. O. Icel. **klekia** *to hatch, bring forth*) *brood of
chickens*, **twelft** *twelfth*, **twelv** *twelve*, **web** *web*, **wed** (OE.
weddian) *to wed, marry*, **wedž** *wedge*, **wel** (noun) *well*,
welp *whelp*, **ouə(r)-welt** (O. Icel. **velta**) *to turn over, upset*,
went *went*, **wet-stn** *whet-stone*.

§ 74. **er** in the combination **er** + consonant has partly
become **ā** and partly **iə**. The reasons for this twofold
development are not clear. It is probable that the words
belonging to the latter category have been influenced by
the literary language :

āt *heart*, **bāk** *to bark*, **bākm** (OE. **beorg** + **ham** N.E.D.
sub **bargham**) *collar of a horse*, **bām** *barm*, **bān** (OE. **bern**)
barn, **dāk** *dark*, **dwāf** *dwarf*, **fāt** (ME. **ferten**) *pedere*, **kāv**
to carve, **smāt** *smart*, **stāv** *to starve*, **wāk** (noun) *work*, **wātə**
(lit. work-day) *week-day*.

Before final **r** we have **āə** : **fāə(r)** (OE. **feorr**) *far*, **stāə(r)**
(OE. **steorra**) *star*, **wāə(r)** (O. Icel. **verre**) *worse*.

iənist *earnest*, **iəþ** *earth*, **jied** (3 feet) *yard*, **jiən** *yearn*,
liən *learn*.

The following words seem to have been borrowed from the literary language : **bēn** *to burn*, **gēn** (with metathesis) *to grin*, **wēþ** *worth*, **sued** (older **swēd**) *sword*.

§ **75.** **ə** has become **iə** before r not followed by another consonant: **biə(r)** *to bear*, **piə(r)** *pear*, **smiə(r)** *to smear*, **spiə(r)** *spear*, **swiə(r)** *to swear*, **wiə(r)** *to wear*, **šiə(r)** *to shear.* The only exceptions are : **tāə(r)** *tar*, **meə(r)** *mare*.

§ **76.** **ə** (i-umlaut of **a**) has become **i** before original **ŋ** (now **ŋ** or **ŋž**): **iŋ** (ME. **hengen**, O. Icel. **hengia**) *to hang*, **iŋž** *hinge*, **iŋlnd** *England*, **iŋliš** *English*, **diŋ** up (O. Icel. **dengia** *to beat, strike*) *to reproach*, **fliŋ** (ME. **flingen**) *to fling, throw*, **kriŋž** *to cringe*, **liŋə(r)** *to linger*, **miŋl** *to mingle*, **siŋž** *to singe*, **sliŋ** *to sling*, **striŋ** *string*, **þink** *to think*, **wiŋ** *wing*.

§ **77.** **ə** has become **i** in : **giv, gi** *to give*, **kil** *to kill*, **milk** *milk*, **rid** *rid*, **siks** *six*, **sikst** *sixth*, **silvə(r)** *silver*, **sistə(r)** (probably from O. Icel. **syster**) *sister*, **sitš** *such*, **šil** (ME. **schellen**, but Prom. Parv. p. 446 has **schillin**, Stratmann) *to shell peas*, etc., **wile** *willow*, **witš** *which*.

§ **78.** **ə** has become **ī** before **ld** : **fīld** *field*, **jīld** *to yield*, **šīld** *shield*, **wīld** *to wield*.

§ **79.** The following words also have **ī** : **bīzm** *besom*, **dī** (ME., Ormulum **deʒen**) *to die*, **wīl** (adv.) *well*, but see § 399, **wīzl** *weazel*, and **gīn** *given*.

§ **80.** **ə** has become **o** in : **fotš** (OE. **feccan**, Town. Myst. **fetche, foche**, inf. **fott**, Sweet, HES. p. 315) *to fetch*, **jole** *yellow*, **jòn** *yon*, **swole** (OE. **swelgan**, ME., Ormulum **swollʒhen**) *to swallow*. We have **oe** in **joen** (OE. **geonian**, also **gānian**) *to yawn*.

§ **81.** **ə** has become **ə** in : **bəri** *berry*, **(ə)levm** *eleven*, **jəst** *yeast*, **jəstədə** *yesterday*, **jət** *yet*.

§ **82.** e has become iə in: əstiəd *instead*, **friət** *to fret*, *bewail, mourn over,* **riəp** *to reap*, but cp. Sievers, OE. Gr. § 382, 3.

§ **83.** OE. eol has become uə in : **juək** *yolk.*

§ **84.** ME. ei from OE. eg, O. Icel. ei has become eə :

breəd (OE. **bregdan**) *to resemble, act like another person,* **geən** (OE. **gegn**) *near, direct*, **leə** *to lay*, **leəd** *laid*, **leən** *lain*, **reən** *rain*, **seə** *to say*, **seəl** *sail*, **weə** *way*, **eweə** *away*.

beən (O. Icel. **beinn**) *near, direct*, **beət** *bait*, **neə** *nay*, **steək** *steak*, **ðeə** (accented form) *they*, **ðeə(r)** (accented form) *their.*

e has also become eə in **feəvr(r)** *fever.*

§ **85.** e(eo) + w has become eu: **eu** *ewe*, **streu** *to strew.*

§ **86.** The combination eht has become eit: **feit** *to fight*, **reit** *right*, **streit** *straight*.

§ **87.** Short e in open syllables has generally become ei :

beid *bead*, **breitš** (O. Fris. **breke**) *a breach*, **eit** *to eat*, **briəd-fleik** (O. Icel. **fleki** *hurdle*) *a hurdle on which oatcakes are dried*, **meil** *meal-flower*, **meit** *meat*, **neid** *to knead*, **neiv** (O. Icel. **knefi**) *fist*, **pei** (ME. **pese**) *pea*, **speik** *to speak*, **bed-steid** *bedstead*, **steil** *to steal*, **steil** (OE. **stel**) *the handle of a pot or jug*, **steim** (OE. **ge-stefnian, a-stemnian** *to give voice for, appoint*) *to bespeak*, **treid** *to tread*, **wei** (OE. **wegan**) *to weigh*, **weik** (ME. **weke**) *the wick of a lamp or candle*, **weiv** *to weave.*

§ **88.** Short e in open syllables has remained in : **brek** *to break*, **get** (O. Icel. **geta**) *to get*, **lek** (O. Icel. **leka**) *to leak.*

i.

§ **89.** OE. i has generally remained :

bid *to invite to a funeral*, pp. **bidn**, **big** *big, large*, **bil**

bill, bin (OE. binnan) *within*, bind *to bind*, biɳ (ME. bing,
O. Icel. bingr) *a bin*, bit *a bit*, bite(r) *bitter*, bitn *bitten*,
bitš *bitch*, biznəs *business*, blind *blind*, blis *bliss*, brim
(ME. brimmen, cp. O. Icel. brimi *burning heat*) *to put the
boar to the sow*, briɳ *to bring*, dig *to dig*, dim *dim*, diš
dish, diðə(r) (ME. diderin) *to tremble, shiver with cold*,
dlitə(r) *to glitter*, drift *drift*, driɳk *to drink*, drivm *driven*,
fidl *fiddle*, fikl *fickle*, film *film*, fin *fin*, find *to find*, fiɳə(r)
finger, fiš *fish*, fit *ready, prepared*, flik *flitch*, flikə(r) *to
flicker*, flint *flint*, gidi *giddy*, gift *gift*, gilt (OE. gilte, O.
Icel. gilta) *a young female pig*, bə-gin *to begin*, grind *to
grind*, grip *grip*, if *if*, ik *to itch*, il *ill*, ilt *hilt*, im *him*, in,
i *in*, ində(r) (occ. inðə(r)) *to hinder*, bi-int *behind*, it *it*, it
to hit, iðə(r) *hither*, iz *is*, iz *his*, kid *kid*, kiɳ-kof *whooping-
cough*, kiɳk (ME. kinkən *to pant, gasp*) *to cough* (of whoop-
ing-cough), kist (O. Icel. kista) *chest, box*, kit (ME. kitte) *a
pail*, kitl (ME. kitelen) *to tickle*, krisp *crisp*, lid *lid*, lig (OE.
licgan) *to lie down*, lik *to lick*, lim *limb*, lip *lip*, liv *to live*,
livə(r) *liver*, midl *middle*, miks *to mix*, mil-dəu *mildew*, mint
mint, mis *to miss*, mizl-tuə *mistletoe*, mist *mist*, mitš *much*,
nibl *to nibble*, niml *nimble*, nit (OE. hnitu) *nit*, pig *pig*, pigin
a small water-can, pitš *pitch*, piþ *pith*, prik *to prick*, prikl
prickle, rib *rib*, ridl (ME. ridil Prom. Parv. p. 433, Stratmann) *sieve*, ridn *ridden*, rift (ME. riften) *to belch, eructate*,
rim *rim*, rind *rind*, riɳ *ring*, riɳ *to wring*, riɳkl *wrinkle*,
rist *wrist*, rizn *risen*, ritn *written*, sift *to sift*, sikl *sickle*,
grun-sil *groundsel*, silk *silk*, sin *since*, sində(r) *cinder*, siɳ
to sing, siɳk *to sink*, sit *to sit*, siv *sieve*, skift *to shift, remove*, skin *skin*, skil *skill*, slidn (pp.) *slid*, sliɳk *to slink*,
slip *to slip*, slipi *slippery*, slitn (pp.) *slit*, smitl *to infect*,
smitn *smitten*, smiþ *smith*, smiði *smithy*, spil *to spill*, spin
to spin, spinl *spindle*, spit *to spit*, spitək *spigot*, spriɳ *to
spring*, stik *stick*, stik *to stick*, stil *still*, stiɳ *to sting*, stiɳk

to stink, stitš *stitch,* strikɒ *stricken,* swift *swift,* swil (OE.
swilian) *to rinse, wash out,* swilinz *thin liquid food for
pigs,* swim *to swim,* swiɒ *to swing,* šift *chemise,* šilin *shilling,* šin *shin,* šip *ship,* šrimp *shrimp,* šriɒk *to shrink,* tik
tick, til *to till,* tin *tin,* tit, titi (OE. tit) *breastmilk,* tlim *to
climb,* tliɒ *to cling,* tlip *to clip,* tšikin *chicken,* tšildə(r)
(only used in the plural, for the sing. bān is always used)
children, tšin *chin,* twig *twig,* twin *twin,* twiɒkl *to twinkle,*
twist *twist,* þik *thick, friendly, in love with,* þiɒ *thing,* þisl
thistle, þrift *thrift,* ðis *this,* wi *with,* widə *widow, widower,*
wik (O. Icel. vik *stirring, moving) quick, alive,* wik *week,*
wil (accented form) *will,* win *to win,* wind *wind,* wind
to wind, wində *window,* wintə(r) *winter,* wiɒk *to wink,*
wispə(r) *to whisper,* wisl *to whistle,* wit *wit,* witl (ME.
þwitel) *large carving knife,* witš *witch,* wizn (OE. wisnian
to dry up) to wither.

§ 90. ir + consonant has become ə̄ + consonant :
bə̄d *bird,* bə̄k *birch,* gə̄sl *gristle,* ə̄d *herd,* tšə̄tš (but
kə̄-gət *kirkgate) church,* þə̄d *third,* þə̄ti *thirty,* wə̄l *to
whirl.*

§ 91. i has become ə in: gosəp *gossip,* jəs *yes,* ·stərək
(OE. stirc, styric) *heifer,* ə(r) *her,* tšərəp *to chirp.*

§ 92. i has been lengthened before ld: mīld *mild,*
wīld *wild.* But tšildə(r) (only used in the plural, for the
sing. bān is used) *children,* owing to the following suffix.

§ 93. ME. iht has become īt: brīt *bright,* līt *light,*
levis, līts *the lungs of animals,* mīt (noun) *might,* nīt *night,*
shortened in fotnit *fortnight,* plīt *plight,* sīt *sight,* slīt
slight, tīt *tight.* weit (OE. gewihte) has been influenced by
wei *to weigh.*

§ 94. Medial OE. ig has become ī in: stī *sty, ladder,*
stīl (OE. stigel) *stile,* tīl *tile.*

§ 95. i has become ai in: ai (accented form, see § 350) *I*.

§ 96. jw has become iu: tliu (OE. cliwe) *a ball of string or worsted.*

§ 97. i has become u in: kud (OE. cwidu) *cud,* ruš *rush,* tul *to.*

§ 98. i has become iǝ in: fliǝ(r) (Norw. flira) *to laugh or sneer at,* striǝk *streak, stripe,* ðiǝz *these.*

§ 99. i has become e in: lenit (ME. lynet, probably from Fr. linotte) *linnet.*

O.

§ 100. OE. o (= West Germanic o) in originally closed syllables has usually remained o; and also when o was originally followed by a single consonant + a suffix containing an l, m, n, r:

blob (see N.E.D.) *a bubble, bulb,* bodm *bottom,* boks *box,* borǝ *to borrow,* brokṇ *broken,* broþ *broth,* dof *to undress,* dog *dog,* dokṇ (OE. docce) *a dock,* dolt *lump of dirt,* don *to dress,* drop *drop,* džogl (cp. ME. joggen) *to shake,* flok *flock,* fog (ME. fogge) *aftergrass,* foks *fox,* folǝ *to follow,* fond (ME. fonned, pp. of fonnen *be foolish) fond,* fotn (pp.) *fought,* frog *frog,* frost *frost,* froþ *froth,* frozn *frozen,* god *god,* gospl *gospel,* kob-web *cob,* kod *cod,* kof *cough,* kok *cock,* kokl *cockle,* kolǝp (ME. colop, cp. O. Swed. kollops) *slice (of bacon),* kopǝ(r) *copper,* kroft (OE. croft) *a small field,* krop *crop,* kros *cross,* loft *loft,* lok *lock,* loks *small pieces of wool which have been detached from the fleece,* lop (OE. lopp) *flea,* lopǝd (ME. lopren *coagulate) clotted, covered with dirt,* lopstǝ(r) *lobster,* lost *lost,* lot *lot,* mos *moss,* mop *moth,* nod (ME. nodden) *nap, short sleep,* nok *to knock*, **not** *knot*, **notš** *notch*, **od** *odd*, **ofl** *offal*, **oft** *oft*, *often*, **og** (ME. **hog**) *the first year's wool of a sheep*, **oks** *ox*, **olǝ** *hollow*, **olin** (OE. **holen**) *the holly-tree, twig of the holly-tree*, **on** (accented form) *on*, **op** *to hop*, **opm** *open*, **otǝ(r)** *otter*, **otšǝd** *orchard*, **ovl** *hovel*, **plot** *plot*, **poks** *pox*, **prod** *to prick, goad*, **rok** *rock*, **rot** *to rot*, **slop** (O. Icel. **sloppr**) *the leg of a pair of trousers*, **slot** (ME. **slot**) *bolt of a door*, **smok** *smock*, **snod** (O. Icel. **snoðinn** *smooth (of hair)*), *smooth, even*, **snodn** *to make smooth*, **snot** *snot*, **sod** *sod*, **sodnd** *saturated, wet through*, **sok** *sock*, **sorǝ** *sorrow*, **spokɒ** *spoken*, **spot** *spot*, **stok** *stock*, **stop** *to stop*, **šop** *shop*, **šot** *shot*, **šotn** (pp.) *shot*, **tlog** *a shoe with wooden soles*, **tlok** *the common black beetle*, **tlok** *to cluck*, **tlot** *clot*, **tlovm** *cloven*, **top** *top*, **topin** (ME. **topping**) *the front part of the hair of the head*, **topl** *to fall over*, **tot** *a small beer glass*, **trodn** *trodden*, **trof** *trough*, **tšozn** *chosen*, **þrosl** (OE. **þrostle**) *thrush*, **þrotl** (ME. **þrotlen**) *to press on the windpipe*, **wovm** *woven*.

§ 101. **oht** has become **out**: **bout** *bought*, **doutǝ(r)** *daughter*, **rout** *wrought*. We have however **o** in **fotn** (§ 100) *fought*.

§ 102. ME. **ow** (= OE. **og**) has become **ou**: **reǝn-bou** *rain-bow*, **floun** *flown*.

§ 103. **ol** + consonant has become **ou** + consonant: **boul** *bowl*, **boustǝ(r)** *bolster*, **bout** *bolt*, **fouk** *folk*, **goud** *gold*, **kouk** (see N.E.D. sub. **colk**) *coke, cinder*, **kout** *colt*, **out** *holt*, **m̍oud-wǎp** *a mole*, **stoun** *stolen*, **toul** *toll*.

But we have **o** in **wod** (accented form) *would*; and **u** in **sud** (accented form) *should*; and **oǝ** in **noǝp** (ME. **nolpen** *to strike*) *to beat, strike*.

§ 104. The development of **o** before a following **r**:

(1) **oǝ**: **boǝn** *born*, **foǝk** *fork*, **koǝn** *corn*, **tǝ-moǝn** *to-*

morrow, **moen, moenin** *morning,* **noeþ** *north,* **oen** *horn,*
oes *horse,* **stoem** *storm,* **swoen** *sworn,* **šoen** *shorn,* **šoet**
short, **toen** *torn,* **þoen** *thorn.*

(2) **ue**: **e-fue(r)** *before,* **smue(r)** (OE. **smorian**) *to smother,
suffocate.*

bued *board,* **e-fued** *afford,* **ued** *hoard.*

(3) **ō**: **spē(r)** *spur,* **wēd** *word,* **wēld** *world.*

§ 105. **o** has become **ue** in: **buekɒ** (ME. **bolkin**) *to
belch, retch,* **fluet** *float,* **kuev** *cove,* **juek** *yoke,* **uep** *hope,* **nuez**
nose, **puek** (OE. **poca**) *sack,* **pueni** *pony,* **puest** (OE. **post**
from Lat. **postis**) *post,* **ruez** *a rose,* **stuev** *stove,* **suek** *to soak,*
suep (OE. **sopa** *sup, small quantity (of water)) a little tea*
or *beer,* etc., **tšuek** *to choke.*

NOTE.—Most, if not all, of the above words are early borrowings from the
literary language.

§ 106. **o** has become **ū** in: **smūk** *to smoke,* **šūl** *shovel,*
stūp (ME. **stolpe**) *a post.*

§ 107. **o** has become **u** in: **dul** *dull,* **foks-dluv** *fox-
glove,* **flute(r)** *to flutter,* **kus** (noun, also used as verb)
kiss, **uvm** *oven.*   It is very probable that the **u** in some of
these words goes back to OE. **y** (§ 121), as has been
pointed out by Prof. Napier in the *Academy,* May 7,
1892, p. 447.

§ 108. **o** has become **e** through loss of stress in: **ðen**
then, **wen** *when.*

§ 109. **o** in originally open syllables has generally
become **oi**: **boil** (O.Icel. **bolr**, ME. **bole**) *bole of a tree,* **foil**
foal, **goit** (ME. **gote**) *channel, mill-stream,* **koil** *coal,* **pig-
coit** (OE. **cot, cote**) *pig-sty,* **loin** (OE. **lone**) *lane,* **loiz** (OE.
losian) *to lose,* **moit** *mote,* **oil** *hole,* **roid** (mostly used in the
plural **roidz**) *a clearing (of a wood),* **soil** (OE. **sol**) *ground,*

earth, **soil** (OE. **sole**, Lat. **solea**) *sole*, **tlois** (OE. **close**) *a*
field, **toidi** *very small*, **þoil** (OE. **þolian** *to endure*) *to give*
ungrudgingly, **þroit** *throat*.

§ 110. Short o in open syllables has remained in : **bodi**
(OE. **bodig**) *body*, **popi** (OE. **popig**) *poppy*.

u.

§ 111. Short u has generally remained unchanged :
bluðe(r) *to cry, weep*, **buk** *buck*, **bul** *bull*, **bulek** *bullock*,
bun (pp. of **bind**) *bound, obliged, beholden*, **bute(r)** *butter*,
busl *to bustle*, **drukɒ** (pp.) *drunk*, **dub** *a small pool of*
water, **dum** *dumb*, **dun** *to urge for payment*, **duɒ** *dung*,
ful *full*, **fule(r)** *fuller*, **fun** (pp.) *found*, **grunsil** *groundsel*,
grunt *to grunt, grumble, find fault*, **grund** *ground*, **grunz**
(pl.) *sediment*, **be-gun** *begun*, **gust** *gust*, **guts** (OE. **gutt**)
entrails, belly, **juɒ** *young*, **krudl** (cp. ME. **cruddin**) *to*
curdle, **krudz** (ME. **crudde**) *curds*, **krum** *crumb*, **krumpl**
to crumple, **kudl** *to embrace*, **kuf** (**kuft**) *cuff*, **kum** *to come*,
kunin *cunning*, **kup** *cup*, **lug** (ME. **luggen**, Swed. **lugga**
to lug, drag) *to pull the hair of the head*, **luɒ** *lung*, **luv**
love, **muml** *to mumble*, **mun** (accented form, O.Icel. **muna**
will, shall) *must*, **musl** *mussel*, **num** *numb*, **nut** *nut*, **pluk**
to pluck, **pund** *a pound*, **rudi** *ruddy*, **ruɒ** *wrung*, **skuft** *the*
nape of the neck, **skul** *skull* (*of the head*), **skute(r)** *to spill*,
sluɒ *slung*, **spruɒ** *sprung*, **spun** *spun*, **stubi** (cp. O.Icel.
stubbi *stock of a tree*) *short and stiff*, **stump** *stump*, **stun** *to*
stun, **stuɒ** *stung*, **stut** (cp. ME. **stutten** *to cease, stay*) *to*
stutter, **sum** *some*, **sume(r)** *summer*, **sumet** (lit. somewhat)
something, anything, **sump** *a puddle or dirty pool of water*,
sun *son*, **sun** *sun*, **sunde** *Sunday*, **sukɒ** *sunk*, **suɒ** *sung*,
swum (pp.) *swum*, **swuɒ** *swung*, **šrukɒ** *shrunk*, **šun** *to shun*,

šuðe(r) (ME. schuderen) *to shudder*, tluŋ *clung*, tluste(r) *cluster*, tub (ME. tubbe) *tub*, tug (ME. tuggen) *to tug, plod*, tuml *to tumble*, tun *tun*, tuŋ *tongue*, tup (ME. tuppe) *a ram*, tusk *tusk*, tšuf *proud, haughty*, ug *to carry*, ugli *ugly*, ugŋ (see Notes and Queries i. 10. 400, Nov. 18, 1854) *hip*, ulz (ME. huls) *bean-swads*, unded *hundred*, unde(r) *under*, uni *honey*, unt *to hunt*, uŋe(r) *hunger*, þune(r) *thunder*, wud *wood*, wulzi *wollen*, wun (pp.) *wound*, wun (pp.) *won*, wund *wound*, wunde(r) *wonder*.

§ 112. u has become ū in : būk, būkþ (ME. bulke, O.Icel. bulki) *bulk, size*, e-būn (OE. on-bufan) *above*, mūfin *muffin*, pūl *to pull*, šūlde(r) (this word has been influenced by the literary language. Most old people still say šūðe(r)) *shoulder*, wūl *wool* (but wulzi *wollen*).

§ 113. u before a following r.

(1) ō : dōst *durst*, kōs *to curse*, skōf *scurf*, snōt (ME. snurtin, cp. Low Germ. snurten *to snort, snore*) *to sneeze, giggle*, tōn *to turn*, tōf *turf*.

(2) e : bere *borough*, eri *row, disturbance, noise*, fere *furrow*.

(3) ue : due(r) *door*, muen *to mourn*. It is highly probable, however, that muen has nothing to do with OE. murnan, but is simply muen *to moan* (§ 122).

§ 114. Medial ug has become ā : fāl (OE. fugol) *fowl*, kāl (OE. cugle) *cowl*, sā (OE. sugu) *sow*.

§ 115. u underwent early lengthening, and then had the same further development as old ū (§ 171) in : ānd *hound*, bāns (ME. bunsen) *to bounce*, drānd (OE. druncnian) *to drown*.

§ 116. u has become iu in : þriu (þrift) *through, from, on account of*.

y.

§ 117. y (=the i-umlaut of u) has generally become i :
bizi *busy*, brig *bridge*, brim *brim*, brimstn *brimstone*, did
did, didl (cp. OE. dyderian) *to cheat*, din *din*, dip *to dip*,
dizi *dizzy*, fil *to fill*, flig (ME. fligge, cp. OHG. flukke *able
to fly*) *to fledge*, flit *to remove*, kiln *kiln*, əkin *akin*, kinl *to
bring forth (of rabbits)*, kinliɲ *firewood*, kiɲ *king*, kripl
cripple, kitšn *kitchen*, ig (OE. hyge *mind*) *mood, temper*,
il *hill*, inš *inch*, ip *hip*, ipin *a cloth placed round the hips of
children*, lift *to lift*, liɲ (O.Icel. lyng) *heather*, lisn *to listen*,
mig *midge*, miln *mill*, nit *to knit*, pilə *pillow*, pit *pit*, rig
(OE. hrycg) *back*, rigin *ridge of a house*, sil *sill*, sin *sin*,
kā-slip *cowslip*, snift *to sniff, scent*, stint *to stint*, tlik (OE.
clycc(e)an, see N.E.D. sub clitch) *to seize, snatch, catch hold*,
tlip *to clip*, trim *to trim*, þin *thin*.

§ 118. yht has become īt : flīt *flight*, frīt *fright*, rīt
wright.

§ 119. y has become ī before ld : bīld *to build*, gīld *to
gild*.

§ 120. y before a following r.

(1) ə̄ : bə̄dn *burden*, bə̄l āt (OE. byrlian) *to draw or
pour out (drink to or for anyone)*, bə̄þ *birth*, ə̄dl *hurdle*,
fə̄st *first*, gə̄dl *girdle*, kə̄nl *kernel*, mə̄þə(r) *to murder*, mə̄ki
mirky, šə̄t *shirt*, tə̄d (cp. OE. tyrdel, Stratmann) *turd*,
wə̄k *to work*, wə̄m *worm*.

(2) ə : beri *to bury*, meri *merry*, sperinz (cp. OE.
spyrian) *banns of marriage*, ste(r) *to stir*, weri *to worry*,
fig-wet *figwort*.

§ 121. y has become u in : bluš *to blush*, bruslz *bristles*,
bunl *bundle*, krutš *crutch*, muk *muck*, stubl *stubble*, šut
to shut, šutl *shuttle*, trunl *trundle*.

2. The Long Vowels.

ā.

§ 122. The normal development of OE. ā in the W. dialect is uǝ :

bruǝd *broad*, **buǝn** *bone*, **buǝ(r)** *boar*, **buǝt** *boat*, **buǝþ** *both*, **druǝn** *drone*, **druǝv** (noun) *drove*, **duǝ** *doe*, **duǝf** *dough*, **duǝfi** *cowardly*, **duǝl** *dole*, **fuǝm** *foam*, **guǝd** *goad*, **gruǝn** *to groan*, **gruǝp** *to grope*, **gruǝv** *grove*, **guǝ** *to go*, **ǝ-guǝ** *ago*, **guǝn** *gone*, **guǝ(r)** *gore*, **guǝst** *ghost*, **guǝt** *goat*, **kruǝk** *to croak*, **luǝd** *load, burden*, **luǝf** *loaf*, **luǝn** *loan*, **ǝluǝn** *alone*, **luǝnsm** *lonely*, **luǝþ** *loath*, **luǝð** *to loathe*, **muǝn** (OE. mǣnan, ME. mǣnen, mānen) *to moan*, **muǝ(r)** *more*, **muǝst** *most*, **nuǝ** *no*, **nuǝn** *none*, **ruǝd** *road*, **ruǝp** *rope*, **ruǝ(r)** *to roar*, **struǝk** *to stroke*, **struǝk** (OE. strāc) *half a bushel*, **stuǝn** *stone*, **suǝ** *so*, **suǝp** *soap*, **suǝ(r)** *sore*, **tluǝþ** *cloth*, **tluǝz** *clothes*, **tluǝð** *to clothe*, **tluǝvǝ(r)** *clover*, **tuǝ** *toe*, **tuǝd** *toad*, **tuǝkn** *token*, **tuǝn** (lit. *the one*) *one of two*, **uǝ** *who*, **uǝk** *oak*, **uǝli** *holy*, **uǝl** *whole*, **uǝm** *home*, **uǝnli** *lonely*, **uǝ(r)** *oar*, **uǝ(r)** *hoar*, **uǝs(t)** (OE. hās) *hoarse*, **uǝts** *oats*, **uǝþ** *oath*, **wuǝ** *woe*.

§ 123. āw has become oǝ :

bloǝ *to blow*, **kroǝ** *crow*, **kroǝ** *to crow*, **moǝ** *to mow*, **noǝ** *to know*, **sloǝ** *slow*, **snoǝ** *snow*, **soǝ** *to sow*, **þoǝ** *to thaw*, **þroǝ** *to throw*, **oǝðǝ(r)** *either*, **noǝðǝ(r)** *neither*.

But we have ou in: **out** (OE. āwiht) *aught*, **nout** (OE. nāwiht) *naught*, **soul** (OE. sāwol) *soul*.

§ 124. ā has become ou in :

lou (O.Icel. lāgr) *low*, **ou** (OE. āgan) *to owe*, **out** (OE. āhte) *ought* ; but oǝ in : **oǝn** (OE. āgen) *own*.

§ 125. ā was shortened to a at an early period in : **as**, **aks** (OE. āscian, ācsian) *to ask*, **alidǝ** (OE. hālig-dæg) *holiday*, **lavrǝk** (OE. lāwerce, ME. laveroc) *lark*, **spatl** (OE. spātl) *spittle*. To **ǝ** in **meš** *mash*, cp. § 59.

And to **o** in **sori** (OE. sārig) *sorry*. But this word has probably been influenced by **sorǝ** (OE. sorg) *sorrow*.

§ 126. ā has become **u** in **ut** *hot*, **wun** *one*, **wuns** *once*.

§ 127. O.Norse **ei** (= OE. ā) has become **eǝ**: **feǝk** (O.Icel. feikr) *trick, deception*, **leǝk** (O.Icel. leika) *to play*, **weǝk** (O.Icel. veikr) *weak*. It is not absolutely necessary to assume that these words are of Norse origin; they may be regularly developed from OE. fācen, lācan, wāc with early shortening of the ā before the following **k**, cp. words like **leitš** *leech* (§ 132), **teitš** *teach* (§ 138), which cannot be of Norse origin.

§ 128. ā has become **ǝ** in the unaccented particles: **ǝn** *an*, **ǝ** *a*, *an*, **ǝ(r)** *or*, **nǝ(r)** *nor*, **nǝt** *not*.

§ 129. The following words remain unclassed: **poul** *pole*, probably an early borrowing from the lit. language; the same is probably the case with **reǝs** *race*, **swīp** *to sweep* (OE. swāpan, pret. swēop) with the vowel of the pret. transferred to the present, **tū** *two*.

Germanic ǣ.

§ 130. Germanic **ǣ** (= WS. ǣ, O.North. ē) has become **ī** in: **grīdi** *greedy*, **īmin** (OE. ǣfnung, ME. ǣfening) *evening*, **nīdl** *needle*, **rīd** *to read*, **sīd** *seed*, **slīp** *to sleep*, **strīt** *street*, **šīp** *sheep*, **tšīz** *cheese*, **þrīd** *thread*.

§ 131. It has become **iǝ** in:

briǝþ *breath*, **briǝð** *to breathe*, **driǝd** *to dread*, **fiǝ(r)** *fear*, **ǝ-fiǝd** *afraid*, **iǝl** *eel*, **iǝrnd** *errand*, **jiǝ(r)** *year*, **miǝl** *meal*, *repast*, **swiǝl** (OE. swǣlan, O.Icel. svǣla) *to gutter (of a candle)*, **ðiǝ(r)** *there*, **wiǝpm** *weapon*, **wiǝ(r)** *where*, **wiǝz** *to wheeze*.

§ 132. Before c(k) it became shortened to ǝ, and then underwent the same further development as old ǝ in open syllables (§ 87): leitš *leech*, speitš *speech*.

§ 133. It has become ǝǝ in : bleǝt *to bleat*, greǝ *gray*, ǝǝ(r) *hair*, weǝv *wave*.

§ 134. It underwent early shortenings to ǝ in : bleðǝ(r) *bladder*, let *to let*, medǝ *meadow*, red (OE. rǣdde) *read*, sed (OE. sǣde, older sægde, Sievers, OE. Gr. § 214, 3) *said*, setǝdǝ (OE. sǣterdæg) *Saturday*, slept *slept*, sez *sayest, says*, šeped *shepherd*, šepstǝ(r) *starling*, wet *wet*.

§ 135. It has become a in : blast *blast*.

§ 136. It has become i in : ridl *riddle*, sili *silly*.

OE. ǣ (= i-umlaut of ā).

§ 137. The normal development of the i-umlaut of ā is iǝ :

briǝdþ *breadth*, diǝl *deal*, dliǝm *gleam*, iǝl *to heal*, iǝlþ *health*, iǝt *heat*, iǝðn *heathen*, liǝd *to lead*, liǝdǝ(r) *tendon*, liǝn *lean*, liǝst *least*, liǝv *to leave*, miǝn *mean*, miǝn *to mean, intend*, riǝ(r) *to rear*, riǝþ *wreath*, siǝ *sea*, siǝt *seat*, swiǝt *to sweat*, šiǝþ *sheath*, tiǝz *to tease*, tliǝn *clean*, wiǝt *wheat*.

§ 138. Before c(k) it became shortened to ǝ, and then underwent the same further development as old ǝ in open syllables (§ 87), cp. also § 132 : bleitš *to bleach*, reik *to reach*, teitš *to teach*.

§ 139. ǣ has also become ei in :
(1) lein *to lean*, spreid *to spread*.
(2) kei *key*, nei *neigh*.

140. ǣht has become out : tout (OE. tǣhte) *taught*.

§ 141. ǣ has become əə in : leədi *lady*, steəz *stairs*,
tleə *clay*.

§ 142. It has become oə in : noeðə(r) *neither*, oeðə(r)
either. These examples rather belong to § 123. See
Sievers, OE. Gr. §§ 346, 348.

§ 143. It underwent early shortening to ə in : emti
empty, fleš *flesh*, left (pret. and pp.) *left*, lent (pret. and pp.)
lent (len to *lend* has its vowel from the pret.) les *less*, ment
meant.

§ 144. It was shortened at an early period to a in : bad
bad, fat *fat*, laðə(r) *ladder*, mad *mad*, madlin *a bewildered
or confused person, stupid fellow*, rasl *to wrestle*, spat
(pret.) *spat*.

§ 145. It has become i in ivə(r) *ever*, ivri *every*, nivə(r)
never.

§ 146. oni (OE. ǣnig) has been influenced by moni (OE.
manig) *many*.

ē.

1. ē (=i-umlaut of ō).

§ 147. ē, the i-umlaut of ō, has become ī : blīd *to bleed*,
brīd *to breed*, dīm to *deem*, fīd to *feed*, fīl to *feel*, fīt *feet*,
gīs *geese*, grīn *green*, grīt to *greet*, īd *heed*, īl *heel*, kīl (OE.
cēlan) *to cool*, kīn *keen*, kīp to *keep*, kwīn *queen*, mīt *to
meet*, sīk *to seek*, sīm to *seem*, slī *sly*, swīt *sweet*, tīm
(O. Icel. tǣma) *to pour out*, tīþ *teeth*, wīp *to weep*.

§ 148. It was shortened early- to ə before consonant
combinations in : bled *bled*, bles to *bless*, bred *bred*, gezlin
gosling, fed *fed*, felt (pret.) *felt*, kept *kept*, met *met*, tem
(pret. of tīm § 147) *poured out*, tem-ful *brimful*.

§ 149. The following forms are irregular : britšəz (OE.

brœc) *breeches*, weest (OE. wǣste) *waste*, wiəri (OE. wǣrig) *weary*.

2. ē (=older īə, partly arising from the i-umlaut of ēa, ēo, and partly arising from ecthlipsis).

§ 150. This ē has also generally become ī: dī *to dye*, drī *dreary*, lītnin *lightning*, bə-līv *to believe*, nīd *need*, sīn *seen*, slīv *sleeve*, stīl *steel*, stīpl *steeple*, šīt *sheet*, tī *to tie*, siks-tīn *sixteen*.

NOTE.—This ē has been shortened to i in: rik *reek*, *smoke*, strip *to strip*.

§ 151. It has become iə before a following r in: iəd *heard*, iə(r) *to hear*, niə(r) (OHG. nioro) *kidney*, stiə(r) *to steer*.

§ 152. ē has been shortened to e at an early period in: nekst *next*.

§ 153. It has become eə in: eə *hay*; and ei in: eit *height*.

3. Germanic ē.

§ 154. let (pret.) *let*, iə(r) *here*. Here may also be placed: mīdles (cp. OE. mēd, older meord *pay, reward*) *troublesome, tiresome, to no purpose*.

4. The OE. ē which arose from lengthening in monosyllables (Sievers, OE. Gr. § 121).

§ 155. This ē has become ī in the following accented forms (§ 350): ī *he*, jī *ye*, mī *me*, ðī *thee*, wī *we*.

ī.

§ 156. OE. ī has regularly become ai: aidl *idle*, aim (OE. hrīm?) *hoarfrost*, ain *hind*, ais *ice*, aivi *ivy*, baid (OE. bīdan) *to endure, put up with, wait, stay, remain*, bait *to bite*, **braidl** *bridle*, **daik** *dike, dyke*, **dlaid** *to glide*, **draiv** *to drive*, **fail** *file*, **faiv** *five*, **graip** *to gripe*, **graim** (ME. grīm) *soot* (*on the kettle*), **kraist** *Christ*, **laif** *life*, **laik** *like*, **laim** *lime*, **lain** *line*, **ǝ-laiv** *alive*, **mai** (accented form) *my*, **mail** *mile*, **main** *mine*, **mait** *mite*, **naif** *knife*, **paik** *pike*, **pail** *pile*, **pain** *to pine*, **paip** *pipe*, **raid** *to ride*, **raip** *ripe*, **rait** *to write*, **raiv** (O. Icel. rīfa *to break*) *to tear*, **raiz** *to rise*, **said** *side*, **sail** (ME. sīlen) *to strain through a sieve*, **saip** (cp. MHG. sīfen) *to ooze* or *drain out slowly*, **saiᵭ** *scythe*, **slaid** *to slide*, **slaim** *slime*, **slaip** *to take away the skin* or *outside covering*, **smait** *to smite*, **snaip** *snipe*, **straid** *to stride*, **straik** *to strike*, **swaim** *to climb up a tree* or *pole*, **swaip** (cp. MHG. swīfen) *to sweep off, remove hastily*, **šain** *to shine*, **šait** *cacare*, **šaiv** (ME. schīve) *slice*, **taid** *feast time*, **taidin** *a present from the feast*, **taik** (O. Icel. tīk *dog*) *a low fellow*, **taim** *time*, **tait** (in the phrase : **es tait** *as soon*, comp. **taitǝ(r)** *sooner, rather*, ME. tīt, O. Icel. masc. tīᵭr, neut. tītt) *soon*, **twain** *twine*, **twais** *twice*, **ᵭai** (accented form) *thy*, **ᵭain** *thine*, **þraiv** *to thrive*, **waid** *wide*, **waif** *wife*, **wail** *a while, time*, **wain** *wine*, **waip** *to wipe*, **wait** *white*, **waiz** *wise*, **fraidǝ** *Friday*.

§ 157. ī before a following r : **aiǝn** *iron*, **spaiǝ(r)** *spire*, **waiǝ(r)** *wire*.

§ 158. Old ī appears as ī in : **sī** *to sigh* (§ 318, *b*), **skrīk** (O. Low Germ. scrīcōn, Swed. skrīka) *to shriek*. And possibly in **stī** (OE. stīg, OHG. stīga) *ladder*, but see § 94.

§ 159. īw has become iu : **spiu** (OE. spīwan) *to spew*, **tiuzdǝ** (OE. tīwesdæg) *Tuesday*.

§ 160. ī underwent early shortening to i in : **bi** (unaccented form) *by*, **dwinl** *to dwindle*, **fift** *fifth*, **fifti** *fifty*, **fipms** *fivepence*, **linin** *linen*, **linsīd** *linseed*, **stif** *stiff*, **wimin** *women*, **midif** *midwife*, **wizdm** *wisdom*.

§ 161. rī has become ō through metathesis in : kōsmes *Christmas*, kōsn *to christen*.

§ 162. ī has become u in : wumn *woman*; ie in : sniek *to sneak*; e in : sterep *stirrup*.

ō.

§ 163. The normal development of ō is ui : bluid *blood*, bruid *brood*, buin *boon*, buit *to boot*, buið *booth*, buizm *bosom*, duin *done*, fluid *flood*, fuid *food*, fuit *foot*, guid *good*, guis *goose*, kruidl *to shrink* or *cower with cold, fear or pain*, kuil *cool*, muid *mood*, muild *confusion, bad temper*, muin *moon*, nuin *noon*, pruiv (OE. prōfian from Lat. probāre) *to prove*, ruid *rood*, ruif *roof*, ruit *root*, skuil *school*, smuið *smooth*, spuin *spoon*, stuid *stood*, stuil *stool*, suin *soon*, suit *soot*, tuil *tool*, tuiþ *tooth*, šuin *shoes*, uid *hood*, uif *hoof*, uin (ME. hōnen) *to harass, treat badly*.

§ 164. ō has become iu before k, m, and when the vowel has come to stand finally in the mod. dialect.

(a) Before k : briuk *brook*, iuk *hook*, kriuk *crook*, liuk *to look*, niuk *nook*, riuk *rook*, šiuk *shook*, tiuk *took*.

būk *book*, and kūk *cook* have been borrowed from the literary language.

(b) Before m : blium *bloom*, brium *broom*, dlium *gloom*, dium *doom*, gium *gum*, lium *loom*.

(c) When final in the mod. dialect : biu *bough*, diu *to do*, driu *drew*, iniu (plural) *enough*, pliu *plough*, sliu *slew*, tiu *too*.

šū *shoe* has been borrowed from the literary language, cp. the pl. form šuin § 163. ō appears as i in inif (sing.) *enough*.

E 2

§ 165. ō has become uə before r: dluə(r) (ME. glōren) *to stare*, fluə(r) *floor*, muə(r) *moor*.

§ 166. ōw has become ou: dlou *to glow*, flou *to flow*, grou *to grow*, stou *to stow*.

§ 167. ōht became oht already in OE. (Sievers, OE. Gr. § 125), and has become out in the W. dialect, cp. § 101: brout *brought*, sout *sought,* þout *thought*.

§ 168. ō has become ou in: skoup *scoop*.

§ 169. Shortenings of old ō.

(*a*) To o: blosm *blossom*, fostə(r) *foster*, foðə(r) *fodder*, kom (OE. cōm) *came*, soft *soft*, šod *shod*, tof *tough*.

(*b*) To u: bruðə(r) *brother*, dluv *glove*, duz *dost, does*, mundə *Monday*, munþ *month*, muðə(r) *mother*, sluf (OE. slōg) *slough*, tuðə(r) *the other*, uðə(r) *other*.

§ 170. ō has become e in wednzdə (OE. wōdnes-dæg) *Wednesday*.

ū.

§ 171. ū has generally become ā: ā *how*, āl *owl*, āmivə(r) *however*, ās *house*, āt *out*, bā *to bow*, bān (O. Icel. būenn, lit. *bound*; generally used in the sense of *going*, as wiə(r) tə bān? *where art thou going?* am bān dān tloin *I am going down the lane*), brā *brow*, brān *brown*, bāt (OE. būtan, be-ūtan) *without*, ə-bāt *about*, dān *down*, dāst *dust*, dlāmi (not the same word as *gloomy* which is dliumi § 164) *sad, downcast*, drāzi *drowsy*, fāl *foul, ugly*, kā *cow*, krād *crowd*, lād *loud*, lās *louse*, mās *mouse*, māþ *mouth*, nā *now*, rām *room*, rāst *rust*, prād *proud*, sāk *to suck*, sāþ *south*, slām (OE. slūma) *slumber*, sprāt (cp. ME. sprūte, M. Low Germ. sprūte) *to sprout*, šrād *shroud*, tān *town*, tlād *cloud*, tlāt *clout*, trāst (ME. trūsten) *to trust*, ðā (accented form) *thou*, pāzn *thousand*.

§ 172. ū has become āə before a following r : āə(r) (accented form) *our*, kāə(r) dān (ME. courən, Swed. kūra *to cower*) *to bend down, sit down*, sāə(r) *sour*, šāə(r) *shower*. But we have ə̄ in pə̄zdə *Thursday*.

§ 173. doən *down, feathers*, seems to have been borrowed from the literary language.

§ 174. ū was shortened to u at an early period in : busk (ME. busken from O. Icel. būask *to get oneself ready*) *to go about from place to place singing and playing for money*, druft *drought*, duv *dove*, fus *fuss*, kud (accented form) *could*, plum *plum*, ruf *rough*, unι-sukl *honeysuckle*, sup *to drink, sup*, šuv *to shove*, pum *thumb*, ulət *owl*, up *up*, uðə(r) *udder*, uz (accented form) *us*, uzbn *husband*.

It has been weakened to ə in the unaccented particle bəd *but*.

ȳ.

§ 175. ȳ, the i-umlaut of ū, has become ai : aid *hide, skin*, aiv *hive*, braid *bride*, brain *brine*, drai *dry*, draip *to drip*, daiv *to dive*, kait *kite*, lais *lice*, mais *mice*, praid *pride*, skai *sky*.

§ 176. It has become aiə before a following r : aiə(r) *to hire*, faiə(r) *fire*, maiə(r) *mire*.

§ 177. It underwent early shortening to i in : fílp *filth*, idn (pp. from which was formed a new present id *to hide*), litl *little*, lits (retained only in the game of lits ən gə̄ts lit. *littles and greats*, a game played by boys with brass buttons, clog clasps, or small pieces of brass of any kind. Two lits have the value of one gēt; cp. P. B. Beitr. ix. p. 365–7). þiml *thimble*, wiš *to wish*.

§ 178. ȳ (?) has become u in þrust *to thrust*.

3. The Diphthongs.

ēa.

§ 179. OE. ēa has generally become iə: biəm *beam*, biən *bean*, biət *to beat*, briəd *bread*, diəd *dead*, diəf *deaf*, diəþ *death*, driəm *dream*, ə-giən *again, against*, iəd *head*, iəp *heap*, iə(r) *ear*, iəst *east*, iəstə(r) *Easter*, liəd *lead*, liəf *leaf*, bə-liəf *belief*, niə(r) *near*, piə-kok *peacock*, siəm *seam*, stiəm *steam*, stiəp *steep*, striə (WS. strēa, O. North. strē, Sievers, OE. Gr. § 250, note 2) *straw*, striəm *stream*, šiəf *sheaf*, tiəm *team*, tšiəp *cheap*, þriəp (OE. þrēapian *to rebuke*) *to contradict*, þriətn *to threaten*.

§ 180. ēaw has become eu: deu *dew*, eu *to hew*, feu (OE. fēawe) *few*, šeu *to show*, teu (OE. tēawian) *to work zealously*.

But we have oə in roə (OE. hrēaw) *raw*; which presupposes a form hrāw (§ 123).

§ 181. It has become ī in: ī (plural īn) *eye*, tšīk *check*. The latter word has probably been borrowed from the literary language.

§ 182. It has become ei in: ei (OE. hēah) *high*, nei (OE. nēah) *nigh, near*. The ME. forms heh and neh would regularly become diphthongized to ei, see § 87.

§ 183. It has become ee in: flee (OE. flēan, Skeat, Etym. Dict. p. 211) *to skin*, neebə(r) *neighbour*.

§ 184. O. Norse au has become ou in : loup (O. Icel. hlaupa) *to leap, jump,* lous (O. Icel. lauss) *loose*; and oə in: goəm (O. Icel. gaum) *heed, care, attention,* goəmles *silly, stupid,* roət (O. Icel. rauta *to roar*) *to bray.*

§ 185. ēa has become ō through absorption of r in : gōt *great.*

§ 186. Shortenings of ēa :
(*a*) To e in: efə(r) *heifer,* lek *leek,* red *red.*
(*b*) To a in: laðə(r) *lather,* tšap *chap.*

ēo.

§ 187. OE. ēo has generally become ī: bī *bee,* bī (accented form) *to be,* bīn *been,* dīp *deep,* dlī *glee,* fīnd *fiend,* flī *to fly,* flī *fly,* flīs *fleece,* frī *free,* frīz *to freeze,* krīp *to creep,* lī *to lie,* līf (OE. lēof) *soon,* līvə(r) *sooner, rather,* līt *a light,* nī *knee,* nīz (O. Icel. hniōsa) *to sneeze,* rīd *reed,* rīl *reel,* prīst *priest,* sī *to see,* sīð *to seethe,* snīz *to sneeze,* tlīv *to cleave,* trī *tree,* bə-twīn *between,* þī *thigh,* þīf *thief,* þrī *three,* wīd *weed,* wīl *wheel.*
But we have tšiuz *to choose* (§ 366).

§ 188. It has become ie before a following r : bie(r) *beer,* die(r) *dear,* drieri *dreary.*

§ 189. Before r + consonant it became shortened to e already in ME., and then had the same further development as old e before r + consonant (§ 87): dālin (OE. dēorling, ME. derrling) *darling,* fādin (OE. fēorðung, ME. ferthing) *farthing.*

§ 190. ēow has become iu: bliu *blew,* briu *to brew,* griu *grew,* jiuþ *youth,* kriu *crew,* niu *new,* niu *knew,* riu *to rue*, **sniu** (§ 377) *it snowed*, **tliu** *clew*, **triu** *true*, **triuþ** *truth*, **siu** *sowed*, **þriu** *threw*.

But in the following words we have **eu** which points to an old **ēaw** (§ 180): **eu** *yew*, **seu** *to sew*, **tšeu** *to chew*. We have **ouə** in: **fouə(r)** (OE. fēower, but ME. fōwer, which would regularly become **fouə(r)** in the dialect, § 166) *four*, **fouət** (OE. fēowerða) *fourth*, **fouətīn** (OE. fēowertēne) *fourteen*. And **āə** in: **jāə(r)** (accented form) *your*. This last word has been influenced by **āə(r)** *our*, § 172.

§ 191. The following two words remain unclassed: **šū** (accented form) *she*, **šuit** *to shoot*.

§ 192. Early shortenings of **ēo**:

(*a*) To **e** in: **brest** *breast*, **fel** (pret.) *fell*, **frend** *friend*, **step-faðə(r)** *step-father*. Anglian **ēo** (=WS. īe) has been shortened to **e** in: **depþ** *depth*, **ten** *ten*.

(*b*) To **o** in: **foti** *forty*, **fotnit** *fortnight*.

(*c*) To **i** in: **divl** *devil*, **sik** *sick*, **ə tūþri** lit. *a two* (or) *three, a few*.

(*d*) To **ə** in: **sə ðə** lit. *see thou, look!* **þrepms** *threepence*.

Elision of ə.

§ 193. The **ə** is elided in the diphthongs and triphthongs **eə, iə, oə, uə, āə, aiə, iuə, ouə**, when they occur finally and the next word begins with a vowel; thus **guə** but **gu uəm** *go home*, **mə ai** *may I*, but **mee wī** (§ 393), **noe** but **a no im** *I know him*, and similarly for the others.

CHAPTER IV.

In the following treatment of the French element in the W. dialect, the present pronunciation of literary English has, in most cases, been taken as the starting point. The transcription of the lit. English vowel sounds is based on that given in Sweet's Primer of Spoken English, pp. 7–8, and is as follows :—

ɒ   as in just, dozen, double.

ā   „   grant, art, master.

ai   „   fine, pie, try.

au   „   doubt, powder.

æ   „   value, rat.

ǝ   „   debt, measure.

ei   „   bacon, bailiff, pay.

eǝ   „   pair, chair.

ə̄   „   furnish, journey.

i   „   dinner, pity.

ij   „   beak, secret, beef, grief.

iǝ   „   fierce, clear.

o   „   jolly, profit.

oi   „   boil, poison.

ou   „   roast, notice.

ō   „   pork, daub, false.

u   „   put, butcher.

uw   „   fruit, blue.

uə   „   sure, poor.

§ 194. Lit. Engl. æ (written a) appears as a : abit *habit*, aktli *actually*, ali *aisle, alley*, arənd (ME. araine, O. Fr. araigne) *spider*, avək *havoc*, baril *barrel*, damidž *damage*, faks *facts*, galək (O. Fr. galc) *lefthand*, galəp *to gallop*, galn *gallon*, garit *garret*, gran-faðe(r), gram-faðe(r) *grandfather*, kap *cap*, kapil (Fr. capel *a little hat*, Cotgr.) *a piece of leather sewn over a hole in a boot* or *shoe*, karit *carrot*, lamp *lamp*, manə(r) *manner*, map (see Skeat, Etym. Dict. sub mop) *a mop*, marə *to match a pattern*, natrəl (natrə-bl) *natural*, pantri *pantry*, ratn (O. Fr. raton) *rat*, salit *salad*, skafl *scaffold*, skaflin *scaffolding*, stati *statue*, tali *to agree, be right*, tə liv tali *to live together without being married*, tšapil *chapel*, vali *valley*, valə *value*.

§ 195. Lit. Engl. has ā where the W. dial. has a in : bastəd *bastard*, branš *branch*, grant *to grant*, pastə(r) *pasture*, plant *plant*.

But ee in⁓ bees *bass*, leerəm *alarum*, meestə(r) *master*, pleestə(r) *plaster*.

§ 196. Lit. Engl. has ei (written a), but W. dial. a in : aprən *apron*, stapl *staple*.

But we have moendž *mange*.

§ 197. a has become e before a following g, ŋ, š, cp. § 59 :

dregŋ *dragon*.

bleŋk *blank*, bleŋkit *blanket*, keŋkə(r) (ME. cancren) *to corrode*, leŋwidž *language*, pleŋk *plank*, reŋk *rank*.

bešfl *bashful*, fešn *fashion*, pešn *passion*, seš *sash*.

§ **198.** al has become oe in the combinations lk, lm, ll, cp. § 62.

goeki (but **galek** § 326) *left handed*, **boem** *balm*, **oeminak** *almanac*, **oemend** *almond*, **boel** *ball*.

§ **199.** al in the combination ld has become ou, cp. § 64: **skoud** *to scald*.

The same sound also occurs in **fout** (ME. **faute**) *fault*.

§ **200.** a has become o before a following n in: **dons** *dance*, **ont** *aunt*, **trons** *trance*, **tšons** *chance*, **tšont** *chant*.

§ **201.** a has become e in: **rediš** *radish*.

§ **202.** a has been retained where in the lit. language it has become o through the influence of the preceding w in: **kwaleti** *quality*, **kwari** *stone-quarry*, **warend** *to warrant*, **walep** (cp. Fr. galoper *to curry, use rudely*, Cotgr.) *to beat, flog*.

§ **203.** ar in the combination r + consonant has become ee, which shows that ar in this combination was pronounced differently in Engl. and Fr. words in the ME. period; cp. § 61.

beebe(r) *barber*, **beedž** *barge*, **beegɒ** *bargain*, **beete(r)** *to barter*, **deet** *to dart*, **eet** *art, skill*, **geed** *guard*, **geedn** *garden*, **geete(r)** *garter*, **keed** *card*, **keekes** (Fr. **carquasse**, Cotgr.) *body, carcase*, **kweet** *quart*, **kweete(r)** *quarter*, **peedn** *pardon*, **peesl** *parcel*, **peet** *part*, **peetne(r)** *partner*, **skeelet** *scarlet*, **tšeedž** *charge*.

§ **204.** Lit. Engl. ei (written a, ai (ay), ei) appears in the W. dial. as ee: **beekɒ** *bacon*, **beel** *bale*, **beeli** (bum-**beeli**, cp. O. Fr. **baili**) *bailiff*, **beet** *to abate*, **bleem** *blame*, **bree** (ME. **braiin**, O. Fr. **breier**) *to beat, pound*, **deendže(r)** *danger*, **deenti** *dainty*, **deet** *date*, **deevi** *affidavit*, **eebl** *able*, **eedž** *age*, **eem** *to aim, intend*, **eenšn** *ancient*, **feed** *fade*, **feel** *to fail,* feənt *to faint,* feəs *face,* feəþ *faith,* feəvə(r) *to favour, resemble in appearance* or *manners,* fleəm *flame,* geə *gay,* iŋgeədž *to engage,* greənz (pl.) *malt which has been used in brewing beer,* greəs *grace,* greət *grate,* keədž *cage,* keəs *case,* leəs *lace,* meəsn *mason,* neətə(r) *nature,* peə *pay,* peədž *page,* peəl *pale,* peən *pain,* peən *pane of glass,* peənt *paint,* peəs *pace,* peəst (but pasti *pasty*) *paste,* pleən *plain,* pleəs *place,* pleət *plate,* preə (but pre-ðə (*1*) *pray thee*) *to pray,* preət *to prate, babble,* preəz *to praise,* reədž *rage,* reət *rate,* seəf *safe,* seəkrid *sacred,* seəm (often called swain-seəm, Ancren Riwle seim, OE. seime *adipe,* Ps. lxii. 6, E. E. T. S. No. 92, from O. Fr. sain) *lard,* seənt (but before names sant) *saint,* seəv *to save,* skeəlz *scales,* steəbl *stable,* streəndž *strange,* teəbl *table,* teələ(r), teəljə(r) *tailor,* teəst *taste,* tleəm *to claim,* treəl (Fr. trailler) *to drag,* treən *train,* tšeəf *to chafe,* tšeəmə(r) *chamber,* tšeəndž *change,* veən *vein,* weət *to wait.*

NOTE.—*contrary* is kontréəri.

§ 205. Before a simple r we have the same development as the lit. language : peə(r) *pair,* peə(r) *to peel,* tšeə(r) *chair.*

ə.

§ 206. ə (written ə, ea) in the lit. language has generally remained in the W. dialect : bezl *to embezzle,* demək (from epidemic) *potato disease,* deməkt *diseased (of potatoes),* det *debt,* dželəs *jealous,* dželi *jelly,* ə-seml *to assemble,* fend *to provide for oneself,* fent *remnant of a piece of cloth,* fezn *pheasant,* geə *to guess,* letə(r) *letter,* letis *lettuce,* mel (Fr. mail) *mallet,* mel (ME. mellen, medlen, O.Fr. medler) *to meddle,* mend *to mend,* mezə(r) *measure,* plezə(r) *pleasure,* prentis *apprentice,* sens *sense,* ses *assessment, tax,* spekteklz *spectacles*, **treml** *to tremble*, **treze(r)** *treasure*, **vente(r)** *to venture*, **vesl** *vessel.*

But **fliem** *phlegm*, **siene** *senna.*

§ 207. **er** has become **ä** before a following consonant : **konsán** *concern*, **pāsn** *parson*, **sādžn** *sergeant*, **sāmen** *sermon*, **sāvnt** *servant*, **sāvis** *service*, **tlāk** *clerk*, **vāment** *vermin*, **vāniš** *varnish.*

In the following two words we have **a** : **arend** (O.Fr. **errant**) *notoriously bad*, **sare** (rarely **sāv**) *to serve*. On **sare** see Behrens, Beiträge zur Geschichte der französischen Sprache in England, p. 91. **ie** in : **ieb** *herb*, and **e** in : **tšeri** *cherry.*

§ 208. **e** has become **a** before a following **r** in **tarie(r)** (ME. **terrere**) *terrier dog*, **vari** *very.*

But **pie(r)** *pear.*

§ 209. **e** has become **i** before a following nasal in : **indžói** *to enjoy*, **indžn** *engine*, **ingeedž** *to engage*, **ink** *ink*, **lints** *lentils*, **simetri** *cemetery*, **šimi** *chemise.*

tribl *treble* (in music) from contamination with **triple**, and **þribl** *threefold* from contamination with **þrī**.

§ 210. **e** has become **a** in **saleri** *celery*, cp. **sallary** sub **celery** in N.E.D.

i.

§ 211. **i** has generally remained in the W. dialect : **dine(r)** *dinner*, **dizml** *dismal*, **finiš** *to finish*, **gimlek** (this word has now almost gone out of use, its place being taken by **gimlit**) *gimlet*, **gizn** *to choke*, **gizn** (Fr. **guisern**, Cotgr. sub **gesier**) *gizzard*, **konsiðe(r)** *to consider*, **limit** *limit*, **list** *list*, **list** *to enlist*, **live(r)** *to deliver*, **ministe(r)** *minister*, **mins** *mince*, **mistšif** *mischief*, **pidžn** *pigeon*, **pik** *pickaxe*, pinien *opinion*, piti *pity*, rivə(r) *river*, sinl *single*, siðez *scissors*, skriptə(r) *scripture*, tift (cp. ME. tiffen from O. Fr. tiffer *to adorn*) *condition, state, order*, tšimli *chimney*, twilt *quilt*.

§ 212. i has become ə in : lenit *linnet*, rebit *rivet*, redžestə(r) *to register*, rens *to rinse*.

§ 213. i has become ə in sperit *spirit* ; and a in krakit *cricket (game)*.

o .

§ 214. Lit. Engl. short o = W. dial. o : boni *nice, pretty*, džoli *jolly*, džosl *to jostle*, kolə(r) *collar*, kotn *cotton*, lodž *to lodge*, mot, moti (French motte, Cotgr., edit. 1673) *a mark at quoits*, obstakl *obstacle*, okə-daik (Fr. oker Cotgr.) *small stream of iron-water*, onə(r) *honour*, rok *rock*, poridž *porridge*, posnit (O. Fr. poçonet) *saucepan*, pot *pot*, profit *profit*, soðə(r) *solder*.

§ 215. o has become u in : nuvl *novel*, nuvis *novice*.

§ 216. Lit. Engl. oi = W. dial. oi : boil *to boil*, džoi *joy*, džoint *joint*, ə-noi *to annoy*, koit *quoit, coit*, loin *loin*, moist *moist*, moistə(r) *moisture*, noiz *noise*, oil *oil*, ointment *ointment*, oistə(r) *oyster*, point *point*, poizn *poison*, soil *soil, ground*, spoil *to spoil*, tšois *choice*, vois *voice*, voiðə(r) *large clothes' basket*.

§ 217. Lit. Engl. ou (written oa) = W. dial. o in : gol (only used in the game of lits en gōts § 177, O. Fr. gaul) *goal*, rost *to roast*.

§ 218. Lit. Engl. ou (written, o, oo, oa) = W. dial. ue in : bruetš *brooch*, kuetš *coach*, nuəbl *noble*, nuetis *notice*, puəni *pony*, puəst *post*, puəzi *nosegay*, ruəb *robe*, ruəg *rogue*, tluək *cloak*.

§ 219. Lit. Engl. ou (written o, oa)=W. dial. oi in :
broitš *to broach*, doit *to dote*, koit *coat*, loitš *loach*, tlois
close, narrow, tloiz *to close*, toist *to toast*.

§ 220. Lit. Engl. ou (written o, oa, ou, ow)=W. dial.
ou in: boul *bowl*, koul (O. Fr. coillir) *to rake*, moud *mould,
model*, poutri *poultry*, poutš *to poach*, roul *to roll*, soudže(r)
soldier.

But we have pŭltis *poultice*.

NOTE.—The first element of the W. diphthong is not the o in not. See § 7.

§ 221. Lit. Engl. uw (written oo)=W. dial. ui: buit
boot, fuil *fool*, gruin (ME. groin, O. Fr. groing) *snout of a
pig*.

§ 222. Lit. Engl. uə (written oor)=W. dial. uə: puə(r)
poor, puəli *poorly, ill*.

§ 223. Lit. Engl. long open ō sound (written or before
a following consonant)=W. dial. uə in: fuədž *forge*, fuəs
force, kuəd *cord*, puək *pork*, puəšn *portion*, puətə(r)
porter.

But we have foefit *to forfeit*, foem *form*, foetn *fortune*,
koənə(r) *corner*, oeðə(r) *order*.

§ 224. uə occurs before single r in dluəri *glory*, stuəri
story. And ə in ferin *foreign*.

§ 225. Lit. Engl. long open ō (written au, aw)=W. dial.
oə in : doəb (ME. daubin, O. Fr. dauber) *to daub, smear*,
džoəm (Fr. jaumbe, Cotgr.) *the side post of a door* or
chimney piece, džoənes *jaundice*, froəd *fraud*, koəsə *causeway*, poə *paw*, poəz (O. Fr. poulser, posser) *to kick*, soəs
sauce.

But we have short o in bə-kos, ə-kos, kos *because*, fols
*false; in reference to a child, implying that it is shrewd
and witty beyond its years.*

u.

§ 226. Lit. Engl. ɒ (written u, o, ou)=W. dial. u :
bukit *bucket*, buldž *to bulge*, butn *button*, buzəd (O. Fr.
busart) *butterfly*, dlutn *glutton*, dubl *double*, duzn *dozen*,
džudž *judge*, džust *just*, frunt *front*, gruml *to grumble*, gulit
gullet, channel for water, gutə(r) *gutter*, guzl *to swallow
greedily*, krust *crust*, kruš *to crush*, kulə(r) *colour*, kumfət
comfort, kumpni *company*, kuntri *country*, kupl *couple*,
kustəd *custard*, kustm *custom*, kuvə(r) *to cover*, kuzin, kuzn
cousin, muni (a commoner word is bras) *money*, muɒril
mongrel, mustəd *mustard*, mutn *mutton*, muzl *muzzle*,
numə(r) *number*, plumə(r) *plumber*, pulp *pulp*, rikuvə(r)
to recover, rubiš *rubbish*, sudn *sudden*, sufə(r) *to suffer*,
sumən *to summon*, supə(r) *supper* ,stuf *stuff*, trubl *trouble*,
truɒk *trunk*, tšuk *to throw, pitch*, tun *tun*, tutš *to touch*,
uml *humble*, uniən *onion*, uɒkl *uncle*.
But we have foisti *fusty*.

§ 227. Lit. Engl. u (written u, and mostly occurring
after labials)=W. dial. u : bušl *bushel*, butšə(r) *butcher*,
bulit *bullet*, puli *pulley*, pulit *pullet*, puš *to push*, put
to put.
But we have siugə(r) *sugar*, see § 310, 1 ; puilpit
pulpit.

§ 228. Lit. Engl. ə̄ (written ur, our before a following
consonant)=W. dial. ə̄, see § 113 *a* : bə̄l (ME. burle) *to
pick out small pieces of straw, etc. from flannel or cloth*,
distə̄b *to disturb*, džə̄ni *journey*, fə̄niš *to furnish*, fə̄nitə(r)
furniture, kə̄n *currant*, nə̄s *nurse*, pə̄s *purse*, tə̄n *to turn*,
tə̄nəp *turnip*, ə̄t *to hurt*.

ai.

§ 229. Lit. Engl. ai (written i, ie, y) = W. dial. ai :
ǝd-vais *advice*, ǝd-vaiz *to advise*, ǝ-plai *to apply*, fain *fine*,
frai *to fry*, kontráiv *to contrive*, krai *cry*, nais *nice*, pai
pie, paint *pint*, prais *price*, praiz *to lift with a lever*, rais
rice, sailm *asylum*, sain *sign*, saizǝz *assizes*, straiv *to strive*,
tais *to entice*, trai *to try*, traifl *trifle*.

But tšienǝ *china ware.*

ai also occurs in: džais (O. Fr. giste) *joist*, paik *to pick,
select.*

ǝ-blīdž (pp. ǝ-blītšt) *to oblige*, and leelǝk *lilac*, still remain
to be explained.

§ 230. Lit. Engl. aiǝ = W. dial. aiǝ: dizaiǝ(r) *desire*,
kwaiǝt *quiet*, raiǝt *riot*, umpaiǝ(r) *umpire*, vaiǝlǝt *violet.*

ij.

§ 231. Lit. Engl. ij (written ea, ei, e, ee, ie) appears in
the W. dial. as iǝ in: biǝk *beak*, biǝst *beast*, but biǝs *cows,*
disiǝt *deceit*, disiǝv *to deceive*, fiǝbl *feeble*, fiǝt *feat*, fiǝst
feast, fiǝtǝ(r) *feature*, griǝs *grease*, iǝgǝ(r) *eager*, iǝgl *eagle,*
iǝkwl *equal*, iǝz *ease*, niǝs *niece*, niǝt *neat, tidy*, piǝl *to
appeal*, piǝs *peace*, pliǝd *to plead*, pliǝz *to please*, riǝl *real,*
riǝzn *reason*, risiǝt *receipt, recipe*, risiǝv *to receive*, siǝkrit
secret, siǝs *to cease*, siǝzn *season*, tiǝ *tea*, triǝt *treat*, triǝtl
treacle, tšiǝt *to cheat*, viǝl *veal.*

§ 232. Lit. Engl. ij = W. dial. ī in: bīf *beef*, ǝ-grī *to
agree*, grīf *grief*, pīp (pp. pǝpt) *to peep*, pīs *piece.*

§ 233. Lit. Engl. iǝ = W. dial. iǝ in: fiǝs *fierce*, tliǝ(r)
clear.

§ 234. Lit. Engl. ij W. dial. ei in: dein *dean*, preitš
to preach.

F

ai in : **bastail** (Fr. **bastille**) *workhouse, union.*

ee in : **konseet** *conceit.*

i in : **pil** *to peel,* **pilinz** *the peels of potatoes,* etc.

e in : **mezlz** *measles.*

au.

§ 235. Lit. Engl. **au** (written **ou, ow**) appears in the W. dial as **ā** : **āl** *to howl,* **āns** *ounce,* **bānti** *bounty,* **dāt** *doubt,* **e-kānt** *account,* **e-lā, lā** *to allow,* **e-mānt** *amount,* **frān** *to frown,* **gān** *gown,* **gāt** *gout,* **kānsl** *to counsel,* **kānt** *to count,* **kātš** *couch,* **krān** *crown,* **lāns** *an allowance of refreshment* or *money,* **mānt** *to mount,* **māt** (Lat. *mūtāre*) *to moult,* **pāᵛe(r)** *powder,* **rānd** *round,* **sānd** *sound, noise,* **stāt** *stout,* **tă-il** (also **tail**) *towel,* **tră-il** *trowel,* **trāns** *to beat, flog,* **vā** *vow.*

au appears as **ū** in : **trūzez** *trousers.*

§ 236. Lit. Engl. **aue** = W. dial. **āe** : **āe(r)** *hour,* **divāe(r)** *to devour,* **flāe(r)** *flower, flour,* **pāe(r)** *power,* **tāe(r)** *tower.*

juw.

§ 237. Lit. Engl. **juw** (written **eau, ue, u, ui, ew, iew**) is **íu** in the W. dialect : **biuti** *beauty,* **diu** *due,* **diuti** *duty,* **fluil** *fuel,* **flute(r)** *future,* **ius** *use,* **iuneti** *unity,* **iunien** *union,* **iusfl** *useful,* **iusles** *useless,* **iuz** *to use,* **miul** *mule, donkey,* **miuzik** *music,* **piu** *pew,* **pius** *puce colour,* **rifíuz** *to refuse,* **siut** *suit,* **stiupid** *stupid,* **viu** *view.*

But we have **ā** in : **kākume(r)** *cucumber.*

jue.

§ 238. Lit. Engl. **jue** (written **ure**) = W. dial. **íue** : **kiue(r)** *cure,* **meniue(r)** *manure,* **piue(r)** *pure.*

uw.

§ 239. Lit. Engl. uw (written ue, ui, u, and mostly occurring after l, r, s) is íu in the W. dialect: bliu *blue*, bliuz (pl.) *delirium tremens*, fliu *flue*, fliut *flute*, seliut *to salute*.

friut *fruit*, griuil *gruel*, rikriut *to recruit*, riubub *rhubarb*, riul *rule*, riume(r) *rumour*, riuin *ruin*.

siu *to sue*, siuit *suet*.

ue.

§ 240. Lit. Engl. ue = W. dial. iue : siue(r) *sure*, siueli *surely*, unsiue(r) *uncertain*.

CHAPTER V.

§ 241. Diphthongs and short and long vowels in un-accented syllables have regularly been weakened to ə, i, or the vowel has disappeared altogether. In the latter case, when an l, m, n followed, it has become vocalic.

1. ə.

§ 242. *a.* In initial syllables followed by the principal accent:

befue(r) *before,* begin *to begin,* and similarly in all other words containing this prefix ; fegetn (pp.) *forgot,* əbāt (also bāt) *about, without,* əbūn *above,* efled *afraid,* efued *to afford,* efue(r) *before,* egeet *in action, at work,* əgien *again, against,* əgrī *to agree,* egue *ago,* əkin *akin,* əkos (also kos) *because,* əlaiv *alive,* əluen *alone,* emeɒ *among,* ənent *opposite,* ənoi *to annoy,* əplai *to apply,* əseml *to assemble,* əstied *instead,* ewee *away,* məniue(r) *manure,* səliut *salute,* tə-moen *to-morrow.*

But we have edikéet *to educate,* əkuedinlái *accordingly,* kontréeri *contrary,* redžéste(r) *to register,* siuəlǐ *surely,* spektéklz *spectacles.*

§ **243.** *b.* In syllables preceded by the principal accent :

basted *bastard,* **baleks** *testiculi,* **bulek** *bullock,* **buzed** *butterfly,* **dželes** *jealous,* **džoenes** *jaundice,* **figwet** *figwort,* **galep** *to gallop,* **gimlek** *gimlet,* **kēsmes** *Christmas,* **kolep** *slice of bacon,* **koese** *causeway,* **kubed** *cupboard,* **kusted** *custard,* **lavrek** *lark,* **leelek** *lilac,* **loped** *clotted, covered with dirt,* **mare** *to match a pattern,* **musted** *mustard,* **otšed** *orchard,* **omest** *almost,* **oles** *always,* **sakles** *silly, foolish,* **sare** *to serve,* **siene** *senna,* **simetri** *cemetery,* **siðez** *scissors,* **spitek** *spigot,* **šeped** *shepherd,* **sterep** *stirrup,* **tēnep** *turnip,* **ulet** *owl,* **unded** *hundred,* **vale** *value,* **winde** *window.*

are *arrow,* **bare** *barrow,* **bore** *to borrow,* **fale** *fallow,* **fole** *to follow,* **fere** *furrow,* **jare** *yarrow,* **jole** *yellow,* **mare** *marrow,* **mede** *meadow,* **nare** *narrow,* **ole** *hollow,* **pile** *pillow,* **sale** *sallow,* **sore** *sorrow,* **spare** *sparrow,* **swole** *to swallow,* **swole** *swallow,* **šade** *shadow,* **šale** *shallow,* **tale** *tallow,* **wide** *widow,* **wile** *willow.*

ame(r) *hammer,* **bleðe(r)** *bladder,* **bute(r)** *butter,* **faðe(r)** *father,* **gane(r)** *gander,* **geðe(r)** *to gather,* **kenke(r)** *to rust, corrode,* **neebe(r)** *neighbour,* **oeðe(r)** *either,* **pleeste(r)** *plaster,* **skute(r)** *to spill,* **slume(r)** *slumber,* **šuðe(r)** *to shudder,* **tarie(r)** *terrier,* **þune(r)** *thunder,* **unsiue(r)** *uncertain,* **une(r)** *hunger,* **wote(r)** *water.*

fénite(r) *furniture,* **flute(r)** *future,* **moiste(r)** *moisture,* **neete(r)** *nature,* **paste(r)** *pasture,* **pikte(r)** *picture.*

meze(r) *measure,* **pleze(r)** *pleasure,* **treze(r)** *treasure.*

But we have **óeminak** *almanac,* **bástail** *union, workhouse,* **óbstakl** *obstacle,* **ríubub** *rhubarb.*

In compounds, some of which have been given above : **beekes** *bakehouse,* **koiles** *coalhouse,* **wākes** *union, workhouse,* **wešes** *washhouse,* **alide** *holiday,* **jestede** *yesterday,* **wāte** (lit. work-day) *week-day,* **sunde** *Sunday,* and similarly for the other days of the week, **nek-ləþ** *neck cloth, hand-kerchief,* **bakəd** *backward,* **forəd** *forward,* **tādz** *towards,* **forədiš** *rather forward,* **oekəd** *awkward,* **oepəþ** *halfpenny worth,* **penəþ** *pennyworth,* **sumət** *something, anything.*

2. i.

§ **244.** *a.* In initial syllables followed by the principal accent :

indžoi *to enjoy,* **iɲgeədž** *to engage,* **disiət** *deceit,* **disiev** *to deceive,* **minístə(r)** *minister.*

§ **245.** *b.* In syllables preceded by the principal accent :

āvis(t) *harvest,* **bleɲkit** *blanket,* **bulit** *bullet,* **damidž** *damage,* **iənis(t)** *earnest,* **inif** (sing.) *enough,* pl. **iniu, ferin** *foreign,* **fotnit** *fortnight,* **gulit** *water channel,* **karit** *carrot,* **lenit** *linnet,* **letis** *lettuce,* **olin** *holly,* **posnit** *saucepan,* **puil-pit** *pulpit,* **pūltis** *poultice,* **salit** *salad,* **spərit** *spirit,* **rebit** *rivet,* **rediš** *radish.*

bāli *barley,* **beəli** *bailiff,* **beli** *belly,* **bəri** *berry,* **bəri** *to bury,* **bodi** *body,* but **nuəbdi** *nobody,* **boni** *nice, pretty,* **dizi** *dizzy,* **emti** *empty,* **evi** *heavy,* **əri** *hurry, row, disturbance,* **kani** *knowing, intelligent, skilful, nimble,* **leədi** *lady,* **məri** *merry,* **moni** *many,* **nevi** *nephew,* **oepni** *halfpenny,* but **oepəþ** *halfpenny worth,* **oni** *any,* **peni** *penny,* but **penəþ** *pennyworth,* **popi** *poppy,* **pratli** *gently, softly,* **rudi** *ruddy,* **sili** *silly,* **slipi** *slippery,* **sori** *sorry,* **snikit** *a small passage,* **stati** *statue,* **šabi** *shabby,* **šimi** *chemise,* **tali** *to agree,* **þəti** *thirty,* **ueli** *holy,* **uenli** *lonely,* **vali** *valley,* **vari** *very,* **wəri** *to worry.*

fādin *farthing,* **gezlin** *gosling,* **īmin** *evening,* **ipin** *a cloth placed round the hips of children,* **kunin** *cunning,* **skaftin** *shafting,* **spərinz** *the banns of marriage,* **swilinz** *thin liquid* *food for pigs,* **šilin** *shilling,* **topin** *the front part of the hair of the head,* **runin** *running,* and similarly in all present participles and words ending in the lit. language in -ing.

3. Loss of Vowel or Syllable.

§ 246. *a.* Initial syllables followed by the principal accent:

bāt *without,* **beet** *to abate,* **kros** *across,* **levm** *eleven,* **piniən** *opinion,* **prentis** *apprentice,* **sailm** *asylum.*

bezl *to embezzle,* **bake** *tobacco,* **kos** *because,* **lāns** *allowance,* **list** *to enlist,* **live(r)** *deliver,* **lotments** *allotments,* **piel** *to appeal,* **saiəti** *society,* **saizəz** *assizes,* **səs** *to assess, tax,* **tais** *to entice,* **twīn** *between,* **vantidž** *advantage.*

deevi *affidavit,* **demək** (lit. epidemic) *potato disease.*

§ 247. *b.* In syllables preceded by the principal accent:

aktli *actually,* **dif-rnt** *different,* **džen-rl** *general,* **kumpni** *company,* **nat-rl, nat-rə-bl** *natural,* **nuəbdi** *nobody,* **navi** (lit. navigation?) *canal,* **oepəþ** *halfpenny worth,* **penəþ** *pennyworth,* **reg-lə(r)** *regular,* **sumdi** *somebody.*

Vocalic l:

anl *handle,* **apl** *apple,* **ginl** *a long narrow uncovered passage,* **gruml** *to grumble,* **kanl** *candle,* **ketl** *kettle,* **kredl** *cradle,* **kudl** *to embrace,* **sinl** *single,* **smitl** *to infect,* **spinl** *spindle,* **þiml** *thimble,* **uml** *humble.*

Vocalic m:

bodm *bottom,* **buism** *bosom,* **evm** *heaven,* **fadm** *fathom,* **fipms** *five pence,* **kustm** *custom,* **luensm** *lonely,* **wizdm** *wisdom, wise,* **wiepm** *weapon.*

Vocalic n:

ādn̯ *to harden,* **brimstn** *brimstone,* **eenšn** *ancient,* **fasn** *to* *fasten*, **fešn** *fashion*, **frozn** *frozen*, **indžn** *engine*, **inlnd** *England*, **fotn** (pp.) *fought*, **foetn** *fortune*, **mutn** *mutton*, **pidžn** *pigeon*, **ratn** *rat*, **sãvnt** *servant*, **seldn** *seldom*, **slidn** (pp.) *slid*, **tšozn** *chosen*, **pãzn** *thousand*.

Vocalic ŋ :

beeŋŋ *bargain*, **beekŋ** *bacon*, **brokŋ** *broken*, **dokŋ** *dock*, **drukŋ** *drunk, drunken*, **rekŋ** *to reckon*, **spokŋ** *spoken*, **sukŋ** *sunk*, **tuekŋ** *token*, **ugŋ** *hip*, **wegŋ** *wagon*, **wokŋ** *to waken*.

Svarabhakti.

§ 248. A vowel has been developed between l, r, and a following consonant in : **galek** (O. Fr. **galc**) *left hand*, **sterek** (OE. **stirc**, also **styric**) *heifer*, **tšerep** (ME. **chirpen**) *to chirp*.

Weak Forms and Particles.

§ 249. The following is a fairly complete list, arranged alphabetically, of words which have weak forms caused by the sentence accent. Any other unaccented forms not given here will be found under the headings of pronouns, auxiliary verbs, adverbs, conjunctions, and prepositions.

The auxiliary verb **diu** is never used in asking questions, except when it begins the sentence: **dije** (**deje**) **þiŋk il** (**el**) **diut**? *do you think he will do it?* but **wile diut, þiŋk je** ? *will he do it, do you think?* The auxiliary verb *have* (**ev, e** ; **ǝv, ǝ**) is often omitted entirely, or perhaps rather has disappeared through assimilation ; thus **a dunt** *I have done it*, **we funt** *we have found it* ; here **fuu** is the pp. and not the pret., *we found it* is **we fant**.

a = *I*. Chiefly used in direct assertions : **a fan em** *I found them*.

abəd *yes but*: abəd ðа mən ger up suin *yes but thou·
must get up soon.*

am, aim, im *I am.*   aim, am are used in principal and
im in subordinate sentences: aim or am nuən bān tə stop
hiə(r) *I am not going to stop here.*   if im wīl inif *if I am
well enough.*

> bi = 1. *be*: wil ðə bi wi əm? *will they be with them?*
>
> = 2. *by*: bi nā *by now.*
>
> bin *been.*
>
> bəd *but.*
>
> —d = 1. *had*: ðed *they had,* ad *I had.*
>
> > = 2. *would, wouldst*: ðad e tə diut *thou wouldst
> > have to do it.*

də, di *do*: dejə or dijə þiɳk əl kum? *do you think he
will come?*

duz, dus (voiceless before the t) *does, dost*: þa duz *thou
dost,* but dus tə? *dost thou?*

e, ev *have*: wis et *we shall have it,* but wis ev əm *we
shall have them.*

ez, es *hast, has*: cp. duz, dus.

> ə = 1. *a*: ə boni bān *a pretty child.*
>
> = 2. *he* (in subordinate sentences and interrogatively, in
> other cases it is ĭ).
>
> = 3. *her* (before consonants): ə faðə(r) *her father.*
>
> = 4. *have* (weakest form): ast ə dunt if id ed ə tšons
> *I should have done it, if I had had a chance.*
>
> = 5. *on*: ə ði rig *on thy back.*
>
> = 6. *of* (may be used before a vowel or a consonant, əv
> only before vowels):

ə pund ə or əv aplz *a pound of apples.*

NOTE.—Through ə being also the unaccented form of on, it often happens
that on is used where we should expect əv, as toəf on əm *the half of
them.*

ed = 1. *had.*

= 2. *would*: it ed or ted tak ə lot *it would take a lot.*

em or rather m (vocalic) *them*: sam em up *pick them up.*

en *an*: en apl *an apple.*

en or rather n (vocalic) =

    1. *and*: Doed en Eels *George and Alice.*

    2. *one*: it wer ə guid en *it was a good one.*

ə(r) = 1. *or.*

    = 2. *are.*

et = 1. *at.* et uem *at home.*

    = 2. *that* (cj.): a sī et im reŋ *I see that I am wrong.*

    = 3. *who, whom* (rel.): im et sed sue *he who said so,*
      ðem et we soe dān trued *those whom we saw*
      down the road.

ev = 1. *have* (weakest form before vowels): ðe med ev ed
      it bi nā *they might have had it by now.*

    = 2. *of* (before vowels): toef ev ə keek *the half of a*
      tea-cake.

ez = 1. *us*: giv ez ə tūþri *give us a few* (lit. *two or three*).

    = 2. *he has*: wen ez wešt isen *when he has washed*
      himself.

    = 3. *he is*: wol ez bān *until he is going.*

    = 4. *as.*

fe(r) *for.*

fre *from.*

i = 1. *in*: i tās *in the house.*

    = 2. *I* (in subordinate and interrogative sentences,
      see a): sali et? *shall I have it?* if i ger it *if I*
      get it.

    = 3. *he* (in direct assertions): i sez *he says.*

inte *into.*

iz *his,* but is before voiceless sounds: a mer iz muðe(r)
I met his mother, but is faðe(r) *his father.*

jə = 1. *ye, you.*

   = 2. *your* (before consonants).

   = 3. *you are* (before consonants) jə bān, āje ? *you are going, are you ?*

jət = 1. *yet.*

   = 2. *you it* : al sel jət *I will sell you it.*

kəd *could.*

kɒ (vocalic ɒ) *can* : ða kɒ seə wot tə laiks *thou canst say what thou likest.*

l *will* : al *I'll,* wil *we will,* etc.

mə = 1. *me* gi(v) mə ə feu *give me a few.*

   = 2. *may* : amə wēk wol i drop fər out ta keəz *I may work until I drop for anything thou carest.*

məd *might.*

mən or rather mn (with vocalic n)

   = 1. *must* : a mən guə *I must go.*

   = 2. *man* : diu it, mən *do it, man.*

mi *my.*

nə(r) = 1. *nor.*

   = 2. *than* (after a comparative).

nət, nt (the form nət is seldom used. The usual form is nt) *not.*

s *us* (after voiceless consonant) : lets ev əm *let us have them.*

s, sl : ðasl, ðas et *thou shalt have it.*

sānt *shall not.*

sant *saint* (before proper names).

sə *so.*

səd, st *should, shouldst* : ða səd or ðast ə dunt *thou shouldest have done it.*

šə *she* (in subordinate and interrogative sentences, in other cases šŭ).

t = 1. *the* : **tman** *the man.*

= 2. *it* : **len met** *lend me it.*

= 3. *art* : **ðat ə fuil** *thou art a fool.*

ta, tə *thou* (in subordinate and interrogative sentences, in other cases **ðä**).

tə, təv (before vowels) *to.*

ðe *there* : **ðez** *there is, there has, there are.*

ðə = 1. *thee* : **a spak tə ðe** *I spoke to thee.*

= 2. *they* : **mun ðə stop ?** *must they stop ?*

= 3. *they (are)* : **ðə nuən sə ritš** *they are not so rich.*

= 4. *they (have)* : **wen ðə funt** *when they have found it.*

= 5. *their* (before consonants).

ði *thy.*

v *have* : **wiv sīnt** *we have seen it.*

wa *why*. The unaccented form of **wai**, cp. **a** beside **ai** *I*, **wol** beside **wail** *while, until*. It is always used when speaking in an encouraging manner to a person : **wa lad, ða mən trai** *why lad, thou must try.*

wə = 1. *we* : **sal wə guə ?** *shall we go ?*

= 2. *our* (before consonants) **wə faðə buits** *our father's boots*, but **wə soə wer ont** *we saw our aunt.*

= 3. *we (are)* : **wə bān tə d'len** *we are going to the Glen.*

= 4. *was, were* : **a wə liukin fojə** *I was looking for you.*

wəd *would.*

wi = 1. *with.*

= 2. *we* (in direct assertions).

= 3. *wilt* : **witə** *wilt thou.*

wol *until*, unaccented form of **wail** (noun) *while.*

z = 1. *is* : **iz** *he is.*

= 2. *has, hast* : **ðaz** *thou hast,* **iz** *he has.*

CHAPTER VI.

The Semi-vowels.

W.

a. Initially.

§ 250. OE. initial w has remained before vowels: **waip** *to wipe,* **weed** *to wade,* **wee(r)** *to spend money,* **wāk** *work,* **wiðe(r)** *to hurl, throw,* **woef** *insipid,* **wote(r)** *water.*

It also appears as w in words of Norse origin: **weeve(r)** *to waver,* **winde** *window,* **wik** *quick, alive,* **wiɒ** *wing,* **wont** *want.*

In words of French origin we have w in some words and v in others, just as in the lit. language: **warend** *to warrant,* **weedž** *wage,* **weet** *to wait,* **walep** *to beat, flog,* **vari** *very,* **viel** *veal,* **vois** *voice,* **voiðe(r)** *a large clothes' basket.*

It has disappeared in the combination wr: **rait** *to write,* **reɒ** *wrong.* Examples for wl- are wanting.

It has also generally remained in the OE. combinations hw, dw, þw, tw, sw, as **wot** *what,* **wīl** *wheel,* **dwinl** *to dwindle,* **dwāf** *dwarf,* **witl** (ME. þwitel) *large carving knife,* **weɒ** (OE. þwang) *thong,* **wak** *to beat, flog,* **twais** *twice,* **twot** *pudendum fem.,* **swiet** *to sweat,* **sweep** *the handle of a machine.*

kw mostly occurs in French words : **kweet** *quart*, **kwari** *quarry*, **kwaleti** *quality*.

Initial **w** has disappeared in the weak forms of **wil** *will*, **wod** *would*, as **al gue** *I will go*, **id diut, if ə kud** *he would do it, if he could*.

w has also disappeared in : **kil** *to kill*, **kud** *cud*, **sued** *sword*, **sitš** *such*, **sump** *a puddle* or *dirty pool of water*. **tū** *two*, **ue** *who*.

b. Medially.

Medial **w** + final vowel have become **ə** after consonants : **swole** (OE. **swalwe**) *swallow*, **spare** (OE. **spearwa**) *sparrow*, **jare** *yarrow*, **wide** (OE. **widwe**) *widow, widower*.

aw > oe : **tloe** (OE. **clawu**) *claw*, § 63.

āw > oe : **bloe** *to blow*, **noe** *to know*, **sloe** *slow*, **snoe** *snow*, § 123.

eow, ew > eu : **eu** (OE. **eowu**) *ewe*, **streu** (OE. **strewian**) *to strew*, § 85.

ēaw > eu : **deu** (OE. **dēaw**) *dew*, **feu** *few*, **eu** (OE. **hēawan**) *to hew*, § 180.

ēow > iu, eu : **triu** *true*, **riu** *to rue*, **briu** *to brew* **eu** *yew*, **seu** *to sew*, § 190.

īw > iu : **spiu** *to spew*, § 159.

ōw > ou : **dlou** *to glow*, **grou** *to grow*, **flou** *to flow*, § 166.

§ **251. w** has disappeared in words compounded with *ward* : **bakedz** *backwards*, **fored** *forward*, **oeked** *awkward*, **tādz** *towards*, § 243; as also in those compounded with *worth*: **oepeþ** *halfpenny worth*, **peneþ** *pennyworth*, **sikspeneþ** *sixpenny worth*, etc.

It has also disappeared in : **midif** *midwife*, **oles** *always*, **sumet** (**et** may here however be the rel. pr.) *something*, *anything*, **anse(r)** *answer*, **grunsil** *groundsel*.

j.

§ 252. OE. initial j, mostly written g, has had the same development as in lit. Engl.: jĭ, jə *ye, you,* jiə(r) *year,* jon *yon,* juək *yoke,* jurɔ *young.*

§ 253. French ü, which has become juw in lit. Engl., appears in the W. dial. as a falling diphthong initially, medially, and finally: ius *use,* iunəti *unity,* fiutə(r) *future,* viu *view,* § 237.

The Liquids.

l.

§ 254. l has generally remained unchanged: lap *to wrap up,* lat *late,* lig *to lie down,* loin *lane,* lium *loom.*

boəld (ME. balləd) *bald,* molt *malt,* fīld *field,* mīld *mild,* wīld *wild,* bīld *to build,* flik *flitch of bacon,* jolə *yellow,* tšeltə(r) *to clot, coagulate (of blood),* twilt *quilt,* nozl *to beat, thrash,* blob *bubble,* galəsəz *braces.*

džoul *to knock, strike,* kāl *to frown,* foəl *to fall,* koil *coal,* teəl *tale,* swiəl *to gutter (of a candle).*

§ 255. al has become oə in the combinations lf, OE. lh, lk, lm, ll, lv. For examples see §§ 62, 198. To these add: oməst *almost,* oəminak *almanac,* oəmənd *almond.*

al has become ou before a following d. For examples see §§ 64, 199.

ol has become ou before a following consonant. For examples see §§ 103, 220.

§ 256. l has also disappeared before a following consonant in: witš (OE. hwelc) *which,* sitš (OE. swelc) *such,* būk *bulk,* stūp (ME. stolpe) *a post.*

It has also disappeared in: wod, wəd, -d (§ 397) *would,*

sud, sed, st (§ 391) *should*, sänt *shall not*, s (§ 391) *shall*, wite ? (§ 397) *wilt thou?* wient *will not*.

In fout (ME. faute, Fr. faute) *fault*, māt (cp. Lat. mūtāre) *to moult*, there probably never was an l in the dialect forms.

§ 257. Consonantal l, when it came to stand finally, has become vocalic after consonants : adl *to earn*, kitl *to tickle*, nibl *to nibble*, ridl *sieve*, satl *to settle*. For further examples see § 247 *b*.

r.

§ 258. r, which is a gently (not strongly as in Scotch) trilled sound, has only remained intact before a following vowel :

raiv *to tear*, reit *right*, ram *to thrust, press*, rīzd *rancid (of bacon)*, briɒ *to bring*, brek *to break*, beri *to bury*, fere *furrow*, sore *sorrow*, sare *to serve*, vari *very*.

r has probably been lost in aim (OE. hrīm?) *hoarfrost*.

§ 259. Before a following consonant it has entirely disappeared : bān (§ 61) *child*, bied (§ 68) *beard*, wǎk (§ 74) *work*, bēk (§ 90) *birch*, boen (§ 104, 1) *born*, bued (§ 104, 2) *board*, dēst (§ 113, 1) *durst*, bēþ (§ 120, 1) *birth*, aien (§ 157) *iron*, dālin (§ 189) *darling*, kweet (§ 203) *quart*, sǎvnt (§ 207) *servant*, oeðe(r) (§ 223) *order*, kēn (§ 228) *currant*, faðe(r) *father*, pl. faðez, swie(r) *to swear*, but i swiez *he swears*.

> NOTE.—The above list contains one example only of the various vowels which have been influenced through the absorption of the r ; for full lists of examples, see the paragraphs enclosed in parentheses.

§ 260. r, which has come to stand finally in the modern dialect, is still slightly trilled, but not so strongly as before a following vowel. This is always the case when

the word containing it is used alone, or stands at the end
of a sentence. In these positions it is never weakened into
a mere voiced glide as in lit. Engl. fear, nor does it disappear altogether as in lit. Engl. far. We thus make a
distinction between **peə** *pay*, and **peə(r)** *pair*, **kā** *cow*, and
kāə(r) *to cover*.

r disappears, of course, altogether in the sentence when
the next word begins with a consonant: **ajə bān?** *are you
going?* **wi wə leəkin** *we were playing*.

Examples of final r are: **wāə(r)** *worse*, **dluə(r)** *to stare
hard*, **smuə(r)** *to smother*, **biə(r)** *to bear*, **piə(r)** *pear*.

§ 261. In addition to the examples in which r has
undergone metathesis in the lit. language as, **bəd** *bird*, **bən**
to burn, **brīt** *bright*, **frīt** *fright*, **oəs** *horse*, **pəd** *third*, we
have **brust** *to burst*, **gən** *to grin*, **gəs** (also OE. **gærs**) *grass*,
gəsl *gristle*, **gət** *great*, **kəsməs** *Christmas*, **kəsn** *to christen*.

§ 262. r has disappeared in **pim-ruəz** *primrose*.

The Nasals.

m.

§ 263. m has generally remained unchanged: **muml**
to mumble, **muin** *moon*, **mistl** *cow-house*, **mizl** *to drizzle (of
rain)*, **mun** *must*, **mūd** *crowded, crammed*.

gami *lame*, **kākumə(r)** *cucumber*, **niml** *nimble*, **treml** *to
tremble*, **tšeemə(r)** *chamber*, **tuml** *to tumble*, **uml** *humble*.

brim *to put the boar to the sow*, **gam** *to gamble*, **krum**
crumb, **rām** *room*, **sam** *up to pick up*.

§ 264. m has become vocalic after consonants: **bodm**
bottom, **fadm** *fathom*, **film** *film*, **kindm** *kingdom*. m is also
vocalic in **əm** (= m) *them*.

G

n.

§ 265. Initial n has remained unchanged: **nate(r)** *to gnaw, nibble*, **nati** *neat, tidy, dexterous (of old people)*, **navi** *canal*, **nīt** *night*, **nie(r)** *kidney*, **noilz** (pl.) *the short hairs taken out of wool by the combing machine.*

§ 266. When n has remained medial in the W. dial., it has generally undergone no change: **dwinl** *to dwindle*, **kanl** *candle*, **sind** *to rinse, wash out*, **spinl** *spindle*, **þune(r)** *thunder.*

§ 267. Medial n has disappeared before **s** in unaccented syllables without compensation lengthening: **estied** *instead*, **Robisn** *Robinson*, **Adkisn** *Atkinson.*

§ 268. n has remained when it has come to stand finally after vowels or was already final in OE.: **ain** (ME. **hīne**) *hind*, **bin** (OE. **binnan**) *within*, **bleen** *blain, boil*, **gruin** *a pig's snout*, **don** *to put on one's clothes*, **len** (OE. **lǣnan**) *to lend*, **nuin** *noon*, **olin** *holly*, **speen** (OE. **spanan**) *to wean.*

§ 269. n has become vocalic after dentals and sibilants: **eenšn** *ancient*, **fešn** *fashion*, **fezn** *pheasant*, **frozn** *frozen*, **miln** (OE. **myln**) *mill*, **ratn** (O. Fr. **raton**) *rat*, **seldn** (OE. **seldon**) *seldom*. For other examples see § 247 *b*.

§ 270. n has become vocalic **m** after labials by assimilation:

apm (lit. *happen*) *perhaps*, **fipms** *fivepence*, **þrepms** *three pence*, etc., **opm** *open*, **wiepm** *weapon*. For further examples see § 247 *b*.

evm *even*, **īmin** *evening*, **sevm** *seven*, **uvm** *oven*, **wovm** *woven.*

§ 271. n has become vocalic **ŋ** after gutturals: **beeŋŋ** *bargain*, **ugŋ** *hip*, **wegŋ** *wagon.*

brokᴅ *broken*, buəkᴅ (ME. **bolkin**) *to retch, belch*, kᴅ (weak form of **kan** *can*, akᴅ diut *I can do it*), spokᴅ *spoken*, stākᴅ *to stiffen*, wokᴅ *to waken*.

§ 272. n generally disappears in ə *on*, i *in*. It has also disappeared in oəpəþ *halfpenny worth*. It has also disappeared by assimilation in amət *am not*.

ᴅ.

§ 273. The guttural ᴅ, written n in OE., only occurred before the gutturals g and c.

It has generally remained in accented syllables in the W. dialect: biᴅ (O. Icel. **bingr** *heap*) *bin*, briᴅ *to bring*, driᴅk *to drink*, iᴅ (ME. **hengen**) *to hang*, liᴅ (O. Icel. **lyng**) *heather*, teᴅz *tongs*, þiᴅ *thing*, piᴅk *to think*, weᴅ *thong*.

fiᴅe(r) *finger*, never fiᴅge(r) as in lit. Engl., iᴅliš *English*, miᴅl *to mingle*, uᴅə(r) *hunger*, siᴅl *single*.

NOTE.—**kindm** (OE. **cynedōm**) but lit. Engl. *kingdom*, through association with *king*.

§ 274. ᴅ has disappeared through assimilation before the following kᴅ in the pp. of verbs ending in ᴅk: drukᴅ *drunk, drunken*, sukᴅ *sunk*, slukᴅ *slunk*, šrukᴅ *shrunk*. But see § 368.

§ 275. ᴅ has become n before the following dental in: lenþ *length*, strenþ *strength*.

§ 276. ᴅ has regularly become n in unaccented syllables: fādin *farthing*, gezlin *gosling*, īmin *evening*, iəzinz *the eaves of a building*, midin (ME. **midding**) *dunghill*, runin *running*, and similarly in all present participles.

§ 277. Palatal ᴅ, written n in OE., only occurred before the palatal forms of g and c.

G 2

In the W. dial. it has become dental n as in lit. Engl.:
drenš (OE. drencan) *to drench*, sinž (OE. sengan) *to singe*.

The Labials.

p.

§ **278.** p has remained in all positions:

pei *pea*, **pimruez** *primrose*, **piek** *perch*, **pāk** *a kind of*
blain, **poem** *palm*, **poez** (O. Fr. **poulser**) *to kick*, **poutri**
poultry, **prog** *to collect wood for the bonfire on the fifth of*
November, **preet** *to prate, babble*, **put** *to put*.

lopste(r) (OE. **loppestre**) *lobster*, **speed** *spade*, **speen** *to*
wean.

dolep *lump of dirt*, **draip** *to drip*, **elp** *to help*, **filep** *to*
beat, flog, **kep** *to catch (a ball)*, **kraps** *the renderings of lard,*
lop *flea*, **noep** (ME. **nolpen**) *to hit on the head.*

§ **279.** Assimilation has taken place as in lit. Engl. in
emti (ME. **empti**, but OE. **ǣmet(t)ig**) *empty*, **kubed** *cup-*
board.

b.

§ **280.** The voiced explosive b has generally remained
in the W. dialect:

bān *child*, **bef** (ME. **beffin**) *to cough*, **bek** *beck*, **ben** (O. Icel.
banga *to hammer*), *to throw, hit violently*, **bid** *to invite to a*
funeral, **boged** *ghost*, **brig** *bridge*, **bun** *bound.*

bleb *blister*, **bluðe(r)** *to weep*, generally used in the phrase
te bluðe(r) en rue(r) lit. *to blubber and roar*, **gab** (cp. O. N.
gabba) *impudence*, **kubed** *cupboard*, **neb** *beak*, **nub** *to nudge*,
nuebdi *nobody*, **web** *web.*

§ **281.** b has disappeared after m: **kuem** *comb*, **lam**
lamb, **tlim** *to climb*, **wuem** *womb.* Also in **sumdi** *some-*
body.

§ 282. b never occurs between m—l or m—r, as in lit. Engl.: eseml *to assemble*, fuml *to fumble*, muml *to mumble*, niml *nimble*, raml *to ramble*, treml *to tremble*, tuml *to tumble*, þiml *thimble*, uml *humble*.

kākumə(r) *cucumber*, numə(r) *number*, slumə(r) *slumber*, tšeemə(r) *chamber*.

f.

§ 283. OE. f was used to re resent both the voiceless (= Mod. Engl. f) and the voiced (= Mod. Engl. v) spirant.

1. Initially it was voiceless and corresponds to Germanic f.

2. Medially it was voiced, except in the combinations ff, ft, fs. See Sievers, OE. Gr. § 192.

3. Finally it was probably voiceless in the historic period even when it corresponded to Germanic ƀ. But when OE. f came to stand medially through being followed by a case, or personal ending, etc., it was voiced, thus wīf *wife*, gen. wīfes, pret. sing. geaf *I, he gave*, pl. gēafon. In this case the W. dial., like lit. Engl., has sometimes generalized the one form, sometimes the other. We shall here treat the sounds in the above order.

1. faðe(r) *father*, feu *few*, flee *to frighten*, flumeks *to confound, cheat*, foil *foal*, foud *fold*, fouk *folk*, fout *fault*, freem *to make a start*, fudl *to confuse*, fuzi *soft, spongy*.

2. eft *haft*, gift *gift*, rift *to belch, eructate*, sift *to sift*, weft *weft*, kuf *cuff*.

delv *to delve*, daiv *to dive*, draiv *to drive*, duv *dove*, evm *heaven*, ive(r) *ever*, kāv *to carve*, kuəv *cove*, live(r) *liver*, neiv (O. Icel. knefi) *fist*, nivə(r) *never*, raiv (O. Icel. rīfa *to break*) *to tear*, siv *sieve*, stāv *to starve*, stuəv *stove*, šeəv *to shave*, šuv *to shove*, þraiv *to thrive*, weiv *to weave*.

ev, ev, ə *have*, and liv *to live* are, of course, not directly developed from OE. habban, libban but from the forms without gemination, as hafaᵹ *he has*, hæfde *he had*, liofaᵹ *he lives*, lifde *he lived*.

It has disappeared as in lit. Engl. in such words as: ez *hast, has*, elte(r) (OE. healfter) *halter*, enent *opposite*, ied *head*, kroel *to crawl*, oek *hawk*, leedi *lady*, loed *lord*, wimin *women*, wumen *woman*.

It has also disappeared in: ebūn *above*, īmin *evening*, steim (ME. stefnen, OE. ge-stefnian and a stemnian *to give voice for, appoint*) *to bespeak a thing*, šūl *shovel*, gīn *given*, oue(r) beside ove(r) *over*, nie(r) beside nive(r) *never*, and generally also in the present gi, pret. ga and e, ə *have*, when the next word begins with a consonant.

The voiced spirant has become b in rebit *rivet*, if the dial. word is etymologically the same as the lit. Engl. word.

3. delf *stone quarry*, kaf *chaff*, oef *half*, ruif *roof*, tᶴf *turf*, þīf *thief*, uif *hoof*, waif *wife*.

aiv *hive*, faiv *five*, greev *grave*, twelv *twelve*.

f has disappeared in: oepni *halfpenny*, ə *of*, sel, sen *self*.

§ 284. te *to* appears as tev when the next word begins with a vowel: tev ə man *to a man*.

The Dentals.

t.

§ 285. Initial t has remained: taid *feast-time*, teem *tame*, temz (ME. temse) *hop-sieve*, teu (OE. tēawian) *to work zealously*, toe *a marble of any kind*, toidi *small, little*, trolep *a dirty, untidy person*, tul (O. Icel. til) *to*.

§ 286. Medial t has mostly remained unchanged:

antm (OE. antefn) *anthem*, getn *got*, nati *neat, tidy, dexterous (of old people)*, ratn *rat*, tluste(r) *cluster*.

It has become d in bodm *bottom*, praid *pride*. It has become r in poreets *potatoes*, has undergone metathesis in witek *wicket*, and disappeared before the b in nobed (lit. *not but*) *only*.

§ 287. t is dropped between s and a following l or n in :

busl *bustle*, bruslz *bristles*, gēsl *gristle*, kasl *castle*, rasl to *wrestle*, þrosl *thrush*, wisl *whistle*, dēsnt *durst not*; but mistl (O. Icel. mjalta-sel *shed for milking*) *cow-house*.

brusn (pp.) *burst*, fasn *to fasten*, lisn *to listen*, oue-kesn *overcast, gloomy (of the sky)*, þrusn (pp.) *thrust*.

ts > ss > s in wisnde *Whitsuntide*. Whitsunday is wisnde sunde.

§ 288. The t in French words which has become tš in lit. Engl. through the influence of the following ü has remained in the W. dialect :

flete(r) *feature*, fēnite(r) *furniture*, flute(r) *future*, foetn *fortune*, kriete(r) *creature*, moiste(r) *moisture*, neete(r) *nature*, natrel *natural*, paste(r) *pasture*, pikte(r) *picture*, vente(r) *to venture*.

§ 289. When t came to stand finally in the W. dial., or was final already in OE., it has generally remained :

fift (OE. fīfta) *fifth*, sikst *sixth*, toist *toast*, twelft *twelfth*.

bāt *without*, feit *to fight*, gēt *great*, goit (ME. gote) *water channel*, mīt *to meet*, out *holt*, slāt *to bedabble*, suit *soot*.

bit *bit*, fat *fat*, it *it*, kot *staples of wool tightly entangled together*, lat (OE. lætt) *lath*, lat *late*, mat *mat*, net *net*, wet *wet*.

§ 290. The t in all verbal forms ending in t preceded by a short vowel, appears as r when the next word begins with a vowel. We regularly say : amīt im ivri dee *I meet*

him every day ; but **amer im ivri dee** *I met him every day.*
Similarly with **get me wun** *get me one*, **ger up** *get up*, **gar**
got, **ir** *to hit*, **ler** *to let*, **pur** *to put*, **sar** *sat*, **ser** *to set*, **sir** *to*
sit, **šur** *to shut*, etc. Also in all the present participles, as
gerin *getting.*

> Note.—This phenomenon is widely spread in Mod. English dialects. See
> EEPr. vol. v. p. 420.

The same is also the case with the pronoun **wot** *whát* :
wotste dun ? *what hast thou done ?* but **wor iz it ?** *what is it?*

§ 291. **t** has become **d** in : **abed** *yes but*, **bed** *but*, **prād**
proud, **buzed** (O. Fr. **busart**), *butterfly*, **Adkisn** *Atkinson*,
warend *to warrant.*

§ 292. It has been dropped in **kōn** *currant*, **sādžn**
sergeant, **džais** (O. Fr. **giste**) *joist*. The older generation
also say **omes** *almost*, **āvis** *harvest*, **bies** (lit. *beast*) *cow*,
cows.

§ 293. A **t** is never pronounced in **eenšn** (Fr. **ancien**)
ancient, **fezn** (O. Fr. **faisan**) *pheasant*, **tairen** *tyrant.*

§ 294. **t** is excrescent in **vāment** *vermin.*

d.

§ 295. Initial **d** has remained : **daiv** *to dive*, **deu** *dew*,
dī *to die*, **died** *dead*, **dof** *to undress*, **don** *to dress*, **dreet** *to* ·
drawl.

§ 296. Medial **d** has also generally remained unchanged :
fidl *fiddle*, **inde(r)** *to hinder*, **midin** (ME. **midding**, Dan.
mögdynge) *dunghill*, **midl** *middle*, **nīdl** *needle*, **ridn** *riden*,
wide *widow*, **sadl** *saddle*, **redi** *ready.*

§ 297. Intervocalic **d** followed by **r** in the next syllable

has become ð: bleðə(r) *bladder*, bluðə(r) *to cry, weep*,
diðə(r) (ME. diderin) *to shiver*, faðe(r) *father*, foðe(r) *fodder*,
geðe(r) *to gather*, tə-geðə(r) *together*, iðə(r) *hither*, konsiðe(r)
to consider, laðe(r) *ladder*, moiðe(r) *to ponder, be anxious
about a thing*, muðə(r) *mother*, pāðə(r) *powder*, šuðə(r) *to
shudder*, tluðə(r) *to get closely together*, uðə(r) *udder*,
voiðe(r) (O. Fr. voider *to void*) *a large clothes' basket*,
weðə(r) *weather*.

NOTE.—The words *thither* and *whither* are not used in the dialect.

The law also holds good when an l or r has disappeared
before the d: soðe(r) *solder*, mā̃ðə(r) *murder*, oeðe(r) *to
order*.

NOTE.—The ð in mā̃ðə(r) is probably not the þ in OE. myrþran, but rþ
became rd (§ 306, 2) and then ð by the above law.

§ 298. d never occurs between n—l, n—r, as in lit.
English:

anl *handle*, dwinl *to dwindle*, kanl *candle*, kinlin *firewood*, spinl *spindle*.

gane(r) *gander*, þune(r) *thunder*.

§ 299. d has disappeared in ansəm *handsome*, anfl
handful, grunsil *groundsel*, gran-faðe(r), gram-faðe(r)
grandfather, lanloed *landlord*, unded *hundred*, but undet
(by assimilation of dt) *hundredth*.

§ 300. OE. final d and the medial d which has come
to stand finally in the W. dial. have generally remained:
bid *to invite to a funeral*, find *to find*, grund *ground*, od
to hold, oud *old*, pund *pound*, roid *a clearing (of a wood)*,
sind *to rinse, wash out*, wund *a wound*, blier-īd *blear-
eyed*.

§ 301. d has disappeared after n in: bran (OE. brand)
niu *quite new*, ən *and*, þāzn *thousand*, uzbn *husband*,

and also in the pret. and pp. of the verbs bind *to bind*, **find** *to find*, **wind** *to wind*, thus : **ban, bun; fan, fun; wan, wun.**

d has also been dropped in **skafl** *scaffold*, **skaflin** *scaffolding*.

§ 302. Final **ndz** has become **nz** : **anz** *hands*, **frenz** *friends*, **senz** *sends*, **grunz** (lit. *grounds*) *sediment*. **pāzn** and **uzbn** may accordingly be new formations from the plural forms.

§ 303. A **d** is never pronounced in **ain** (ME. **hīne**) *hind*, **bān** (O. Icel. **būenn**) *going*, as **wie te bān ?** *where art thou going ?*, **len** (OE. **lǣnan**) *to lend*.

§ 304. **d** is excrescent in **arend** (ME. **aranie**, O. Fr. **araigne**) *spider*, **drānd** *to drown*.

§ 305. **d** has become **t** in **wāte** (lit. *work-day*), *week-day*, **wēsit** *worsted*, **st** the weak form of **sud** *should*. In **be-int** *behind*, the t is probably due to the t in **frunt** *front* ; for similar examples see Paul-Braune's Beiträge, xiii. p. 590. In the phrase **iust te wod** or **wed** *to be wont* or *willing*, the t is due to assimilation with **te** : **ða iust te wed diu e bit e wāk** *thou wast formerly wont to do a bit of work*.

þ.

§ 306. OE. **þ**, also written **ð**, was a voiceless spirant like the **th** in lit. Engl. **thin**, initially, finally as also medially except probably between voiced sounds. Between voiced sounds it was probably voiced like the **th** in lit. Engl. **breathe**. See Sievers, OE. Gr. § 201.

We shall here adopt the following order : 1. Initially. 2. When the sound or its further development has remained medial in the W. dialect. 3. When it has become final in

the W. dialect. In this case two subdivisions are necessary according as we have now the voiceless or the voiced
sound. Cp. § 283, 3.

Fifty years ago f for þ and v for ð were quite general
throughout the Township of Idle, but they have now practically disappeared except as an individualism. When I
was a boy þ and ð were regularly used among the younger
Windhill people, but f and v were still generally used in
Thackley and Idle, which are only about a mile distant
from W. I well remember how we used to twit the
Thackley and Idle people about their pronunciation of
these sounds: **fakle** *Thackley*, **fiŋk** *think*, **fəd** *third*, **leev**
barn, **smivi** *smithy*, etc.

1. þ has remained voiceless except in pronouns and the
adverbs derived from them:

þak *thatch*, **þiŋk** *to think*, **þoil** *to give ungrudgingly*,
þraiv *to thrive*, **þriəp** (OE. þrēapian *to rebuke*) *to contradict,
dispute*.

In the pronouns and the adverbs derived from them
there originally existed double forms: the stressed forms
with þ and the unstressed forms with ð. The W. dial., like
lit. Engl., has generalised the latter, which are now used
both as the stressed and unstressed forms. See the Chapter
on the pronouns:

ðă *thou*, **ði** *thy*, **ðat** (only as demonstrative, the rel. pr.
and cj. is **ət** which is of Norse origin) *that*, **ðem** (mostly
as demonstrative, the pers. pr. is **em**) *those*, **ðis** *this*, etc.;
ðiə(r) *there*, **ðen** *then*, etc.

The def. art. is generally t and is attached to the following
word, thus **tman** *the man*, **toudn** *the old one*, **tkoilz** *the
coals*. We make a clear distinction between **teəbl** *table*
and **t'teəbl** *the table*, **eit** *eight and* **eit'** *eighth*, the former is
the ordinary Engl. t and the latter is a suspended t. ð has

become t in the nom. of the second pers. sing. of the pers.
pronoun when used interrogatively and in subordinate
sentences (§ 350): **es-tə**? *hast thou?* **sal-tə**? *shalt thou?* **witə**? *wilt thou?* **kantə diut**? *canst thou do it?* **þa kɔ gue
wen tet redi** *thou canst go when thou art ready.*

þ has disappeared before **w** in: **wak** *to beat severely*, see
Skeat, Et. Dict., **witl** (ME. **þwitel**) *large carving knife*,
wen (OE. **þwang**) *thong.*

Occasionally the **þ** is omitted in the pres. tense of **þink**,
as a **iɔk** *I think.*

2. Between vowels we have **ð**: **feðə(r)** *feather*, **laðə(r)**
foam, froth, **leðə(r)** *leather*, **reəðə(r)** *rather*, **smiði** *smithy*,
weðə(r) (OE. **weðer**) *the wool of a sheep which has already
been shorn at least once before.*

It has become **d** medially after **r** in: **bēdn** *burden*, **fādin**
farthing, **əfued** *to afford.*

It has also become **d** in: **fadm** *fathom*, **snodn** *to make
smooth*, **snod** (O. Icel. **snoðenn** *smooth (of hair)*, **bald**)
smooth, even.

ð has disappeared in **moek** (O. Icel. **maðkr**) *maggot*, and
besk (O. Icel. **baðask**) *to bask.*

3. **baþ** *bath*, **dieþ** *death*, **froþ** *froth*, **gēþ** *girth*, **ielþ** *health*,
paþ *path*, **smiþ** *smith*, **swāþ** (O. Icel. **swörðr**) *the skin of
bacon*, **wēþ** *worth.*

brieð *to breathe*, **buið** *booth*, **leeð** (O. Icel. **hlaða**) *barn*,
saið *scythe*, **smuið** *smooth.*

§ 307. It has disappeared before the **s, z** in **muns**
months, **tluez** *clothes.* And also in **wi** *with.*

§ 308. The **d** in **beed** *to bathe* has probably been influenced by **weed** *to wade.*

§ 309. The ordinal numerals, except **seknd** *second*, **þēd**
third, all end in t. Regular forms are **fēst** (OE. **fyresta**),

first, **fift** (OE. fīfta) *fifth*, **sikst** (OE. **siexta**) *sixth*, **twelft** (OE. **twelfta**) *twelfth*, after the analogy of which have been formed **fouet** (OE. fēowerða) *fourth*, **naint** *ninth*, **tent** *tenth*, etc.

Sibilants.

s.

§ 310. Initially and finally as also medially (except between voiced sounds) OE. s was a voiceless spirant like the s in Mod. English sin. Medially between voiced sounds it was possibly voiced like the s in Mod. English rise. See Sievers, OE. Gr. § 204.

The development of s in the W. dialect is parallel with that of f (§ 283) and þ (§ 306), so that we shall here distinguish the three positions: 1. Initially. 2. When the sound has remained medial in the W. dialect. 3. When the sound was already final in OE. or has become final in the W. dialect. Here two subdivisions are necessary according as we have now the voiceless or the voiced spirant. Cp. § 283.

1. Initial s has remained both before vowels and consonants: **sā** *a drain, sough*, **sāk** *to suck*, **sam up** *to pick up*, **seem** *lard*, **set** *to set*, **sī** (OE. **sēon** = OHG. **sīhan**) *to stretch*, **sin** *since*, **sind** *to rinse, wash out*, **slate͘(r)** *to spill*, **smuið** *smooth*, **snod** *smooth, even*, **snikit** *a small passage*, **speik** *to speak*, **spitek** *spigot*, **steim** *to bespeak*, **stedi** *steady*, **strie** *straw*, **swāþ** *the skin of bacon*, **sweep** *the handle of a machine*.

s (?) has become **š** in **šŭ**, **še** *she*.

s has also remained before ü in French words, whereas in the lit. language it has become **š**: **siuge͘(r)** *sugar*, **siue(r)** *sure*.

2. Medially between voiced sounds we have z: **bīzm**
besom, **biznəs** *business*, **buzəd** *butterfly*, **dlazn** *to glaze*, **fezn**
pheasant, **frozn** *frozen*, **fuzi** *soft, spongy*, **mizl** *to drizzle (of
rain)*, **rīzd** *rancid (of bacon)*, **rizn** *risen*, **þāzn** *thousand*,
uzbn *husband*, **wizn** *to wither*.

z has also remained before ü in French words, but has
become **ž** in the lit. language: **mezə(r)** *measure*, **plezə(r)**
pleasure, **trezə(r)** *treasure*.

The **ð** in **siðəz** *scissors* is difficult to explain. It is just
possible that it may have been influenced by **saið** *scythe*,
just as **mud** *might* (verb) has probably been influenced by
kud *could*, **sud** *should*, and **bə-int** *behind* by **frunt** *front*,
and **beəd** *to bathe* by **weəd** *to wade*.

In combination with voiceless sounds **s** has been retained:
bəsk *to bask*, **blosm** *blossom*, **fasn** *to fasten*, **kist** *a chest*,
kə̄sn *to christen*, **musl** *muscle*, **rasl** *to wrestle*, **rust** (O.Icel.
röst) *rest, repose*, **trāst** *to trust*, **þrosl** (OE. **þrostle**) *thrush*.

3. **ās** *house*, **dlas** *glass*, **džais** (O.Fr. **giste**) *joist*, **gīs** *geese*,
kə̄s *to curse*, **kus** *kiss*, **lās** (pl. **lais**) *louse*, **mās** (pl. **mais**)
mouse, **muns** *months*, **oəs** *horse*, **uəs(t)** *hoarse*, **ðis** *this*.

anz *hands*, **bleəz** *blaze*, **duz** *dost, does*, but **dus tə?** *dost
thou?* **greəz** *to graze*, **iuz** *to use*, **loiz** (OE. **losian**) *to lose*,
nuəz *nose*, **raiz** *to rise*, **ruəz** *rose*, **temz** (ME. **temse**) *hop-
sieve*, **tluəz** *clothes*.

Final **z** is very common in originally unstressed forms,
as **iz, z** *is*, **ðaz** *thou hast*, **ĭz** *he has, he is*, **əz, uz** *us*, never **us**
even as stressed form, **əz** *us*.

§ 311. **s** has disappeared in: **pei** (ME. **pese**) *pea*, **ridl**
(ME. **redels**) *riddle*, **šimi** *chemise*, **tšeri** (O.Fr. **cerise**)
cherry.

The Gutturals.

C.

§ 312. Germanic **k**, generally written **c** in OE., remained a guttural initially before the guttural vowels **a, ā, o, ō, u, ū** and their mutations **e, ǣ, e, ē (œ̄), y, ȳ**, but became a palatal before the palatal vowels **æ, ǣ** (=OHG. **ā**), **e** (=Germanic **e**) **ea, eo, ēa, ēo, i, ī** and their mutations **e, ie** (=i-umlaut of **ea, eo**), **īe** (i-umlaut of **ēa, ēo**).

Medial **c** and **cc** remained a guttural before a following **a, o, u**, but became palatal when an **i** or **j** originally followed, as **sēc(e)an**=Goth. **sōkjan** *to seek*, **þecc(e)an** from older **þakjan to cover*, **bryce** from older **brukiz breach*. See Sievers, OE. Gr. §§ 206-7.

But already at an early period the palatals became gutturals again in many cases in the Anglian dialects, e. g. **sēcan** *to seek*, **þencan** *to think*, **cāld** *cold*. See Sweet, HES. § 535, Kluge, Grundriss der germanischen Philologie, i. pp. 836-41.

1. Initial **c** before consonants.

c has disappeared before **n** : **neid** *to knead*, **naif** *knife*, **nī** *knee*.

It has remained before **r** : **kraps** *the renderings of lard*, **kreev** *to crave*, **krinž** *to cringe*, **kriuk** *crook*, **kroe** *craw*.

It has become **t** before **l** : **tlād** *cloud*, **tlam** *to famish*, **tlāt** *clout*, **tleg** (Lowland Scot. **clag**) *to clog*, **tleŋk** *to flog, box on the ears*, **tlie(r)** *clear*, **tliet** *coltsfoot*, **tlien** *clean*, **tlim** *to climb*, **tliŋ** *to cling*, **tlip** *to clip*, **tliu** *a ball of string* or *worsted*, **tlīv** *to cleave*, **tloe** *claw*, **tloek** *to scratch with the fingers* or *claws*, **tlok** *to cluck*, **tlomp** *to tread heavily*, **tluek** *cloak*, **tlueþ** *cloth*, **tlueve(r)** *clover*. **k** has disappeared in **nek-leþ** *neckcloth, handkerchief*.

2. Initially before vowels.

kā *cow*, kaf *chaff*, kaind *kind*, kait *kite*, kanl *candle*, kāt *cart*, kāv *to carve*, keǝk *bread of every kind*, keǝ(r) *care*, kei *key*, kek *hemlock*, kemp (ME. kempe *shaggy*) *small coarse white hairs in wool*, kep *to catch (a ball, etc.)*, kest (ME. kesten) *to cast*, ketl *kettle*, kōgǝt *kirkgate* (but tšētš *church*), kōnl *kernel*, kōs *to curse*, kōsmǝs *Christmas*, kīl *to cool*, kil (OE. cwellan) *to kill*, kiln *kiln*, ǝ-kin *akin*, kīn *keen*, kindm (OE. cynedōm) *kingdom*, kiŋ-kof (cp. ME. kinken *to pant, gasp*), *whooping cough*, kīp *to keep*, kist *a chest, box*, kit (ME. kitte, cp. Mid. Du. kitte) *a pail*, kitl *to tickle*, kitl *to bring forth kittens*, kitšn *kitchen*, koef *calf*, koǝl *to call*, kal *to gossip*, koǝn *corn*, koit *coat*, koud *cold*, kouk (see NED. sub colk) *coke*, kout *colt*, kubǝd *cupboard*, kud (OE. cwidu) *cud*, kuǝm *comb*, kūk *cook*, kum *to come*.

tšaid *to chide*, tšap *chap*, tšavl *to nibble at, gnaw, chew*, tšeu *to chew*, tšētš *church*, tšiǝp *cheap*, tšīk *cheek*, tšikin *chicken*, tšildǝ(r) *children*, tšin *chin*, tšǝrǝp *to chirp*, tšīz *cheese*, tšiuz *to choose*, tšoǝk *chalk*, tšoul (ME. chavel, O. Low Germ. kafal) lit. *jaw*, only used in the phrase tšīk ǝn tšoul *said of two people walking closely together*, tšuǝk *to choke*, tšuf *proud, haughty*.

3. Initial sc.

skab *scab*, skaftin *shafting*, skelp (ME. skelpen) *to beat, flog*, skep (O. Icel. skeppa) *a large wicker basket for holding spinning bobbins*, skeǝlz *scales*, skōf *scurf*, skai *sky*, skift *to shift, remove*, skil *skill*, skin *skin*, skoup *scoop*, skuft *the nape of the neck*, skuil *school*, skul *skull of the head*, skutǝ(r) *to spill*, skraml *to scramble*, skreǝp *to scrape*, skrat (ME. scrattin) *to scratch*, skriǝm *to scream*, skrīk (O. Low Germ. scrīcōn) *to shriek*.

šak *to shake*, šait *cacare*, šaiv (ME. schīve, M. Low Germ. schīve) *a slice*, šakl *shackle*, šap *shape*, šel *shell*, šelf *shelf*, šeed *shade*, šeem *shame*, šee(r) *share*, šie(r) *to shear*, šil (ME. schellen, but Prom. Parv. p. 446 has schillin) *to shell peas*, šin *shin*, šip *ship*, šiuk *shook*, šop *shop*, šot *shot*, šut *shut*, šuðe(r) *to shudder*, šuv *to shove*, šreŋk *shrank*, šrimp *shrimp*, šriŋk *to shrink*.

Initial sc has become s in: sal, sl, s *shall*, sud, səd, st *should*.

4. When medial c has not become final in the W. dialect.

eskəd (cp. ME. aske *lizard*) *newt*, fikl *fickle*, kokl *cockle*, miks (by metathesis from OE. miscian) *to mix*, sikl *sickle*, twiŋkl *to twinkle*.

flikə(r) *to flicker*, neekt *naked*, snikit *a small passage*, wokŋ *to waken*.

kitšn *kitchen*.

meed *made*, musl *mussel*, teen *taken*, feseen *forsaken*.

5. When c or its further development is final in the W. dialect.

bek *beck*, beek *to bake*, brek *to break*, briuk *brook*, daik *ditch*, dreek *drake*, fleek *flake (of snow)*, briəd-fleik (O. Icel. fleki *hurdle*) *a hurdle on which oat-cakes are dried*, flik *flitch of bacon*, flok *flock*, ik (cp. Low Germ. hicken) *to hitch*, iuk *hook*, kok *cock*, lavrek *lark*, lek *to leak*, leek *to play*, lik *to lick*, liuk *to look*, lok *lock*, mak *to make*, muk *muck*, nek *neck*, niuk *nook*, nok *to knock*, pak *bundle*, pluk *pluck*, prik *to prick*, reek *rake*, reik *to reach*, rik *smoke*, sāk *to suck*, sek *sack*, seek *sake*, slek *small coal*, slek *to extinguish a fire with water*, slumək *a dirty, untidy person*, sneek *snake*, snek (ME. snekke) *latch of a door*, spek *speck*, speik *to speak*, steek *stake*, suek *to soak*, tak *to take*, tik *tick*, tiuk *took*, tlik (OE. clyccan) *to clutch, seize, catch hold*, þak *thatch*, þik *thick*, weik (ME. weke) *the wick of a lamp or candle*, wāk (noun) *work*, wōk *to work*, wik (O. Icel. vik (noun) *stirring, moving*) *quick, alive*.

H

bŏək *balk, beam*, tŏək *to talk*, wŏək *to walk*.

bɘŋk *bench*, drɪŋk *to drink*, ɘŋk *hank*, spɘŋk *to hit*, þɪŋk *to think*.

bāk *bark*, bēk *birch*, fŏək *fork*, māk *mark*, mŏək *maggot*, stāk (OE. stearc *strong, severe*) *very, quite*, wāk (OE. wærc, O. Icel. verkr) *ache, pain*.

Palatal nc has become nš : drenš (OE. drencan) *to drench*.

bitš *bitch*, bleitš *to bleach*, breitš *breach*, britš *breech*, etš *to hatch*, fotš *to fetch*, krutš *crutch*, latš *latch*. leitš *leech*, meitš *to measure*, mitš *much*, notš *a run at the game of cricket*, pitš *pitch*, sitš *such*, speitš *speech*, stitš *stitch*, stretš *to stretch*, swetš (OE. swæcc *a taste*) *a sample of cloth*, tletš (cp. O. Icel. klekja *to hatch*) *a brood of chickens*, teitš *to teach*, witš *which*, wotš *to watch*.

6. Final sc.

ask (ME. harsk, cp. Dan. harsk) *dry, rough, harsh*, besk *to bask*, busk *to go about from place to place singing and playing for money*.

eš *ash-tree*, fiš *fish*, fleš *flesh*, freš *fresh*, peš (ME. paschen, cp. Swed. paska) *to knock about, smash, dash*, reš *rash*, weš *to wash*, wiš *to wish*.

sc has become s in as (OE. æsce) *ash*, as-midin *ash-pit*, as beside aks (OE. āscian. ācsian) *to ask*, mens (OE. mennisc *dignity, honour*) *neatness, tidiness*.

§ 313. k has disappeared through assimilation in kḡgət *kirkgate*, kiŋ-kof *whooping cough*, beside kiŋk (ME. kinken *to pant, gasp*) *to cough* (of *whooping cough*), wātə (lit. *work day*, kd > kt > tt > t) *week day*. ŋks > ŋs in the phrase þiŋs tə? *thinkest thou?* as ədnt'ə out tə (ə) dunt, þiŋs tə? (lit. *hadst not thou ought to have done it, thinkest thou?*) *don't you think you ought to have done it?* Many people pronounce it as if it were þiŋ stə?

§ 314. The relation, if any, of **bleg**, plural **blegz**, to *blackberry* is difficult to explain. It may be that **blakbəri** became **blagbəri** by assimilation, and that then **bəri** was dropped. **blag** would regularly become **bleg** in the W. dial., see § 59.

g.

§ 315. OE. initial **g** was a voiced spirant before both vowels and consonants. Before guttural vowels and their mutations (cp. § 312) it was a guttural spirant, as also before **æ** (Sievers, OE. Gr. § 212), but before the palatal vowels **ə** (= Germanic e), **ea, eo, ēa, ēo, i, ie** it was a palatal spirant. At a later period the guttural spirant became an explosive before consonants, guttural vowels, and **y̆** (= i-umlaut of **ŭ**), **ē** (= i-umlaut of **ō**); but the palatal spirant remained. On forms like Mod. Engl. **give, get, begin**, etc., see Sweet's New English Grammar §§ 817–8, and Kluge in Paul's Grundriss I. pp. 843–4.

Medially between vowels it was a voiced spirant. After **n** (= ŋ) it was an explosive. And when geminated (written **cg**) it was also a voiced guttural or palatal explosive according as it was originally followed by a guttural or palatal vowel.

During the OE. period final **g** became **h** after long guttural vowels and **r, l**, Sievers § 214.

1. Initial **g** before consonants.

It has disappeared before **n** : **nəəg** *to gnaw,* **nat** *gnat.*

It has remained before **r** : **gēsl** *gristle,* **grəə** *grey,* **grīn** *green,* **grund** *ground.*

Before **l** it has become **d** : **dlad** *glad,* **dlāmi** *sad, downcast,* **dlas** *glass,* **dlium** *gloom,* **dlue(r)** (ME. **glōrən**, Swed. **glōra**) *to stare,* **dlumpi** *sulky, morose.*

H 2

2. Initially before vowels.

Initially before vowels it has had the same development as in lit. Engl. :

gab (cp. O. Icel. **gabba**) *impudence, cheek*, **gane(r)** *gander*, **gavlek** (OE. **gafoluc** *spear*) *crowbar*, **geep** *to gape*, **geet** *gate*, **gest** *guest*, **get** *to get*, **gilt** (O. Icel. **gilta**) *a young female pig*, **be-gin** *to begin*, **giv, gi** *to give*, **goit** *a water channel, mill-stream*, **guet** *goat*, **goud** *gold*, **guid** *good*.

jād *yard*, **jān** *yarn*, **jel** *to yell*, **jelp** *to yelp*, **jest** *yeast*, **jestede** *yesterday*, **jīld** *to yield*, **joen** *to yawn*, **jole** *yellow*, **juek** *yolk*.

3. When **g** or its further development has not become final in the W. dial.

æg has become **ee**: **breen** *brain*, **eel** *hail*, **feen** *fain*, *gladly*, **fee(r)** *fair*, **meen** *main*, **neel** *nail*, **peel** *pail*, **sleen** *slain*, **sneel** *snail*, **teel** *tail*, see § 65. But we have **sed** (OE. **sæde** beside **sægde**) *said*.

ag has become **oe**: **doen** *to dawn*.

āg has become **oe** in **oen** *own*.

eg has become **ee** and has thus fallen together with **ee** from **æg**: **breed** (OE. **bregdan**) *to resemble, act like another person*, **geen** (O. Icel. **gegn**) *near, direct*, **geen** *gain*, **leed** *laid*, **leen** *lain*, **reel** *rail*, **reen** *rain*, **seel** *sail*. See § 84.

ig has become **ī**: **stīl, stī** *stile*, **tīl** *tile*, cp. also **stī** *ladder*. But we have **sail** from **sigelian** *to drain through a sieve*, **saið** from **sigþe** *scythe*. **ig** cannot have become **ī** at a very early period in the North, otherwise it would have become **ai** like old **ī**. Cp. also Easther, A Glossary of the Dialect of Almondbury and Huddersfield, sub **sile** and **stigh**.

og has become **ou**: **floun** *flown*.

ug has become **ā**: **fāl** *fowl*, **kāl** *cowl*.

4. When **g, cg**, or their further development have become final in the W. dialect.

a. g has combined with the preceding vowel along with which it has become a long vowel or a diphthong.

æg: dee *day*, mee (emphatic form) *may*.

ag: droe *to draw*, loe *law*.

āg: lou *low*, ou *to owe*.

ǣg: gree *grey*, tlee *clay*; kei *key*, nei *to neigh*.

eg: wee *way*, wei *to weigh*.

ēg: dī *to dye*, drī *dreary, gloomy, tedious*, tī *to tie*.

ĭg: stī *sty*, stī *ladder*.

og: bou (OE. boga) *bow*.

ōg: biu *bough*, driu *drew*, iniu (pl.) *enough*, as este inuf bried? *hast thou enough bread?* But este iniu poreets? *hast thou enough potatoes?* pliu *plough*, sliu *slew*.

ōͤg: slī *sly*.

ug: sā *sough, drain*; but **suf-oil** *manhole of a drain*, bā *to bow*, sā (OE. sugu) *sow*.

ȳg: drai *dry*.

ēag: ī (pl. īn) *eye*.

ōog: flī *to fly*, flī *fly*, lī *to tell a lie*.

b. After l we have e, i: **bele** *to bellow*, **fole** *to follow*, **gales** *gallows*, **swole** *to swallow*, **tale** *tallow*, **beli** *belly*.

After r we have e, i: **bore** *to borrow*, **mare** *marrow*, **sore** *sorrow*, **beri** *berry*, **beri** *to bury*, **weri** *to worry*.

c. Final ig in unaccented syllables has become i: **bodi** *body*, **dizi** *dizzy*, **evi** *heavy*, **moni** *many*, **oni** *any*, **rudi** *ruddy*.

d. We have f in: **duef** *dough*, **duefi** *cowardly*, lit. *doughy*, **dwāf** *dwarf*, **inif** (sing.) *enough*, **sluf** *slough*, **suf-oil** *manhole of a drain*, **trof** *trough*, **uf** *displeasure, an offended manner, rage*.

Here may conveniently be placed **druft** (OE. drūgaþ) *drought*, **sterep** (OE. stīg-rāp) *stirrup*, **bākm** (OE. beorg + ham, see N.E.D. sub bargham) *the collar of a horse*.

NOTE.—sā *drain*, and iniu (pl.) *enough*, are from the inflected forms.

e. The W. dialect has **g** :

dreeg *to drawl,* **eeg** *the berry of the hawthorn,* **ig** (OE. **hyge** *mind*) *mood, temper,* **meeg** *maw,* **neeg** *to gnaw,* **seeg** *a saw.*

beg *bag,* **big** *big, great,* **breg** *to brag,* **brig** *bridge,* **brigz** *a trivet, in brewing, to put across a tub to support the hop-sieve,* **deg** (cp. Swed. **dagga** *to bedew*) *to besprinkle with water,* **dig** *to dig,* **dog** *dog,* **dreg** *to drag,* **dregz** *drags,* **eg** {ME. **eggen**} *to incite, urge on,* **eg** *egg,* **flig** (ME. **fligge,** cp. OHG. **flukke** *able to fly*) *fledge,* **flog** *to flog,* **fog** (ME. **fogge** *rank grass*) *after-grass,* **frig** *coire,* **frog** *frog,* **geg** (ME. **gaggin**) *to gag,* **ie-wig** *earwig,* **leg** *leg,* **lig** *to lie down,* **lug** (ME. **luggen,** Swed. **lugga** *to lug, drag*) *to pull the hair of the head,* **mig** *midge,* **og** *the wool of a sheep which has been shorn for the first time,* **pig** *pig,* **prog** *wood collected for the fire on the fifth of November,* **reg** *rag,* **rig** *back,* **rigin** *ridge of a house,* **seg** *sedge,* **seg** (ME. **saggin**) *to distend,* **šeg** *shag,* **tug** (ME. **tuggen**) *to tug, plod,* **twig** *twig,* **ug** *to carry,* **weg** *to wag.*

f. The W. dialect has **dž** in : **edž** *hedge,* **edž** *edge,* **sledž-ame(r)** *sledge-hammer,* **wedž** *wedge.*

g. Palatal **ng** has become **nž** : **inž** *hinge,* **krinž** *to cringe,* **sinž** *to singe.*

h. **bai** (OE. **bycgan**) *to buy,* **lee** (OE. **lecgan**) *to lay,* **see** (OE. **secgan**) *to say* are from the forms without gemination.

h.

§ 316. OE. initial **h** was an aspirate like the **h** in Mod. Engl. hand. In other positions it was a spirant like the **ch** in German nach, ich.

§ 317. *a.* Initial **h** has disappeared in the W. dialect :

ap (ME. happen) *to wrap up*, eft *haft, handle*, oil *hole*, uel *whole*, ut *hot*.

loup (O.Icel. hlaupa) *to jump*, luef (OE. hlāf) *loaf*.

nit (OE. hnitu) *nit*, nut (OE. hnutu) *nut*.

riŋ (OE. hring) *ring*, riuk (OE. hrōc) *rook*.

wie(r) *where*, wiet *wheat*, wāf *wharf*, wen *when*, wot *what*.

§ 318. *b.* Medial and final h have disappeared except in the examples under *c, d* :

eit *eight*, eit *height*, feit *to fight*, reit *right*, streit *straight*, weit *weight*.

brīt *bright*, flīt *flight*, frīt *fright*, līt *light*, līts (ME. lihte) *the lungs of animals*, mīt (noun) *might*, nīt *night*, plīt *plight*, rīt *wright*, sīt *sight*, slīt *slight*, tīt *tight*.

bout *bought*, brout *brought*, doute(r) *daughter*, out *aught*, out *ought*, nout *naught*, rout *wrought*, sout *sought*, tout *taught*, þout *thought*.

ei *high*, but efe(r) (OE. hēahfore) *heifer*, nei *nigh*, but neebe(r) (OE. nāah-gebūr) *neighbour*.

sī *to sigh*, see Mayhew OE. Phonology, § 814, soe *he saw*, þī *thigh*.

fere (OE. furh, ME. furh, furwe) *furrow*, ole (OE. holh, ME. holwe) *hollow*.

§ 319. *c.* h has become f in : draft *draught, draft*, kof *cough*, laf *laugh*, ruf *rough*, tof *tough*, woef (OE. walh *sickly taste*) *insipid*.

lafte(r) *laughter*, slafter *to slaughter*.

Beside þriu (OE. þurh) we have also þrif *through*.

§ 320. *d.* hs has become ks : nekst *next*, oks *ox*, siks *six*, woks *to grow*.

The French Element.

§ 321. The consonants of the French words occurring in the W. dialect have for the most part been already treated along with the other consonants. There therefore only remain to be added a few examples of **k, g, š, tš, dž**.

k.

§ 322. **k** has remained : **koul** (O. Fr. **coillir**) *to rake*, **koəsə** (O. Norm. Fr. **causie**) *causeway*, **keəd** *card*, **keəs** *case*, **keisn** (lit. *occasion*) *need, necessity*, **kontréəri** *contrary*, **kreək** *to creak*.

skafl *scaffold*, **skaflin** *scaffolding*, **skoud** *to scald*, **skeəlit** *scarlet*, **kwaləti** *quality*, **kwari** *stone quarry*, **kwaiət** *quiet*, **kweət** *quart*, **keəkəs** *body, carcase*, **bleŋkit** *blanket*, **bleŋk** *blank*, **iŋk** *ink*, **reŋk** *rank*, **avək** *havoc*, **biək** *beak*, **leəlek** *lilac*, **paik** *to pick, choose, select*, **puək** *pork*, **fakt** *fact*, but pl. **faks**.

§ 323. **kl** has become **tl** in **tlãk** *clerk*, **tleəm** *claim*, **triətl** *treacle*. The change of initial **kl** to **tl** is quite regular in native English words also (§ 312, 1), but **triətl** is the only example I know where medial or rather final **kl** has become **tl**.

§ 324. **kw** has become **tw** in : **twil** *quill, pen*, **twilt** *quilt*, **twilt** *to beat, thrash*.

§ 325. **wišin** *cushion*, seems to be the same as the literary word originally, but I cannot for the present offer a satisfactory explanation of the exact relation in which they stand to each other.

gurion

g.

§ 326. g has remained: **gāl** *the matter which gathers in the corner of the eye* (see Florio, s.v. cispa *a kind of waterish matter in sore eyes*, called of some **Gowl**. Or it is **cispi** *waterish* or **gowly** *eyes*), **galək** (O. Fr. galc) *left hand*, **garit** *garret*, **geəte(r)** *garter*, **gizn** *to choke*, **gol** *goal*, only used in the game of **lits ən gōts** (§ 177), **grant** *grant*, **egrivéet** *to aggravate, vex*, **eəgifái** *to argue, dispute*.

š.

§ 327. We regularly have š in cases where the lit. language has this sound : **fešn** *fashion*, **pešn** *passion*, **rediš** *radish*.

finiš *finish*, **vāniš** *varnish*, **blemiš** *blemish*.
branš *branch*, **eənšn** *ancient*.

dž.

§ 328. dž has generally remained in words where the lit. language has this sound. In the W. dial. dž also occurs after **n** : **džais** *joist*, **dželəs** *jealous*, **dželi** *jelly*, **džoul** *to knock, strike*, **džoint** *joint*, **džoəm** *the side post of a door* or *chimney piece*, **džoənəs** *jaundice*, **eədž** *age*, **damidž** *damage*, **fuədž** *forge*, **indžói** *to enjoy*, **leɔwidž** *language*, **pidžn** *pigeon*, **soudže(r)** *soldier*.

indžn *engine*, **moəndž** *mange*, **moəndži** *mangy, peevish*, **streəndž** *strange*, **tšeəndž** *change*.

§ 329. dž has become d in: **Doəd** *George*, **Duəd** *Joe*, **Duəz, Duəzi** *Joshua*, **doi** *joy, darling*, a pet word applied to children. This last word gives a clue to the explanation of

the change, which is no doubt due to the imperfect pronunciation of children being imitated by grown-up persons.
The proper names must originally have been used in
addressing children only, just as **doi** still is, and then afterwards have become used for grown-up persons.

tš.

§ 330. We regularly have **tš** in the same words in
which the literary language has it: **tšapl** *chapel*, **tšeedž**
to charge, **tšeeme(r)** *chamber*, **tšeri** *cherry*, **tšimli** *chimney*,
tšois *choice*, **tšons** *chance*, **tšont** *chant*.

preitš *to preach*, **poutš** *to poach*.

ACCIDENCE.

—⋅⋅—

CHAPTER VII.

A. Formation of the Plural.

1. Plurals in -əz, -z, -s.

§ 331. Nouns ending in s, š, z, ž add əz to form the plural, as las *lass* lasəz, fees *face* feesəz, but ās *house* has āzəz; diš *dish* dišəz, wotš *watch* wotšəz; nuəz *nose,* nuəzəz, saiz *size* saizez; edž *hedge* edžəz, džudž *judge* džudžəz.

§ 332. Nouns ending in a vowel or voiced consonant other than z, ž add z, as: lad *lad* ladz, gam *game* gamz, ratn *rat* ratnz, leeð *barn* leeðz, dee *day* deez. But nouns ending in -nd, (-r) lose the -d, (-r) before the plural ending §§ 302, 259, as frend *friend* frenz, faðe(r) *father* faðəz.

§ 333. Nouns ending in a voiceless consonant other than s, š add s, as lat *lath* lats, kap *cap* kaps, dieþ *death* dieþs, māþ *mouth* māþs, wāf *wharf* wāfs, ruif *roof* ruifs.

But nouns ending in **f** preceded by a vowel or diphthong (except **ui**) which was long in OE., and nouns originally ending in -**lf** change the **f** into **v** and add **z** in the plural, as **luef** *loaf* **luevz**, **naif** *knife* **naivz**, **koef** *calf* **koevz**.

2. Plurals in -**n**.

§ 334. There are only three nouns which have -**n** in the plural: **ī** *eye* **īn**, **oks** *ox* **oksn**, **šū** *shoe* **šuin**.

3. Plural in -**r**.

§ 335. The only example of this class is **tšildə(r)** *children*. In the singular we use **bān**, the plural of which is **bānz**, and is in more general use than **tšildə(r)**.

4. Plurals with umlaut.

§ 336. These are: **fuit** *foot* **fīt**, **guis** *goose* **gīs**, **lās** *louse* **lais**, **man** *man* **men**, **mās** *mouse* **mais**, **tuiþ** *tooth* **tīþ**, **wumən** *woman* **wimin**.

5. Singular and Plural alike.

§ 337. **as** *ash, ashes*, **fiš** *fish, fishes*, **šīp** *sheep*.

Nouns expressing time, space, weight, measure, and number, when preceded by a cardinal numeral, as **iz nət bin sīn fə ten jiə(r)** *he has not been seen for ten years*, but **its jiəz sin ə wə sīn** *it's years since he was seen*, and similarly with **munþ** *month*, **wik** *week*. **þrī mail þrə Koəvlə** *three miles from Calverley*, but **mailz þrə ðiə(r)** *miles from there*, and similarly for **inš** *inch*, **fuit** *foot*, **jiəd** *yard*, **eəkə(r)** *acre*, etc. **ten pund ə meit** *ten pounds of meat*, cp. lit. Engl. *a ten-pound note*, but **ðe wə punz ont weəstəd** *there were pounds of it wasted*, and similarly with **āns** *ounce*, **stuən** *stone*, **undəd weit** *hundred weight*, etc. **tū kweət ət best** *two quarts of the best (ale)*, **siks galn** *six gallons*, **nain šilin** *nine shillings*, etc. **fouə skuə(r)** *four scores*, but **skuəz on əm** *scores of them*, etc.

6. Miscellaneous.

§ **338.** Some nouns are only used in the plural as: **kruds** *curds*, **laps** *a kind of woollen waste made in spinning*, **līts** *lungs of animals*, **loks** *small pieces of wool which have been detached from the fleece*, **mezlz** *measles*, **noilz** *the short hairs taken out of the wool by the combing machine*, **roidz** *clearings (of a wood)*, now only used in the phrase **West Roidz** *West Royds*, **siðez** *scissors*, **sperinz** *banns of marriage*, **terz** *tongs*, **trūzez** *trousers*. Others have a different meaning in the singular and the plural, as **brig** *bridge* pl. **brigs** *bridges, a trivet to put across a tub to support the hop-sieve*, **green** *grain* **greenz** *malt which has been used in brewing beer*, **grund** *ground* **grunz** *sediment*.

Nouns with double plural endings are rare, but we have them in: **belesez** *bellows*, **galesez** *braces*, **stepsez** *steps*.

In speaking of cows the form **bies** is generally used, as **ā moni bies eje nā?** *how many cows* (lit. *beasts*) *have you now?*

poridž *porridge*, always, and **broþ** *broth*, frequently, require the plural form of the verb as **ðem poridž worent ez guid ez ðe out te (e) bīn**, lit. *them porridge were not as good as they ought to have been.*

B. Formation of the Genitive Case.

§ **339.** The sign of the genitive both singular and plural is generally omitted when one noun qualifies another; the two nouns thus forming a kind of compound, as **ðemz mi faðe buits** *those are my father's boots*; but **ðem buits e mi faðez** *those boots are my father's*, **tlad faðe buits** *the boy's father's boots*, but **tbuits e tlad faðez** *the boots of the boy's* *father*, ðem bānz (never bānzez) muðe(r) *those children's mother.*

When the genitive is not followed by another noun, the gen. singular and plural have the same form as the nom. plural. The only exceptions are that nouns which end in -vz in the plural have -fs in the gen. singular, **waifs** *wife's*, and the two umlaut-plurals **men, wimin** have sing. **manz, wumenz**, plural **menz, wiminz**.

CHAPTER VIII.

ADJECTIVES.

1. The Articles.

§ **340.** The indefinite article ө *a*, **өn** *an*, differs from lit. Engl. in so far that ө may be used before both vowels and consonants. It is equally right to say : **av etn ө** or **өn apl** *I have eaten an apple.* In **nidiөt** *idiot* and **noreišn** *row, disturbance,* the initial n has come from the indef. article, **ðis nidiөt** *this idiot,* **wots tmiөnin ө čis noreišn ?** *what is the meaning of this* (lit. *oration*) *row?* Cp. lit. Engl. **newt** for **ewt.** Observe the phrase : **a wөr i sitš өn ө steөt** *I was in such (an) a state.*

§ **341.** The definite article t *the* is generally attached to the following word, as **tman** *the man,* **tkoilz** *the coals,* **tak tguid өnz** *take the good ones,* **tloөd ө tmane(r)** *the lord of the manor,* **a duөnt noө wot tman did wit** *I don't know what the man did with it,* **a no(ө) uө tman wo(r)** *I know who the man was.*

When the word following the definite article begins with t or d, the only trace of the article is that t and d become suspended or popularly expressed lengthened. We make a clear distinction between **teөbl** *table* and **t'eөbl** *the table,* **dlium** *gloom* and **d'lium** *the gloom.*

Cp. the similar distinction between eit *eight*, and eit' *eighth*.

We however always use ðə before loed when it means *God*, as ðez nuebdi bed ðə loed ən mī, noez wot iv ed tə baid *there is nobody but the Lord and myself, know what I have had to suffer.* ðə (never t) is also used after ue *who*, wot *what*, in such expressions as : ue ðə divl did ðat? *who the devil did that?* wot ðə ɒment duz ə wont? *what the hangment does he want?* a duent noe wot ðə ɒment i did wit *I don't know what the hangment he did with it.*

Note.—In order to obtain information on this difference in the use of t and ðə in some other Yorkshire dialect, I wrote to Mr. Bradley, the Joint Editor of the New English Dictionary, who is thoroughly conversant with the Sheffield dialect; and from his kind communication I learn that the distinction in the Sheffield dialect is practically the same as in my own. I venture to quote the following extract from his letter, which will be found interesting and instructive.—'t' lord o' t' manor—(decidedly). When "Lord" means God, the association of liturgical and Bible reading generally cause the full pronunciation (ðə) to be used. But I have, though rarely, heard t' Lord, in rather off-hand, irreverent speech; and "Lord knows" without any article at all is common enough. A don't know what t' man did wi' it—(certainly not ðə man, nor man without article). What the hangment, What the devil, What the plague, etc.— (always ðə, never t or omitted). A know who t' man wor—(certainly not ðə, nor omitted).'

2. Comparison of Adjectives.

§ 342. The comparative is formed by adding -ə(r) and the superlative by adding -ist to the positive. This rule also holds good for familiar adjectives of two or more syllables. But unfamiliar adjectives of more than one syllable sometimes form the comparative and superlative by prefixing mue(r), muest.

fāe(r) *far*, fāre(r), fārist; juɒ *young*, juɒe(r), juɒist or juɒst ; uelsm *wholesome*, uelsm-ə(r), uelsm-ist; biutifl *beautiful*, biutifl-er, biutifl-ist.

§ **343.** The following adjectives are compared irregularly as in lit. Engl. :

bad *bad* ⎫ **il** *ill* ⎭	**wäe(r)**	**wäst**
guid *good*	**bete(r)**	**best**
lat *late*	**late(r)**	**latist, last**
litl *little*	**les**	**liest**
moni *many* ⎫ **mitš** *much* ⎭	**mue(r)**	**muest**
nie(r) *near*	**niere(r)**	**nierist, nekst**

NOTE.—The use of vari before adjectives is the same as in lit. Engl.: vari guid *very good*. But instead of using vari we sometimes repeat the adjective with əz *as*: guid əz guid *very good*, dāk əz dāk *very dark*.

3. Numerals.

§ **344.** *a.* Cardinal and ordinal numerals.

Cardinal.	*Ordinal.*
wun *one*	**fēst**
tū *two*	**seknd**
þrī *three*	**þēd**
foue(r) *four*	**fouet**
faiv *five*	**fift**
siks *six*	**sikst**
sevm *seven*	**sevnt**
eit *eight*	**eit˙**
nain *nine*	**naint**
ten *ten*	**tent**
(ə)levm *eleven*	**(ə)levnt**
twelv *twelve*	**twelft**
þētīn *thirteen*	**þētīnt**
fouetīn *fourteen*	**fouetīnt**

I

Cardinal.	Ordinal.
fiftīn *fifteen*	fiftīnt
sikstīn *sixteen*	sikstīnt
sevntīn *seventeen*	sevntīnt
eitīn *eighteen*	eitīnt
naintīn *nineteen*	naintīnt
twenti *twenty*	twentit
twenti wun *twenty-one*	twenti fə̄st
twenti tū *twenty-two*	twenti seknd
þə̄ti *thirty*	þə̄tit
foti *forty*	fotit
fifti *fifty*	fiftit
siksti *sixty*	sikstit
sevnti *seventy*	sevntit
eiti *eighty*	eitit
nainti *ninety*	naintit
unded *hundred*	undət
þāzn *thousand*	þāznt

§ **345.** The old form **uen** *one* is still retained in the phrase **tuen** *the one of two*, as **tuen on əm est**, lit. *the one of them has it*, i. e. *one of the two has it*. The unaccented form is **ən** or rather vocalic **n**, as it **wer ə guidn** *it was a good one*. We may also note **wun-ā** *somehow*, **wun-ā ər ənuðə(r)** *somehow or other*.

On the suspended t' in **eit'** *eighth*, see §§ 341, 306.

m for older **n** (§ 270) is regularly heard in **sevm, (ə)levm**; but in **sevnt, (ə)levnt, sevntīn**, etc., **m** for older **n** is seldom, if ever, heard.

All the ordinals, except **seknd** and **þə̄d**, end in t. Most of these are, of course, new formations made after the analogy of **fə̄st, fift, sikst, twelft** which had t in OE. See § 309. In a similar manner the lit. Engl. ordinals *fifth,* *sixth, twelfth,* and all those ending in *-nth* are new formations made after the analogy of such forms as *fourth,* OE. fēowerᵈa.

§ 346. In playing at games, e. g. *marbles* toəz, boys have the following ordinals, denoting the order in which each is to begin the game. The boy who calls out fəri has the first turn. The order is fəri *first*, səki *second*, þədi *third,* lari *last.*

> NOTE.—toə is used for a marble of any kind. When made of marble or alabaster it is called ə wait ali, if streaked with red veins ə bluid ali; when of glass ə glas ali; when made of powdered stone ə stuəni; when made of clay ə pot donək.

§ 347. *b.* Fractional numerals: kweətə(r) *quarter,* ə fouət or wun peət āt ə fouə(r) *a fourth,* ə þəd or wun peət āt ə þrī *a third,* and similarly tū þədz or tū peəts āt ə þrī *two thirds,* oəf *half,* as ə oəf pund, oəf pund, or oəf ə pund *half a pound,* oəpni *halfpenny,* oəpəþ *halfpennyworth.*

§ 348. *c.* Multiplicatives : simpl *simple,* dubl *double,* tribl, þribl *threefold,* fouə-foud *fourfold,* wuns *once,* twais *twice,* þrī taimz *three times.*

§ 349. *d.* Numerals in composition : ə tūþri lit. *a two* (or) *three, a few,* as lər əm əv ə tūþri *let them have a few,* tupms *two pence,* fipms *fivepence,* þrəpms *three pence,* etc.

CHAPTER IX.

PRONOUNS.

1. Personal.

§ 350.

FIRST PERSON.

Singular.	*Plural.*
Nom. ai, (a, i)	wī, (wi, we)
Obj. mī, (me)	uz, (ez, s)

SECOND PERSON.

Nom. ðā, tā, (ða, ta, te)	jī, (ji, je)
Obj. ðī, (ðe)	jī, (je)

THIRD PERSON.

Singular.

Masc.	*Neut.*	*Fem.*
Nom. ī, (i, e)	it, (t)	šū, (šu, še)
Obj. im	it, (t)	ē(r), (e(r).

Plural.

Nom. ðee, (ðe, ðe)
Obj. ðem, (em, m).

The weak forms are in parentheses. They are far more frequently employed than the strong ones; the latter are only used to express special emphasis.

The weak form i *I* is older than a, it arose from the shortening of ī before the latter became ai, whereas a is the regular weak form of ai, cp. the weak forms abəd *yes but*, wol *until*, wa *why*, beside the strong forms aibəd, wail (noun) *while*, wai. Examples of the first person are:

muni guə wi jə? *must I go with you?* sali et temoən? *shall I have it to-morrow?* if id nobəd ə bit ə bras, a wodnt (or ad nət) diu sitš wāk *if I had only a little brass (money), I would not do such work,* al kum ən sī jə, wen i ger ə bit ə taim *I will come and see you, when I get a bit of time,* as ə dun inā *I shall have done presently,* a fan əm i tloin *I found them in the lane,* gi m(ə) ə feu *give me a few,* ðə təld mə ða wər iə(r) *they told me (that) thou wast here.* wi or we bān dān til *we are going down the hill,* sud wə len im it? *should we lend him it?* ðel or ðəl stop wol wə kum *they will stop until (while) we come.* lets as im *let us* or *me ask him,* šə þeŋkt əz fə tpeənz wid teən wit *she thanked us for the pains we had taken with it.* The z in the strong form uz is never voiceless as it is in lit. Engl. The weak form s is only used when it is attached enclitically to a preceding voiceless consonant.

The strong form tā and the weak forms ta, tə can only be used interrogatively and in subordinate sentences, as wil tá weš it? *wilt thou wash it?* witə len mət? *wilt thou lend me it?* wiəs tə kum þriu? (lit. *where hast thou come through*) *where do you come from?* kan tə diut bi ðisen? *canst thou do it by thyself?* wen tət redi wil send ðət *when thou art ready we will send thee it.* as or asl gi ðə (ə) oəpni if tə elps mə, *I shall give thee a halfpenny if thou helpest me,* ðat nuən sə wīl əs tə wo(r) *thou art not so well*

as thou wast, ðal (never tal or tel) find im ət iz wāk *thou
wilt find him at his work.* At first sight one might be
inclined to assume that the forms tă, te have arisen from
assimilation with verbal forms ending in -t, e. g. ăt (§ 396)
art, out (§ 394) *oughtest,* dəst (frequently dəs § 390) *durst ;*
but these are the three solitary instances in which the
second person singular ends in -t where assimilation could
take place. See the personal endings (§ 385). It is far more
probable that the forms have arisen from their unaccented
position in the sentence. If this is right then the def. art.
t has a similar origin. However the t of the article arose,
I certainly do not believe that it is a clipped form of ðat
that, which is regularly used as a demonstrative (§ 354), but
never as a rel. pronoun or conjunction ; the latter are
expressed by ət (§§ 356, 401). am bān te tak ðe wi me
I am going to take thee with me. ji or je sed ət im it ren
you said that I am in the wrong, wot did je see tul im?
what did you say to him? wil je sam me ðem tluez up ?
will you pick up those clothes for me? jev etn oel tmeit sue
jel e te diu bāt nā wol setede *you have eaten all the meat
so you will have to do without until Saturday,* if je (not ji)
sī mi faðe(r), as im te kum uem *if you see my father, ask
him to come home,* wi soe je i tmiln *we saw you in the mill.*
The old objective form of the second person plural has
entirely died out; cp. on the other hand the disappearance
in Modern English of the old nom. ye except in liturgical
and the higher literary language. The pronoun of the
second person singular is still extensively used, but it is
not so general now as it was twenty years ago. When I
was a lad the following was the rule : ðā was used in every
case except that jī was used (1) in addressing strangers,
especially grown-up people, or as a mark of respect to
masters and old people; (2) children in addressing their

parents ; (3) people who had made each other's acquaintance
after they had grown up usually employed jī in speaking
to each other.

The masc. of the third person singular is the only pronoun
which has not at least two forms for the obj. case. im is no
doubt used as a weak form so as to prevent confusion with
the obj. case of the plural. t is attached to the preceding
word. The nominative of the feminine presents great
difficulties. Dr. Sweet in his New English Grammar
(§ 1068) gives the following explanation for the lit. Engl.
form she : the old demonstrative sēo became shō through
the intermediate stage seō(sjoo), then shō became contaminated with the old personal pronoun hēo, which gave
rise to the form shēo which would regularly become she in
Mod. English. This explanation may or may not be right
for the lit. language, but a form shēo could not possibly
become šū, but only šī in the W. dial. as also in the other
dialects round about Windhill; cp. the Dialect Tests in
Ellis, EEPr. v. On the other hand, the uncontaminated
form shō would not become šū but šiu in the modern
dialect, cp. tiu *too*, diu *do*, etc. § 164 *c*; unless we may
assume, which I do not believe is the case, that the one
solitary example (šū *shoe*, but pl. šuin §§ 163–4 *c*) containing ū from older ō has not been borrowed from the lit.
language. On the various origins of W. ū see § 40. For
the present the form šū *she* still remains a riddle. The
strong form ðem is from OE. ðǣm (ðām), the dat. plural of
the demonstrative pronoun sē, sēo, ðæt, whereas the weak
forms em, m are from OE. heom, the dat. plural of the
personal pronoun hē, hēo, hit.

Examples of the third person are: iz bīn on trant oel
twik *he has been on the spree all the week*, eze fotšt ðat flik
ə beekɒ ? *has he fetched that flitch of bacon ?* i ied it wen ə

wer et jär ās *he heard it when he was at your house*, tiznt
main *it is not mine*, eze funt? *has he found it?* gimet *give
me it*, estet? *hast thou it?* wots e dun wit? *what has he done
with it?* šuz iu e mad ig *she is in a bad temper*, šu or še
oles wešez e tmunde *she always washes (the clothes) on the
Monday*, eše or es še sared tpigz? *has she served the pigs?*
stop wol še kumz *stop until she comes*, ðed or ðed e gīn me
ten šilin fot *they would have given me ten shillings for it*,
wil ðe suin bi ie(r)? *will they soon be here?* ðel suin bi ier if
ðe kum reit uem *they will soon be here if they come straight
(right) home*, al sel jem *I will sell you them*, kan je diu
bāt em? *can you do without them?*

It is hardly possible to give a very clearly defined and
accurate rule for the use of the weak nominative forms:

> a, wi; ji; i; šu; ðe beside
> i, we; je; e; še; ðe.

The former set is mostly used in making direct assertions,
and the latter in interrogative and subordinate sentences.
i *I* and e *he* are never used in making direct assertions, but
the other pairs are, and when the one form and when the
other is used, seems to depend upon sentence rhythm.

The obj. case of all persons is often used reflexively, as
al weš me nā *I will wash myself now*, am džust bān te don
me *I am just going to dress myself*, i leed im dān i tfīld
he lay down in the field, kum fored lad en sit ðe dān en al
set tketl on *come forward lad and sit (thee) down and I
will set the kettle on (and make some tea).*

We always use the obj. case where in refined lit. Engl.
the nom. is used:

ɪ. After the substantive verb, as its mī, þī, ē(r), im, uz,
jī, ðem, lit. *it is me, thee, her, him, us, you, them.* Note
ðemz em et i want *those are the ones that I want.*

2. When the verb refers to different persons, as **im ən mī** went *he and I went,* **Bil ən imz guən dān truəd** *Bill and he have gone down the road,* **uz ən ðem we tegeðər oəl d'ee** *we and they were together all the day.*

3. When the subject of the principal sentence is separated from the predicate by a subordinate sentence, as : **im ət did ðat out tə eɴ** *he who did that ought to be hanged,* **uz əts dun se mitš for im me guə tə d'ogz fər out ī keez** *we who have done so much for him may go to the dogs for aught he cares.*

2. Possessive.

§ 351. *a.* Conjoint : **mai, (mi)** *my ;* **āo(r), (wo(r))** *our ;* **ðai, (ði)** *thy ;* **jāə(r), (jə(r))** *your ;* **iz, is** *his ;* **it** *its,* **ē(r), (ə(r))** *her,* **ðee(r), (ðə(r))** *their.*

The weak forms are in parentheses. As in the personal pronouns so also here the weak forms are far more frequently used than the strong ones. **mi, ði, ðə(r)** are from the Middle English weak forms mi, ði, ðer, and not Modern weakenings of the strong forms ; otherwise we should have had **ma, ða** for our mi, ði, see § 350. **wə(r)** has been formed from **we** after the analogy of **jə** *ye,* **jə(r),** thus **jə : jə(r) : : wə : wə(r).** **iz** is used before vowels and voiced consonants and **is** before voiceless consonants, as **iz ās** *his house,* **iz oən** *his own,* **iz muðə(r)** *his mother,* **is koit** *his coat,* **is faðə(r)** *his father,* **estə sīn it faðə(r)?** *hast thou seen its (= the child's) father?* **it iəd wāks** *its head aches.*

§ 352. *b.* Absolute : **main** *mine,* **āz** *ours,* **ðain** *thine,* **jāz** *yours,* **iz** *his,* **its** *its,* **ēz** *hers,* **ðeez** *theirs.*

3. Reflexive.

§ 353.

FIRST PERSON.

Singular.	*Plural.*
misen	wesen
misel	wesenz
miseln	wesel
	weseln

SECOND PERSON.

ðisen	jesen
ðisel	jesenz
ðiseln	jesel
	jeseln

THIRD PERSON.

Singular.

Masc.	*Neut.*	*Fem.*
i(s)sen	itsen	esen
i(s)sel	itsel	esel
i(s)seln	itseln	eseln

Plural.

ðesen
ðesenz
ðesel
ðeseln

The stress is always on the second syllable. When these pronouns are used emphatically the stress on the second syllable is of course stronger than when they are used reflexively. All the forms -sel, -seln, -sen are often heard without any distinction in meaning.

Such a variety of forms must be quite modern, and is probably due to importation from neighbouring dialects. The -sen-forms are far more common than either of the other two. In the Eastern North Midland dialects, to which Windhill belongs (Ellis, EEPr. v. pp. 364–408), I find the following forms: -seln at Huddersfield and Halifax; -sen at Bradford, Leeds, Dewsbury, Rotherham, Sheffield, Wakefield. In this division of dialects no -self-forms seem to be known.

In order to find out the areas of the -sel, -seln, and -sen-forms I have carefully examined all the classified word-lists and comparative dialect specimens in Ellis, EEPr. v, with the following results. -sel is the only form that occurs in all the North Northern, West Northern, and East Northern dialects, except at Holderness (S.E. Yorkshire) and South Ainsty, where we find -sen. The North North Midland, West North Midland, and South North Midland dialects have only -sel. The Border Midland dialects, which embrace the county of Lincolnshire, have only the -sen-form. The -sen-form does not seem to occur south of Lincolnshire. -self is regularly found without exception in all the Eastern dialects. The Mid Southern dialects have -self, -zelf, except at Much Cowarne (nine miles N.E. of Hereford) we find -sel and in Western Dorset -zel. The North Border Southern, Mid Border Southern, and South Border Southern dialects have only -self. In the East Southern dialects, which embrace almost the whole of Kent, with East Sussex, examples are wanting except that -saaf, pl. -saavz occurs at Faversham (eight miles W.N.W. of Canterbury). The Northern West Southern dialects regularly have -zel. In the Southern West Southern dialects all three forms, -sel, -zel, and -self, occur. For the Western West Southern dialects examples are wanting.

The South Western dialects seem to have -self, but more examples are wanting to be certain, as only one example of the reflexive occurs in this division, viz. at Docklow (five miles E. S. E. of Leominster). For the North Western dialects there is only one example given in Ellis, viz. -sel for Pulverbach (seven miles S.W. of Shrewsbury).

wesen, etc. have been formed from the weak possessive we(r) *our*, which is itself a .new formation, § 351. There is no difference in meaning or usage between wesen and wesenz, ðesen and desenz. jesen is used for the sing. and plural *yourself, yourselves*, but jesenz *yourselves* has always a plural meaning.

The simplex self occurs in the dialect, as e tself seem dee *on the self same day*.

4. Demonstrative.
§ 354.

Sing.	ðis *this*	ðat *that*	jon *yon.*
Plural.	ðiez *these*	ðem *those*	jon *yon.*

ðis and ðiez are often followed by ie(r) *here*, and ðat, ðem by ðie(r), *there*, as ðis ier ās wonts e lot e tlienin *this house wants a lot of cleaning*, dus te laik ðiez ie(r)? *dost thou like these?* a kānt eit ðat ðie meit *I can't eat that meat*, i ga me ðat ðie koit *he gave me that coat*, ðem ðier aplz kost tupms *those apples cost twopence*, ðemz vari guid bed ðiez ez or e bete(r) *those are very good but these are better*.

ðem is the only word used for *those*, a form ðuez would be quite foreign to the dialect.

5. Interrogative.

§ 355.

Masc. and Fem.   *Neut.*

Nom., Obj. **uǝ** *who*   **wot** *what*, **witš** *which.*

Gen. **uǝz** *whose.*

uǝm *whom* is never used in the W. dialect.   Beside **wot**
we have also **wor**, on which see § 290.

6. Relative.

§ 356. The relative pronoun is expressed either by **ǝt**
for all genders and numbers, or by **uǝ** for the masc. and
fem., **wot** for the neuter.   **ǝt** is invariably used when the
antecedent is expressed ; in other cases we always use **uǝ**,
wot.   Thus : **im ǝt sed suǝz reɒ** *he who said so is wrong,*
tman ǝt i soǝ jǝstǝdǝ *the man whom I saw yesterday,* **tlas
ǝt i gav ǝ pund ǝ aplz tul ǝz ǝtn ǝm oǝl** *the lass to whom
I gave a pound of apples has eaten them all,* **tkoilz ǝt tǝ
bout dān i Windil ǝ vari guid** *the coals which thou boughtest
down in Windhill are very good,* **did jǝ sī ðem ǝt did it?**
did you see those who did it? **ðem men ǝt tǝ so(ǝ) i trued
wǝr on trant** *those men whom thou sawest in the road were
on the spree.*

a no(ǝ) uǝz dunt *I know who has done it,* **we no(ǝ) uǝz
it iz** *we know whose it is,* **a noǝ wot tǝ sez** *I know what
thou sayest,* **a kǝn or kɒ ges uǝ ðaz bīn wi** *I can guess with
whom thou hast been,* **a duǝnt belīv wot ǝ sez** *I don't
believe what he says;* but **a duǝnt belīv ǝ wēd (ǝt) i sez**
I don't believe a word (that) he says.

The obj. case of **ǝt**, but never of **uǝ**, **wot**, is often omitted :
tman i soǝ *the man (whom) I saw,* **tkoilz ǝ bout** *the coals
(which) he bought.*

ət is of Norse origin and was originally only used as a
conjunction with the meaning of *that*. But already in Old
Icelandic it came to be used both as a relative pronoun and
conjunction just as it still is in the W. dialect: a no(ə) ət
im i tgeet *I know that I am in the way*. See Noreen,
Altisländische und altnordische Grammatik, § 402. ət occurs as a rel. pronoun in the Northern English dialects so
early as the thirteenth century, see J. A. H. Murray, The
Dialect of the Southern Counties of Scotland, p. 194.

It may be useful to note here that ðat is never used in
the dialect either as a rel. pronoun or as a conjunction.

7. Indefinite.

§ 357.

sum *some*, sumdi *somebody*, sumət (lit. *somewhat*) *something, anything*.

out *aught*, nout *naught, nought*.

inif, pl. iniu *enough*: gim(ə) ə feu, nee ðaz ed iniu *give
me a few, no thou hast had enough*, ejə bried inif? *have you
enough bread?*

feu *few*, ivri *every*, oel *all*, els *else*, sitš *such*, uðə(r)
other.

oəðə(r) (OE. āwðer) *either*, noeðə(r) (OE. nāwðer) *neither*.
Cp. § 123 and see Sievers, OE. Grammar, §§ 346, 348.

oni (OE. ǣnig) *any*, onibodi *anybody*, moni (OE. monig,
manig) *many*. The o in oni is due to the influence of the o
in moni. The following question would be quite unintelli-
gible to anyone but a North countryman: ez or ez oni on
jə oni on jə? inquired a man of a company of persons, after
asking two or three of them individually for a match, lit.
has any on you any on you? i. e. *has any of you got one?*

tuen (lit. *the one*) *one of two* or *more*: tuen on jez dunt *one of you has done it.* Strong form **wun** (nom.), weak form **ən** (obj.) *one,* pl. **ənz** *ones,* **wun ənuðə(r)** *one another,* **nuə,** weak form **nə** *no,* **nuəbdi** *nobody* ; **nuən** *none* has no weak form. **nuən** is often used in the place of **nət**: **am nuən bān** *I am not going,* **ðat nuən tfuil ət tə liuks** *you are not the fool you look to be.*

　　u(ə)-ivə(r) *whoever,* **wotivə(r)** or **tšiuz-wot** (lit. *choose-what*) *whatever.*

CHAPTER X.

§ 358. The verbs are divided into two great classes : — Strong and Weak—according to the formation of the preterite and past participle. Besides these two great classes of strong and weak verbs, there are a few others which will be treated under the general heading of *Minor Groups.*

§ 359. The strong verbs form their preterite by means of ablaut. In order to facilitate the use of the book for philologists I have sub-divided them into seven classes and have adopted the order given in Sievers' Old English Grammar, §§ 382-97.

A great many verbs which were strong in OE. are now weak in the dialect ; on the other hand a few, which were originally weak, have become strong. The lists contain all the strong verbs in general use. When two forms of the preterite and past participle are in existence, the less usual one is enclosed in brackets. Some verbs, which now usually have a weak preterite, still retain the old strong past participle, e. g. **feseen** *forsaken*, **fretn** beside **frieted** *fretted, mourned.*

There is only one form for the singular and plural of the preterite just as in lit. Engl. The present and the past participle of all classes have, as a rule, been regularly developed from their corresponding OE. forms. But the preterite of some classes, e. g. the whole of the first and second, are new formations made after the analogy of the pret. of the fourth and partly the fifth classes. Some few verbs have passed over from one class into another. All these points will be discussed in their proper places.

§ 360. The preterite and the past participle of weak verbs end in -ed, -d, -t. See §§ 380-3. Many verbs, originally weak, have both a strong and a weak past participle. See §§ 380-3.

A. Strong Verbs.

§ 361.

CLASS I.

Infin.	Pret. Sg.	Pret. Pl.	P. P.
OE. ī	ā	i	i
W. ai	ee		i
aid *hide*	eed		idn
baid *endure*	beed		bidn
bait *bite*	beet		bitn
daiv *dive*	deev		divm
dlaid *glide*	dleed		dlidn
draiv *drive*	dreev		drivm
kontraiv *contrive*	kontreev		kontrivm
raid *ride*	reed		ridn
rait *write*	reet		ritn
raiv *tear*	reev		rivm
raiz *rise*	reez		rizn
slaid *slide*	sleed		slidn
straid *stride*	streed		stridn
straik *strike*	streek		strukn
straiv *strive*	streev		strivm

K

Infin.	*Pret. Sg.*	*Pret. Pl.*	*P. P.*
šain *shine*	šeen		šaind
šait *cacare*	šeet		šitn
þraiv *thrive*	þreəv		þrivm

§ 362. The pret. of all verbs of this class is a new formation. The eə can arise neither from the OE. singular nor plural form. From the former we should have had uə (§ 122) and from the latter i (§ 89). The only classes of verbs which regularly have eə in the pret. are the fourth (§ 371) and part of the fifth (§ 372). To merely say that the pret. of Class I has been formed after the analogy of Class IV and part of Class V would be avoiding the real difficulty, which consists in giving a satisfactory reason why they should have had such an influence, seeing that they had no forms in common with Class I in OE. One might perhaps be inclined to think that the identity of the vowel in a pp. like ʒifenn *given* (Ormulum, i. 71) with that in a pp. like **risenn** *risen* (Ormulum, ii. 47) may have given rise to the new formation. But that would not do. In the dialect the pret. of **gi(v)** is **ga(v)**=Ormulum ʒaff, **gaff**, ii. 16. At present I cannot even suggest a satisfactory explanation.

§ 363. The pp. of **šain** is always weak, and I have also occasionally heard a weak pret. **šaind**. For the pret. of **straik** I have often heard **striuk**, **strak**, the latter of which seems to be a shortening of the Northern ME. form **strāk**; the pp. of this verb corresponds to the early Mod. Engl. lit. form **struken**.

§ 364. **aid** (OE. **hȳdan**) and **daiv** (OE. **dȳfan**) were weak in OE. **raiv** (O. Icel. **rīfa**) and **þraiv** (O. Icel. **þrīfa**) are of Norse origin. **straiv** (O. Fr. **estriver**) was already strong in ME. **kontraiv** must be a late borrowing from

lit. Engl., the ME. form **controuen** (u = v) from O. Fr.
controver would not have become **kontraiv** in the W.
dialect.

CLASS II.

§ 365.

	Infin.	*Pret. Sg.*	*Pret. Pl.*	*P. P.*
OE.	ēo	ēa	u	o
W.	ī		eə	o
	iu (§ 187)		eə	o
	ī		eu	ou
	frīz *freeze*		freəz	frozn
	tlīv *cleave, split*		tleəv	tlovm
	tšiuz *choose*		tšeəz	tšozn
	flī *fly*		fleu	floun

§ 366. All the other verbs, which formerly belonged
to this class, have become weak.

OE. **cēosan** would regularly have become *tšīz (§ 187) in
the dialect. **tšiuz** seems to be an early borrowing of the
ME. West Midland form **chüsen**, which would regularly
become **tšiuz** in the dialect.

The **eə** in the pret. is not regularly developed from OE.
ēa, which has become **iə** (§ 179), but is due to the analogy
of such verbs as **weəv** *wove*, **neəd** *kneaded*. Just as we
have the pp. **wovm**, **nodn**, pret. **weəv**, **neəd**, so to the pp.
frozn, **tlovm**, **tšozn** there has been formed a new preterite
freəz, **tleəv**, **tšeəz**.

CLASS III.

§ 367. This class had in OE. four sub-divisions:
1. Verbs having a medial nasal + a consonant.

2.	,,	,,	l +	,,
3.	,,	,,	r or h +	,,

K 2

4. When the stem vowel was followed by two consonants other than a nasal, l, r, or h + a consonant. Sievers,
OE. Gr. §§ 386–9.

All verbs originally belonging to 2. have become weak.
The same also applies to sub-divisions 3. and 4. with the
exception of **feit** *fight*, and **brust** *burst*.

	Infin.	*Pret. Sg.*	*Pret. Pl.*	*P.P.*
1.	OE. i	o (a)	u	u
	W. i	a		u
	i	e (§ 59)		u
	begin *begin*	**began**		**begun**
	spin *spin*	**span**		**spun**
	swim *swim*	**swom** § 58 (swam)		**swum**
	win *win*	**wan (won)**		**wun**
	bind *bind*	**ban**		**bun**
	find *find*	**fan**		**fun**
	wind *wind*	**wan (won)**		**wun**
	run *run*	**ran**		**run**
2.	**briŋ** *bring*	**breŋ**		**bruŋ**
	diŋ *reproach, revile*	**deŋ**		**duŋ**
	fliŋ *throw*	**fleŋ**		**fluŋ**
	iŋ *hang*	**eŋ**		**uŋ**
	riŋ *wring*	**reŋ**		**ruŋ**
	riŋ *ring*	**reŋ**		**ruŋ**
	siŋ *sing*	**seŋ**		**suŋ**
	sliŋ *sling*	**sleŋ**		**sluŋ**
	spriŋ *spring*	**spreŋ**		**spruŋ**
	stiŋ *sting*	**steŋ**		**stuŋ**
	striŋ *string*	**streŋ**		**struŋ**
	swiŋ *swing*	**sweŋ**		**swuŋ**
	tliŋ *cling*	**tleŋ**		**tluŋ**
	driŋk *drink*	**dreŋk**		**drukŋ**

Infin.	Pret. Sg.	Pret. Pl.	P.P.
siŋk *sink*	seŋk		sukŋ
sliŋk *slink*	sleŋk		slukŋ
stiŋk *stink*	steŋk		stukŋ
šriŋk *shrink*	šreŋk		šrukŋ

Infin.	Pret.	Pret. Pl.	P. P.
3. W. Sax. eo	ea	u	o
O. North. e	æ	u	o
W. ei (§ 87)		ea	o
feit *fight*		feet	fotn

Infin.	Pret. Sg.	Pret. Pl.	P. P.
4. OE. e	æ	u	o
W. u		a	u
brust *burst*		brast	brusn
þrust *thrust*		þrast	þrusn

§ 368. On the present form run, see Sweet NE. Gr.
§ 1382. The pret. and pp. ban, fan, wan and bun, fun,
wun are very widely spread in the Midland and Northern
dialects, see the Word-lists in Ellis, EEPr. v. The pret.
breŋ and pp. bruŋ are no doubt new formations after the
analogy of forms like seŋ, suŋ; the weak pret. and pp.
brout is also much used, but is not so common as the
strong forms. iŋ (ME. hengen, O. Icel. hengja) and riŋ (OE.
(h)ringan) were originally weak verbs. diŋ (O. Icel. dengja),
fliŋ (O. Icel. flengja), sliŋ (O. Icel. slöngva) are of Norse origin.
striŋ seems to be quite a modern formation from the noun.

The pp. of verbs whose stem ends in ŋk regularly lose
the medial guttural ŋ in the W. dialect. I have assumed
in the Phonology (§ 274) that ŋ has disappeared through assimilation before the following kŋ in the pp. of these verbs.
This is possible and not at all improbable; but we must
not exclude the possibility that some of these pp. may be

of Norse origin, e.g. drukɲ (O. Icel. drukkenn), sukɲ
(O. Icel. sokkenn), and that the remaining ɲk-verbs may
have followed the analogy of these. This is a point well
worth investigating, but of the five verbs ending in -ɲk in
the present and preterite, Ellis has unfortunately only the
pp. of driɲk, and I have accordingly read through all his
Word-lists, Dialect tests, and Comparative Specimens to see
how far the form without medial ɲ in the pp. extends.
The following is the result: The medial ɲ is retained in
all the Eastern, Western, and Southern dialects, with
the exception of South Devon (Ellis, p. 163), which is
probably a mistake on the part of Dr. Ellis' informant.
All the Border Midland, Southern, North Midland, Western
Mid Midland, Eastern Mid Midland, East Mid Midland,
Western South Midland, Eastern South Midland, Northern
North Midland, and Western North Midland dialects have
medial ɲ except at Colne Valley and at Burnley, where
double forms—without and with medial ɲ—seem to occur
(pp. 334 and 351). In the Eastern North Midland division
to which my own dialect belongs the form without medial
ɲ is found at Huddersfield, Halifax, Dewsbury which have
drufen, at Keighley, Bradford, Leeds, Rotherham, Elland,
and Calverley where the nasal has disappeared before the
following k ; but medial ɲ occurs at Barnsley, Sheffield, and
Marsden (seven miles S. W. of Huddersfield). In the East
Northern division, Mid Yorkshire, North Mid Yorkshire,
New Malton, Lower Nidderdale, Washam River district,
South Cleveland, North East Coast, Danby and Skelton
in Cleveland, and Whitby, all have the form without medial
ɲ, but Market Weighton, Holderness, Malton, Pickering,
and The Moors, Sutton and Goole retain the medial
guttural nasal. All the West Northern dialects—for which
there are a great number of examples in Ellis—lose the

medial ꞃ except at Upper Swaledale. The same is also the
case for the North Northern dialects, except that at New-
castle-on-Tyne the medial ꞃ seems to exist (Ellis, p. 647).
For the Lowland division of English dialect districts in
Scotland only forms without medial ꞃ are registered. It
is however important to note that Dr. Murray, The Dialect
of the Southern Counties of Scotland, has pp. drunk beside
drukken, and only slunk, stunk, sunk, schrunk (scrynkit).
This would certainly seem to favour the idea that our
drukꞃ is of Norse origin, and that the pp. of the four other
verbs have been formed after the analogy of it.

In feet *fought* the vowel of the singular seems to have
been carried over to the plural at an early period. The
latter form then became generalized. The short o in the
pp. is quite regular (§ 100).

On the forms brust, brast, brusn see Sweet, NE. Gr.
§ 1354, and on þrust (ME. þrusten, þrusten, O. Icel. þrȳsta)
see loc. cit. § 1348.

CLASS IV.

§ 369.

	Infin.	*Pret. Sg.*	*Pret. Pl.*	*P.P.*
W. Sax.	e	æ	ǣ	o
O. North.	e	œ	ē	o
1. W.	ei (§ 87)	ee (§ 70)		ou (§ 103)
	steil *steal*	steel		stoun
2. W.	ie (§ 75)	ee		oe (§ 104a)
	bie(r) *bear*	bee(r)		boen
	swie(r) *swear*	swee(r)		swoen
	šie(r) *shear*	šee(r)		šoen
	wie(r) *wear*	wee(r)		woen
3. W.	e (§ 88)	a		o
	brek *break*	brak		brokꞃ

§ 370. To this class also belongs **kum** (OE. **cuman**) *come*, **kom** (**kam**), **kum** (**kumd**).

§ 371. **wie(r)** (OE. **werian**) was originally a weak verb, but has become strong after the analogy of **bie(r)**, **šie(r)**. Similarly **swie(r)** (OE. **swerian**, pret. sing. **swōr**) has passed over from the sixth class into this.

The **ee** in the preterite is due to levelling. The vowel of the pret. singular of strong verbs was often extended to the plural already in ME. Then this **a** being in an open syllable became lengthened and was afterwards levelled out into the singular; so that the preterites with **ee** in this and the fifth class are really generalized plural stem-forms. The old pret. pl. form with **ǣ** (**ē**) would have become **ī** in the dialect, § 130. On the other hand, **brak** is the old sing. form. The same is also the case with the **a** in the pret. of verbs of Class V.

CLASS V.

§ 372.

	Infin.	*Pret. Sg.*	*Pret. Pl.*	*P.P.*
W. Sax.	e	æ	ǣ	e
O. North.	e	æ	ē	e
1. W.	ei (§ 87)		ee (§ 371)	o
	neid *knead*		need	nodn
	speik *speak*		speek (spak)	spokɒ
	spreid *spread*		spreed	sprodn
	treid *tread*		treed	trodn
	weiv *weave*		weev	wovm
2. W.	ei (§ 87)		ee	e (§ 73)
	eit *eat*		eet	etn
3. W.	e (§ 88)		a (§ 371)	e (§ 73)
	get *get*		gat	getn
4. W.	i (§ 77)		a (§ 371)	ī
	gi(v)		ga(v)	gīn (§ 79)

1. **spreid** was a weak verb in OE. (**sprǣdan**, pret. **sprǣdde**). The pp. of this sub-division have been formed after the analogy of verbs of the fourth class. The pret. **spak** is very often heard.

2. The pret. **eet** is a new formation made after the analogy of **weiv**, etc. The OE. form sing. **ǣt**, pl. **ǣton** would have become *ī*t (§ 130).

4. Instead of **gīn** I have very often heard **gen**, which is no doubt due to the influence of **etn, getn.**

§ 373.

	Infin.	Pret. Sg.	Pret. Pl.	P.P.
W. Sax.	i	æ	ǣ	e
O. North.	i	æ	ē	e
1. W.	i	a (§ 371)		i
	bid *invite to a funeral*	bad		bidn
	it *hit*	at		itn
	nit *knit*	nat		nitn
	sit *sit*	sat		sitn
	slit *slit*	slat		slitn
	spit *spit*	spat		spitn
	split *split*	splat		splitn
2. W.	i	e (§ 59)		u
	dig *dig*	deg		dug
3. W.	i	a		u
	stik *stick*	stak		stuk

1. **it** (O. Icel. hitta *find*), **nit, slit, spit, split** were originally weak verbs. I have also often heard the weak pret. and pp. **nited**; **bidn** (OE. beden, but already ME. bidden with i from the present), **sitn** (OE. seten, but already ME. siten).

2. **dig** was formerly weak (ME. diggen, diggede). The pp. **dug** is difficult to explain. According to Sweet, NE.

Gr. § 1370, the lit. form **dug** does not occur until towards the end of the Early Modern English period (1500–1650). The pp. **dugɒ** is also sometimes heard.

3. **stik** (OE. stician) was originally a weak verb. The pp. **stuk** may owe its **u** to the influence of **stuɒ**, Sweet, NE. Gr. § 1376.

§ 374. To this class also belongs **sī** (OE. sēon) *see*, pret. **soə** (§ 63), pp. **sīn** = Old North. **gesēn**.

CLASS VI.

§ 375.

Infin.	*Pret.*	*P. P.*
OE. a	ō	a
1. W. a (§ 71)	iu (§ 164)	eə (§ 312, 4)
tak *take*	**tiuk**	**teən**
2. W. oə (§ 63)	iu (§ 164 c)	oə
droə *draw*	**driu**	**droən**
3. W. a	ui (§ 163)	ui
stand *stand*	**stuid**	**stuidn**

stuidn has its vowel from the preterite. A weak pret. and pp. **standəd** is not uncommon. I have also heard a pp. **studn**, the vowel of which seems to be due to the influence of the literary form **stood**.

§ 376.

Infin.	*Pret.*	*P.P.*
OE. ēa	ō	a(æ)
W. eə	iu (§ 164 c)	eə (§ 65)
sleə *slay*	**sliu**	**sleən**

The **eə** of the present is from the past participle. **šak** *shake* generally has the weak pret. and pp. **šakt**; but pret. **šiuk** (§ 164) and pp. **šakɒ** are not uncommon. The pp. of **fəsak** *forsake* is **fəseən** (§ 312, 4).

CLASS VII.

§ 377.

	Infin.	*Pret.*	*P. P.*
OE.	ā	ēo	ā
W.	oə (§ 123)	iu (§ 190)	oə
	bloə *blow*	bliu	bloən
	kroə *crow*	kriu	kroən
	moə *mow*	miu	moən
	noə *know*	niu	noən
	snoə *snow*	sniu	snoən
	soə *sow*	siu	soən
	þoə *thaw*	þiu	þoən
	þroə *throw*	þriu	þroən

þoə was a weak verb in OE. (þāwian or þāwan); snoə (OE. snāw) is the noun used as a verb, which has formed its pret. and pp. after the analogy of the other verbs of this class.

§ 378.

	Infin.	*Pret.*	*P. P.*
OE.	ō	ēo	ō
W.	ou (§ 166)	iu (§ 190)	ou
	grou *grow*	griu	groun

§ 379.

	Infin.	*Pret.*	*P. P.*
OE.	ea(a)	ēo	ea(a)
W.	oə (§ 62)	e (§ 192 a)	oə
	foəl *full*	fel	foəln

B. Weak Verbs.

§ 380. The weak verbs are best classified according to their formation of the preterite and past participle. We thus distinguish three classes:—1. -ed, 2. -d, 3. -t.

Paragraphs 381–3 contain a fairly complete list of verbs which either differ from literary English in the preterite and past participle, or are interesting from other points of view. When the pret. or pp. has two forms, the less usual one is enclosed in brackets.

CLASS I.

§ **381.** The preterite and past participle generally take -ed when the present ends in -t or -d. But a few verbs with short stem-vowels, whose present ends in -t, have the same form in the pret. and past participle; and a few others with a long stem vowel in the present have a short vowel in the pret. and pp.

Infin.	*Pret.*	*P.P.*
bend *bend*	**bended (bent)**	**bended (bent)**
bīld *build*	**belt (bīlded)**	**belt (bīlded)**
blīd *bleed*	**blīded (bled)**	**blīded (bled)**
bluid *bleed*	**bluided**	**bluided**
brīd *breed*	**brīded (bred)**	**brīded (bred)**
ət *hurt*	**ət (əted)**	**ət (ətn)**
fīd *feed*	**fīded (fed)**	**fīded (fedn)**
grund *grind*	**grunded**	**grunded**
kost *cast*	**kost (kosted)**	**kosted (kesn)**
lied *lead*	**lieded (led)**	**lieded (ledn)**
melt *melt*	**melted**	**melted**
od *hold*	**oded (eld)**	**odn (oded)**
send *send*	**sended (sent)**	**sended (sent)**
skrat *scratch*	**skrated**	**skrated (skratn)**
spend *spend*	**spended (spent)**	**spended (spent)**
šuit *shoot*	**šuited**	**šuited (šotn)**
kost *cost*	**kost (kosted)**	**kost (kosted)**
kut *cut*	**kut**	**kut (kutn)**

Infin.	*Pret.*	*P. P.*
let *let*	let	let (letn)
put *put*	put	put (putn)
set *set*	set	set (setn)
šut *shut*	šut	šut (šutn)
wed *marry*	wed	wed (wedn)
wet *wet*	wet (weted)	wet (weted, wetn)
līt *light*	let (līted)	let (letn, līted)
mīt *meet*	met	met (metn)
rīd *read*	red	red
tīm *pour out*	tem (temd)	tem (temd)
biet *beat*	bet	bet (betn)
friet *fret*	frieted (fret)	frieted (fretn)
swiet *sweat*	swieted (swet)	swieted (swetn)
tšiet *cheat*	tšieted (tšet)	tšieted (tšetn)
triet *treat*	tret (trieted)	tretn (trieted)

When I was a boy pret. and pp. forms like **bent, bled, led, spent,** etc., were hardly ever heard, but through the spread of elementary education they are now much used, especially among the younger generation, and will no doubt in the course of time entirely supplant the other forms. In like manner the strong pp. **kesn, putn, fretn,** etc., were far more common twenty years ago than they are now.

Forms like **let** *lit, lighted,* **belt** have been formed after the analogy of such pret. as **met, red,** etc., where the vowel was shortened before the double consonants (e. g. pret. **mette**) already in ME.

Class II.

§ 382. The preterite and past participle generally take -d when the present ends in a voiced sound other than -d.

Infin.	*Pret.*	*P. P.*
bə̄n *burn*	bə̄nd	bə̄nd
briu *brew*	briud	briud (briun)
diəl *deal*	diəld (delt)	diəld (delt)
driəm *dream*	driəmd (dremt)	driəmd (dremt)
eŋ *hang*	eŋd	eŋd
eu *hew*	eud	eud (eun)
fīl *feel*	fīld (felt)	fīld (felt)
iə(r) *hear*	iəd	iəd
leə *lay*	leəd	leəd (leən)
lein *lean*	leind	leind
len *lend*	lend	lend
liən *learn*	liənd	liənd
liəv *leave*	liəvd (left)	liəvd (left)
lig *lie down*	ligd	ligd
loiz *lose*	loizd (lost)	loizd (lost)
miən *mean*	miənd (ment)	miənd (ment)
nīl *kneel*	nīld (nelt)	nīld (nelt)
riu *rue*	riud	riud (riun)
seə *say*	sed	sed
sel *sell*	seld	seld
seu *sew*	seud	seud (seun)
siəz *seize*	siəzd (seəz)	siəzd
smel *smell*	smeld	smeld
spel *spell*	speld	speld
spil *spill*	spild	spild
spoil *spoil*	spoild	spoild
streu *strew*	streud	streud (streun)
swel *swell*	sweld	sweld
šeəv *shave*	šeəvd	šeəvd
šeu *show*	šeud	šeud (šeun)
šū *shoe*	šūd	šūd
tel *tell*	teld	teld

Infin.	*Pret.*	*P. P.*
tlueð *clothe*	tlueðd	tlueðd
tšeu *chew*	tšeud	tšeud (tšeun)
wokɒ *wake, awake*	wokɒd	wokɒd
gue *go*	went	guən
bai *buy*	bout	bout

The forms delt, felt, left, lost, ment, nelt, and in Class III krept, slept, swept, are the literary forms which are now very commonly used among the younger people.

We regularly use leə, leəd, leəd (leən) in speaking of a hen, pigeon, etc.; but in other cases leə and lig are equally used transitively or intransitively without any distinction in meaning: al lig i bed wol brekfəs(t) taim *I will lie in bed until breakfast time,* al lig me dan *I will lie (me) down,* al lig it ə tflue(r) *I will lay it on the floor,* ðe leəd or ligd wol ðə we tə lat fə ðə wāk *they lay until they were too late for their work,* wi ligd or leəd əz dān *we lay down,* ðev leəd (ligd or leən) oəl tbleəm ə mī *they laid all the blame on me.*

<h2 align="center">CLASS III.</h2>

§ 383. The preterite and past participle generally take t when the present ends in a voiceless consonant other than t.

Infin.	*Pret.*	*P. P.*
elp *help*	elpt	elpt
katš *catch*	katšt	katšt
krīp *creep*	krīpt (krept)	krīpt (krepm, krept)
kus *kiss*	kust	kust (kusn)
reik *reach*	reikt	reikt
slīp *sleep*	slīpt (slept)	slīpt (slept)
swīp *sweep*	swīpt (swept)	swīpt swept

Infin.	*Pret.*	*P. P.*
šap *shape*	šapt	šapt
teitš *teach*	teitšt (tout)	teitšt (tout)
weš *wash*	wešt	wešt
pīp *peep*	pept (pīpt)	pept (pīpt)
sīk *seek*	sīkt (sout)	sīkt (sout)
þiŋk *think*	þout	þout
wōk *work*	wōkt (rout)	wōkt (rout)
mak *make*	meed	meed

Verbal Endings.

§ 384.

Present : The first person singular and the whole of the plural generally have no special endings, except when the subject of the sentence is a relative pronoun. See § 395, p. 156. The second and third persons singular end in -ez, -z, -s. -ez is used after the spirants s, z, š, ž, as misez *missest, misses*, raizez *risest, rises*, wišez *wishest, wishes*, sinžez *singest, singes*; -z after voiced sounds, as weivz *weavest, weaves*, lenz *lendest, lends*, duz *dost, does*; -s after other voiceless sounds, as elps *helpest, helps*, wōks *workest, works*, eits *eatest, eats*.

On the personal endings of the verbs *have* and *be*, see §§ 395, 6.

Preterite : The singular and plural of strong verbs have no special endings. The singular and plural of weak verbs end in -ed, -d, -t for all persons. See §§ 380, 385.

Participles : The present participle ends in -in (§§ 276, 385). The past participle of strong verbs ends in vocalic -n after dentals (§ 269), -ŋ after gutturals (§ 271), and -m after labials (§ 270). The past participle of weak verbs ends in -ed, -d, -t. See §§ 381–3.

Infinitive : The infinitive has no special ending just as in lit. Engl.

Paradigms.

§ 385. The conjugation of eŋ *hang* and **brek** *break* will serve as models.

Indic. Pres. Sing. 1.	eŋ	brek
2.	eŋz	breks
3.	eŋz	breks
Plur.	eŋ	brek
Indic. Pret. Sing.	eŋd	brak
Plur.	eŋd	brak
Imper. Sing. and Plur.	eŋ	brek
Infin.	eŋ	brek
Pres. Part.	eŋin	brekin
Past Part.	eŋd	brokŋ

§ 386. The future, the perfect tenses, and the passive voice are formed the same as in lit. Engl. The subjunctive mood has entirely gone out of use.

§ 387. TABLE OF TENSES.

Tense.	Indefinite.	Imperfect and Continuous.	Perfect.	Perfect and Continuous.
Present	**a brek** *I break*	**am brekin** *I am breaking*	**av brokn** *I have broken*	**av bĭn brekin** *I have been break-ing*
Preterite	**a brak** *I broke*	**a we brekin** *I was breaking*	**ad brokn** *I had broken*	**ad bĭn brekin** *I had been break-ing*
Future	**as brek** *I shall break*	**as bĭ brekin** *I shall be breaking*	**as e brokn** *I shall have broken*	**as e bĭn brekin** *I shall have been breaking*

NOTE.—The full conjugation of the auxiliary verbs will be found : *shall* (§ 391), *will* (§ 397), *be* (§ 396), *have* (§ 395).

C. Minor Groups.

a. Preterite-Presents.

§ 388. In tenses where it has been thought advisable I have added the affirmative and interrogative forms with and without negation. On the various forms assumed by the personal pronouns, see § 350.

1. *can.*

§ 389. Pres. strong form **kan**, weak forms **kən, kŋ**. Pret. strong form **kud**, weak **ked**. The weak form **kŋ** is mostly used in combination with the personal pronouns.

AFFIRMATIVELY.

Present.

Sing.			*Plur.*		
ai, a, i	kan or kŋ		wǐ, we	kan or kŋ	
ðǎ, tǎ, tə	,,	,,	jǐ, je	,,	,,
ǐ, ə	,,	,,	ðee, ðe, ðə	,,	,,
šǔ, še	,,	,,			

Pret.

Sing.			*Plur.*		
ai, a, i	kud or ked		wǐ, we	kud or ked	
ðǎ, tǎ, tə	,,	,,	jǐ, je	,,	,,
ǐ, ə	,,	,,	ðee, ðe, ðə	,,	,,
šǔ, še	,,	,,			

Affirmatively with *not.*

Pres.	Pret.
ai, a, i, kanet or kǎnt	ai, a, i kudnt or kednet
etc.	etc.

INTERROGATIVELY.

Present.

Sing.   *Plur.*

kan ai, a, i ?   kan wĭ, wө ?

„ ŏă, tă, tө ?   „ jĭ, jө ?

„ ĭ, ө ?   }
                                       „ ŏeө, ŏө, ŏө ?
„ ŏŭ, šө ? }

Pret.

kud ai, a, i ?   kud wĭ, wө ?

etc.   etc.

Interrogatively with *not*.

Pres   Pret.

kanөt or kănt ai, a, i ?   kudnt ai, a, i ?

etc.   etc.

kud, kөd are used both as an infin. and past part.,
unless, as is more probable, the use of kud, kөd, in such
cases, is due to the contamination of two constructions, as a
ius tө kud or kөd diut *I used to be able to do it*, ad ө dunt
if id kud (never kөd) *I would have done it if I had been
able.*

2. *dare.*

§ 390. This verb presents no special peculiarities. I shall
therefore only give the first person singular of each tense in
use. The final t regularly disappears in the pret. before
the following negative. A weak form dө only occurs in the
phrase a dө see *I dare say*.

Present.   Pret.

ai, a, i dāө(r)   ai, a, i dĕst

ai, a, i dārөnt   ai, a, i, dĕsnt

dāөr ai, i ?   dĕst ai, i ?

dārөnt ai, i ?   dĕsnt ai, i ?

3. *shall.*

§ **391.** Present strong form **sal**, weak **sl, s.**   Pret. strong form **sud,** weak **sed, st.**

AFFIRMATIVELY.

Present.

Sing.	*Plur.*
ai, a sal	wĭ sal
aisl, asl	wĭsl, wəsl
ais, as	wĭs, wəs
ðắ sal	jĭ, jə sal
ðắsl	jĭsl, jəsl
ðắs	jĭs, jəs
ĭ sal	
ĭsl	ðee, ðe, ðə sal
ĭs	ðeesl, ðesl, ðəsl
sŭ, šə sal	ðees, ðes, ðəs
šŭsl, šəsl	
šŭs, šəs	

Pret.

ai, a, i sud or sed	wĭ, we sud or sed
aist, ast	wĭst, west
ðắ, tắ, tə sud or sed	jĭ, jə sud or sed
ðắst	jĭst, jəst
ĭ, ə sud or sed	
ĭst	ðee, ðe, ðə sud or sed
šŭ, šə sud or sed	ðeest, ðest, ðəst
šŭst, šəst	

Affirmatively with *not*.

Present.

Sing.	Plur.
ai, a salnt	wĭ, we, salnt
ai, a sänt	wĭ, we sänt
aisl, asl net	wĭsl, wesl net
ais, as net	wĭs, wes net
ðă̆ salnt or sänt	jĭ, je salnt or sänt
ðă̆sl, ðă̆s net	jĭsl, jesl net
	jĭs, jes net
ĭ salnt, sänt	
ĭsl, ĭs net	
šŭ, še salnt or sänt	ðꝺee, ðꝺe, ðꝺe salnt or sänt
šŭsl, šesl net	„ „ „ slnet
šŭs, šes net	ðꝺees, ðꝺes, ðꝺes net

Pret.

Sing.	Plur.
ai, a sudnt	wĭ, we sudnt
ai, a sed net	wĭ, we sed net
aist, ast net	wĭst, west net
etc.	etc.

INTERROGATIVELY.

Present.

sal ai, a, i ?	sal wĭ, we ?
„ ðă̆, tă̆, te ?	„ jĭ, je ?
„ ĭ, e ?	
„ šŭ, še ?	„ ðꝺee, ðꝺe, ðꝺe ?

Pret.

sud ai, a, i ?	sud wĭ, we ?
„ ðă̆, tă̆, te ?	„ jĭ, je ?
„ ĭ, e ?	
„ šŭ, še ?	„ ðꝺee, ðꝺe, ðꝺe ?

Interrogatively with *not*.

Pres.	Pret.
salnt, sānt ai, a, i ?	sudnt ai, a, i ?
etc.	etc.

There is no difference in meaning between the weak forms s, st and sl, sed, but only in usage. The former are never used except in combination with the personal pronouns, as aset bi tə-moen *I shall have it by to-morrow*, ðest ə guen if ðed kud *they should have gone if they had been able*, tmen sl (never s) et *the men shall have it*, ði faðe sed gim(ə) ə feu *thy father should give me a few*. But the difference in use between s and sl, st and sed in combination with pronouns seems to be due to sentence rhythm.

4. *must*.

§ 392. To express lit. Engl. *must*, we have two words which are never confounded in use:

1. Strong form mun, weak men which expresses a necessity dependent upon the will of a person, as a men get mi wāk duin bi tə-nīt *I must get my work done by to-night*, je men tel im wen ə kumz et as bi bak inā *you must tell him when he comes that I shall be back presently*, mun i guə wi je ? *must I go with you?*

mun, men is sometimes used to express *may, can*, as ða men þink wot tə laiks bed ðal e tə diut *you may think what you like but you will have to do it*, mun ðe stop ? may mean either *must they stop?* or *may they stop?*

The weak form med (§ 393), which generally means *might*, is also used as a preterite of mun, as šu sed ðe med oeðer eit ðat e diu bāt out *she said they must either eat that or do without anything*.

mun is of Norse origin, O. Icel. inf. mono, later munu

shall, will, pres. sing. **mon,** later **mun,** pl. **monom,** later **munum,** pret. **munda.** The verb presents no peculiarities, so that only the first person is given here.

Sing.	*Plur.*
ai, a, i mun or mɘn	wĭ, wɘ mun or mɘn
„ „ „ munɘt or muɘnt	„ „ munɘt or muɘnt
mun ai, a, i ?	mun wĭ, wɘ ?
munɘt or muɘnt ai, a, i ?	munɘt or muɘnt wĭ, wɘ ?

2. For *must* we use **must,** which has no weak form, when it implies a logical or natural necessity, as ða must bi ɘ fuil if tɘ þiɳks im bān tɘ diut *you must be (surely you are) a fool if you think I am going to do it,* ðem ɘt sed ðat must bi reɳ i ðɘr ied *those who said that must be wrong in their heads.* In these and similar cases **mun, mɘn** is never used. Cp. ðe múst kum ðis wee = Lowland Scotch *thay byd cum thys way* with ðe mɘn kum ðis wee = Lowland Scotch *thay mæn cum this way*; the former implying that there is no other road, the latter that they are under personal restraint to take this road. On the Scotch verbs **byd, mæn** see The Dialect of the Southern Counties of Scotland, by Dr. Murray, pp. 217–8.

5. *may.*

§ 393. Present strong form **mee,** weak **mɘ.** Preterite strong form **mud,** weak **mɘd. mud** is a new formation made after the analogy of **sud** *should,* **kud** *could.*

AFFIRMATIVELY.
Present.

Sing.	*Plur.*
ai, a, i mee or mɘ	wĭ, wɘ mee or mɘ
etc.	etc.

Pret.

Sing.   Plur.

ai, a, i mud or med   wĭ, we mud or med
etc.   etc.

Affirmatively with *not.*

Pres.   Pret.

ai, a, i meent   ai a, i mudnt
„ „ „ menet   „ „ „ mudnet
etc.   etc.

INTERROGATIVELY.

Present.

Sing.   Plur.

me ai, a, i ?   mee wĭ, we ?
mee dă, tă, te ?   etc.
etc.

The e of mee regularly disappears before a following
vowel (§ 193). After the analogy of me i ? *may I?* me e ?
may he? I have often heard me we ? *may we?* etc.

Pret.

mud ai, a, i ?   mud wĭ, we ?
etc.   etc.

Interrogatively with *not.*

Pres.   Pret.

meent ai, a, i ?   mudnt ai, a, i ?
etc.   etc.

6. *ought.*

§ 394. out remains uninflected for all persons, so that it
will be sufficient to give the first person only : ai, a, i out,
outnt or outnet. out ai, a, i ? outnt ai, a, i ?

b. *have.*

§ 395. Pres. strong forms ᴇv, ᴇ, weak ᴇv, ᴇ. Pret. strong
form ᴇd, weak ᴇd.

The present forms ᴇ, ᴇ are regular only before consonants : as ᴇ dun inā *I shall have done presently,* a sᴇd ᴇ
guᴇn bᴇd fᴇ ᴆī *I should have gone but for thee;* but we
always say, ai ᴇv ᴇm *I have them,* as ᴇt or ᴇv it *I shall have
it.* In combination with the pronouns we now use the v
form before consonants, as a or av dun *I have done.*

The vowel disappears in the weak forms ᴇv, ᴇd when
preceded by the nom. of the personal pronouns, av *I have,*
wĭv *we have,* etc. ᴇd sīn im *I had seen him,* but tmᴇn ᴇd
sīn im *the men had seen him.* And sometimes the verb
disappears altogether, as a faiv on ᴇm *I have five of them,*
ᴆe guᴇn uᴇm *they have gone home,* ᴆe stoun ᴇm *they have
stolen them,* wi or wᴇ funt *we have found it;* but wi or wᴇ
fant *we found it.* See § 249.

The final -z in the second and third persons singular
becomes -s before voiceless consonants, as ᴇstᴇ ? *hast thou?*
if tᴇs tᴇ diut *if thou hast to do it.*

AFFIRMATIVELY.

Present.

Sing.	*Plur.*
ai, a, i ᴇv or ᴇ } aiv, av, iv }	{ wĭ wᴇ ᴇv or ᴇ { wĭv wᴇv
ᴆă, tă, tᴇ ez } ᴆăz, tăz, tᴇz }	{ jĭ, jᴇ ᴇv or ᴇ { jĭv, jᴇv
ĭ, ᴇ, ez } ĭz, ez }	
	{ ᴆe, ᴆᴇ ᴇv or ᴇ
šŭ, šᴇ ez } šŭz, šez }	{ ᴆeᴇv, ᴆᴇv, ᴆᴇv

Pret.

Sing.   *Plur.*

ai, a, i, ed }   { wĭ, we ed
aid, ad, id }   { wĭd, wed

ŏă, tă te ed }   { jĭ, je ed
ŏăd, tăd, ted }   { jĭd, jed

ĭ, e, ed }
ĭd, ed }   }   { ŏe, ŏe ed
šŭ, še ed }   { ŏeed, ŏed, ŏed
šŭd, šed }

Infin. ev, e }
          ev, e }

Present Part. evin

Past   „   ed, ed, d.

Affirmatively with *not.*

Pres.   Pret.

ai, a, i evnt }   { ai, a, i ednt
aiv, av, iv net }   { aid, ad, id net
     etc.   etc.

INTERROGATIVELY.

Present.

Sing.   *Plur.*

ev ai, a, i ?   e wĭ or we ?

ez ŏă, es tă or te ?   e jĭ or je ?

ez ĭ or e ?

es šŭ, es še ? }
     eše ?   } }   e ŏee, ŏe or ŏe ?

Pret.

ed ai, a, i ?   ed wĭ, we ?
     etc.   etc.

Interrogatively with *not*.

Pres.	Pret.
evnt ai, a, i ?	ednt ai, a, i ?
etc.	etc.

The plural forms of the present, given above, are only
used in combination with the personal pronouns, in other
cases we use ez, ez, z, s (after voiceless consonants) just as
in the second and third person singular, as ðem menz bĭn
vari guid te me *those men have been very good to me*, tladz
ez gen me sumet *the boys have given me something*, uz ets
dun se mitš for im *we who have done so much for him*, ez ðem
men sīn ðe ? *have those men seen thee?* es taplz guen bad ?
have the apples gone bad? The same also applies to the
first person, as its mī ets dunt *it is I who have done it*, mī
ets ed se mitš te baid *I who have had so much to endure.*

The endings -z, -s for the whole of the singular and
plural are now chiefly confined to the verbs *have* and *be*
(except the second person singular).

With other verbs we now generally only use these
endings in combination with the relative pronoun et, as
ðem men diu ðe wāk vari wīl *those men do their work very
well* ; but ðemz tmen et duz ðe wāk tbest *those are the men
who do their work the best.* Although this is the normal
usage, I have often heard the -z, -s forms used under the
same circumstances as they are for the verb *have.* In the
older stage of the dialect the endings -z, -s must have been
used for all verbs in the manner they are still used for
have. Already in OE. the Northern dialects had the plural
ending -as beside -að, e. g. bindas beside bindað.

As it may possibly interest some readers to learn how
far the plural endings -z and -s extend, I have examined the
Comparative dialect specimens in Ellis, EEPr. v. The

second and sixth sentences contain the point in question.
The sentences are : (2) 'Few men die because they are
laughed at.' In the dialect specimens this is often rendered
as if it were : 'there are few men who die because they are
laughed at.' In the statistics given below, this sentence
will be referred to as without relative and ending, without
relative with ending, with relative and no ending, with
relative and ending. The sixth sentence is : (6) 'And the
old woman herself will tell any of you that laugh now.'

Western Mid Southern division : at Tedbury with rel. and
ending -z ; at Ledbury and Much Cowarne without rel. and
ending, but (6) with rel. and endings -s -z ; at Eggleton rel.
with ending -z. Eastern Mid Southern : at Hamstead
Norris without rel. and ending, but (6) rel. without ending ;
Southampton to Winchester without rel. with ending -z
and (6) with rel. and ending -s. Northern Border Southern :
at Banbury without rel. with ending -z, and (6) with rel.
and ending -s. Mid Border Southern : at Handborough rel.
and endings -z, -s. Southern Border Southern : no examples.
East Southern : at Faversham without rel. and ending, and
(6) with rel. and no ending. Northern West Southern : at
Wellington (West Somerset) (6) with rel. and no ending.
South West Southern : at Iddesleigh without rel. and
ending, and (6) with rel. and no ending, the same also in
South Devon. Western West Southern : no examples.
South and North Western divisions : no examples. West
Eastern : at Aylesbury (p. 190) *father and mother n (=are)
lame.* Mid Eastern : at Ware without rel. and ending, and
(6) with rel. and no ending, the same also for Mid Bedford-
shire and East Haddon. South and North Eastern
divisions : no examples. East Eastern : in South Norfolk,
East and West Suffolk without rel. and ending, and (6)
with rel. and no ending. Border Midland (the county of

Lincolnshire) : no examples. Southern North Midland : at
Stalybridge without rel. with ending -n, and (6) with rel.
and ending -s ; at Glossop with rel. and ending -n, and (6)
with rel. and **er** along with the pres. part. ; at Chapel-en-le-
Frith (2 and 6) with rel. and ending -n. Western North
Midland : at Skelmersdale (2 and 6) rel. and endings -z, -s ;
at Westhoughton without rel. with ending -z, and (6) with
rel. and **iz** along with the pres. part. ; at Leyland without
rel. with ending -n; at Burnley without rel. with ending -z,
and (6) with rel. and -s along with the pres. part. Northern
North Midland : at Poulton without rel. and ending, but (6)
with rel. and -s ; at Goosnargh without rel. and ending, but
(6) with rel. and **iz** along with the pres. part. Eastern
North Midland : at Huddersfield, Halifax, Keighley, Bradford, Leeds, Dewsbury, Rotherham, both in (2) and (6) with
rel. and endings -z, -s ; but at Sheffield without rel. and
ending, and (6) with rel. and no ending. Western Mid
Midland : at Middlewich both (2) and (6) with rel. and
ending -n ; the same at Shrigley ; at Tarporley (6) with rel.
and ending -n; at Burslem (6) with rel. and ending -s.
Eastern Mid Midland : at Taddington rel. with ending -n,
and (6) rel. with ending -s ; at Ashford rel. with ending -z,
and (6) rel. with **iz** along with the pres. part. ; at Winster
(2) and (6) with rel. and endings -z, -s ; at Ashbourne rel.
with ending -z, also without rel. with ending -z, and (6)
with rel. and ending -s ; at Brampton (2) and (6) with rel.
and ending -n ; at Repton (2) and (6) with rel. and endings
-z and -s. East and Western South Midland divisions : no
examples. Eastern South Midland : at Cannock Chase
without rel. and ending -n, but (6) with rel. and ending
-n ; at Dudley without rel. with ending -z ; at Ather-
stone (2) and (6) with rel. and no ending, at Waltham
without rel. and ending ; and (6) with rel. and no

ending. East Northern: at South Ainsty and Holderness
without rel. with ending, -z, and (6) with rel. and ending
-s. Mid Yorkshire, North Mid Yorkshire, New Malton,
Lower Nidderdale, Washburn River, South Cleveland,
North East Coast, and Market Weighton, all have (2) and
(6) with rel. and endings -z, -s. West Northern: at Upper
Swaledale, the Upper Mining Dales, Upper Craven with
Upper Nidderdale, Skipton, and Mid Craven, we have for
(6) rel. with ending -s; at Hawes, Kirkby, Lonsdale, Dent,
Sedburg, Kendal, Orton, Kirkby Stephen, Crosby Ravens-
worth, Langwathby, and Keswick, we have the form without rel. with ending -z; but at Lower-Holker-in-Cartmel,
Coniston, Long Sleddale, Temple Sowerby, Clifton, Holme
Cultram, Carlisle, and Knaresdale without rel. and ending;
at Milburn, Ellonby, and Upper Swaledale with rel. and
ending -z. All the dialects in this division have for (6) rel.
with ending -s except at Coniston, where we have with rel.
and no ending. North Northern: at South Shields (6) with
rel. and ending -s; at Newcastle and Berwick-upon-Tweed
without rel. and ending, and (6) with rel. and no ending.
The Lowland division: at Bewcastle, Hawick, Edinburgh,
Arbroath, Keith, and Dunrossness without rel. and with
ending -z, but (6) with rel. and ending -s; at Stranraer and
Wick without rel. and ending, but for (6) with rel. and no
ending. The above are the only comparative specimens of
the Lowland division given in Ellis. But Dr. Murray, The
Dialect of the Southern Counties of Scotland, pp. 211–2,
states that the plural and first pers. singular without -s are
only used when the verb is accompanied by its proper
pronoun; when the subject is a noun, adjective, interrogative or relative pronoun, or when the verb and subject are
separated by a clause, the verb takes the termination -s in
all persons. Dr. Murray informs me that the persons who

supplied Dr. Ellis with the comparative specimens for Stranraer and Wick have given inaccurate versions with regard to the verbal endings. The probability is that Dr. Ellis has misunderstood the versions, because in a note (p. 683) he distinctly says that he took down the two versions hurriedly, and was afraid that some of the finer shades might have escaped him.

c. be.

§ 396. The vowel disappears in the weak forms of the present, and when followed by a consonant the verb disappears altogether in the plural, as **wil guθ wen tθt redi** *we will go when thou art ready,* **ðer at it θgiθn** *they are at it again*; but **ðe bān uθm** *they are going home,* **we selin θm θt oθpni θ kweθt** *we are selling them at a halfpenny a quart.* The -z in the third person becomes -s before and after voiceless consonants, as **tbriθd θt tθ bouts nuθn guid** *the bread which thou boughtest is not good,* **šθs þiɳkin θ gu(θ)in** *she is thinking of going.*

Present.

Sing.	Plur.
ai, a, i am ⎱ aim, am, im ⎰	⎱ wĭ, we āθ(r) ⎰ wĭ(r), we(r)
ðă āt, tθ āt ⎱ ðăt, tăt, tθt ⎰	⎱ jĭ, jθ āθ(r) ⎰ jĭ(r), jθ(r)
ĭ iz, θ iz ⎱ ĭz, θz ⎰ ⎱ šŭ iz, šθ iz ⎱ ⎰ šŭz, šθz ⎰	⎱ ðeθ, ðθ, ðo āθ(r) ⎰ ðeθ(r), ðθ(r), ðθ(r)

Pret.

Sing.   *Plur.*

ai, a, i wo(r) or we(r)   wĭ, we wo(r) or we(r)
etc.   etc.

Infin.   bĭ, be
Pres. Part. bĭ-in
Past   „   bĭn

AFFIRMATIVELY WITH *not.*

Present.

Sing.   *Plur.*

ai, a, i amet   ⎫   ⎰ wĭ, we ānt
aim, am, im net ⎭   ⎱ wĭ, we net
ðă, tă, te ātnt   ⎫   ⎰ jĭ, je ānt
ðăt, tăt, tet net ⎭   ⎱ jĭ, je net
ĭ, e iznt   ⎫
ĭz, ez net ⎭ ⎫
šŭ, še iznt ⎫⎬   ⎰ ðee, ðe, ðe ānt
šŭz, šez net ⎭⎭   ⎱ ðee, ðe, ðe net

Pret.

ai, a, i wornt   wĭ, we wornt
ai, a, i we-net   wĭ, we we-net
etc.   etc.

INTERROGATIVELY.

Present.

am ai, a, i?   ăwĭ, ăwe?
ăðă, ătă, ăte?   ăjĭ, ăje?
izĭ, ize?
iz šŭ, še? ⎫
išŭ, iše? ⎭   ăðee, ăðe, ăðe?

Pret.

Sing.   *Plur.*

wor ai, a, i ?   wowĭ, wowə ?

woðă, wotă, wote ?   wojĭ, wojə ?

wor, ĭ, ə ?   } woðeə, woðe, woðə ?

wošŭ. wošə ?   }

INTERROGATIVELY WITH *not.*

Present.

amət ai, a, i ?   ānt wĭ, wə ?

ătnðă, ătntă ?   } ānt jĭ, jə ?

ătntə ?   }

iznt ĭ, ə ?   } ānt ðeə, ðe, ðə ?

iznt šŭ, šə ?   }

Pret.

wornt ai, a, i ?   wornt wĭ, wə ?

etc.   etc.

In forms like ātnt *art not,* wornt *was, were not,* the n is vocalic.

The above forms of the present are mostly used in combination with the pronouns, in other cases we generally use iz, əz, z, s, cp. § 395, as tkoilz iznt dun jət *the coals are not done yet,* ðez lots on əm dān truəd *there are lots of them down the road,* ðemz or ðem ə vari guidnz *those are very good ones,* tladz əz or ə bān wi jə *the lads are going with you,* ðez fouks əts or ət er oləs grumlin *there are people who are always grumbling,* mĭ əts sə puəli *I who am so poorly,* ðĭ əts nout tə diu məd elp mə ə bit *thou, who hast nothing to do, mightest help me a bit.*

d. *will.*

§ 397. Present, strong form wil, weak əl which loses its vowel in combination with the pronouns.

Preterite, strong form **wod**, weak forms **wəd**, **əd**, the latter loses its vowel in combination with the pronouns, as **ad lən ðət, bəd a kānt diu bāt it džust nā** *I would lend thee it, but I cannot do without it just now*, **tladz wəd** or **əd fotš it, if jə ast əm** *the lads would fetch it, if you asked them.*

wod, wəd is used as an infin. in the phrase: **ius tə wod** *to be formerly wont* or *willing to do a thing*, as **ðə ius tə wəd əlp mə nā ən ðen** *they were formerly wont* or *willing to help me now and then.* **wod** is also in common use as a past participle, **a kud** or **kəd ə dunt if id wod** *I could have done it if I had wished.* But see the end of § 389.

AFFIRMATIVELY.

Present.

Sing.	Plur.
ai, a wil ⎱ ail, al ⎰	⎰ wĭ, wə wil ⎱ wĭl, wəl
ðǎ, tǎ, tə wil ⎱ ðǎl, tǎl, təl ⎰	⎰ jĭ, jə wil ⎱ jĭl, jəl
ĭ, ə wil ⎱ ĭl, əl ⎰ ⎫ šǔ, šə wil ⎱ ⎬ šǔl, šəl ⎰ ⎭	⎰ ðee, ðə, ðə wil ⎱ ðeəl, ðəl, ðəl

Prət.

ai, a, i wod or wəd ⎱ aid, ad, id ⎰	⎰ wĭ, wə wod or wəd ⎱ wĭd, wəd
ðǎ, tǎ, tə wod or wəd ⎱ ðǎd, tǎd, təd ⎰	⎰ jĭ, jə wod or wəd ⎱ jĭd, jəd
ĭ, ə wod or wəd ⎱ ĭd, əd ⎰ ⎫ šǔ, šə wod or wəd ⎱ ⎬ šǔd, šəd ⎰ ⎭	⎰ ðee, ðə, ðə wod or wəd ⎱ ðeed, ðəd, ðəd

M 2

AFFIRMATIVELY WITH *not*.

Present.

Sing.	*Plur.*
ai, a wilnt or wient	wĭ, we wilnt or wient
etc.	etc.

Pret.

ai, a, i wodnt }	wĭ, we wodnt }
aid, ad, id net }	wĭd, wed net }
etc.	etc.

INTERROGATIVELY.

Present.

wil ai, a, i ?	wil wĭ, we ?
wil ŏă, tă, te ? }	
wită, wite ? }	wil jĭ, je ?
wil ĭ, e ? }	
wil šŭ, še ? }	wil ŏee, ŏe, ŏe ?

Pret.

| wod ai, a, i ? | wod wĭ, we ? |
| etc. | etc. |

INTERROGATIVELY WITH *not*.

Present.

| wilnt, wient ai, a i ? | wilnt, wient wĭ, we ? |
| etc. | etc. |

Pret.

| wodnt ai, a, i ? | wodnt wĭ, we ? |
| etc. | etc. |

e. *do.*

§ 398. As an independent verb **diu** has its full conjugation like any other verb. The pret. **did** is used for all

persons singular and plural. Present part. **diu-in**, which
has been reformed from the inf., otherwise we should
have had *du(i)in (§ 163); past part. **duin, dun.** Present
wit *not* is **duent, dunet,** pret. **didnt.**

When used interrogatively as an auxiliary verb we have
diu for the first person singular and for the plural strong
form **diu**, weak forms **de, di.** When *do* is used affirmatively as an auxiliary verb it has, of course, no weak
forms.

PRESENT.

Affirmatively.

Sing.	*Plur.*
ai, a, i diu	wĭ, we diu
ðă, tă, te duz	jĭ, je diu
ĭ, e duz ⎫	
šŭ, še duz ⎭	ðee, ðe, ðe diu

Interrogatively.

diu ai, a, i?	de or di wĭ, we?
duz ðă, dustă, duste?	de or di jĭ, je?
duz ĭ, e? ⎫	
duz šŭ, duše? ⎭	de or di ðee, ðe, ðe?

The verb *do* is not used so frequently in asking questions as in lit. Engl.: **wot þinste, sal we gue?** lit. *what
thinkest thou, shall we go?* **wod e diut, þink je?** *would he
do it, do you think?* See § 249.

APPENDIX.

CHAPTER XI.

Adverbs, Prepositions, and Conjunctions.

I. ADVERBS.

§ **399.** 1. Adverbs of manner and degree: The adverbs of manner mostly end in -li, as **ādli** *hardly*, **oekədli** *awkwardly*; but we have the stress on the suffix in **siuəlĭ** *surely*, **ekuədinlái** *accordingly*.

ā *how*, **ā-ivə(r)** old people say **āmivə(r)** *however* which seems to have been contaminated with **āsəmivə(r)** *howsoever*, with the particle **səm** = the O. Dan. **sum**, O. Icel. **səm**; **apm** (lit. *happen*), **mə bi** *perhaps*, **nobəd** lit. *not but, only*, **oləs** *always*, **oməst** *almost*, **tiu** *too, also* (instead of **tiu** we very often use **ən oəl** lit. *and all*, it **wər ə vari guidn ən oəl** *it was a very good one too*, **aim bān ən oəl** *I am going too*), **vari** *very*, **wīl** *well*. But when *well* begins the sentence we use **wel** just as in lit. Engl., as **wel**, a **nivər iəd sitš ən ə þiŋ i oəl mi boən deəz** *well, I never heard such (an) a thing in all my born days*; but its **oəl vari wīl** *it is all very well*, **šuz nuən sə wīl tə-dee** *she is not very well to-day*.

suə, weak form **sə** *so*. Instead of **suə** we often use **ðat**, as i **wə ðat mad** *he was so angry*, **šə wə ðat week wol šə kudnt stand** *she was so weak that* (lit. *while*) *she could not stand*.

The adverbs *also, thus, why* are not used. To express

also we use tiu, ən oəl, *thus* is i ðis weə, and *why*, wot fo(r), wots ə guən fo(r)? *why has he gone?*, a duənt noə wot əz dun ðat fo(r) *I don't know why he has done that.*

Adverbs of place : oniwiə(r) *anywhere*, iə(r) *here*, iðə(r), *hither*, jondə(r) *yonder*, sumwiə(r) *somewhere,* ðiə(r) (weak forms ðe(r), ðə(r)) *there*, wiə(r) *where*.

Adverbs of time : inā *bye-and-bye, presently*, binā *by this time*, ivə(r) *ever*, jestedə *yesterday*, jestənīt *last night*, jet *yet*, nā *now*, nivə(r) *never*, oft *often*, sin *since*, suin *soon*, tə-dee *to-day*, tə-moən *to-morrow*, tə-moən-tnīt *to-morrow (the) night*, tə-nīt *to-night*, ðen *then*, wen *when*.

Affirmative and negative particles : ai *yes* (jes is also used but it is not so common as ai), nee *no* (nou *no* has been borrowed from the literary language), nət *not* (instead of nət we often use nuən) ; cp. § 357.

2. PREPOSITIONS.

§ 400. aftə(r) *after*, bə-fuə(r), ə-fuə(r), fuə(r) *before*, bə-twīn, twīn *between*, bi, weak bə *by*, bə-int *behind*, bin *within*, dān *down*, ə, əv (before vowels) *of*, ə-bāt, bāt *about, without*, ə-būn, būn *above*, ə-giən, giən *against*, ə-leᴎ ə *along of, on account of*, ə-meᴎ *among*, ə-nent *opposite*, ə-said, bə-said *besides*, ə-stiəd ə, stiəd ə *instead of*, fo(r) *for*, fre, frə *from*, in, i *in* (i is very common before both vowels and consonants), intə, intəv (before vowels), intul *into*, niə(r) *near*, nobəd *except*, on (weak form ə) *on, of*, ouə(r), ovə(r) *over*, sin *since*, tə, təv (before vowels) *to*, þriu, þre *through, from*, undə(r) *under*, up *up*, wi *with*, wiðāt *without*.

3. CONJUNCTIONS.

§ 401. The following are the chief conjunctions in addition to those prepositions and adverbs which may be

used as conjunctions : **bǝd** *but*, **bǝ-kos**, **kos** *because*, **ǝn** *and*,
ǝt *that* (**ðat** is never used as a conjunction in the dialect), **if**
if, **noǝðǝ(r)** *neither*, **oǝðǝ(r)** *either*, **nǝ(r)** *nor* (after compara-
tives *than*, **betǝ nǝr i þout** *better than I thought*), **o(r)**, **ǝ(r)**
or, **ðoǝ** *although*, **wol** *until*, *that* (**stop wol ǝ kumz** *stop
until he comes*, **šǝ wǝ ðat badli wol ðǝ þout šǝd nivǝ mend**
she was so ill that they thought she would never get better).

SPECIMENS.

It was originally my intention not to give any specimens of the dialect in this volume, but to reserve them for
a second which was to contain a complete glossary of
such dialect words as are not in use in the Modern literary
language, together with extensive specimens of the dialect.
With this end in view I have been collecting materials for
a great number of years; but various circumstances prevent me from entertaining the hope of being able to
publish them for some years to come. I have therefore
decided to give a few specimens in the present volume,
trusting that they may be found useful to those readers
who may wish to make themselves familiar with the
dialect. To anyone who takes the trouble to read them
I venture to say that they will be found both amusing and
instructive.

There is a great quantity of stories and poems printed
in the dialect, but as they stand they are practically
worthless for the purposes of this book. The transcription is neither accurate nor consistent. All the specimens
given here are from printed sources. To number III.
I have added the original in order to show the kind of
transcription usually employed in such books.

The sources are:—III. (The Yorkshireman's Comic An-
nual, 1884, pp. 37–38), IV. (ditto, 1885, pp. 14–17), V.
(ditto, 1882, pp. 24–26), VI. (Yorkshire Sketches, by Wil-
liam Cudworth, pp. 11–17), VII., VIII., IX. (Dialect and
other Poems, by Ben Preston, pp. 31–33, 11–12, 1–10).

I.

Comparative Specimen.

See Ellis, EEPr. vol. v. p. 7*.   In this and the Dialect Test I have inserted the forms in parentheses in the literary English Specimens in order to facilitate the reading of the dialect versions.

ı. wel, neəbə(r), jī ən im mə buəþ laf ət ðis niuz ə main. uə keəz ?   ðats noəðər iə nə ðiə(r).

2. feu men dī kos ðə laft at, wī noə, duənt wə ?   wot səd mak əm ?   its nət vari laikli, iz it ?

3. āsəm·ivə ðiəz ə tfaks ə tkeəs, suə džust od jə din, frend, ən bi kwaiət wol iv dun.   ākɲ !

4. ·aim siuər a iəd əm seə—sum ə ðem fouks ət went þriu tuəl þiɲ frə tfēst ðəsenz,—þat a did, [seəf] siuər i·nif,—

5. ət tjuɲist sun isen, ə gēt lad ə nain, niu is faðə voiz ət wuns, ðo(ə) it ·wo sə kwiər ən skwiəkin, ən ad trāst ·im tə speik t'riuþ oni deə, ai, a ·wod ðat.

6. ən toud wumən əsen l tel oni on jə ət laf nā, ən tel jə streit of, tiu, bāt mitš boðə(r), if jəl nobəd as ə(r), oə ! wiənt šə ?—

7. ət oni reət šu teld it ·mī wen i ast ə(r), tū ə þrī taimz ouə(r), šu did, ən ·šū outnt tə bi reɲ i sitš [ən] ə point əz ðis, wot þiɲk jə ?

I.

Comparative Specimen.

1. Well, neighbour, you and he may both laugh at this news of mine. Who cares? That is neither here nor there.

2. Few men die because they are laughed at, we know, don't we? what should make them? It is not very likely, is it?

3. Howsoever these are the facts of the case, so just hold your [din] noise, friend, and be quiet till I have done. Hearken!

4. *I* am [sure] certain I heard them say—some of [them] those folks who went through the whole thing from the first themselves,—that did I, [sure] safe enough,—

5. That the youngest son himself, a great [lad] boy of nine, knew his father's voice at once, though it *was* so queer and squeaking, and I would trust *him* to speak the truth any day, aye, I *would* [that].

6. And the old woman herself will tell any of you that laugh now, and tell you straight off, too, without much bother, if you will only ask her, oh! won't she?—

7. [at any rate] leastways she told it *me* when I asked her, two or three times over, did she, and *she* ought not to be wrong on such a point as this, what do you think?

8. wel əz a wə se(ə)-in, ˙šūd tel jə, ā, wiər ən wen šə fan d'rukɳ ānd ət šə koəlz ər uzbn.

9. šu sweə šə so(ə) im wi ər oən īn, ligin reit ət ful lenþ, ə tgrund, in iz guid sundə koit, tlois bi d'uɔr ə tās, dān ət tkoənər ə jon loin.

10. i wə ruərin ə˙weə, sɔz šū, fər oəl twōld laik ə puəli bān, ər ə litl las in ə friət.

11. ən ðat apmd, əz ɔr ən ə doutər-i-loə kom þriu tbak jād frə iɳin twet tluəz āt tə drai ə tıwešin deə.

12. wol tketl wə boilin fə t'iɔ, wun fain brīt sumər aftənuin, nobəd ə wik sin kum tnekst þēzdə.

13. ən, di jə noə? a nivə liənd nə muə nə ðis ə ðat biznəs up tə tə˙deə, əs siuər əz mi neəm z džon šepəd, ən a ḍuənt wont tiu oəðə(r), ðiə nā!

14. ən su(ə) am bān uəm tə mi supə(r). guid nīt, ən duənt bi sə redi tɔ kro(ə) ouər ə bodi ə˙giən, wen ə toəks ə ðis ðat ə tuðə(r).

15. its ə weək fuil ət preəts bāt riəzn. ən ðats mai last wēd. guid bai.

8. Well as I was saying, *she* would tell you, how, where, and when she found the drunken [hound] that she calls her husband.

9. She swore she saw him with her own eyes, lying [right] stretched at full length, on the ground, in his good Sunday coat, close by the door of the house, down at the corner of yon lane.

10. He was [roaring] whining away, says she, for all the world like a [poorly barn] sick child, or a little [lass] girl in a fret.

11. And that happened, as she and her daughter-in-law came through the back yard from hanging out the wet clothes on [the] a washing day.

12. While the kettle was boiling for [the] tea, one fine bright summer afternoon, only a week [since] ago come next Thursday.

13. And, do you know? I never learned [no] any more [nor] than this of that business up to to-day, as sure as my name is John Shepherd, and I don't want to either, there now!

14. And so I am going home to [my supper] sup. Good night, and don't be so [ready] quick to crow over a body again, when he talks of this that or t' other.

15. It is a weak fool that prates without reason. And that is my last word. Good bye.

II.

Dialect Test.

See Ellis, p. 8*, and compare the version given below with the one in Ellis (p. 389), which contains several strange mistakes both in the version and the notes to it. If his rendering of the dialect test of other dialect speakers is as inaccurate as that of the Windhill dialect, the value of these tests for phonetic and philological purposes is not very great. The classified word-list (pp. 391-4) also contains many mistakes. The only way in which I can account for these inaccuracies is partly through the hurried manner in which the dial. test and classified word-list were taken down and partly through their not having been revised.

1. su(ə) a seə meəts, jə sī nā ət im reit ə·bāt ðat litl las kumin frə tskuil jondə(r).

2. šuz gu(ə)-in dān truəd ðiə þriu tred geət ə tleft and said ə tweə.

3. siuər i·nif, tbān z guən streit up tə d'uər ə tren ās,

4. wiə šl tšons tə find ðat drukn diəf wiznd felə (more commonly tšap) ə tneəm ə toməs.

5. wi oəl no(ə) im vari wīl.

6. wiənt toud tšap suin teitš ə nət tə diu it ə·giən, puə þin !

7. liuk! iznt it triu ?

II.

Dialect Test.

1. So I say, mates, you see now that I am right about that little [lass] girl coming from the school yonder.

2. She is going down the road there through the red gate on the left hand side of the way.

3. Sure enough, the [barn] child has gone straight up to the door of the wrong house,

4. where she will chance to find that drunken deaf [wizzened] shrivelled fellow of the name of Thomas.

5. We all know him very well.

6. Won't the old chap soon teach her not to do it again, poor thing!

7. Look! Isn't it true?

III.

TBATL ǝ T'LUƷZ LAINZ.

ai, Greǝs, las, it wǝr oǝl ouǝr ǝ bit ǝv ǝ tluǝs kuǝd. am
nǝt wun ǝ tsuǝt tǝ guǝ peilin up ǝn dān diɲin fouk ouǝ(r),
ǝz ǝ riul ; ða noǝz ðat. wot ·ai wont is piǝs ǝn kwaiǝtnǝs,
bǝd if fouk wiǝnt let mǝ ev it [or et], al mak ǝm sit up fot,
5 ǝz oni wumǝn ·wod ǝt ǝd ǝr oǝn weǝ tǝ mak i twēld, ǝn ǝ lot
ǝ bānz tǝ mak ǝn mend fo(r), nivǝ neǝm ǝ uzbn ǝt nivǝ
blakliǝdǝd ǝ greǝt ǝ wešt ǝ windǝ sin wǝd wǝ wo(r). ða
noǝz ǝz wīl ǝz ·ai noǝ wot ǝ gōt wešin ai ev ivri wik—ǝ lot
ǝ muki smoks ǝn skōts, ǝt jǝ mǝ boil ǝn betǝ boil, ǝn ðen bi
10 niǝli ǝz bad ǝz wen jǝ bǝ·gan. ðe duǝnt koǝl it tgriǝzi miln
fǝ nout. tiuzdǝ z olǝs bīn mai wešin deǝ fǝ ðiǝz siks jiǝ bak
ǝ muǝ(r). a olǝs put t'luǝs tǝ stīp tnīt ǝ·fuǝ(r), ǝn gct up ǝt
faiv ǝ·tlok i tmoǝnin, ǝ·fuǝ Ben ǝn tbānz guǝz tǝ ðǝ wāk,
ǝn gcts tsetpan ǝ·gcǝt, ǝn z ivri tlāt āt suin aftǝ brekfǝs
15 taim, if ðǝz ǝ guid druft, fǝr if ðǝz wun þiɲ muǝ nǝr ǝ·nuðǝr
ǝt maks Ben liuk blak its ǝ lot ǝ tluǝz iɲin ǝ·bāt.

ðats bin mai we(ǝ) ǝ gu(ǝ)in on, ǝn šuz noǝn it ǝz wīl ǝz
iv noǝn it misen. wol ðis apmd wi wǝr ǝz guid neǝbǝz ǝz
nīd bī. wi mud fratš ǝ bit nā ǝn ðen ouǝ tbānz—fǝ ðat
20 Siuzi ǝ ōz iz ǝ reit ·teǝstril ov ǝ las, ǝn giz āǝ Džoni sum reǝ
slaps sumtaimz—bǝd wiv nivǝr ed nǝ boðǝ tǝ miǝn out wol
nā. ǝn if tǝl bǝ·līv mǝ, las, av dun muǝ fǝ ðat ðiǝ wumǝn
nǝr if šǝd bīn mi oǝn sistǝ(r). a neg·lektǝd mi oǝn ɲǝm tǝ

III.

AY, Grace, lass, it wor all ovver a bit of a tloaze cord.
I'm nut one o' t'soart to go peylin' up an' dahn dingin'
fowk ovver, as a rule; thah knaws that. What I want is
peace an' quietness, but if fowk weant let me hev it, I'll
mak' 'em sit up for it, as onny woman wod 'at hed her awn 5
way to mak' i' t'world, an' a lot o' barns to mak' an' mend
for, nivver name a husband 'at nivver blackleeaded a grate
or weshed a winda sin' wed we wor. Thah knaws as weel
as I knaw what a gurt weshin' I hev ivvery week—a lot
o' mucky smocks an' skirts, 'at ye may boil an' better 10
boil, an' then be nearly as bad as when ye began. They
don't call it t'greasy miln for nowt. Tuesday's awlus been
my weshin' day for these six year back or more. I awlus
put t'tloaze to steep t'neet afore, an' get up at five o'clock
i' t'mornin', afore Ben an' t'barns goes to ther wark, an' 15
gets t'set-pan agate, an' hez ivvery claht aht sooin after
brekfast time, if ther's a gooid druft, for if ther's one
thing more nor another 'at mak's Ben lewk black it's a lot
o' tloaze hingin' abaht.

That's been my way o' goin' on, an' shoo's knawn it as 20
weel as I've knawn it mysen. Whol this happen'd we wor
as gooid nabors as need be. We mud fratch a bit nah an'
then ovver t'barns—for that Susey o' hers is a reyt tay-
strill of a lass, an' gives ahr Johnny some rare slaps sometimes—bud we've nivver hed no bother to mean owt whol 25
nah. An' if ta'll believe me, lass, I've done more for that
theer woman nor if shoo'd been my awn sister. I ne-

N

weət on ə wen šə wə ligin in ɔ tlast bān ; av swild tpasidž
25 duznz ə taimz wen its bīn ɔ̄ tōn ; ən a wə nivər ə·giən takin
keər ə tās for ɔ wen šəz wontəd tə guə tə tmītin. šūz ə
grand ən tə guə tɔ tmītin, šū iz ẟat ; bəd a oləs sed, ən al
se(ə) ə·giən, ət ẟem ət prə·fesəz tə bi sə piuər ən guid əz oləs
twāst wen ẟə kum tə bi reit rekŋd up. a wuns niu ə pāsnz
30 doutər ət didnt no(ə) ā tə freəm tə weš ə pot up, ən šə kəd
fešn tə guə tə t'šapil ivri sundə i twik. bəd jə duənt no(ə)
u(ə) is sānd wol jəv bodmd əm reit; ən if onibodi kəd ə
teld mə þrī wik sin ət Meəri Džeglz əd ə dun əs šu ɔz dun tə
mə, ast ə þroən d'ištlāt i ẟə feəs ən teld əm ẟə wə nuən
35 wot ẟə out tə bī. bəd ẟəz nout tə bi sed fot. ẟes sum
fouk əd disiəv ə maiklskoup, ẟe sə dīp.

   wel, əz a wə telin ẟə, av oləs wešt ə t'iuzdə ẟis moni ə
jiə(r), fər a laik tə gu(ə) āt ɔ bit əv ə mundə, wen iv getn
əm ẟə sundə tluəz brušt ən saidəd ə·weə, ən a mak nout ə
40 wešin ən beəkin tə-geẟər ət tbak end ə twik, wen
jə səd bi tliənin. suə tiuzdə z mai deə, ən šu noəz it.
wel, ə fotnit sin kum jəstədə, a gat up ət faiv ə·tlok, əz
iuzl, ən went at it laik ə oəs wol ə·bāt brekfəs taim. ẟen
a tiuk t'luəs kuəd ən þout ad bi getin ə tūþri þiŋz āt. bəd,
45 wod tə bə·līv it ? Meəri əd guən ən putn ər oən kuəd āt
ən getn it ful ə tluəz. a kəd ādli bə·līv mi oən īn. a nivə
niu ə weš wol wednzdə ə·fuər i ool mi laif, su(ə) a guəz up
tul ər, ən a sez, ' wots tmiənin ɔ ẟis laik ? ' ' tmiənin ə
wot ? ' šu sez, əz inisnt əz ə stuft miul. ' didnt tə no(ə) it
50 wɔ mai wešin moənin ? ' a sez. ' apm a did,' šu sez, ' ən
apm a didnt, bəd a spuəz av əz mitš reit tə iŋ mai tluəz āt
əz ẟā̃ əz tə iŋ ẟain.' ẟis netld mɔ ; su(ə) a sez, ' ẟa noəz

glected my awn hoam to wait on her when shoo wor liggin'
in o' t'last barn; I've swilled t'passidge dozens o' times
when it's been her turn; an' I wor nivver ageean takkin' 30
care o' t'hahse for her when shoo's wanted to go to t'meetin'.
Shoo's a grand un to go to t'meetin', shoo is that; bud I
awlus said, an' I'll say ageean, 'at them 'at professes to be
so pure an' gooid is awlus t'warst when they come to be
reyt reckoned up. I once knew a parson's dowter 'at 35
didn't knaw hah to frame to wesh a pot up, an' shoo could
feshan to go to t'chapel ivvery Sunday i' t'week. Bud ye
doan't knaw who is sahnd whol ye've bottom'd 'em reyt;
an' if onnybody could ha' teld me three week sin' 'at Mary
Jaggles wod ha' done as shoo hez done to me, I sud ha' 40
thrawn t'dishclaht i' ther face an' teld 'em they wor noan
what they owt to be. But ther's nowt to be said for it.
Ther's some fowk 'ud deceive a michaelscowp, they're so
deep.

Well, as I wor tellin' tha, I've awlus weshd o' t'Tuesday 45
this monny a year, for I like to go aht a bit of a Monday,
when I've gotten 'em ther Sunda' tloaze brushed an' sided
away, an' I mak' nowt o' weshin an' bakin' together at
t'back end o' t'week, when ye sud be tleanin'. So Tuesday's my day, an' shoo knaws it. Well, a fortnit sin' come 50
yesterday, I gat up at five o'clock, as ushal, an' went at it
like a horse whol abaht brekfast time. Then I tewk
t'tloaze cord an' thowt I'd be gettin' a toathree things aht.
Bud, wod ta believe it? Mary hed goan an' putten her
awn cord aht an' gotten it full o' tloaze. I could hardly 55
believe my awn een. I nivver knew her wesh whol Weddinsday afore i' all my life, so I goes up tul her, an' I says,
'What's t'meanin' o' this like?' 'T'meanin' o' what?'
shoo says, as innocent as a stuffed mule. 'Didn't ta knaw
it wor my weshing mornin'?' I says. 'Happen I did,' 60
shoo says, 'an' happen I didn't, bud I suppose I've as mitch
reyt ta hing my tloaze aht as tha hez ta hing thine.' This
nettled me; so I says, 'Thah knaws varry weel 'at Tues-

vari wil ət tiuzdə z mai deə, ən su(ə) al þeɪŋk ðə tə get ðem
tlāts ə ðain āt ə truəd əs suin əs tə kan.' 'uə tə toəkin
55 tul?' šu sez. 'ða noəz vari wil u(ə) im toəkin tul,' a sez,
'suə let s e nə boðə(r).' ðen šu tōnz rānd ən šu sez, 'av əz
mitš reit tə ðis grund ən tə ðat tluəspuəst əz ðā ez, ən al sī
ðə fat ə·fuər al tak əm dān, suə nā ða noəz.' 'al pūl əm
dān if tə duznt,' a sez. 'if tə duz ðal get ði topin pūld,' šu
60 sez. 'ən uəl pūl it?' a sez; 'uəl pūl it, Meəri Džeglz?'
ən a went up tul ə tə šeu ər a wə nuən fleəd on ə(r), nər oni
sitš laik. 'ðal sī uə,' šu sez, 'suə get intə tās wi ðə.' a wə
sum ən mad, ða mə bi siuə(r), su(ə) a sez, 'get intə tās
ðisen, jə oud þiɪŋ ; uə stāvd tkat?' 'uə kudnt þoil tə kīp
65 wun?' šu sez. 'uə boild d'ištlāt up wi tbroþ?' sez ai.
'uə senz ðə bānz āt i regz?' sez šū. 'uə z reɪŋ i ðər iəd?'
sez ai. 'ðā āt, ən oəl bə·leɪŋin ðə,' šu sez.

a wornt bān tə stand sitš leɪŋwidž əz ðat oni loɪŋə(r),
su(ə) a þriu mi kuəd dān ən ran intə tās ən gat tkāvin
70 naif. ðen a fliu ət ə kuəd wi it in ə džifi. bəd ad nə suinə
bə·gun ə seəgin wi it nə šə rušəz at mə wi tloɪŋ bruš ən
ramz it intə mi feəs, fər oəl it wə kuvəd wi wet ən muk.
ad sitš ən ə muki feəs əz ða nivə soə sin tə wə boən. bəd
a wə nuən bān tə bi bet, su(ə) a fotšt mi oən loɪŋ bruš, ən
75 aftə rubin it i tsludž i tmidl ə truəd a went ən peəntəd ivri
reg ət šəd iɪŋin āt wi it. Meəri ðen fotšt ə peəlful ə sudz ən
þriu əm ouər āə duəstnz, bəd a gat ə pigin ful ə tseəm suət
ə stuf ən let ər əv it feər i tfeəs. ə reglə krād əd getn rānd
bi ðis taim, ən tladz kept siɪŋin āt oəl suəts ə lou stuf, ən
80 wot əd ə bīn tupšot on it oəl a duənt no(ə) if āə Ben ednt
apɪŋd tə kum ɯəm təv iz brekfəs džust ðen.

day is my day, an so I'll thenk tha to get them clahts o'
thine aht o' t'road as sooin as ta can.' 'Who're ta talkin' 65
tul?' shoo says. 'Thah knaws varry weel who I'm talkin'
tul,' I says, 'so let's hev no bother.' Then shoo turns
rahnd an' shoo says, 'I've as mitch reyt to this grund an'
to that tloaze-post as thah hez, an' I'll see tha fat afore I'll
tak' 'em dahn, so nah thah knaws.' 'I'll pool 'em dahn if 70
ta doesn't,' I says. 'If ta does thah'll get thy toppin'
pooled,' shoo says. 'An' who'll pool it?' I says; 'who'll
pool it, Mary Jaggles?' an' I went up tul her to show her
I wor noan flayed on her, nor onny sitch like. 'Thah'll
see who,' shoo says, 'so get into t'hahse wi' tha.' I wor 75
some an' mad, thah may be suar, so I says, 'Get into
t'hahse thysen, ye owd thing; who starved t'cat?' 'Who
couldn't thoil ta keep one?' shoo says. 'Who boiled
t'dishclaht up wi' t'broth?' says I. 'Who sends ther barns
aht i regs?' says shoo. 'Who's reng i' ther heead?' says I.
'Thah art, an' all belongin' tha,' shoo says.

I worrant bahn to stand sitch langwidge as that onny
longer, so I threw my cord dahn an' ran into t'hahse an'
gat t'carvin' knife. Then I flew at her cord wi' it in a
jiffy. Bud I'd no sooiner begun o' sawin' wi' it nor shoo 85
rushes at me wi' t'long brush an' rams it into my face, for
all it wor covered wi' wet an' muck. I'd sitch a mucky
face as thah nivver saw sin' ta wor born. Bud I wor noan
bahn to be bet, so I fotched my awn long brush, an' after
rubbin' it i' t'sludge i' t'middle o' t'road I went an' painted 90
ivvery reg 'at shoo hed hingin' aht wi' it. Mary then
fotched a pailful o' suds an' threw 'em over ahr doorstuns,
bud I gat a piggin' full o' t'same soart o' stuff an' let her
hev' it fair i' t'face. A reggalar crahd hed gotten rahnd
by this time, an' t'lads kept singin' aht all soarts o' low 95
stuff, an' what 'ad ha' been t'upshot on it all I don't knaw
if ahr Ben heddant happened to come hoam to his brekfast
just then.

'What's up nah?' says Ben; so I at it an' tell'd him,

'wots up nā ?' sez Ben ; su(ə) a at it ən teld im, ol·ðoə šə
wər ektərin ə·weə laik mad ivri bit ə t'aim. fə wuns Ben
tiuk mai said, ᴏn i tiuk ə tluəz, ᴏn tkuəd, ən ivriþiŋ džust
85 əz it wo(r), ən beŋd əm slap ᴏn təv ər oən duəstnz. ðe
wər ə bit ə kwaiətnəs ðen fər ə bit, ᴏn a gat mi oən kuəd
ful ə tluəz āt ə·fuə Ben went bak ə·giən təv iz wāk. in ə
wail ət aftə(r), ā-ivə(r), a iəd ə lafin noiz, su(ə) a popt mi iəd
āt ə d'uə(r), ən ðiər if toud bīzm ᴄdnt guᴏn ən kut mi lain
90 dān, ᴏn oəl mi tluəz wə ligin ə tfluə(r). a faiəd up ən a
wᴄnt təv ᴏr ās, bᴏd šu slamd d'uər i mi feəs ən put tlatš
dān su(ə) əz i kudnt gᴄt in. 'al mak ðə peə fə ðis, jə
treš !' a šātəd þriu tkei-oil. 'mak ᴏn !' šu šātəd bak, ən ad
tə gu(ə) ən sam mi tluəz up ən weš əm ouər ə·giən. wᴏt əd
95 ə kum tə pas if it ᴄdnt tēnd āt tə bi ə wᴄt dᴄə a kānt tel ;
bᴏd it kom dān laik kats ǝn dogz, ᴏn wi buəþ ed tə drai wo
tluəz i tās.

wᴄn nīt kom a wə fleəd ðəd bī ə boni rumpəs, fə Ben wə
boilin wi reədž. if oni ə Meəri bānz kom niər āəz šu fotšt
100 ᴏm in wi ə tlatə(r), ən þriətnd tə kil əm if ivə ðə leəkt wi
ðᴄm þiŋz oni muə(r). 'wir əz guid əz jī !' sez āə Dik.
'bᴏd jāə muðoz ə bad ən ; šuz bān tə bi teᴏn tə tlokup,' sᴄz
Meəriz juŋist las. þiŋz gat tə sitš ən ə pitš, indīd, wᴏl āᴏ
Bᴄn went ən ofəd tuəl famli, big ən litl, āt tə fᴄit. ā-ivə(r),
105 Meᴏri uzbn z ᴏ nais kwaiət suət əv ə tšap, ən av nout tə
sᴄ(ə) ə·giən ·im, ən i wodnt oəðə mᴄl nə mak. ᴏn ðats wᴏt
wiv gᴄtn tul, ᴏn ā wis kum ᴏn tnᴄkst tiuzdə ðə loəd uᴏnli
noᴏz. bəd as nivə fə·giv ᴏ(r) ; nivə wᴏl i liv ; tnasti guid-
fə-nout ! aftər oəl ət iv dun for ər ᴏn oəl, ᴏn nivə tšeədžd
110 ᴏr ᴏ oəpni pīs.

wornt ðat ᴏ nok ət d'uᴏ(r) ? a þout it wo(r). kum in.
wᴏl, if it iznt Meᴏri ! ða sez ða þout it wo wᴄdnzdə ? ᴏn

although shoo wor hectorin' away like mad ivvery bit o' 100
t'time. For once Ben tewk my side, an' he tewk her
tloaze, an' t'cord, an' ivverything just as it wor, an' beng'd
'em slap on to her awn doorstuns. Theer wor a bit o'
quietness then for a bit, an' I gat my awn cord full o'
tloaze aht afore Ben went back agean to his wark. In a 105
while at after, hahivver, I heeard a laughin' noise, so I popt
my heead aht o' t'door, an' theer if t'owd besom heddant
goan an' cut my line dahn, an' all my tloaze wor liggin' o'
t'floor. I fired up an' I went to her hahse, but shoo
slammed t'door i' my face an' put t'latch dahn so as I 110
couldn't get in. 'I'll mak tha pay for this, ye tresh!'
I sharted threw t'keyhoil. 'Mak' on!' shoo sharted back,
an' I hed to go an' sam my tloaze up an' wesh 'em ovver
agean. What 'ud hev come to pass if it heddant turned
aht to be a wet day I can't tell; bud it com' dahn like 115
cats an' dogs, an' we both hed to dry wer tloaze i' t'hahse.

When neet com' I wor flay'd there'd be a bonny rumpus,
for Ben wor boilin' wi' rage. If onny o' Mary's barns com'
near ahrs shoo fotched 'em in wi' a clatter, an' threaten'd
to kill 'em if ivver they laikt wi' *them things* onny more. 120
'We're as gooid as ye!' says ahr Dick. 'Bud yahr
mother's a bad un; shoo's bahn to be ta'en to t'lockup,'
says Mary's youngest lass. Things gat ta sitch a pitch,
indeed, whol ahr Ben went an' offered t'whoal family, big
an' little, aht to feyt. Hahivver, Mary's husband's a nice, 125
quiet sort of a chap, an' I've nowt to say agean *him*, an'
he woddant awther mel nor mak'. An' that's what we've
getten tul, an' hah we sal com' on t'next Tuesday the Lord
oanly knaws. Bud I'se nivver forgive her; nivver whol
I live; t'nasty gooid-for-nowt! After all 'at I've done for 130
her an' all, an' nivver charged her a hawpney piece.

Worrant that a knock ot t'door? I thowt it wor. Come
in. Well, if it isn't Mary! Thah says thah thowt it wor
Weddinsday? An' thah wants to be reyt? So dew I.
I don't knaw what we've hed to fall aht abaht; an' I've 135

ða wonts tə bi reit ? suə diu ai. a duənt noə wot wəv ed
tə foəl āt ə·bāt ; ən av džust bin se(ə)in ət if ivə ðə wər ə
115 wumən ət i þout out ə·bāt it wə ðī. kum in wi ðə. av
bin evin ə bit ə frendli tšat wi Greəs iə(r). tketl z on,
ən av ə fati keək i tuvm, ən a dāə seə ðcz ə drop ə
Džəmeəkə sumwiə(r). sit ðə dān, laƨ.

just been sayin' 'at if ivver theer wor a woman 'at I thowt
owt abaht it wor thee. Come in wi' tha. I've been
hevin' a bit ov a friendly chat wi' Grace here. T'kettle's
on, an' I've a fatty cake i' t'oven, an' I dar' say theer's a
drop o' Jamaica somewheer. Sit tha dahn, lass.   140

IV.

TKUKŪ TLOK.

a wə dān ət Līdz tuˤðə wik, ən bi-in reəˤðə drai aftə
liukin rānd t'ān, a apmd tə pop intəv ə eələs nət fāə frə
tsteišn, wiə ˤðə wə bān tə bī ə rafl fər ə̂ kukū tlok.   a də
seə jəl noə wot ə kukū tlok iz ; ā-ivə(r), its ə tlok əts getn
5 ə oil i tfeəs ont wiər ə bə̄d pops āt ivri āər ən šāts ' kukū '
ə·stiəd ə straikin, ən šāts wuns ivri oəf āər əz wīl.   nā it
wə tseəm ət ˤðis rafl oz it iz ət ivri uˤðə(r)—ˤðe wər oəl
wontin tə bi twinə(r).   ˤðe wə niəli oəl juɲ tšaps ət wər in,
ən ət ɔ·bāt sevm ə·tlok ˤðe bə-gan ə mustrin tə·geˤðə(r).   wol
10 ˤðə wə weətin ˤðiə fər əm oəl tēnin up, ˤðe kəd toək ə nout
nobəd ˤðis kukū tlok.   ' am siuər ai sl win it,' sed Ned ə
oud Bilz.   ' ˤðal nət win ˤðis,' sed Krakə(r).   ' av nət bīn in
ə rafl jət bəd wot iv wun.'   ' ˤðat tlok l bi ·main tə·nīt, ər els
am tšet,' sed Džim Tanə(r).   ' ə diəl on jəl find jəsenz
15 mis·teən,' sed juɲ Stroəbəri, kos av kum þrī mail ə pāpəs
tə fotš it.'   t'aim kom ət last for əm tə šak, ən if jəd nobəd
sīn əm eɲin on t'eəbl tə sī wot numəz wə tēnd up, jəd aktli
ə þout ˤðə wə bān tə swol·ə tbeəsin.   trafl wər ouər ət last,
ən Bili Mušrəm wə di·kleəd tə bi twinə(r).   wen (ə)levɪn
20 ə·tlok kom, tlanloəd teld əm it wə taim tə bi skiftin, suə
Bili gat is tlok ən went uəm.   nā Bili didn't no(ə) ət it wər
ə kukū tlok, ən id niə sīn wun ə·fuə(r), su(ə) it koəzd im ə
diəl o trubl, əz al tel jə in ə bit   ' so ˤðə, Džini wot iv brout
ˤðə,' i sed tə twaif, əz i tlapt t'lok on t'eəbl wen ə gat uəm.
25 ' wiər es tə getn ˤðat þriu, Bili ? ' šu sed.   ' av wun it,' sed
Bili.   ' ai, its ə boni ən.   av niə sīn wun laik ˤðat ə·fuə(r).
bəd let s bi šapin fə bed, Bili, fər its getin lat.'   ' al iɲ t'lok

up ə·fuər i guə,' sed Bili, əz ə wont fər ə neəl ɔn tamə(r).
aftər əd uɔ it up ə·giən twoəl, ən set tpendləm wegin, ðe
went tə bed ; bəd ðed nuən bīn in moni minits ə·fuə ðə iəd 30
sumət šāt ' kukū ! ' ' wot ðə erɔment s ðat ? ' sed Bili.
' neə, ai kānt tel,' sed Džini. ' am siuər a iəd ɛumdi šāt
kukū,' sed Bili. ' suə did ai, Bili,' sed twaif. Bili gat up,
strak ə līt, ðen went dān-tsteəz. i liukt oəl up ɔn dān,
bə·int d'uəz, intə tkubəd ən tkoil oil, bəd kəd find nout, 35
su(ə) i went ən gat intə bed ə·giən. in ə bit i iəd ' kukū '
twelv taimz. ' iə ðə, Džini,' i sed, ' ðats pleən i·nif, bi
gum ! ' ən džumpt āt ə bed, strak ə līt, ran dān-tsteəz, gat
od ə tpuəkər ən bə·gan tə unt up ən dān ɔ·giən. ' a kɔ sī
nout dān iə(r), Džini,' i sed, aftə liukin up ən dān fər ə·bāt 40
ten minits, ' džust fīl if ðəz onibodi undə tbed.' ' neə, bi
gum, Bili ; briɔ tlıt ən kum ən liuk fə ðisen.' ' ðat nuən
fleəd, ā tə ? ' sed Bili, bə·ginin tə bi frītnd isen, ən diðərin
wol ə kəd ādli od tkanl i tstik. ' neə, am nɔt ə bit fleəd,'
šu sed, ' bəd av iəd fouk se(ə) ət twelv ə·tlok ət nīt s t'aim 45
ət bogədz bə·gin tə nok ə·bāt, ən its džust o·bāt twelv nā.'
ðat wər i·nif fə Bili. tkanl flopt āt ə tstik, ən i rušt upsteəz
ən tumld intə bed əz if sumdi wər aftər im. ' oə, mōðə(r) ! '
skriəmd Džini, þiɔkin Bili əd sīn sumət. Bili kuvəd iseln
ouə tiəd wi t'luəz ən krepc dān tə tbodm ə tbed. id getn 50
sə fāə dān ət wun ɔv is fīt uɔ ə bit ouə tbodm, ən tkitlin
bi-in upsteəz ən wontin sumət tə leək wi, gat od ə Bili tuəz
wi it tloəz. ' mēðə(r) ! ' Bili šātəd, əz i dregd iz leg up.
' þīvz ! ' skriəmd Džini, əs šu kuvəd o·sen ouə tiəd. noəðor
on əm dēst stō fər ə·bāt ten minits. ət last Džini sed, 55
' Bili ! Bili ! ' ' od ði din las.' ' dus tə þiɔk ðis ās əz
oəntəd, Bili ? ' ' am siuər it iz,' sed Bili, ' ən al flit tfēst þiɔ
ə mundə moənin. a niə bə·līvd i bogədz ə·fuə(r), bəd a kɔ
bə·līv it nā, bə·kos av felt wun.' ' felt wun ? ' sed Džini.
' ai e fə siuə(r), las.' ' ən wot wor it laik ? ' šu sed. ' a kānt 60
tel. it kom ən gat od ə mi tu(ə) ə bit sin.' Džini flopt ouə
tiəd ɔ·giən, ən Bili þiɔkin šəd sīn sumət, flopt ouə tiəd tiu.
in ə bit, ivriþiɔ bi-in kwaiət, Džini popt ər iəd āt ə bed

ə·giən. ' Bili, a wiš it wə moənin,' šu sed. ' suə diu ai,'
65 sed Bili, əz ə flopt iz iəd āt. ' am feən ðā iəd it əz wīl əz
mī, ər els ða məd apm ə þout ad bin driəmin.' ' it wə nuə
driəmin, Bili, fə noəðər on əz əd bīn ə·slīp.' ðe buəþ lœd
lisnin, on ivriþiŋ wə so kwaiət ðe kəd iə t'lok tikin dān-
tsteəz. ' kukū !' wə šātəd ə·giən. ' jonz tseəm din ə·giən,'
70 šu sed ; ' am siuər its dān-tsteəz. gu(ə) ən ev ə·nuðə liuk.'
' a duənt noə wiə tkanl iz,' i sed ; ' it tumld āt ə tstik
sumwiə(r).' ' wel, itl nuən bi fāər of ; get up ən liuk fot.'
Bili gat up, went on iz anz ən nīz, ən bə·gan gruəpin ə·bāt
tfluə fə tkanl. nā Džini əd uŋ ə frok ən skōts on ə neəl ət
75 t'op ə tsteəz, ən Bili apmd tə tutš əm wen i wər untin
fə tkanl, ən ðe kom tumlin on im. i džumpt intə bed
wi sitš fuəs ət i nokt iz waif āt ə tuðə said. ' məðə(r) !
þīvz !' skriəmd Džini, ən šu opmd twində ən šātəd ' elp !'
ə plīsmən ət wə džust pasin, þiŋkin sumət wə reŋ i tās,
80 brast d'uər opm ən went in. ' wot s tə diu iə(r) ?' i sed.
' kan jə sī onibodi ðiə(r) ?' Džini šātəd. ' ā kan i sī i d'āk ?'
i sed, əz i šut d'uə tə kīp onibodi frə gu-in āt. ' stop ðiə
wol Bili gets ə līt,' šu sed, ' kos ðəz oəðə þīvz ə bogədz i
tās.' Bili gat ə līt, ən im ən tplīsmən siətšt buəþ upsteəz
85 ən dān, bəd kəd find nout. ' jə fo·gat tə liuk undə tbed,'
sed Bili. ə·weə tplīsmən went upsteəz, ən Bili ən twaif
krept aftər im. nout wə fun undə tbed, suə tplīsmən sed ət
ðə must ə bin mis·teən. wol ðə wər upsteəz tbād šātəd
' kukū ' ə·gien. dān kom tplīsmən, tū steps ət wuns, ən
90 Bili ən twaif krept aftər im. ə siətš wo ðen meəd i ivri
niuk ən koənə(r), īvm undə t'iəpot ən tsoltselə(r), bəd
nout wə fun. ' ðes sumət kwiər ə·bāt ðis,' sed tplīsmən.
' ðes sumət vari kwiə(r),' Džini sed. ' e jə ivər iəd
sitš dinz əz ðem i tās ə·fuə(r) ?' tplīsmən ast. ' nivər ə·fuə
95 tə-nīt,' Džini sed. ' wel,' sed tplīsmən, bə·ginin tə bi əs
flœd əz oəðə Bili ə twaif, ən gu-in əz wait əz ə šīt, ' as bi
rānd ə·giən in ə·bāt ən āo(r), ən al liuk in,' bəd i wə feən tə
get āt, ən ðev nət sīn im sin. Bili ən twaif krept upsteəz
ə·giən, ən džust əz ðed gctn intə bed ðe iəd ' kukū ' wuns

muə(r). 'wel, ðis kaps oəl ət i ivər iəd tel on,' sed Bili. 100
'its tlast nīt i ðis ās fə mī,' sed Džini. 'a wodnt stop iər
if ðəd let mə liv rent-frī.' 'its nu(ə) ius gu-in dān-tstcəz
ə·giən, iz it, las, wi kɔ find nout?' 'neə, wi məd džust əz
wīl stop wiə wə āər ən kīp wokɔ wol moənin.' ðe wispəd
tə wun ən·uðə wol tū ə·tlok, ən ðen ðc iəd 'kukū' twais. 105
'bi gum, its jondər ə·giən!' Bili sed, ən it oləs sānz i tseom
pleəs. av ə guid maind tə sit dān-tsteos ə bit ən sī if i kɔ
find it āt.' 'diu, Bili,' šu sed. Bili let tkanl, krept pratli
dān-tsteoz, ən piəkt isen i trokin tšcə(r), bəd i suin fel
ə·slīp. i didnt iə tbōd šāt wcn it wər oəf past tū, nɔ Džini 110
noəðə(r), fə šəd guən tə slīp tiu. Bili wokɔd džust o·fuə
þrī ə·tlok, ən findin id bīn ə·slīp, i dlanst rānd tās, bəd i soə
nout. in ɔ bit tbōd kom āt ən šātəd 'kukū' þrī taiɯz.
Bili kest iz īn up ət t'lok wen ə iəd it fōst taim, ən ðen i
gat up tul it wen it šātəd tsekn taim, ən wen it šātəd 115
tþōd taim id ə guid liuk at it wol it popt in ən wə šut up.
'oə, av fun ðə āt ət last, ev i?' i sed. 'Džini! Džini! av
fun tbogəd āt; kum dān ən liuk at it.' 'wot iz it, Bili?'
šu sed. 'its ə bōd getn intə t'lok,' sed Bili. Džini kom
dān-tsteəz, ən ðen Bili went tə t'lok ən traid tə opm d'uə 120
wiə tbōd wo(r), bəd i kudnt manidž it. 'ā ðə crɔments ez
it gotn ðiə(r)?' Džini sed. 'neə, a kan nət tel,' sed Bili.
ðe buəþ traid tə get ət tbōd wol oəf past þrī, wcn it popt āt
ən šātəd 'kukū,' ən ðeɯ went in ə·giən. Bili traid to get
od ont, bəd it wə tə šāp for im. 'ðat ən oud fešnd raskl, 125
bi gum!' sed Bili, 'bəd ðal apm nət bi sə fleəd wen təz bīn
iər ə de(ə) ɔ tū.' 'wel, Bili,' sed twaif, 'a nivə niu sitš ən
ɔ þiɔ i mi laif. av oməst ə guid maind tə nok it nek āt fə
frītnin əz ən kīpin əz wokɔ niəli oəl tnīt. kil it fōst þiɔ,
ən let s e nə muə boðə wi it.' tlast ət i iəd ə·bāt Bili ən is 130
kukū tlok, i wə fiksin ə fāntn for it tə driɔk āt on, ən ə
boks for it tə eit āt on, o·said ə toil wiər it kept popin it iəd
āt.

V.

ðis oz ə kwešn ət oft kumz up fə dis·kušn, ən wen ə niuli
wed kupl es tə di·said it ðe sumtaimz a loɳ wail ə·bāt it. i
mi juɳ deoz, wen a wə wēkin ət tmiln, niuz wə brout intə
tməkanik šop ət Sam Wilmən ən An Aris wə bān tə bi wed əs
5 tnekst sundə. ðis niuz wə brout in džust ə·fuə tindžn stopt
ət brəkfəs taim, ən suə wen wəd getn naisli set dān tə wə
moənin miol oud Dik Tšəri seɳ āt tə Sam—'wot, a ges ðat
bān tə bi wed tnekst sundə.' 'wa,' sed Sam, 'am þiɳkin ə
sumət ə tsuot.' 'wel, nã,' sez oud Dik, 'if tə miənz tə gu(ə)
10 on smuiðli ən bī ə api man, duənt spoil ði waif wi pamprin
ə(r), oz if šə wər ə sik bān, bəd bə·gin əs tə miənz tə kari
on ; if tə duznt, ðal e tə riu. ət tvari taim ot oud Dik wə
givin ðis əd·vais tə Sam, ə lot ə wed wimin əd geðəd rānd
An Aris i tweivin šeəd, ən ðe sed təv ə(r), 'nā, An, las,
15 wotivə tɔ duz, sī ət tə stanz up fə ði reits; duənt gi weə
tul im ən inš. if tə wuns bə·ginz tɔ nukl undər il mak ə
kum·pliot sleəv on drudž on ðə ; its oləs tbest weə tə bə·gin
oz wə in·tend tə kari on.' its oft bin sed ət fouk rekɳz
nout ə əd·vais unles ðə guə təv ə loəjər ən peə siks ən
20 eitpms fot ; bəd buəþ Sam ən An þout təd·vais ðed getn wə
wōþ aktin on. rent deəz ən wedin deəz ·wil kum ət last,
ðoo lanloodz ən braidgriumz þiɳks ðe kum on ət ə sneəl
galop, ən wen tnekst mundə moənin kom rānd Sam ən An
wə man ən waif. 'its siks ə·tlok bi ðis wotš ə ðain,' sed
25 Sam, 'a þiɳk its ə·bāt taim tə gat up ən let tfaiə(r).' 'a
wə džust þiɳkin,' sed An, 'ət ·tād leəd reəðə tə loɳ, get up
wi ðə, ðal find sum kinlin i tuvm. 'a mən e ðī tə get up,'
sed Sam ; 'es tə fə·getn wot tə sed jostədə—didnt tə promis

tə luv, onɔr ən ə·beə ?' 'am prə·peəd tə diu ɔəl i promist,'
sed An, 'bəd ə bodi kānt diu ivriþiŋ ət wuns, al luv ən 30
onə ðə nā, if tl get up ən līt tfaiə(r), ən wen tketl boilz ða
mən koəl mə dān-tstcəz ən al ə·beə ðə.' 'kum, kum,' sed
Sam, 'if tə þiŋks tə kŋ traifl wi mə i ðis weə ðal find āt ði
mis·tak. a as ðə tə diu nout ət i kānt bak up wi skriptə(r),
fə sant Pītə sez—"waivz, nukl undə tə jər uzbnz."' 'duz 35
ə ?' sed An. 'al bə·līv it wen i sī it.' 'ðen ða sl suin sī it,'
sed Sam, ən i bānst āt ə bed ən ran dān-tstcəz in is šōt.
wol ə wə rumidžin ɔ·bāt fə t'estiment, wot duz An diu bəd
nip intə t'lozit, sam up oəl iz wātə tluəz, fliŋ əm dān tə
tbodm ə tsteps, bout t'šcəmə duər i tinsaid, ən ðen krīp bak 40
ə·giɔn intə bed. in ə bit, Sam in iz əri tə get bak, gat wun
əv is fɪt feltəd iu iz dudz, ən fel forəd, bumpin iz nuəz
ə·giɔn tšāp edž ə wun ə tsteps. ðis put im intəv ə bit əv ə
pešn, ən wen ə gat tə tsteəz iəd, ən fan d'uə fest, i sweər ə
gōt uəþ, ðoə id bīn ət t'šapil tnīt ə·fuə(r). 'ðiə lad,' sed 45
An, 'if təs swoən wi t'estiment i ði and, a wodnt bi ðī fər
oəl tbras i tbeŋk, ðez nuəbdi sə ādnd əs tə diu ðat nobəd
trif-raf ət gets intə tkuət-ās.' 'a tə bān tə opm d'uə ən
liuk ət ðis tekst ?' sed Sam. 'al liuk at it, wen tə lets mə
no(ə) ət tketl z boilin, its nu(ə) ius getin up ə·fuə(r),' ən An 50
kuvəd ər iəd up i tbed tluəz ən feə kiŋkt ə·giən wi lafin, tə
þiŋk ā šəd bafld im ; bəd wen šə iəd tās duə guə tul wi
ə gōt beŋ, it put ə bit əv ɔ dampər on ə məriment.
'wiərivə kan tmadlin bi of tul ?' sed šū, 'a oməst wiš id
getn up misen ən let tfaiə(r), its nuə gōt džob, ən if id jīldəd 55
ðe wod ə bīn piəs bə·twīn əz. wišt! a þiŋk a iər is
fuit kumin up tsteps. if ə pīps þriu tlok-oil il bi eəbl
tə sī mə. al rekŋ tə bi ə·slīp'. suə šu leəd wi ə feəs tə d'uər
ən stātəd ə snuərin laik ə peər ə blaksmiþ bcləsəz ət əd getn
ə bad koud. in ə bit šu stātəd up ən lcind on ər elbou ən 60
āknd. šu iəd ə soft, pərin noiz ən nā ən ðen ə sānd əz if
suməct wə skratin wud. 'oə diə(r),' šu sed, 'its nuən im, its
nobəd tkat ət s mīdləs fər ə drop ə milk.' it wə nu(ə) ius
An trai-in tə foəl ə·slīp, šu kudnt, suə šə dond ə·sen ən krept

65 reit pratli dān tsteəz. oəl wər əs koud ən sailnt əz ə tšǎtš
əv ə wikdeə. Sam wə nuəwiə tə bi sīn, bəd iz wātə dudz
wə guən, suə šə niu id set of sumwiə(r)—bəd wiə(r)? šu
samd up tfaiə šūl, þiŋkin šud guə tə tbodm ə tjäd tə tkoil-
oil ən fotš ə šūlfl ə koilz, nət ət šə þout ə lītin tfaiə(r), oə,
70 nou, šud eit it suinə(r), bəd šud get oəl redi fər im, su(ə) əz
ə kəd ev ə bleəz in ə minit. bəd, bə-oud! wen šə wontəd
tə gu(ə) āt šu fan ət d'uə wə fest, ən šu kudnt opm it. šu
wər ə priznə lokt up i tās. wen šə boutəd ə bed-rūm duər
ən bafld ər uzbn, šu laft reəli, þiŋkin it wər ə vari guid
75 džuək; bəd wen šə wə bafld ən bestəd ə·sen šu kudnt laf.
uðə fouk məd apm ə sīn tfun ont, bəd An didnt—šu brast
āt ə ruərin. if šəd ed oni wūk tə guə tul šud ə guən tə
tmiln, if šə kəd ə getn āt ə tās; bəd šu ed nə wāk, šud gīn
up ə liumz, fə Sam əd sed, 'ðasl nivə guə tə tmiln ə·giən,
80 las, əz loŋ əz a kŋ kīp ðə. wen šə bə·þout ər ə ðem wōdz
šu ruəd āðə nər ivər ən pūld sum eər of ər iəd ən fleŋ it on
tfluə(r), əz if ðat, sumā, kəd mend matəz. oəl ət wuns šə
bə·þout ər ət tnekst duə neəbər əd ə kei ət əd opm ðeə
duə(r), suə wen šəd baþt ər īn wi koud wotə(r), šu stātəd ə
85 pundin tfaiə bak wi tpuəkə(r). In ə bit tneəbə wumən kom
āt ən steəd in ət twində tə sī wot wər up. 'am lokt in,'
sed An, 'a wont jə tə opm d'uə wi jāə kei.' tneəbə ran uəm
fə tkei ən opmd d'uər in ə krak. 'wotivə did jər uzbn lok
jə in fo(r)?' sed tneəbə(r). 'wa,' sed An, trai-in tə laf, it
90 sīmz id fəgetn mə, it iznt twenti fouər āəz jət sin wi wə tīd
tə·geðə(r), ən ə man kānt get intə niu weəz oəl ət wuns. a
də se(ə) it əd tliən slipt iz maind ət i ed ə waif, su(ə) iz lokt
d'uər ən teən tkei in is pokit əz iuzl. Samz ə tšap ət boðəz
iz iəd ə guid bit wi tpə·petiuəl muəšn. ən av īvm noən im
95 set of tə tpump wi tfaiə šūl in iz and ən ðen kum sliŋkin
bak fə twotə kit. puər An sed oəl ðis in ə məri of-and weə
ət əd ə di·siəvd tvari oud lad iscn, bəd it didnt blind
twumən ət livd tnekst duə(r). əs šə went bak təv ər oən ās
šu sed, lou dūn, 'ðat wumən z bin ruərin, ðez ə fratš on bi
100 nā.' wel, a diu þiŋk ət ðat deə wə tloŋist, drī-ist, ən muəst

mizrəbl deə ət ivər An əd past sin šə wə boən. wot əd
bəˈkum ə Sam šu kudnt imˈadžn. i didnt kum niə fər ə
bait ə dinə(r), ət givin ouə taim i nivə tōnd up, ən ət ten
əˈtlok ət nīt šəd nivə sīn is feəs. if šə went wuns tə tentri
end, šu went ə undəd taimz i tāə tə ākᴚ fər is fuit, bəd it 105
wər oəl i veən. Sam wə noəðə tə bi iəd nə sīn. twāst ont
wo(r), šu kudnt fešn tə guə sīk for im, šu felt əz if šəd
reəðə dī nər oni ə tᴍiln lasəz səd no(ə) ət Sam əd left ə
tvari de(ə) aftə twedin deə. oəl þouts ə koᴚkrin ər uzbn ən
setin up fə tmeəstə wə skatəd tə twind ; it wə fāə betə tə 110
bi oni suət əv ə drudž ən sleəv nə liv ðat weə ; su(ə) ət aftə
ten əˈtlok ət nīt, šu kinld tfaiər on meəd əz nais ə supər əz
anz kəd mak, nət fər əˈseln, bəd fə Sam. əs fər ə šu ednt etn
ə māþfl oəl ðat blesid deə, nə kudnt ; ðe wər ə lump in ə
þroit sə big ət šə kudnt swolə ət oəl. əs fə Sam, wiər edˈi 115
bīn ən wot ed ˈī bin diu-in ? aftə liəvin uəm i went streit
təv iz wāk, gat iz brekfəs ən iz dinər ət ə kofi-šop, ən ət oəf
past faiv ət nīt wondəd up ən dān tstrīts əz dezələt ən
mizrəbl əz oni man wīl kan bī. əz ə wə moəndrin up ən
dān i ðis weə i gat mikst up wi ə krād ə fouk oəl gu-in i 120
wun diˈrekšn. i went wi tstriəm, fər i didnt keə mitš wiər
ə went, ən ət last fan isen in ə tšapil. in ə wail ən oud
man, wi ə feəs laik ən eəndžilz, stuid up ən preitšt laik ən
eəndžil, preitšt piəs boˈtwīn kuntri ən kuntri, piəs bəˈtwīn
man ən man, ən last əv oəl, piəs bəˈtwīn man ən waif. it 125
sīmd tə Sam əz if, sumweə, toud man əd getᴎ tə noə wot
wər up bəˈtwīn im ən twaif, fər i liukt streit ət im ən teld
im ðe səd bi nə strugl fə tmeəstəšip bəˈtwīn man ən waif, bəd
ət in oəl þiᴚz, big ə litl, luv səd bi tmeəstə(r). wen Sam
gat āt ə ðat tšapil iz āt bəˈgan tə sofᴎ tād iz juᴚ waif, tə 130
mak eksˈkiusəz fər ə kondukt, on aftər ə desprət batl wi is
praid ət lastəd wol əˈlcvm p.m. i þout id gu(ə) uəm ən trai
tə fəˈget ən fəˈgiv. wen ə gat niə tentri end, i tutšt ə duə
step wi is fuit, ən wə vari niə foəlin. An so(ə) im ən ran
intə tās riᴚin ər anz ən krai-in ˈoə diə(r), iz drukᴚ, iz 135
drukᴚ.' tpuə las dōsnt feəs im i likə(r), suə šə id əˈsen

o

ə·bak ə tkitšin duə(r). in ə bit Sam kom in, bəd nət drukᴎ,
i wə soubər i·nif ən sorəfl i·nif. i sat im dān i tām tšeer ən
liukt rānd.   tfaiəsaid wə wām ən brīt ən taidi, ə nais supə
140 wə redi, is slipəz leən bi tfendə(r), ivriþiᴎ dun fər is
kumfət ət wumən kud diu.   i leind bak in is tšeer ən šu
kəd sī t'ioz wun aftər ə·nuðə run slooli dān is feos.   in ə bit
An ventəd tə kum āt ən sed pitifli, 'Sam!' i tōnd iz iəd, iz
legz peətəd, ən i eld āt iz āmz.   i les nər ə tik-tak šə wə
145 siətəd on iz nī, wi ər āmz rānd iz nek, sobin əz if ər āt əd
brek.   aftə ðat ðo wə nivə nout sed əs tə 'uə z tə bi
tmeəstə(r)'; buəþ sed 'luv sl bi tmeəstə(r),' ən ðat satld it.

VI.

'tɛ̄nd fifti!' bi tmɛgz, bəd its taim tə bi liukin rānd
tkoənəz nū, ən nuə mis·tak. džust ə bit loɔɔr ən as bi ʍun
ə ðem leɔki tšaps bāt šuin, ən stokinz ivə so mitš tə big, ət
Wiliəm toəks ə·bat i tpleə. bəd a nuən laik it, ən ðat s
flat. ʍen ə tšap kuɔz tə ðat, ʍot kuɔz təv im? ʍa, īz 5
nokt ə·bat þriu pilə tə puəst, ən tmuəst ət fouk se(ə) on iɔ
iz—'ai, puər oud tšap, īs sīn iz best deəz.' its tšiəfl, kum-
fətin toək iz ðat fər ə tšap ət s muild ən broild, ən duin iz
best tə kīp bodi ən soul tə·geðə(r), ən apm riəd ə lot ə juɔ
ənz tə elp tə kari on twōligig biznəs ə twōld. aftər oəl its 10
laik stopin ət ə guid beətin šop ʍen ə tšap s reikt iz oəf
sentri, əz it giz im ə tšons ə samin isen tə·geðə laik, ən
makin ə dženrəl baləns up ə oəl iz dun ən left undun. a
ʍundər ā moni on əz l bi eəbl tə stand it ən kum of wi ə
baləns ə treit said! am fit tə þiɔk ðɔz nobəd iər ən ðiə ʍun. 15
əs fə misen, al tak tult ən mak nə buənz ə·bāt it—av bīn ə
reglə raskl þriu tfɔ̄st wik a ʍə boən. mi muðə s sed suə
moni ə taim, su(ə) it mun bi triu. ā-ivər a kəd fešn tə liuk
ər it feəs aftə t'aimz šəs teld mə ðat, a kanət imadžin, ən
am nuən bān tə dis·piut it, nət ai. ðez moni þāzn muə bīn 20
teld tseəm teəl. su(ə) as nuən bi bāt kumpni. bəd liəvin
džuəkin ə·said, a riəli ən onistli bə·līv a ʍər ə raskl i mi juɔ
deəz. tnumər ə kitlinz iv þrotld, duks iv traid tə mak
piək, doɔkiz teəlz iv prikt, prə·sāvz iv stoun, tluəs-kuədz iv
snikt, windəz iv brokɔ, fati-keəks iv etn, ən misdə·miənəz 25
bāt numər ət əd ə bīn ə eɔin džob i toud fešnd taimz ʍen
eɔin ʍə fešnəbl. oəl ðiəz kraimz ən moni muə raiz up

O 2

laik guəsts kundžəd bi ðem tū wədz—'tōnd fifti.' a meə
bi þout ə braznt ānd, bəd ðes sum ə mi triks al bi eɳd if
30 im sori fo nā! a wodnt giv ə tos fər ə juɳstər ət eznt ə spāk
ə divlri ə·bāt im. wot if ə duz galəp þriu ə siut ə tū ə tluəz
ə jiə(r). ad reəðə peə fər ɔ siut ə kuədiroi nər ə wudn ən
oni taim. ðe wər ə trik a wuns pleəd toud skuil misis, oud
Mali Begstə wī koəld ɔ(r). ə reər oud las wə Mali i d'eəz
35 bə·fuə skuil buədz ən buəd skuilz wə þout on. šu wər ə·bat
tšap əv ə beəl ə botni, wi ə feəs laik ə raizin sun stikin āt
ə t'op; litl fat āmz, ən anz əz big əz ə šūldər ə mutn. šu
kəd noəðə rīd nə rait, bəd ðat didnt matər i ðem deəz. šu
·wor eəbl tə beək avə-keək, ā-ivə(r), ən ðat wər ə muə
40 konsikwens tə Mali. wel, wot bə·twīn beəkin avə-keək ən
liukin aftər ə·bāt twenti bānz, Mali əd ə wāk set. a duənt
no(ə) ā šəd ə getn on, if šə ednt ɔ ed tə iuz ɔ þibl i tavə-
keək biznəs. it kom in sə andi tə wokɳ uz juɳ ənz up wi,
ən kīp əs þriu fratšin. it wər ə bit oəkəd sumtaimz wen
45 Mali əd bin stəriɳ tþin uət-meil, ən sudnli snigd tþibl āt tə
gi sum on əz ə swiləkər on tsaid ə tfeəs. toud las wə reəðə
fond ə wopin mī, bəd a di·tāmind tə e mi ri·vendž, ən wun
de(ə) ad ə fain tšons. Mali wə dān ɔ wun fuit, ət reəðə
spoild ə woəkin. ðe wər ə peər ə kats ət toud las wə vari
50 fond on, suə wot did i diu bəd tī buəþ ðə teəlz tə·geðər ən
iɳ əm ouə tband wiə Mali uɳ ər avə-keək. a niu šəd fleər
up di·rektli šə soə tkats i ðə kwiə pə·zišn. a niu tiu ət šəd
mak streit fə mī wi tþibl, suə di·rektli a so(ə) ə kumin a
wopt ə soft avə-keək on tə tfluə reit i toud las weə, ən dān
55 šə kom əs flat əz ə flāndə(r). bai gou, wornt ðər ə meələk
i tmiul-oil oəl in ə minit. toud wumən fiumd ən rould
ə·bāt, wi ə šoət leg stikin up i teə(r); tkats splutəd ən feət;
tladz ən lasəz ran skamporiɳ āt intə tstrīt; ən ai wər ə·bāt
tfəst on əm, fər a niu wot əd apm if i didnt kut mi stiks.
60 eə diə(r), ðem oud fešnd taimz! ðez nuə sitš meələkin i
ðiəz deəz! ast laik tə sī tlad wi tpluk tə sāv sitš ən ə trik
oɳ ə skuil buəd misis! wa, id bi wōþ iz weit i Džiudi Barit
umbugz. wel, aftər id ed ə fəst-reət skuilin, sitš əz ladz

gat i ðem deəz, a wə put prentis təv ə gruəsə(r). nā, a duənt
no(ə) ə muə trai-in sitiweəšn fər ə lad wi ə weəknəs fə swīt 65
stuf nər evin trun əv ə gruəsə šop—ðat iz, wol ə gets ə
reglə siknər ən ðen il wiš isen ət tnoəþ poul, ə sum sitš spot
wiə ðə sāk ais-šaklz fə ðə foənuin driŋkin. litl Nati Belšə
wə mi meəstə(r), ən a wə wot ðə koəl ə induə prentis, witš
ment nout bəd wāk, de(ə) in ən de(ə) āt, ən sleəvin ə·weə tū 70
ə þrī nīts bə·said, wen ðə wər out tə diu i wei-in punz ə
siuɡər ən penəþs ə suəp, ən sitš laik. a didnt sə mitš keə fə
ðat ət fēst, kos ad ə fain tšons ə pitšin intə figz ən reəzinz,
ən siuɡə kandi, ən traiflz ə ðat suət, bəd, bi gou, ðat suət ə
þiŋ duznt last fər ivə(r). its kapin ā suin swīt stuf gets əz 75
bitər əz goəl wen ə tšap ez is ful swiŋ at it. ai imadžin its
ə·bāt tseəm wi wot ðə koəl tplezəz ə ðis wōld i dženrəl.
ā-ivər it tiuk ə bit ə taim tə briŋ mə tə tstoəleisn point,
apm ə bit loŋə nər it əd ə dun sum ladz, ən bə·fuər it did
ad reəðər ə kwiər əd·ventə(r). mi misis wər ə bit əv ə 80
skriu, ən kəd ādli þoil mə i·nif tə eit, su(ə) a tiuk it āt i
siuɡə kandi ər out ət i laikt i tšop, ən nout bəd reit,
noəðə(r). ā iz ə grou-in lad tə þraiv bāt džok? wel, it
apmd wun sundə tmoənin ət i felt oəfl pekiš aftə mi
brekfəs, ən ad etn ivri moəsl up ət toud las put āt. a 85
dəsnt as fə nə muər ər els ast ə getn ə flī i mi iər-oil. ad
getn dond redi fə t'šapil, fə toud las wə vari pə·tiklər ə·bāt
mə bi-in reit brout up, šu sed, if šə did pinš mə i vitlz. i
ðem deəz ladz laik mī weə beləs-kaps wi taslz on, ən rānd
krimpt koləz, ən al stand it a wər əs fain əz onibodi mi saiz, 90
bəd wot s ðat wen ə tšap s pinšt in iz džok. wel, it wə
getin vari niə tšapil taim, ən a niu a səd e tə meətš i tfrunt
ə Nati ən twaif, bəd if jəl bə·līv mə, ad ðat kreəvin i mi
insaid a kəd əv etn ə bit ə rainosərəs, aid ən oəl. suə wot
did i diu bəd nip intə tšop tə get suмət tə lain mi stuмək 95
wol dinə taim. a niu ad nə biznəs ðiər ə sundəz, bəd
uŋə(r), ðe seə, iz ə šāp þoən, ən bi gou its triu. wel, a ednt
bin i tšop ə minit wen i iəd tmisis siŋin āt—'Džosiuə!
Džosiuə!' ðat wə mi neəm, ən toud las wə sīkin mə. bəd

100 a wə nuən bān tə liəv bāt sumət, su(ə) a seəz od əv ə šaiv ə
unikeək ət toud las ius tə mak up tə sel—reit swīt stuf it
wo(r)—slapt it intə mi beləs-kap āt ɔ tsīt, ən gat tə d'uə
džust əs tmisis wə bə·ginin tə bel āt ' Džosiuə'! ə·giən. su(ə)
of wi set tə t'šapil. eə, diə(r)! it wə twāst diu ivər i ed,
105 wə ðat. it wə reəðər ə wām moənin ən a wə swiətin laik ə
brok fə fiə toud las səd sə·spekt sumət. a dəsnt tak mi kap
of, kos a wə wookin džust i tfrunt ə buəþ tmeəstər ən
tmisis, bəd it wər ə roki ruəd tə Džoədn, wə ðat woək! əz
a wāmd up a kəd fīl tunikeək stərin ə mi iəd əz if it wə
110 wik, bəd on a məd guɔ. ət last wi gat tə tprimitiv šop, ən
əf kuəs a ed tə dof mi beləs-kap. wel, wot wi twām
moənin ən mī swiətin, tunikeək wə stuk fest on t'op ə mi
iəd, ən wə bə·ginin tə swiol dān tsaidz ə mi feəs tə ðat
də·grī wol ad ə unikeok wig ən nuo mistak. a wiənt tel
115 oəl id tə undəguə þriu ðat džob, bəd a bloəm tmisis fər it
oəl i nət findin mə džok i·nif. av stoun moni ə anfl ə figz,
ən reəzinz, ən þirɔz ə ðat suət, if ðə koəl it steilin, bəd ai
duənt wen ə grou-in lad eznt i·nif grub gīn im, aftər iz adld
it əz ai did wi Nati Belšə(r). eə wel; ā ðiəz ladiš teəlz kum
120 təv ə bodiz maind; ən a nobəd menšn əm tə šeu ət ladz—
rasklz əz ðə āə(r)—ānt suə wiðāt koəz sumtaimz. ðez nuə
tū weəz ə·bāt it; moni on əm əd bi vari difrnt if ðə wə reit
duin tul. am þiŋkin ðes sum əv uz oud boiz ev ə lot tə
ansə for i ðat biznəs. bəd a dārənt gu(ə) on ə bit loɯə(r),
125 ðoə its kapin wot ɔ lot ə þirɔz duz kum intəv ə tšaps iəd
wol is smūkin ə paip ən þiŋkin ə·bat bi-in tānd fifti.

VII.

TOUD SĀM TIUN.

sum kouks wāmd mi nīz wi ðə dul red iət
wen id swoləd mi milk ən pobz,
suə tlois up tə tſendər a pūld mi siət
ən a plantəd mi fīt ə tobz.

ðen lītin mi šoot blak paip, a swuɳ   5
reit bak i mi oud ām tšeə(r),
ən a sat wotšin trik əz it reəz ən uɳ
laik ə spərit i tmidnīt eə(r).

sistə Mali ən tbānz wər əˑslīp upsteəz—
ðə wə piəs wi ðat bleətin kriu—   10
su(ə) a smūkt ən a þout ə mi weəstəd jiəz,
ən ə twūk ət wə jət tə diu.

əz a liukt ət ðis laif ən ət tlaif tə bī,
a sed tə misen, " ðā as !
wi kumfət ða noəðə kən liv nə dī,   15
fə ðas seəvd noəðə soul nə bras."

ðen spai-in oud Seətn əˑstraid ə t'lād
ət wər uɳ undə t'šeəmə fluə(r),
a dubld mi neiv ən sed, "āk ðə, lad,
al bi didld wi ðī nə muə(r);   20

if mi sinz bi laik liəd, ən laik koək mi pəs,
wa ðəz nuəbdi bəd ðī tə þeɳk ;
bəd wen twēldz ə wik oudə(r), ðā gēnin kēs,
as e bīn buəþ tə t'šētš ən tə tbeɳk."

ðen sum minits past ouə mə, sad ən drī,   25
ən mi þouts griu ez dāk əs tnīt,
wen sum drukŋ oud alz ət əd bīn on tsprī
kom siŋin laik mad up tstrīt.

wi ðər anz ən ðə fīt ðe kept biətin t'aim
ez ðər āmz intə teə wə fluŋ,   30
eə! ən twēdz əv ə godləs ən sili raim
təv ən oud sām tiun ðe suŋ.

ai! t'aimz ət iv džoind i ðat grand oud eə(r),
wen oud frenz ət mi said wə sīn,
wen mi laif wər ə sunšaini alidə,   35
ən ðis wiznd oud wōld wə grīn.

i tlīt əv ə sun əts loŋ sin set
a sī t'sapil ə P(r)imruəz Brā,
ən wot frenz on ə sabəþ deə ðiər əz met
ət fər ivər əs peətəd nā.   40

ðe kum ən ðe smail ən ə·wcə ðe pas,
bəd ðe oləs liəv wun i viu—
ə puə litl faðələs kuntri las,
ət wuns sat i tsiŋəz piu.

wun kām sumə nīt əz wə seŋ tlast im   45
šu liukt i mi feəs reit ād ;
ən ə lips wə wait ən ər īn wə dim
wen i džoind ər i t'šapil jād.

ən šu sed tə mə, "Ben, a fīl feənt ən il,
ða mən gi mə ði ām, oud lad ;"   50
ən šu wispəd sum wēdz ət i þiŋk on stil,
fə ðe meəd mə reit prād ən dlad.

su(ə) a elpt ə wi keər ouə reəl ən stail,
wol wə gat təv ə geədin duə(r),
ðen šu eld mə bi tand sitš ə loŋ, loŋ wail—   55
ən a so(ə) ər ə·laiv nə muə(r).

wel, ðis wēld gets əs koud ən əz ād əs stil,
ən ət taimz a fīl feən šəz diəd,
fə šəd ād tə sleəv ət ə lium ən wīl
fər ə moəsil ə onist briəd.   60

muə nə twenti jiə šuz bin diəd ən guən,
bəd wiərivə mi lot mə bī,
wen tās əz oəl wišt ən im left ə·luən,
šu oləs kumz bak tə mī.

av wišt ət id təld ə bi tgeədin duə(r)   65
ā dīp wə mi luv ən triu,
fər ə frenz, puə las, ðe wə feu ən puə(r)—
bəd nuə matə(r), a þiŋk šə niu.

ā! if ivər i get tə jond pleəs əbūn,
wiər i leŋ i mi āt tə bī,   70
džust tə iər ə wuns muə siŋ ðat oud sām tiun
əl bi evm əv itseln tə mī.

VIII.

it wə misti ən frosti ən dāk əz ə buit,
ən sə koud jəd ə pitid ə tuəd,
wen i iəd tə mi þiŋkin ə līt litl fuit
pit-patin bə-int mə ə truəd.

nã, ət faiv ər oəf past, əv ə koud wintə moən,   5
ad nuə þouts əv ə kumreəd ət oəl,
su(ə) a stuid wol ðə kom up ə bit əv ə bān,
laik ə pegi-stik eərin ə šoəl.

'olou, las,' a sed, əz a tapt ər ə tkrān,
'ðal bi duin for i trivər ə tkiln;   10
wot ātə, jə muŋki, ən wiər ātə bān?'
sez šū, 'ə šoət taimə tə tmiln.'

'if ðat meəstər ə ðain z oni tšildə(r)' a sed,
'a səd laik əm tə meətš ət ði bak;
bəd, a ges, if təd leəd ən āə loŋər i bəd   15
ət treəd əd bə·gin tə bi slak.'

'ai! meəstə,' šu sed, 'av iəd tguvnə swiər
ət iz meəd nout bi t'reəd fə ðis eədž,
ən iz oəsəz ən karidžəz nips im sə beə
wol ə ādli kən þoil tə gi weədž.   20

'ðen iz bout ən i·steət, ən iz bīldin ə ās,
eə! ən tkost ont nə moətl noəz jət;
if wə pinš wol wə kubədz wiənt peəstər ə mās
i kən nobəd džust stand on is fīt.

'i sez fərinəz latli əz meəd ə gēt spriŋ,   25
ən ðe liv on tšopt kabidž ən seəm;
su(ə) it uinz im, jə sī, tɔ šut bras laik ə kiŋ,
ən ðen sel i tseəm meəkits wi ðɛm.

'if wɔ duənt wōk fɔ litl, wi muənt wōk ət oəl,
ən mi granfaðə sed jəstənīt   30
if it wornt fə tšoət taiməz ət tsistm ɔd foəl,
ən tpliušeə kum bak intə tstrīt.'

a liukt of tī end ət ðat wiznd oud bān,
ən a sed, 'it əˑpiəz laik tə mī
ət tfaktri ən tmanšn ən tmeən ə tkonsān   35
əz upodn bi midžez laik ðī.

iər a peətəd wi tbān, ən a kudnt bəd laf,
ðo(ə) a felt nuən sə mitš ət mi iəz,
fər a þout tə miseln—its ə boni kum of
if wə propt bi sitš piləz əz ðiəz.   40

IX.

NATƎRIN NAN.

nuə dāt jəl oəl əv iəd ə·bāt
təpolə Belvədiə(r),
ə stati þout bi sum tə bī
frə ivri feəlin tliə(r).

oəl reit ən streit i mak ən šap,   5
ə moud fə treəs ə men :
ə dānreit, upreit, beɔup tšap,
nət mitš unlaik misen.

nā, ðoə jə no(ə) iz nout bəd stuən,
i liuks sə grand ən big,   10
ət litl dōst je pūl iz nuəz,
ə lug is twistəd wig.

pratli, reit pratli ouə tfluə(r)
ə tip-ə-tuəz jə woək,
ən od jə briəþ fə vari oə,   15
ən wispə wen jə toək.

ðiəz ðat ə·bāt im—bəd a noənt
nət reitli ā tə seə t—
ət maks jə fīl əz smoəl əs þīvz
ə·nent ə madžistreət.   20

jəv sīn ðat dolt ə muki tleə
ə tfeəs ə Pudsə Duəz ;
toud madlin z woən it oəl iz laif,
ən fansid it ə nuəz.

jond props əz laik ə peər ɔ teɪɔz   25
ə Saiksəz, jət, bi tmɒgz,
wen i wə soubər əz ə džudž
av iəd im koəl əm legs.

su(ə) evm bi preəzd fə self konseət;
wiðāt it, a səd seə,   30
wist eət wəsen wi oɔl wə mīt
fər ivər ən ɔ deə.

wen weəstəz liuks ət tmābl god,
īgoi! ā waid ðe geəp,
ən wundə witš ðe feəvə tmuəst—   35
ə bogəd ər ən eəp.

ən sum wì envi ən wi spait
get fild tə ðat də·grī
ðəd nok iz nuəz of, if ðə dēst,
ə giv im ə blak ī.   40

ī sumā kɒsts ə līt ə þiɪɔz
ət fouk nuən wonts tə sī;
ðez feu laiks tɒlin wot ðə āə(r),
ɔ wot ðə out tə bī.

wa, wa, pə·fekšn nivə did   45
tə Admz bānz bə·leɪɔ;
ən liuk ət moətlz wen wə wil,
wis find ə sumət reɪɔ.

oud Adm gat sə mešt wi tfoəl
ət oəl ə tiumən reəs   50
grouz sadli āt ə šap i tmaind,
i tkeəkəs, ən i tfeəs.

ðez nuən sə blind bəd ðeə kɪɔ sī
ə fout i uðə men;
av sumtaimz met wi fouk ət þout   55
ðə soə wun i ðəsen.

ən tbest ə tšaps l find ðəsen
ət taimz i tfouti tlas ;
av dubld neiv əˑfuə tə-deə
ət tfuil i tsīmin dlas.   60

bəd twūst ə fouts ət aiv sīn jət,
i wumən ər i man,
is twiəri, neəgin, neɯin tə̄n
ət pleəgd puə natərin Nan.

a went wun sumər aftənuin   65
tə sī ə puər oud man.
ən ādli ed i dākɯd d'uə(r),
wen twərit ðus bəˑgan :

'eə ! wa! did ivə(r)! wot ə triət
tə sī ði faðəz sun ;   70
kum forəd, lad, ən sit ðə dān,
ən al set tketl on.'

'neə, neə,' a sez, 'am nuən ə ðem
ət koəlz ət t'aim bi t'lok,
ən bumps əm dān i tkoənə tšeə(r),   75
ən dluəz reit ād ət tdžok.'

ðā nuənkeət, wi tə od ði tuɯ?
il suin bi iər a þiɯk,
suə, if tə l sit ən līt ði paip,
al fotš ə suəp ə driɯk.   80

'oud las,' sez ai, 'ðat ei i buən,
ən reəðə lou i bīf.'
'ai, bān,' sez šū, 'ðis jiər ə tū
av ed ə diəl ə grīf.

'am not o wumən ət oft speiks,   85
ə siɯz fouk duəlfl seɯz,
bəd ai kɯ tel mi maind tə ði,
ða noəz wot þiɯz bəˑleɯz.

'ðaz nuətist ai nuəu liukt sə stāt,
ən ai kɩɔ triuli soə,   90
frə tlast bak ɔnd ə tjiə tə nā
av nɔt bīn wīl ə deə.

'ən wɔt wi siknəs, wɔt wi grīf,
am duin ða meə di·pend—
its bīn ə wiəri muild ən teu,   95
bəd nā it gɔts niə tend.

'av bout oəl tsistər ət i ev
ə blak məraino gān;
fouks þiɳks am reəli of, bəd, lad,
am þeɳkfl ət im bān.   100

wi twɛ̄ld, ən ivriþiɳ ɵt ɛ int,
am krost tə ðat də·grī
ət moni ə taim i d'eə av preəd
tə lig mə dān ən dī.

'wɔt aiv tə tak frə tliəst i tās̀   105
əz muə nə fleš kən biə(r);
it iznt džust ə taim bi tšons,
bəd ivri dɔ(ə) i tjiə(r).

nuə livin soul ətop ə tiəþ
wə traid əz aiv bin traid;   110
ðez nuəbdi bəd ðə Loɔd ən mī
ət noəz wɔt iv ed tə baid.

frə twind i tstumək, triumətizm,
ən teɳin peənz i tgium,
frə kofs ən kouds ən tspain i tbak,   115
av sufəd mātədium.

bəd nuəbdi pitiz mə ə þiɳks
am eəlin out ət oəl;
tpuə sleəv mən tug ən teu wi twāk
wol ivə šū kən kroəl.   120

'ən Džoni z tmuəst unfilin briut
ət ivə weər ə iəd:
i wodnt weg ə and ə fuit
if ai wər oəl bəd diəd.

'i tmidst ə oəl iv ed tə ↲iu   125
ðat ruəg wə nivə tman
tə fotž ə koil, ə skāər ə fleg,
ə weš ə pot ə pan.

'fouk sez āə Sal l suin bi wed,
bəd tþouts ont tānz mə sik ;   130
ad reəðər iɔ ər up bi tnek,
ə sī ə bərid wik.

'ən if i þout ə bān ə main
wə boən tə liəd mai laif,
a sudnt þiɔk it wor ə sin   135
tə stik ə wi mi naif.

'av ast āə Džoni twenti taimz
tə briɔ ɔ swīp tə d'uə(r) ;
bəd nā ə·fuər il speik ə·giən
al sit i tās ən smuə(r):   140

'ən ðen—guid greišəs, wot ə wind
kumz wiuwin þriu d'uə snek ;
a felt it oəl tlast wintə(r), laik
ə witl ət mi nek.

'ðat siɔk paip, tiu, gat stopt wi muk   145
ə·būn ə fotnit sin,
su(ə) ivri āər i d'eə wi tslops
am trešin āt ən in.

'oə! wen i þiɔk ā aiv bin tret,
on ā i teu ən straiv—   150
tə tel ðə tonist triuþ, am kapt
tə find miseln ə·laiv.

'wen īz bin reɔkin āt ə tnīt,
ət tmeəkit ər ət tfeə(r),
sitš þouts ɔs kum intə mi iəd   155
əz liftəd up mi eɔ(r).

'av þout, "ai, lad, wen tā kumz uəm,
ðal find mə uɪɔ bi tnek ; "
ən ðen av me bi þout ə·giən
ət kuəd əd apm brek.   160

'ər els av mutəd, "if it wornt
sə dāk, ən koud, ən wet,
ad guə tə tnavi ə tə d'am
ən drānd miseln tə-nīt."

'its grīf, lad, nout ət oəl bəd grīf,   165
ət weəsts mə deə bi deə ;
suə Seətn temps mə, kos im weɔk,
tə put miseln ə·weə.'

toud tšap iəd peət ə wot šə sed
əz i kom tlompin in,   170
ən šātəd in ə red feəst reədž,
'od, rot it! od ði din.'

ðen Nan bə-gan tə froþ ən fium,
ən fiz laik botld driɳk ;
'wot, ðen, ðaz entəd tās ə·giən,   175
ða ofld liukin sliɳk!

'ða nivə kumz ðiəz duəz wiðin
bəd ðā mən kās ən swiə(r),
ən straiv tə briɳ mə tə mi greəv
wi brīdin əriz iə(r).   180

'frə ðī ən ðain sin wed wə wo(r)
av teən nu(ə) end ə grīf,
ən nā ða stamps mə undə tfuit,
ðā məðərin ruəg ən þīf.

P

'ðā viln, gi mə wot i brout   185
ðat de(ə) ot wī wə wed,
ən nivə muə wi wun laik ðī
wil ai set fuit i bed.'

iə d'oudi liftəd təv ər īn
o jiəd ə linin tšek,   190
ən sobd ən ruəd ən rokt əson,
əz if ər āt əd brek.

ən ðen šu reəv reit up bi truits
ə anfl əv ər eə(r),
ən fitəd laik ə dī in duk,   195
ən šutəd āt ə t'šeə(r).

'aə! Džoni, run fə d'oktə(r), lad,
a fīl a kānt tel ā;'
sez Džoni, 'līt ði paip ə'giən
šul kum ə'bāt i-nā.'   200

bəd betər ed it bīn fər im
if īd niə stəd ə peg;
mai geətəz! wot ə poəz i gat
frə Nanz riumatik leg.

suin, vari suin, šu kom ə'bāt   205
ən fluɔ ən teər ən reəv,
i sitš ə we(ə) əs feu kəd diu
wi wun fuit i ðə greəv.

ðen at it went ə tuɔ ə'giən
ðat minit šu gat iəz,   210
'ðā viln, ða, ða noəz ði weəz
brinz on sitš gādz əz ðiəz.

'aɔ! if təd straik mə stif ət wuns,
o stab mə tə mi āt,
a ðen kəd dī kontent, fɔ fonk   215
wəd noɔ reit wot tə āt.

'unfīlin briut! unfīlin briut!
a niə wə wīl ən strɔŋ;
ðez nobəd wun þiŋ tšiəz mə nā—
a kan nɔt last sə long.   220

'tə stand up fər ə þiŋ ət s rcit
it iznt i mi neətə(r);
ðcz fouk ət noəz i oləs wo(r)
ɔ puɔ(r), soft, kwaiət kriətə(r).

'wun þiŋ ai kŋ seə, if tə-nīt   225
mi laif səd end it liəs,
av duin mi diuti ən ða noəz
av oləs strivm fə piəs.

'a no(ə), a no(ə), ət lm i tgeət—
ðaz uðər uəts tə þreš,   230
suə, wen im duin fo(r), ðā mə wed
jond guid fə nout juŋ treš.'

ðen Nan pūld sumət āt ə d'roə(r),
wait əz ə sumə tlād,
sez ai tə Džoni, 'wot s ðat ðiə(r)?'   235
sez Džoni, 'its ə šrād.

'on kofin kom tiu, bəd a sweə(r)
a wodnt ct i tās;
suə wen šəz miuld šə seuz ət ðat,
əs kwaiət əz ə mās.'   240

puə Nan liukt at mə wi ə liuk
sə jondəli ɔn sad:
'ðal kum tə tbɔrin?' 'jɔs,' a sed,
'a sal bi vari dlad.'

'ðen bid ði muðə(r), Džoni kraid,   245
'on as ði uŋkl Ben;
ɔn oəl ɔ preəz fə sudn diəþ
sl c mibest "cəmcn."'

P 2

NOTES.

The (˙) denotes that the following syllable has the strong stress, thus asem·ivə (I. 3), ·aim (I. 4). Before beginning the Specimens the reader is advised to read over §§ 249, 260, 341, 350 in the Grammar. In order to facilitate the reading of the Specimens, I have written **get up** instead of **gər up**, **wot iz it?** instead of **wor iz it?** etc. See § 290.

III.

Line 4, **fot** *for it.* 11, **jiə** (§ 337). 17, on forms like **we(ə)** see § 193. 22, **ðiə** see § 354. 26, **tmītin** *class meeting, prayer meeting.* 34, **nuən** (§§ 357, 399). 37, on **wel** beside **wīl** see § 399. 63, **sum ən mad** (lit. *some and mad,* a very common phrase) *very angry.* 73, **sitš en ə** (§ 340). 80, **on** (see page 73 note). 89, **bīzm** (lit. *besom*) *good-for-nothing.* 99, **āəz** read **āz** *ours.* 100, **wi ə tlatə(r)** *and at the same time inflicted blows upon them.* 101, **þiɒz** here used contemptuously of Grace's children. 106, **mel nə mak** pleonastic for *meddle.* 107, **ðə** (see page 112). 109, **en oel** (§ 399). 118, **Džəmeəkə** *Jamaica rum.*

IV.

Line 2, **eeles** *ale-house, beer-house.* 3, **də** (§ 390). 5, **ont** *of it.* 11, **Ned ə oud Bilz** *Ned (the son) of old Bill.* 14, **tšet** (§ 381). 23, **səðə** (lit. *see thee*) *look!* 34, **dān-tsteez** lit. *down the stairs.* 38, **strak** (§ 363). 52, **Bili** (§ 339). 88, **must** (§ 392). 108, **let** (§ 381). 128, **it** (§ 351).

V.

Line 14, **tweivin šeed** *the weaving shed.* 25, **tə** *thou*
(§ 350). 46, **tes** *thou hast.* 56, **wišt** *hush!* 104, **tentri end**
the end of the passage. 136, **likə(r)** (lit. *liquour*) *drink.*

VI.

Line 8, **muild ən broild** *struggled hard.* 25, **snikt** *cut.*
32, **wudn ən** (lit. *wooden one*) *coffin.* 42, **if sə ednt ə ed**
(lit. *if she had not have had*) *if she had not had.* This con-
struction only occurs in subordinate sentences, and has
probably arisen from contamination with such phrases as,
šud or **šed ə dunt** *she would have done it*; **tladz ed ə guən**
the boys would have gone. We generally say **ad ə lend jet
if jed nobed ə ast mə** *I would have lent you it, if you had
only (have) asked me.* Cp. the end of §§ 389, 397. 48,
we dān ə wun fuit *was down of one foot,* i. e. *one of her legs
was longer than the other.* 59, **kut mi stiks** *make myself
scarce.* 86, **ə flī i mi iər-oil** *a box on the ears.* 93, **ðat**, see
§ 399. 100, **seez** (§ 382). **med** (§ 392).

VII.

Line 53, **stail** is the lit. Engl. form, see § 315. The same
is also the case with **midžez** (VIII. 36).

IX.

After line 200 the following four lines have been inad-
vertently omitted in our Specimen :—

> sez ai, 'a nivə so(ə) ə tšap
> sə iəzifl ən fat ;
> ðal siuolī len ə elpin and
> tə lift ər of ə tplat.'

INDEX.

antm *anthem*, 57, 286.
anvil *anvil*, 57.
anz *hands*, 302, 310.
ap *to wrap up (with clothes)*, 57, 317.
âp *harp*, 61.
apl *apple*, 57, 247.
apm (lit. *happen*) *perhaps*, 270, 399.
apren *apron*, 196.
are *arrow*, 57, 243.
arend *notoriously bad*, 207.
arend *spider*, 194, 304.
as *ash, ashes*, 57, 312, 337.
as (aks) *to ask*, 125, 312.
âs *house*, 171, 310.
âsemive(r) *howsoever*, 399.
ask *dry, rough, harsh*, 312.
as-midin *ash-pit*, 57, 312.
at *hat*, 57.
ât *heart*, 74.
ât *out*, 171.
ât *thou art*, 61.
avek *havoc*, 194, 322.
ave(r)-meil *oat-meal*, 57.
âvis, âvist *harvest*, 61, 245, 292.
âz *ours*, 352.

bâ *to bow*, 171, 315.
bad *bad*, 144, 343.
bad (pret.) *invited*, 57, 373.
bai *to buy*, 315, 382.
baid *to endure, put up with, wait, stop, remain*, 156, 361.
bait *to bite*, 156, 361.
bak *back*, 57.
bâk *bark*, 61, 312.
bâk *to bark*, 74.
bake *tobacco*, 246.
baked *backward*, 243.

bakedz *backwards*, 251.
bâkm *collar of a horse*, 74, 315.
bak-stn *the iron plate on which oat cakes are baked*, 70.
baleks *testiculi*, 243.
bâli *barley*, 61, 245.
bâm *barm*, 74.
ban (pret.) *bound*, 57, 301.
bân *child*, 61, 259, 280.
bân *barn*, 74.
bân *going*, 171, 303.
band *string, cord*, 57.
bâns *to bounce*, 115.
bânti *bounty*, 235.
bare *barrow*, 57, 243.
baril *barrel*, 194.
bas *door mat, hassock*, 57.
bastail *workhouse, union*, 234, 243.
basted *bastard*, 195, 243.
bât *about, without*, 171, 242, 246, 289, 400.
baþ *bath*, 57, 306.
bed *bed*, 73.
bed-steid *bedstead*, 87.
beebe(r) *barber*, 203.
beed *to bathe*, 70, 308.
beedž *barge*, 203.
beegn *bargain*, 203, 247, 271.
beek *to bake*, 70, 312.
beekes *bakehouse*, 243.
beekn *bacon*, 204, 247.
beel *bale*, 204.
beeli *bailiff*, 204, 245.
been *near, direct*, 84.
bee(r) *bare*, 70.
bee(r) (pret.) *bore*, 70, 369.
bees *bass*, 195.
beet *bait*, 84.
beet *to abate*, 246.

biuti *beauty*, 237.
bizi *busy*, 117.
bīzm *besom*, 79, 310.
biznəs *business*, 89, 310.
blak *black*, 57.
blast *blast*, 135.
bleb *blister*, 280.
bled *bled*, 148.
bleed *blade*, 70.
bleem *blame*, 204.
bleen *blain, boil*, 268.
bleet *to bleat*, 133.
bleetin kriu *noisy children.*
bleez *blaze, to blaze*, 70, 310.
bleg *blackberry*, 59, 314.
bleitš *to bleach*, 138, 312.
blemiš *blemish*, 327.
blend *to blend*, 73.
bleŋk *blank*, 197, 322.
bleŋkit *blanket*, 197, 245, 322.
bles *to bless*, 148.
bleðə(r) *bladder*, 134, 243, 297.
blīd *to bleed*, 147, 381.
bliər-īd *blear-eyed*, 300.
blind *blind*, 89.
blis *bliss*, 89.
bliu *blew*, 190, 239.
blium *bloom*, 164.
bliuz (pl.) *delirium tremens*, 239.
blob *a bubble, bulb*, 100, 254.
bloe *to blow*, 123, 250, 377.
blosm *blossom*, 169, 310.
bluid *blood, to bleed*, 163, 381.
bluid ali, see § 346 note.
bluš *to blush*, 121.
bluðə(r) *to cry, weep*, 111, 280, 297.

bodi *body*, 110, 245, 315.
bodm *bottom*, 100, 247, 264, 286.
boek *balk, beam*, 62, 312.
boel *ball*, 198.
boeld *bald*, 62, 254.
boem *balm*, 198.
boen *born*, 104, 259.
bogəd *ghost*, 280.
boil *bole of a tree*, 109.
boil *to boil*, 216.
boks *box*, 100.
boni *nice, pretty*, 214, 245.
borə *to borrow*, 100, 243, 315.
botni *Botany wool.*
bou *bow*, 315.
boud *bold*, 64.
boul *bowl*, 103, 220.
boustə(r) *bolster*, 103.
bout *bolt*, 103.
bout *bought*, 101, 318.
brā *brow*, 171.
braid *bride*, 175.
braidl *bridle*, 156.
brain *brine*, 175.
brak (pret.) *broke*, 57, 369.
brakŋ *a kind of fern*, 57.
brān *brown*, 171.
bran niu *quite new*, 57, 301.
branš *branch*, 195, 327.
bras *brass*, 57.
brast (pret.) *burst*, 57, 367.
brat *pinafore*, 57.
braznt *brazen, impudent*, 57.
bred *bred*, 148.
bree *to beat, pound*, 204.
breed *to resemble, act like another person*, 84, 315.
breen *brain*, 65, 315.
breg *to brag*, 59, 315.

dāk *dark*, 74.
dākɒ *to enter*.
dālin *darling*, 189, 259.
dam *large pond of water*, 57.
damidž *damage*, 194, 245, 328.
dān *to darn*, 61.
dān *down*, 171, 400.
dān-reit *downright*.
dāst *dust*, 171.
dāt *doubt*, 235.
deə *day*, 65, 315.
deəl *dale*, 70.
deendžə(r) *danger*, 204.
deenti *dainty*, 204.
deət *to dart*, 203.
deət *date*, 204.
deəvi *affidavit*, 204, 246.
deəzi *daisy*, 65.
deg *to sprinkle with water*, 59, 315.
dein *dean*, 234.
delf *a stone quarry*, 73, 283.
delv *to delve*, 73, 283.
demək *potato disease*, 206, 246.
deməkt *diseased (of potatoes)*, 206.
deɒ (pret.) *reviled, reproached*, 59, 367.
depþ *depth*, 192.
det *debt*, 206.
deu *dew*, 180, 250, 295.
də *do*, 398.
dēsnt *durst not*, 287.
dēst *durst*, 113, 259, 390.
di *do*, 398.
dī *to die*, 79, 295.
dī *to dye*, 150, 315.
did *did*, 117.
didl *to cheat, deceive*, 117.
died *dead*, 179, 295.

dief *deaf*, 179.
diel *deal, to deal*, 137, 382.
die(r) *dear*, 188.
dieþ *death*, 179, 306.
dif-rnt *different*, 247.
dig *to dig*, 89, 315, 373.
dim *dim*, 89.
dīm *to deem*, 147.
din *din*, 117.
dine(r) *dinner*, 211.
dinɒ *up to reproach, revile*, 76, 367, 368.
dip *to dip*, 117.
dīp *deep*, 187.
disiət *deceit*, 231, 234.
disiev *to deceive*, 231, 244.
distēb *to disturb*, 228.
diš *dish*, 89.
diðe(r) *to tremble, shiver with cold*, 89, 297.
diu *to do*, 164, 398.
diu *due*, 237.
dium *doom*, 164.
diuti *duty*, 237.
divāə(r) *to devour*, 236.
divl *devil*, 192.
dizaiə(r) *desire*, 230.
dizi *dizzy*, 117, 245, 315.
dizml *dismal*, 211.
dlad *glad*, 57, 315.
dlaid *to glide*, 156, 361.
dlāmi *sad, downcast*, 171, 315.
dlas *glass*, 57, 310, 315.
dlazn *to glaze*, 57, 310.
dlazne(r) *glazier*, 57.
dleə(r) *to stare hard*, 70.
dlī *glee*, 187.
dliəm *gleam*, 137.
dlite(r) *to glitter*, 89.
dlium *gloom*, 164, 315.
dlou *to glow*, 166, 250.

dlue(r) *to stare*, 165, 260, 315.
dlueri *glory*, 224.
dlumpi *sulky, morose*, 315.
dlutn *glutton*, 226.
dluv *glove*, 169.
doeb *to daub, smear*, 225.
Doed *George*, 329.
doen *dawn, to dawn*, 63, 315.
doen *down, feathers*, 173.
dof *to undress*, 100, 295.
dog *dog*, 100, 315.
doi *joy, darling*, a pet word applied to children, 329.
doit *to dote*, 219.
dokŋ *a dock*, 100, 247.
dolep *lump of dirt*, 278.
dolt *lump of dirt*, 100.
don *to dress*, 100, 268, 295.
dons *dance*, 200.
doudi *a scolding, irritable woman.*
doute(r) *daughter*, 101, 318.
draft *draught, draft*, 57, 319.
drai *dry*, 175, 315.
draip *to drip*, 175, 278.
draiv *to drive*, 156, 283, 361.
drānd *to drown*, 115, 304.
drāzi *drowsy*, 171.
dreeg *to drawl*, 70, 315.
dreek *drake*, 70, 312.
dreet *to drawl*, 295.
dreg *to drag*, 59, 315.
dregŋ *dragon*, 197.
dregz *dregs*, 73, 315.
drenš *to drench*, 73, 277, 312.
drenk *drank*, 59.
drī *dreary, gloomy, tedious*, 150, 315.
dried *to dread*, 131.

driem *dream*, 179, 382.
drieri *dreary*, 188.
drift *drift*, 89.
drink *to drink*, 89, 273, 312, 367.
driu *drew*, 164, 315.
drivm *driven*, 89.
droe *to draw*, 63, 315, 375.
drop *drop*, 100.
druen *drone*, 122.
druev (noun) *drove*, 122.
druft *drought*, 174, 315.
drukŋ *drunk, drunken*, 111, 247, 368.
dub *a small pool of water*, 111.
dubl *double*, 226, 348.
dudz *clothes.*
due *doe*, 122.
Dued *Joe*, 329.
duef *dough*, 122, 315.
duefi *cowardly*, 122, 315.
duel *dole*, 122.
due(r) *door*, 113.
Duez, Duezi *Joshua*, 329.
duin *done*, 163, 398.
dul *dull*, 107.
dum *dumb*, 111.
dun *to urge for payment*, 111.
dun *done*, 398.
duŋ *dung*, 111.
duv *dove*, 174, 283.
duz *dost, does*, 169, 310.
duzn *dozen*, 226.
dwāf *dwarf*, 74, 250, 315.
dwinl *to dwindle*, 160, 250, 266, 298.
džais *joist*, 229, 292, 310, 328.
dželes *jealous*, 206, 243, 328.
dželi *jelly*, 206, 328.

guts *entrails, belly*, 111.
guzl *to swallow greedily*, 226.

i *I*, 350.
i *in*, 89, 272, 400.
ĭ *he*, 155, 350.
ī (pl. īn) *eye*, 181, 315, 334.
id *to hide*, 177.
id *I would*, 250.
īd *heed*, 147.
idn (pp.) *hid*, 177.
ī-end *corner of the eye*.
iəb *herb*, 207.
iəd *head*, 179, 283.
iəd *heard*, 151.
iəgə(r) *eager*, 231.
iəgl *eagle*, 231.
iəkwl *equal*, 231.
iəl *to heal*, 137.
iəl *eel*, 131.
iəlþ *health*, 137, 306.
iənis, iənist *earnest*, 74, 245.
iəp *heap*, 179.
iə(r) *ear*, 179.
iə(r) *to hear*, 151, 382.
iə(r) *here*, 154, 354, 399.
iərin *herring*, 68.
iərnd *errand*, 131.
iəst *east*, 179.
iəstə(r) *Easter*, 179.
iət *heat*, 137.
iəþ *earth*, 74.
iəðn *heathen*, 137.
iə-wig *earwig*, 315.
iəz *ease*, 231.
iəzinz *the eaves of a building*, 276.
if *if*, 89, 401.
ig *mood, temper*, 117, 315.
īgoi, an exclamation of surprise or wonder.
ik *to hitch*, 89, 312.

il *hill*, 117.
il *ill*, 89, 343.
īl *heel*, 147.
ilt *hilt*, 89.
im *him*, 89, 350.
īmin *evening*, 130, 270, 276, 283.
in *in*, 89, 400.
inā *presently*, 399.
ində(r) (occ. inðe(r)) *to hinder*, 89, 296.
indžn *engine*, 209, 247, 328.
indžói *to enjoy*, 209, 244, 328.
inif (sing.), *enough*, 164, 245, 315, 357.
iniu (pl.) *enough;* 164, 245, 315, 357.
inš *inch*, 117, 337.
intə, intəv, intul *into*, 400.
inž *hinge*, 76, 315.
iŋ *to hang*, 76, 273, 367, 368.
iŋgeedž *to engage*, 204, 209, 244.
iŋk *ink*, 209, 322.
iŋk *think*, 306.
iŋliš *English*, 76, 273.
iŋlnd *England*, 76, 247.
ip *hip*, 117.
ipin *a cloth placed round the hips of children*, 117, 245.
is *his*, 351.
i(s)sen, i(s)sel, i(s)seln *himself*, 353.
it *to hit*, 89, 373.
it *it*, 89, 289, 350.
it *its*, 351.
i tgeet *in the way*.
its *its*, 352.
itsen, itsel, itseln *itself*, 353.
iðə(r) *hither*, 89, 297, 399.
iuk *hook*, 164, 312.

iuneti *unity*, 237, 253.
iunien *union*, 237.
ius *use*, 237, 253.
iusfl *useful*, 237.
iusles *useless*, 237.
iuz *to use*, 237, 310.
ive(r) *ever*, 145, 283, 399.
ivri *every*, 145, 357.
iz *his*, 89, 351, 352.
iz *is*, 89, 310.
ĭz *he has, he is*, 310.

jād *yard*, 61, 315.
jāe(r) *your*, 190, 350.
jān *yarn*, 61, 315.
jare *yarrow*, 57, 243, 250.
jāz, *yours*, 352.
jel *yell*, 73, 315.
jelp *yelp*, 73, 315.
je *ye, you*, 252, 350.
je(r) *your*, 351.
jes *yes*, 91, 399.
jesen, jesel, jeseln *your-self, yourselves*, 353.
jesenz *yourselves*, 353.
jest *yeast*, 81, 315.
jestede *yesterday*, 81, 243, 315, 399.
jestenīt *last night*, 399.
jet *yet*, 81, 399.
jĭ *ye, you*, 155, 252, 350.
jied (3 feet) *yard*, 74, 337.
jien *to yearn*, 74.
jie(r) *year*, 131, 252, 337.
jīld *to yield*, 78, 315.
jiuþ *youth*, 190.
joen *to yawn*, 80, 315.
jole *yellow*, 80, 243, 254, 315.
jon, jond *yon*, 80, 252, 354.
jondeli *vacant, beside one-self*.
jonde(r) *yonder*, 399.

juek *yolk*, 83, 105, 252, 315.
juɔ *young*, 111, 252.

kā *cow*, 171, 312.
kāe(r) dān *to bend down, sit down*, 172.
kaf *chaff*, 57, 283, 312.
kaind *kind*, 312.
kait *kite*, 175, 312.
kākume(r) *cucumber*, 237, 263, 282.
kal *to gossip*, 57, 312.
kāl *cowl, to frown*, 114, 254, 315.
kan *can*, 57.
kan (verb) *can*, 57, 389.
kani *knowing, skilful, nim-ble*, 57, 245.
kanl *candle*, 57, 247, 266, 298, 312.
kānsl *to counsel*, 235.
kānt *to count*, 235.
kap *cap*, 57, 194.
kap *to surprise*.
kapil *a piece of leather sewn over a hole in a boot or shoe*, 194.
karit *carrot*, 194, 245.
kasl *castle*, 57, 286.
kā-slip *cowslip*, 117.
kat *cat*, 57.
kāt *cart*, 61, 312.
katš *to catch*, 383.
kātš *couch*, 235.
kāv *to carve*, 74, 283, 312.
keed *card*, 203, 322.
keedž *cage*, 204.
keek *bread of any kind*, 70, 312.
keekes *body, carcase*, 203, 322.
kee(r) *care*, 70, 312.

liede(r) *tendon*, 137.
lief *leaf*, 179.
lien *lean*, 137.
lien *to learn*, 74, 382.
liest *least*, 137, 343.
liev *to leave*, 137, 382.
līf *soon*, 187.
lift *to lift*, 117.
lig *to lie down*, 89, 254, 315, 382.
lik *to lick*, 89, 312.
lim *limb*, 89.
limit *limit*, 211.
linin *linen*, 160.
lints *lentils*, 209.
liᴅ *heather*, 117, 273.
liᴅe(r) *to linger*, 76.
lip *lip*, 89.
lisn *listen*, 117, 287.
list *list*, 211.
list *to enlist*, 211, 246.
līt *light, levis*, 93.
līt *light, to light*, 187, 381.
litl *little*, 177, 343.
lītnin *lightning*, 150.
lits lit. *littles*, 177.
līts *the lungs of animals*, 93, 318, 338.
liuk *to look*, 164, 312.
lium *loom*, 164, 254.
liv *to live*, 89, 283.
live(r) *to deliver*, 211, 246.
live(r) *liver*, 89, 283.
lodž *to lodge*, 214.
loe *law*, 63, 315.
loed *lord*, 283.
loft *loft*, 100.
loin *lane*, 69, 109, 254.
loin *loin*, 216.
loitš *loach*, 219.
loiz *to lose*, 109, 310, 382.
lok *lock*, 100, 312.

loks *small pieces of wool which have been detached from the fleece*, 100, 338.
loᴅ (leᴅ) *long*, 59.
lop *flea*, 100, 278.
loped *clotted, covered with dirt*, 100, 243.
lopste(r) *lobster*, 100, 278.
lost *lost*, 100.
lot *lot*, 100.
lotments *allotments*, 246.
lou *low*, 124, 315.
loup *to leap, jump*, 184, 317.
lous *loose*, 184.
lued *load*, 122.
luef *loaf*, 122, 317.
luen *loan*, 122.
luensm *lonely*, 122, 247.
lueþ *loath*, 122.
lueð *to loathe*, 122.
lug *to pull the hair of the head*, 111, 315.
luᴅ *lung*, 111.
luv *love*, 111.

m *them*, 350.
mad *mad*, 144.
madlin *a bewildered or confused person*, 144.
mai *my*, 156, 351.
maie(r) *mire*, 176.
maiklskoup *microscope*.
mail *mile*, 156, 337.
main *mine*, 156, 352.
mais *mice*, 175.
mait *mite*, 156.
mak *to make*, 71, 312, 383.
māk *mark*, 61, 312.
man (pl. men) *man*, 57, 336.
mane(r) *manner*, 194.
mānt *to mount*, 235.
map *a mop*, 194.

miuzik *music*, 237.

mizl *to drizzle (of rain)*, 263, 310.

mizl-tuǝ *mistletoe*, 89.

moǝ *to mow*, 123, 377.

moǝk *maggot*, 63, 306, 312.

moǝn *morning*, 104.

moǝndǝ(r) *to wander about without any definite aim in view.*

moǝndž *mange*, 196, 328.

moǝndži *mangy, peevish*, 328.

moǝnin *morning*, 104.

moist *moist*, 216.

moistǝ(r) *moisture*, 216, 243, 288.

moit *mote*, 109.

moiðǝ(r) *to ponder over, be anxious*, 297.

molt *malt*, 58, 254.

moni *many*, 58, 245, 315, 343, 357.

mos *moss*, 100.

mot, moti *a mark at quoits*, 214.

moþ *moth*, 100.

moud *mould, model*, 220.

moud-wǎp *a mole*, 103.

mud (verb) *might*, 393.

mūd *crowded, crammed*, 263.

muǝn *to moan*, 122.

muǝn *to mourn*, 113.

muǝnt *must not*, 392.

muǝ(r) *moor*, 165.

muǝ(r) *more*, 122, 343.

muǝst *most*, 122, 343.

mūfln *muffin*, 112.

muid *mood*, 163.

muild *confusion, bad temper*, 163.

muild ǝn teu *hard labour, continuous toil.*

muin *moon*, 163, 263.

muk *muck*, 121, 312.

muml *to mumble*, 111, 263, 288.

mun *must*, 111, 263, 392.

mundǝ *Monday*, 169.

muni *money*, 226.

muns *months*, 307, 310.

munþ *month*, 169, 337.

munǝ(r) *monger*, 59.

munril *mongrel*, 226.

musl *muscle*, 310.

musl *mussel*, 111, 312.

must *must*, 392.

mustǝd *mustard*, 226, 243.

mutn *mutton*, 226, 247.

muðǝ(r) *mother*, 169, 297.

muzl *muzzle*, 226.

nǎ *now*, 171, 399.

naif *knife*, 156.

nain *nine*, 344.

naint *ninth*, 309, 344.

nainti *ninety*, 344.

naintīn *nineteen*, 344.

naintīnt *nineteenth*, 344.

naintit *ninetieth*, 344.

nais *nice*, 229.

nap *nap*, 57.

narǝ *narrow*, 57, 243.

nat *gnat*, 57, 315.

natǝ(r) *to gnaw, nibble*, 265.

natǝrin *scolding, fault-finding in a small vexatious manner.*

nati *neat, tidy, dexterous (of old people)*, 265, 286.

nat-rl, nat-rǝ-bl *natural*, 194, 247, 288.

navi *canal*, 247, 265.

neb *bill, beak*, 73, 280.

neǝ *nay*, 84, 399.

pain *to pine*, 156.
paint *pint*, 229.
paip *pipe*, 156.
pak *pack, bundle*, 57, 312.
pāk *a kind of blain*, 278.
pāk *park*, 61.
pan *pan*, 57.
pantri *pantry*, 194.
pāsn *parson*, 207.
paste(r) *pasture*, 195, 228, 243.
pasti *pasty*, 204.
paþ *path*, 57, 306.
pāð̌e(r) *powder*, 235, 297.
pee *pay*, 204.
peedn *pardon*, 203.
peedž *page*, 204.
peel *pail*, 65, 315.
peel *pale*, 204.
peen *pain*, 204.
peen *pane of glass*, 204.
peent *paint*, 204.
pee(r) *pair*, 205.
pee(r) *to peel*, 205.
pees *pace*, 204.
peesl *parcel*, 203.
peest *paste*, 204.
peeste(r) (lit. *pasture*) *to feed.*
peet *part*, 203.
peetne(r) *partner*, 203.
pegi-stik *the handle of a* pegi (an instrument used in washing clothes, having a long handle inserted at right angles to the plane of a wooden disc, in which are set several pegs).
pei *pea*, 87, 278, 311.
peil up en dān *to go about, hurry up and down.*
pen *pen*, 73.

peneþ *pennyworth*, 243, 247, 251.
peni *penny*, 73, 245.
peš *to knock about, smash, dash*, 59, 312.
pešn *passion*, 197, 327.
pēs *purse*, 228.
pidžn *pigeon*, 211, 247, 328.
piek *perch, to perch*, 278.
pie-kok *peacock*, 179.
piel *to appeal*, 231, 246.
pie(r) *pear*, 75, 208, 260.
pies *peace*, 231.
pig *pig*, 89, 315.
pigin *a small water-can*, 89.
pig-koit *pig-sty*, 109.
pik *pickaxe*, 211.
pikte(r) *picture*, 243, 288.
pil *to peel*, 234.
pile *pillow*, 117, 243.
pilinz *the peels of potatoes, etc.*, 234.
pim-ruez *primrose*, 262, 278.
pinien *opinion*, 211, 246.
pīp (pret. and pp. pept) *to peep*, 232, 383.
pīs *piece*, 232.
pit *pit*, 117.
piti *pity*, 211.
pitš *pitch*, 89, 312.
piþ *pith*, 89.
piu *pew*, 237.
piue(r) *pure*, 238.
pius *puce colour*, 237.
plant *plant*, 195.
plat *floor, ground.*
pleen *plain*, 204.
plees *place*, 204.
pleeste(r) *plaster*, 195, 243.
pleet *plate*, 204.
plenk *plank*, 197.
pleš *to splash*, 59.

R

swīt *sweet*, 147.
swoən *sworn*, 104.
swolə *swallow*, 58, 243, 250.
swolə *to swallow*, 80, 243, 315.
swom *swam*, 58.
swon *swan*, 58.
swop *to exchange, barter*, 58.
swum (pp.) *swum*, 111.
swuŋ (pp.) *swung*, 111.

šabi *shabby*, 245.
šadə *shadow*, 57, 243.
šāə(r) *shower*, 172.
šaft *shaft*, 57.
šain *to shine*, 156, 361, 363.
šait *cacare*, 156, 312, 361.
šaiv *slice*, 156, 312.
šak *to shake*, 71, 312, 376.
šakl *shackle*, 71, 312.
šalə *shallow*, 57, 243.
šap *shape*, 57, 312, 383.
šāp *sharp*, 61.
šeg *shag*, 59, 315.
šeəd *shade*, 70, 312.
šeəm *shame*, 70, 312.
šeə(r) *share*, 70, 312.
šeəv *to shave*, 70, 283, 382.
šel *shell*, 73, 312.
šelf *shelf*, 73, 312.
šeŋk *shank*, 59.
šepəd *shepherd*, 134, 243.
šepstə(r) *starling*, 134.
šeu *to show*, 180, 382.
šə *she*, 350.
šət *shirt*, 120.
šiəf *sheaf*, 179.
šiə(r) *to shear*, 75, 312, 369.
šiəþ *sheath*, 137.
šift *chemise*, 89.
šil *to shell peas, etc.*, 77, 312.
šīld *shield*, 78.

šilin *shilling*, 89, 245, 337.
šimi *chemise*, 209, 245, 311.
šin *shin*, 89, 312.
šip *ship*, 89, 312.
šīp *sheep*, 130, 337.
šīt *sheet*, 150.
šiuk *shook*, 164, 312.
šod *shod*, 169.
šoəl *shawl*.
šoən *shorn*, 104.
šoət *short*, 104.
šop *shop*, 100, 312.
šot *shot*, 100, 312.
šotn (pp.) *shot*, 100.
šrād *shroud*, 171.
šreŋk *shrank*, 312.
šreŋk (pret.) *shrunk*, 59.
šrimp *shrimp*, 89, 312.
šriŋk *to shrink*, 89, 312, 367.
šrukŋ (pp.) *shrunk*, 111, 274, 368.
šŭ *she*, 191, 310, 350.
šū (pl. šuin) *shoe*, 164, 334.
šū *to shoe*, 382.
šuin *shoes*, 163.
šuit *to shoot*, 191, 381.
šūl *shovel*, 106.
šūldə(r) (šŭðə(r)) *shoulder*, 112.
šun *to shun*, 111.
šut *to shut*, 121, 312, 381.
šutə(r) *to fall*.
šutl *shuttle*, 121.
šŭðə(r) *to shoulder*, 111, 243, 297, 312.
šŭðə(r) (šūldə(r)) *shoulder*, 112.
šuv *to shove*, 174, 283, 312.
swiə(r) *to swear*, 75.

t *the*, 306, 341.
t *it*, 350.

twilt *quilt*, 211, 254, 324.
twilt *to beat, thrash*, 324.
twin, *twin*, 89.
twīn *between*, 246, 400.
twiɳkl *to twinkle*, 89, 312.
twist *twist*, 89.
twot *pudendum fem.*, 250.

þak *thatch*, 57, 306, 312.
þāzn *thousand*, 171, 247, 301, 302, 310, 344.
þāznt *thousandth*, 344.
þəd *third*, 90, 261, 344.
þədi *third*, 346.
þeɳk *to thank*, 59.
þəti *thirty*, 90, 245, 344.
þətīn *thirteen*, 344.
þətīnt *thirteenth*, 344.
þətit *thirtieth*, 344.
þēzdə *Thursday*, 172.
þī *thigh*, 187, 318.
þibl *a smooth round stick used to stir porridge with.*
þīf *thief*, 187, 283.
þik *thick, friendly, in love with*, 89 312.
þiml *thimble*, 177, 247, 282.
þin *thin*, 117.
þiɳ *thing*, 86, 273.
þiɳk *to think*, 76, 273, 306, 312, 383.
þisl *thistle*, 89.
þoə *to thaw*, 123, 377.
þoən *thorn*, 104.
þoil *to give ungrudgingly*, 109, 306.
þout *thought*, 167, 318.
þraiv *to thrive*, 156, 283, 306, 361.
þrast (pret.) *thrust*, 57.
þreɳ *busy, throng*, 59.

þrəpms *threepence*, 192, 270, 349.
preš *to thresh*, 73.
prešld *threshold*, 73.
prə *through, from*, 400.
prī *three*, 187, 344.
pribl *threefold*, 209, 348.
prīd *thread*, 130.
priəp *to dispute, contradict*, 179, 306.
priətn *to threaten*, 179.
prif *through*, 319.
prift *thrift*, 89.
prift (priu) *through, from, on account of*, 116.
priu *threw.* 190.
priu (prift) *through, from, on account of*, 116, 319.
proə *to throw*, 123, 377.
proit *throat*, 109.
prosl *thrush*, 100, 287, 310.
protl *to press on the windpipe, choke*, 100.
prusn (pp.) *thrust*, 287.
prust *to thrust*, 178, 367, 368.
pum *thumb*, 174.
punə(r) *thunder*, 111, 243, 266, 298.

ðǎ *thou*, 171, 306, 350.
ðai *thy*, 155, 351.
ðain *thine*, 156, 352.
ðat (demon. pr. and conj.) *that*, 57, 306, 354. Cp. also 399.
ðǎz *thou hast*, 310, 395.
ðe *they*, 350.
ðeə *they*, 84, 350.
ðeə(r) *their*, 84, 351.
ðeəz *theirs*, 352.
ðem (demon. and pers. pr.) *them, those*, 306, 350, 354.

Oxford

HORACE HART, PRINTER TO THE UNIVERSITY

www.ingramcontent.com/pod-product-compliance
Lightning Source LLC
Chambersburg PA
CBHW020348030726
47496CB00007B/2049